**T**HEY'RE TORTURING HIM," FARIDEH SAID QUIETLY. SHE TURNED HER head. "That's what I dream about. Devils cutting up Lorcan. And I can't stop it, and when I try to, they capture you too."

"That does sound more like something you'd vomit about," Havilar said after a moment. "You're right, though, it's just a dream. Why would a devil want me anyhow?"

Farideh shut her eyes. Tell her, she thought. Tell her, tell her now.

"Havi . . . what would you do if a devil offered you a pact?"

"What, like Lorcan?"

"Another devil," she said. "One you didn't know. One who offered you anything you wanted. What would you do?"

Havilar's eyes flicked over Farideh's face, as if she were gauging the seriousness of the question. As if she were trying to decide what her answer ought to be and not what it truly was, Farideh noted.

"Tell them to heave off," Havilar said finally. "I don't want to be a warlock, and I don't want to be indebted to a devil." She slipped an arm around Farideh and hugged her tightly. "I don't want you to be either. Do you think he's making you dream that? Like if he wanted you back?"

"Not his style." Lorcan's attention made the lines of her brand ache—but no matter how shaken or ill she felt whenever she awoke, her arm and shoulder were fine. If he wanted to lure her back, he would have started by needling at the brand. If he wanted to get her back, he would have let her know he was alive.

# FORGOTTEN REALMS

## ALSO BY ERIN M. EVANS

Ed Greenwood Presents Waterdeep:
*The God Catcher*

*Brimstone Angels*

*The Adversary*
The Sundering, Book 3
(December 2013)

# FORGOTTEN REALMS

# ERIN M. EVANS

# BRIMSTONE ANGELS
# LESSER EVILS

**BRIMSTONE ANGELS
LESSER EVILS**
©2012 Wizards of the Coast LLC.

All characters in this book are fictitious. Any resemblance to actual persons, living or dead, is purely coincidental.

This book is protected under the copyright laws of the United States of America. Any reproduction or unauthorized use of the material or artwork contained herein is prohibited without the express written permission of Wizards of the Coast LLC.

Published by Wizards of the Coast LLC.

FORGOTTEN REALMS, DUNGEONS & DRAGONS, D&D, WIZARDS OF THE COAST, and their respective logos are trademarks of Wizards of the Coast LLC in the U.S.A. and other countries. Hasbro SA, Represented by Hasbro Europe, Stockley Park, UB11 1AZ, UK.

All Wizards of the Coast characters and their distinctive likenesses are property of Wizards of the Coast LLC.

PRINTED IN THE U.S.A.

The sale of this book without its cover has not been authorized by the publisher. If you purchased this book without a cover, you should be aware that neither the author nor the publisher has received payment for this "stripped book."

Cover art by: Min Yum
First Printing: December 2012

9 8 7 6 5 4 3 2

ISBN: 978-0-7869-6376-8
ISBN: 978-0-7869-6136-8 (ebook)
620A2670000001 EN

U.S., Canada, Asia Pacific, & Latin America, Wizards of the Coast LLC, P.O. Box 707, Renton, WA 98057-0707, +1-800-324-6496, www.wizards.com/customerservice

Europe, U.K., Eire & South Africa, Wizards of the Coast LLC, c/o Hasbro UK Ltd., P.O. Box 43, Newport, NP19 4YD, UK, Tel: +80457 12 55 99, Email: wizards@hasbro.co.uk

Visit our web site at www.wizards.com

# DEDICATION

For Idris, who changed everything,
For my mother, Andriea, who helped things stay the same,
And for Kevin, always.

Welcome to Faerûn, a land of magic and intrigue, brutal violence and divine compassion, where gods have ascended and died, and mighty heroes have risen to fight terrifying monsters. Here, millennia of warfare and conquest have shaped dozens of unique cultures, raised and leveled shining kingdoms and tyrannical empires alike, and left long forgotten, horror-infested ruins in their wake.

## A LAND OF MAGIC

When the goddess of magic was murdered, a magical plague of blue fire—the Spellplague—swept across the face of Faerûn, killing some, mutilating many, and imbuing a rare few with amazing supernatural abilities. The Spellplague forever changed the nature of magic itself, and seeded the land with hidden wonders and bloodcurdling monstrosities.

## A LAND OF DARKNESS

The threats Faerûn faces are legion. Armies of undead mass in Thay under the brilliant but mad lich king Szass Tam. Treacherous dark elves plot in the Underdark in the service of their cruel and fickle goddess, Lolth. The Abolethic Sovereignty, a terrifying hive of inhuman slave masters, floats above the Sea of Fallen Stars, spreading chaos and destruction. And the Empire of Netheril, armed with magic of unimaginable power, prowls Faerûn in flying fortresses, sowing discord to their own incalculable ends.

## A LAND OF HEROES

But Faerûn is not without hope. Heroes have emerged to fight the growing tide of darkness. Battle-scarred rangers bring their notched blades to bear against marauding hordes of orcs. Lowly street rats match wits with demons for the fate of cities. Inscrutable tiefling warlocks unite with fierce elf warriors to rain fire and steel upon monstrous enemies. And valiant servants of merciful gods forever struggle against the darkness.

[FORGOTTEN REALMS]

# A LAND OF
# UNTOLD ADVENTURE

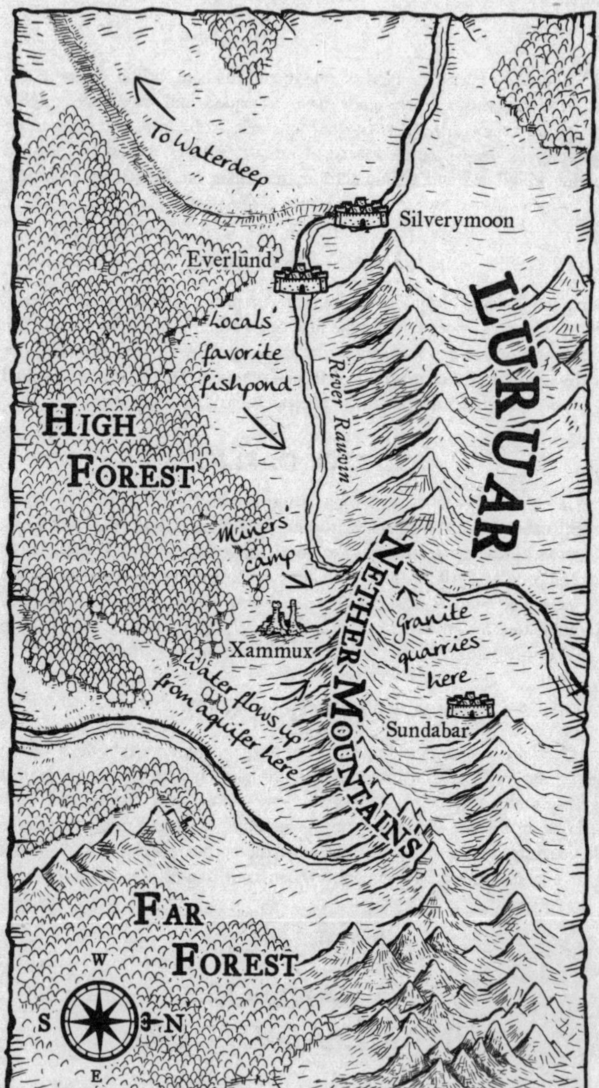

To Waterdeep
Silverymoon
Everlund
Locals' favorite fishpond
River Rauvin
LURUAR
HIGH FOREST
Miners' camp
NETHER MOUNTAINS
Granite quarries here
Xammux
Water flows up from aquifer here
Sundabar
FAR FOREST
W
S
N
E

# PROLOGUE

*Malbolge, the Sixth Layer of the Hells*

*The Year of the Dark Circle (1478 DR)*

LORCAN OUGHT TO HAVE COUNTED HIMSELF LUCKY. BOUND FROM knees to chest in a chain devil's restraints, dragged across the hungry nightmare landscape of the Sixth Layer of the Hells—still, the half-devil son of Fallen Invadiah was not dead.

He was not dead, and he would soon be locked away in his sister's newly claimed domain, far from their vengeful mother's weakened reach, far from the notice of the archdevils, and farthest of all from those mortals who knew better than to let Lorcan slip the noose, after what had happened in Neverwinter. Lucky, indeed.

But that luck only counted for these few breaths.

*All my life*, he thought, watching the skull palace of Osseia recede as the chain devil hauled him toward the fingerbone towers, leaving a trail of raw, oozing ground in their wake. *All my life avoiding the hierarchy and this is how they catch me. Beshaba shit in my eyes.*

The goddess of ill luck could count herself proud of this mess: the only reason he was alive was that he had been caught in the tangled interplay of the Lord of the Sixth, Glasya, and her father, Asmodeus, king of the Hells and the risen god of evil. Their schemes and counter-schemes made a knotted net that trapped devils in every layer. Lorcan had long made an art of staying out of the cutthroat hierarchy they created. And now he was square in the middle of it.

*Do be careful, little Lorcan.*

Glasya's words as he'd been hauled out of the court moments earlier pounded in his thoughts like a heavy hammer. She might, for all appearances, have given his freedom to his sister Sairché, a reward for all her help in twisting the collapsing pieces of Glasya's schemes in Neverwinter into a suitable place. But wherever Sairché locked him away, Glasya owned Lorcan.

*Your sister may be persuasive, but you and I know your warlock kept things in check.*

Which meant Glasya owned Farideh too, he thought.

Osseia's empty sockets watched him until the chain devil hauled him into the farthest fingerbone tower, as if waiting for Lorcan to make the next move.

There were erinyes in the tiny room at the tip of the tower—his half sisters, Cissa and Aricia—and more chains. Bad, bad, bad, he thought. The chain devil's appendages withdrew, dumping Lorcan unceremoniously onto the marrow-slicked floor.

"Already?" he cried. Ruby-eyed Cissa seized him by the joint of his wing and yanked him forward. He cursed. "Were you crouching in Sairché's shadow all this time?"

Aricia hooked the chain onto the nearest bone spur. "The time her lordship held the lot of you was enough to tell where the plane tilts."

"If Baby Sister wants to play at commander," Cissa said, shoving him to his knees and turning him around, "we'll wait it out."

"Who knows?" Aricia said, as he struggled. She smiled around a broken fang. "Maybe she'll take out a few of the *pradixikai* when she goes. Make some room for the rest of us."

"Watch your tongue," a new voice growled. Lorcan lifted his head. In the lacuna of the doorway stood his mad sister, Bibracte. Still armored and splattered in the gore of Neverwinter's denizens, the maddest member of the elite *pradixikai* made the lesser erinyes grow still with caution.

Bibracte stepped aside to admit Sairché—the half-devil daughter of Fallen Invadiah and master of her holdings. The erinyes might have towered over her cambion half sister, might have crushed Sairché as easily as a dry leaf instead of following Glasya's orders. But she guarded over Sairché as if Sairché had never been anything but commander of the *pradixikai*. Bibracte gave him a vicious grin.

Bad, bad, bad, Lorcan thought.

Red-skinned Sairché stood with her wings curled around her. She'd had the good sense not to deck herself in Invadiah's treasures at least, only a pair of bracers—silver, to match the tracery of tattoos that laced her bare scalp and the needle-sharp eyelashes she affected.

"Well, aren't you prepared," he said, as if there weren't terrible things in store for him. As if he didn't know exactly what Sairché wanted. "I didn't realize you were so steeped in the hierarchy, to know Asmodeus's mind before he speaks it."

Sairché smirked. "Idiot. No one was ever going to lay the blame on you when they could lay it on Mother."

"You've made an enemy of Invadiah, and *I'm* the idiot?" Cissa pressed down on his wing joint and he let out a gasp of pain.

"Careful, Lorcan," Sairché said. "One might think you were growing a spine."

"Much as one might think you were getting soft."

Lorcan's memory didn't go back far enough to recall a time before Sairché, before knowing that his sister was never going to be an ally, even if she might suffer just as much under the erinyes' notice. *That* Sairché would not have wasted so much of her time needling him.

"A pity for you I'm not," she said.

"Really? I suspect you're the one to pity."

Sairché laughed. "How adorable! Is that something you picked up, grubbing around on Toril? I've won, brother dear. Pity my wickedness all you like, it doesn't matter."

"What on every plane do you take me for?" he said. "I've no pity for your *means*. You've achieved more than any of us could have imagined, particularly while under Invadiah's thumb. You—a cambion—have control of the *pradixikai* and a good portion of Malbolge's erinyes. You have all of Invadiah's treasures—not the least of which is being the archduchess's ear. Truly, no one would have thought you could rise so high."

Sairché narrowed her eyes. "Many thanks."

He smiled despite himself. "But you cannot 'win' at the hierarchy, and you know that. Now they're all watching you, looking for the weak point that will bring you down again." He looked up at Aricia and Cissa. "Found it yet?"

Neither erinyes had taken her eyes off Bibracte. She grinned at her half sisters and cracked her knuckles.

"Not now," Sairché snapped. She scowled at Lorcan. "So I let her kill them and leave you with much better odds? You do think I'm an idiot." To Aricia and Cissa, "Pin his wings."

Cissa held his wings together. The cold iron spike ripped through the membranes, one after the other—*pop, pop*—so fast, Lorcan couldn't cry out before it was already done. Aricia slid a loop over the ends of the bolt and twisted. A rush of magic ran down Lorcan's bones, like a flow of lava. They let him up, his wings pulling against the pin as he tried to find his balance.

"Now," Sairché said. "Are you going to cooperate? Or do I let Cissa and Aricia prove their loyalty?"

Long years of survival instinct made his wings flex against the iron bar—*flee, flee, flee.* But even if he could remove the bolt, even if his wings weren't torn and bloodied, he'd have nowhere to run. He no longer had a portal out of the Hells. He had no allies. Malbolge was growing every day. The *pradixikai* would find him and tear him to shreds. He made himself still, pressed the urge to run down deep.

"That depends on what you want."

Sairché's stare didn't waver. "The Kakistos heir. What else?"

Lorcan held her gaze and smiled, even though his heart was in his throat. Even though he was imagining another set of eyes—one silver, one gold. Another voice whispering, *Run. Come with us. They'll kill you.*

"Now why," he drawled, "would you want her?"

Sairché watched him, unblinking, but Lorcan was certain after long years of practice that there was nothing to see. "I don't like loose ends."

"What end is she to you? She's *my* warlock."

"And Rohini's doom. I don't need to repeat the *pradixikai's* reports for you—you were there, after all. A warlock, I don't care about. A Brimstone Angel, I care a little for. A Brimstone Angel who throws off a succubus's domination and runs her through with so little effort? That I—and plenty of other devils—would be much more interested in." Sairché smirked. "And then there's the fact that she's yours, as you say."

He didn't so much as blink, but he was overtaken by the memory of the slender tiefling warlock standing entranced before

Rohini, motionless in the middle of the battle of aberration and devil, moments from death. Lorcan in the air high above, waiting for her to die—there was *nothing* he could do . . .

And then the charm snapping, almost audible, and Farideh releasing a burst of magic, a slash of blood spraying from Rohini's burned face as Farideh lashed out with the heavy rod. Relief he would never, ever, voice starting his heart again.

"Was it Zela who came up with that nonsense?" he asked. "You've met Farideh—Hells, you dragged her around that crater of a city for half a day trying to woo her away. Do you really think she could have resisted someone like Rohini? Struck her down? The girl couldn't corrupt a lord in a whore's parlor."

"She did well enough resisting me," Sairché said.

Lorcan snorted, recalling the vicious, calculating succubus Rohini who'd nearly brought Neverwinter—and Glasya—to ruin. Sairché was certainly formidable, and Farideh had done well to ignore Sairché's entreaties and promises. But Rohini had been a gem of another water—a foe far beyond Sairché's skills.

Sairché wasn't entirely wrong. No, Farideh hadn't been the one to kill Rohini. So far as Lorcan knew, the succubus wasn't even dead. And quick as Farideh might be to strike out, she'd never have lasted a moment trying to fight Rohini like a rogue in the street had other forces not been in play.

But it couldn't be denied: that domination would have held firm on any of his other warlocks. And Sairché knew that much by now.

Sairché, and possibly half the Hells.

"All you have to do," Sairché said, "is renounce the pact. Give her up."

The night after he'd made her pact, he'd gone back to Toril to find Farideh, weeping beside a campfire in the foothills beyond the sty of a village she'd been hiding in all her years. It had been simple to claim her and simpler still to steer her with sweet words and sure hands—she was a girl who wanted what she couldn't have and he was the sort of devil to gift her with it.

But then she was also the sort of girl to stand in his arms and ask, first of all, if this would hurt him. She was not a proper warlock or a proper Brimstone Angel.

*Do be careful, little Lorcan.*

"Who are you collecting for?" he asked. "Not Glasya—"

"Where is she, Lorcan?"

Tell Sairché, he thought, and risk Glasya's fury—whatever Sairché wanted Farideh for, it wasn't for the archduchess's secretive plans. Keep quiet and risk Sairché's fury—an anger that would lead to much quicker retributions.

Keep quiet, he thought, and you might keep her a little longer.

"I might be able to get you another one."

"Liar," Sairché said. Her wings closed tight against her delicate frame. "All four of the Kakistos heirs are claimed. Besides, yours is the one I need. Where is she?"

Quicker retributions, Lorcan thought, all too aware of the blackened chains. But Sairché's irritation with him was all genuine—she needed Farideh for some reason. And, for now, she thought she needed Lorcan. Until that changed she wouldn't kill him. If he gave up Farideh, he gave up his only bargaining chip.

*Does it hurt?* Farideh had asked. *I'll be fine,* he'd told her.

"I haven't the faintest idea," he said, grinning at his sister.

Sairché narrowed her eyes. "Cissa, Aricia: chain him up and give him an idea." She didn't break her gaze as they hauled him to his feet and backward toward the suppurating wall. "But don't be *too* eager proving your loyalty. The others will want a turn."

# CHAPTER ONE

*WATERDEEP*

*28 KYTHORN, THE YEAR OF THE DARK CIRCLE (1478 DR)*

"Fᴵᴿˢᵀ ᵀᴴᴱᴿᴱ ᵂᴱᴿᴱ ᵀᴴᴿᴱᴱ," ᴬ ᵂᴼᴹᴬᴺ'ˢ ᵛᴼᴵᶜᴱ ˢᴬʸˢ, ᴬᴺᴰ ᴵᵀ ˢᴴᴬᴷᴱˢ *Farideh's bones like a bell pealing over her head. The red glow of poisonous clouds isn't enough to illuminate her, shrouded in the shadows of broken Neverwinter. "And then you found the fourth. What a shame you kept her."*

*The cambion pinned to the wall cannot answer—the hellwasps have smashed his teeth and torn out his tongue. He is screaming, wordless, and so is Farideh.*

*"The fifth one is mine," the woman's voice says over the din, and she says it to Farideh. From the shadows, Farideh's sister, garbed in the armor of erinyes, steps out, her eyes flashing gold and her grin someone else's. "The fifth Brimstone Angel."*

Farideh opened her eyes to a night pallid with rain clouds and the reflected light of the City of Splendors, to a forest she hardly recalled, her mind overflowing with the echoes of a dreamland Hells, of broken Neverwinter, and horrors she thought she might never forget.

Every nerve of her body was taut as a tripwire, every vein carrying fire to her limbs. Farideh squeezed her eyes shut against the twisting memory and tilted her head so her horns pressed into the ground and made her head ache where they anchored to her brow. You're awake, she thought. It was a dream. Havi's safe. Havi's safe.

Still ill at ease, Farideh sat up and regarded her twin sister's sleeping form on the other side of the fire. Havi's safe, she told herself again. No one could have said, as peaceful as the tiefling girl slept, that she'd been possessed by a devil and nearly sacrificed to the god of evil a tenday prior.

She's the one who ought to be having nightmares, Farideh thought. Not me.

*The woman's voice starts laughing when they catch him. Lorcan screams and the blood starts flowing.*

*Farideh cannot run, she cannot wake. She casts blast after blast at the hellwasps the voice in the shadows sends, but they are legion. They break his wings and his fingers. She casts and casts, but the wasps ignore her flames. They pluck out Lorcan's eyes, smash his teeth. Blood—blacker than the night—pours down his face, over his red skin. He is screaming and so is she.*

*"First there were three," the woman's voice sings. "And then you found the fourth."*

None of that's happened, she told herself, staring up at the tips of the evergreens stretching up toward the grayish sky. The clouds didn't turn red, didn't boil with hellwasps, didn't boom with the terrible voice she'd imagined for Lorcan's liege-lady. All her imagination.

Please let it be my imagination, she thought.

High above, a pine cone dangled at the tip of a ragged branch. Farideh pointed two fingers at it. *"Assulam."*

Energy welled through her frame and streaked out her outstretched arm. A pop, and pinecone fragments rained down on their campsite. Farideh relaxed a little—if the spell worked, then Lorcan was still alive and channeling the powers of the Hells to her through her warlock pact and the brand that marked it.

Or perhaps she didn't know how the pact worked at all. As much as she'd found Lorcan kept her in the dark, either might be true. She shut her eyes again, and slipped a hand up her sleeve to trace the raised skin of her warlock brand.

*. . . the wasps come when the erinyes scream and shatter into a dozen of the enormous insects; wasps with cunning eyes and swords for arms. The air is full of swords and monsters. Lorcan grabs her arm and shoves her back—Run, darling, he cries, run fast and run far—*

*The wasps swoop down and pierce his shoulders, pin his wings to the crumbling walls.*

*The woman starts laughing. Lorcan screams and the blood starts flowing.*

**LESSER EVILS**

"Here."

Farideh sat up, drawing the powers of the Hells up in her surprise, but it was just Tam who kneeled beside her bedroll, holding a steaming tin cup. She eyed the priest of Selûne a moment, ready for him to transform into a devil or a cultist or something worse.

"It's just tea," he said gently. "It will help you sleep."

She shook her head. "I have to take watch next."

"I'll spell you," he said, pressing the cup into her hands. The steam that wafted off the liquid's surface smelled floral and bitter . . .

*Draw the rune, Lorcan says. She looks up at him, his wicked smile, his black, black eyes. The horns that mimic hers and the skin, red as hot irons. Say* laesurach.

*The word burns her mouth, a surge of Hellish powers courses up through the soles of her feet, thrilling every limb, and sets her tongue ablaze. It pours out the rod, out the cloudy quartz crystal at its point, as she traces the shape of the Infernal rune. The ground opens under the erinyes hooves, a lake of lava, a fountain of magma. The mouth of a volcano that devours the devil women, swallows them whole.*

*The erinyes scream and they shatter into wasps . . .*

She gulped the tea, trying to wash the phantom taste of the burning erinyes from her mouth. It was scalding hot and as bitter as it smelled, and it only made the image of Lorcan having his tongue torn out echo through her thoughts. Tam raised his eyebrows.

"We don't burn easily," she reminded him quietly. "That goes for tea too."

"I forget," he apologized. "My experience with tieflings has been . . . largely academic."

She turned the mug in her hands. "You had it ready," she noted.

"You're not the only one having trouble sleeping." He returned to his spot beside the fire, which still burned high, and the clutter of belongings strewn beside him—curling sheets of parchment, a stylus and ink, his haversack spilling all manner of bottles and pouches, and a great, fat tome.

Farideh frowned and moved to sit beside the fire as well. "I don't mean to be rude," she said after a moment, "but you can't keep much of a watch this close to the light. And while you write your . . ." She glanced at the sheets. *Netherese scouts sighted, expect larger numbers in surrounding wood . . .* "Letters," she decided.

The corner of Tam's mouth, crooked by a small scar, twitched into a smile. "I would have said 'sermons.' "

Farideh flushed. The Selûnite priest didn't seem like a spy, but neither did he seem all that much like a priest. The spiked chain he carried was fit for someone far more barbaric, and his gentle, paternal demeanor lay at odds with the sure and secretive nature he displayed at times. He knew, she was sure, that *she* knew he was not only a priest, but it didn't seem to matter. When he spoke, she couldn't shake the sensation that he was secretly laughing at her.

She looked over at the bulk of Mehen, her dragonborn foster father, sleeping solidly just out of the fire's light, closest to the bounty they escorted to Waterdeep. If Mehen of all people trusted the priest, then surely she ought to too.

"I laid a circle," Tam said, shuffling the curling parchments beside him into a neater pile. "Setting a watch is largely a formality with that. Finish your tea."

Farideh sipped the brew, eyeing the faint shimmer of runes that crept over the forest floor in an arc twenty feet wide. Tam's haversack lay open and an array of bottled powders, inks, and incenses lay on the ground beside a thick book—the remnants of the ritual that had made the circle.

"Does it keep us in?" she asked. "Or keep things out?"

"This one keeps things out. Anything fiendish, in particular."

She blushed a little harder. If Tam would have preferred she not know he was a spy, Farideh would rather he still assumed she was not a warlock.

Tam settled back, his knees folded in a fashion Farideh wouldn't have expected a man his age to find comfortable. The Planes knew Mehen couldn't manage, and the human had years on him.

"Will you tell me what you're dreaming of?" he asked.

*. . . the erinyes are a thunderstorm, unstoppable and rolling toward them out of nothing. Their hooves crack the cobbles, shatter the rune. Their crowns of horns threaten to spear the moon. Their swords are fire. Their swords are hungry . . .*

*Lorcan ignores them, leans close, his mouth on the edge of her ear. He runs the tips of his fingers up her spine—Draw the rune, he says, say* laesurach.

Farideh shifted. "I don't think you'll appreciate it."

"It's Neverwinter, isn't it?" When she looked away, he added. "There's nothing to be ashamed of. It's common, you know, a madness that chases after ordeals and upsets."

"I don't have the battle-shock," she said tersely. "That wasn't my first combat."

Tam shrugged. "No. But will you tell me the other times you crossed swords with someone, or something, were as bad?"

Farideh didn't answer. She'd killed the erinyes at her very feet with the eruption of lava. She'd watched an army of them march on Neverwinter. She'd seen Lorcan captured by hellwasps. She'd found Havilar possessed by a devil and ready to kill her—the same devil who'd sent Mehen, under a charm, to kill her. She knew there were devils looking for her—and looking for Havilar, as soon as Lorcan stopped keeping her a secret.

*You wanted this, Lorcan says, pulling her closer. She looks down at her hands, at the rune-carved rod that's suddenly there. She did. She does. She raises her arm as she had so long ago in the crumbled village, lets Lorcan's burning hands mold her fingers—smaller two wrapped around the implement, longer two extended, thumb curled over—and draws her hand down to point directly at the rune he had drawn in the frost and lichen that coats the street.*

*Draw the rune, darling, he says, say* laesurach.

*In the shadows, something watches. When she tries to catch it, the darkness just stares back, a great dark eye that fills every nook, every alley.*

*You cannot run, the woman's voice. All the planes are looking for you. The erinyes' hooves crack the cobbles and shatter the rune back into the frost . . .*

"When I was your age," Tam said, "maybe a little older, I ran with a band of adventurers. Six of us, thick as thieves. One summer, we were headed down into the wilds of Akanûl, looking for a ruin we'd heard rumors of—a Chondathan palace. It took us into the path of a Netherese scouting party.

"They killed every one of my friends," he said as mildly as such a thing could be said. "I fell to an arrow in the initial attack and rolled into a briar, out of sight. But I watched the shadar-kai draw my comrades' deaths out to gain every thrill they could. The shade that commanded the party picking through our gear as if at the market, while my friends screamed and screamed, and died. The clerics of the Lady of Loss standing over it all, just watching. I lay there, with only the Moonmaiden for company, until they'd gone on their way and I could crawl out and find my way back to a town." He kept watching the fire. "I thought I'd seen a lot of things, but that . . . you can imagine."

"I'm sorry," Farideh said after a moment.

"I dreamed of it for months," he said. "Nearly a year. Still do, sometimes, especially when my days are running rough. You choose a certain kind of life—or it chooses you—and eventually you'll run into your Shadovar. Your Neverwinter." He prodded the fire, sending a swirl of embers into the smoke. "The tea will help. Buries the dreams for a bit."

"Thank you for that," she said. "But I'm sure I'll be fine."

Tam sighed softly. "Do you know how long you'll stay in Waterdeep?"

"Hours, if that. Mehen knows of a portal to Cormyr. He'll want to take her through as soon as possible." *And there is no time soon enough*, she thought. Constancia Crownsilver, the fugitive knight of Torm they'd been tracking when they entered Neverwinter, had been difficult every day of their return trip, sneering and snapping and cruel at times.

"Will Brin go?" Tam asked.

"I don't know," she said. "I wouldn't, if I were him." The young man who'd joined their unlikely party had turned out to be the cousin of their bounty and was wrapped up in a political tangle that had sent him on the run. She'd be sad if they parted ways—in all their days wandering the world, she and Havilar hadn't made friends as easily as they had with the Cormyrean boy—but he'd fled Cormyr and Constancia for reasons he was still being tight-lipped about.

Farideh yawned, fatigue suddenly swallowing her like an overlarge cloak she couldn't struggle out of. Tam gave her another crooked smile.

"Go to sleep," he suggested. "I'll give your father more of the tea."

"I told you," she said, "it isn't the battle-shock. I'm not fainting over my first blood."

"Even if you've stood against a hundred foes and slain a thousand dragons," he said, "you've stood and watched people you love suffer and risk death and be turned against you. That will take time to settle itself." He hesitated. "And, I gather, you lost . . . someone you called a friend."

*She looks up at Lorcan, his wicked smile, his black, black eyes. The horns that mimic hers and his skin, red as hot irons.*

*The cambion holds out a hand, beckons her nearer. Cobblestones sprout from the hard-pack under her feet, and even though the ground crunches with the frost of a winter night—the night he showed her the spell that unleashed the vent of flames—the air thickens and warms. The air is Neverwinter's and a battle is coming.*

*You wanted this, he says, and she does.*

Farideh finished the cup of tea. "He's not lost yet," she said firmly, even if the echoes of the archdevil's laughter mocked her certainty.

.:⌒:.

The day they reached Waterdeep, Brin had still not settled things with Constancia.

When Brin had fled the Citadel of Torm, he hadn't had much of a plan—just get as far as possible before anyone noticed and leave as little a trail as he could. But despite making it halfway across the continent of Faerûn, despite dyeing his hair and lying about his name and taking every precaution he could think of, his cousin, Constancia, had caught up with him and the odd friends he'd made in the bounty hunters chasing her down.

He watched Mehen leading Constancia's big charger, Squall, down the cobbled road, his cousin riding, but carefully shackled. They needn't have bothered, he knew. Constancia wouldn't compound the embarrassment of having a bounty on her head like a common fleeing criminal.

Havilar dropped back to walk beside him as they passed into the city. "Have you been to Waterdeep before?"

He nodded. "Once. I was here a few days before I found the caravan to Neverwinter."

"Is Suzail like this?" she asked. "Or nicer?"

"Different," he said, as they passed by a gargantuan statue, frozen mid-stride, its ankles plastered with a variety of handbills. "Suzail's Cormyrean. Waterdeep's . . . a little of everything. I like it better." He smiled. "But maybe that's just because it's different from what I know."

She slipped her arm through his in that disconcerting way she had, too comfortable for him to make sense of what it meant. "I wish you could show us what's different. I wish we were staying longer."

He stopped walking and she stepped out of his arm. "What do you mean? How long are you staying?"

She shrugged. "An hour? Maybe a few? Mehen just wants to sell the horse, get some supplies and head straight for the portalkeeper."

"You're taking the new portal? Are you in such a hurry to get to Cormyr?"

Havilar shifted uneasily. "Your cousin . . . is not the most pleasant bounty."

"She has good points," Brin said stiffly.

"Maybe if she likes you." Havilar jerked her head up the street at Constancia, who was giving them both a glare that might once have shamed Brin into punishing himself. He scowled back.

"That makes less difference than you think."

"She does *not* like us," Havilar added. "Anyway, it won't take long this way. Maybe you can show us around Suzail instead."

"Maybe," he said. But his stomach was clenching tight as he said it. He didn't want to go back to Cormyr. He *couldn't* go back to Cormyr.

"Come on," Havilar said, slipping her arm through his again. "Let's catch up."

They found a stable willing to buy Squall, albeit for a tragic sum. The great gray charger bucked and stamped when they took his rider, as if he knew Constancia wouldn't be returning for him. Havilar and Mehen helped the stable boy master the reins and get a hood over

Squall so they could lead him into the yard. Constancia's dark eyes burned into Brin.

"I wish we didn't have to," Farideh murmured beside him. "I didn't think you could break a horse's heart."

"Would that have stopped you, devil child?" Constancia asked. Farideh's mouth went tight, and the faint banners of a shadowy protection curled out around her frame.

"What would you have them do?" Tam asked. "The portal is expensive, and I doubt its keepers want his hooves cracking their fine floors."

"Better they take me home the way I came."

"Better you avoided the bounty in the first place," Tam answered. Brin felt a flush of shame rush over him: Constancia's bounty came from his disobedience. If he hadn't run, she wouldn't have pursued, and his Aunt Helindra wouldn't have assumed Constancia'd had a hand in his disappearance.

"What will you do?" Tam asked him.

"I wish you wouldn't do that," Brin said, irritably. "It's like you're in my head."

The priest chuckled. "Apologies. You just have the look of a man deciding something unpleasant."

Farideh turned to regard them both. "You aren't coming to Cormyr, are you?"

"You stop it too," Brin admonished. "I haven't . . . I don't know." Constancia was watching him warily. "I'd hate it if I never saw you two again."

"But you ran for a reason," Farideh finished.

"I ran for very good reasons," he agreed, still watching Constancia.

Across the city, the enormous clock they called the Timehands began to chime the hour. Tam swore. "Day just burns by. I need to get to my rooms before midday. If you do stay," he said to Brin, "I'll be at the Blind Falcon Inn, just north of Dock Ward." He paused. "But ask the innkeeper for 'Yahyn.'"

Mehen returned then with Havilar, and Tam said his good-byes. The rest of them headed across Sea Ward to the portal that led to the other side of the continent.

"Farideh thinks he's some sort of secret mercenary," Havilar told Brin as they parted ways with Tam. "He doesn't seem like a priest."

"No," Brin agreed, with a last glance at the Harper agent as he disappeared into the street traffic. "Not *just* a priest, anyway."

"Neither do you, though."

"I told you," he said irritably. "I'm not a priest." The very idea would have a true holy champion of Torm laughing in a thoroughly undignified way. Only Torm himself could say why Brin of all people could manage to heal in His name—occasionally—despite failing so utterly in training to serve the god of duty.

Havilar snickered. "I know. I'm teasing." She looked away, up the road. "You're not a priest," she said, and this time there was no doubting she was serious. "You're 'His Grace.' "

Brin didn't respond. Of all the things he didn't want to have to speak—an apology for Constancia, a request for passage back to Suzail, a good-bye to the twins, a good-bye to Havilar—why Constancia had called him "His Grace" was still right at the top of the list.

They reached the portal all too soon, a narrow, gray stone building with enormous wooden doors. Brin's stomach dropped as—one arm still hooked through Havilar's—he was pulled into the entryway.

"Hells and broken planes," Mehen sighed, seeing the masses of people ahead of them in the hall beyond. "Girls, go stand in line, while I get our papers in order. Brin"—the dragonborn's cold, yellow eyes pinned him in place—"hang on to her shackles."

"Bye, Brin," Farideh said, squeezing his arm.

"You're coming, right?" Havilar asked, releasing him.

"I might . . . ," he said, taking hold of Constancia's chains.

"Good!" Havilar said, and she passed into the larger hall with her twin. Mehen stepped aside and set his haversack on a bench carved into the wall below a fresco of Suzail at dawn, pulling out permits and bounty sheets. Brin swallowed against the knot forming in his throat. This was all happening too fast.

And still he had not made his peace with Constancia.

"I never meant for them to blame you for my leaving," Brin said softly so only she could hear. "Honest."

"At least there is that," she said in clipped tones. She tossed her head, shaking the blunt bob of her dark hair out of her face. "Thank

Torm. I should like to die here and now, if you turned out to be cruel and stupid as well as disrespectful of your duty."

Brin looked away. "This is a different sort of duty."

"A coward's duty, perhaps," Constancia said.

*Coward*—the truth of it stung. He'd run instead of telling the Crownsilvers he wasn't what they wanted him to be—an eager heir for the Crownsilvers' share of the royal line. He'd run rather than face his Aunt Helindra down. He'd left Constancia to take the blame and never warned her it was coming. He'd met the twins because they'd had to save him from orcs, and when Havilar was captured by cultists in Neverwinter, he hadn't been able to do a thing. Brin was certainly a coward.

"*What* were you thinking, Aubrin?" she said. "Do you have any idea how *terrified* I was to find you missing?"

"I left a note," Brin said lamely.

"And what good did you think a note would be against Aunt Helindra's ire?"

"I'm sorry," he tried again. "I couldn't stay and face it all."

"You will have to face it all," she said. "Do you think this is something that will just go away? You could flee to Abeir and you'd still owe your duty to the family."

Constancia meant the tangled tree of Crownsilvers, the aunts and uncles and cousins and greybeards who spread through the courts of Suzail and the markets beyond, with his great-aunt Helindra carefully watering and pruning them. To those varied branches of Crownsilvers, Brin was sure he mattered as much as a shipment of lumber or an invitation from the Clerk of Protocol to visit after the most recent festival—precious, critical to Helindra's orders, but only so long as he played his part. Only Constancia—a second cousin on his father's side, who Helindra had made Brin's guardian when his father died, and Brin had been spirited away to the Citadel of Torm—really counted in Brin's mind as "family." Constancia who'd been kind to him, in her own way, and defended him when he faltered before Helindra, and never made him feel as if he were something she'd been stuck with. Not even at the beginning, when he'd been a lonesome and terrified child, and she, a squire pulled out of training to be his guardian.

"This is to help the family," Brin said. "Aunt Helindra hasn't considered—"

"I guarantee you that she has considered *everything*."

She probably had. Helindra Crownsilver had probably considered Brin from every possibly viewpoint, every angle . . . and deemed the chaos a hitherto unknown lord would bring to Suzail a necessary evil. He wanted to stop it all before he ended up like his father, shot full of arrows by rival families before Brin could so much as hold a shield—all for suddenly becoming the Crownsilvers' best claim to the throne.

Brin had heard often enough how Cormyr was civilized beyond such pettiness, how every lord stood behind their king. On the face of it, it might have been true . . . but that said not a word for those who stood behind the lords. Even if no one was so treacherous as to assassinate the king outright—and Brin had his doubts about that—there was nothing simpler than killing the lords who stood between one and the throne. Just in case. Just for *influence*.

"I think you ought to do a little more considering," Constancia said. "For example, stop thinking of Helindra's ambition and start thinking about Cormyr's needs. You are a bright young man with a fair future—you might control the Crownsilvers' fortunes someday, and someday soon, Cormyr may have need of it."

"Stop talking like a nursery story," Brin said. "What do you think I'm going to do? Free a magic sword and lead armies against Shade when nothing else will save us?"

Constancia was quiet a moment. "To be truthful? Yes. Something like that, with a little less scorn." She regarded him solemnly. "Before I left, the word was that two of the Purple Dragons' palisade forts in the Marshes of Tun had been razed, slain down to a soul."

" 'Destroyer of the Marauding Bullywugs.' It does have a ring to it."

"Monsters don't wipe out seasoned soldiers that way," Constancia snapped. "And not twice over. Not with bodies left behind. There may be no evidence to mark Shade's fault, but it doesn't take the likes of Vangerdahast to see who makes gains by erasing the defenses along the border."

No matter where you came from, there was something, someone out in the world or under the bed that frightened you as a child. The dark shapes that lurked on the edge of the world, the ones you knew were real because even adults feared them—because the adults had grown up fearing them. On the edges of the Sea of Fallen Stars, it was the aboleths and their servitors, reaching out from the Far Realm to spread madness and destruction. Near the Underchasm it might be the drow raiders. North, far north, children might worry that the orcish kingdom of Many-Arrows might assault their village one day, without warning.

In Cormyr, Brin had grown up with the fear of Netheril deep down in the marrow of his bones. From the City of Shade, the twelve princes ruled the growing kingdom of Netheril, pressing its borders right up to Cormyr's frontier. Any day might bring the advance that pressed into Cormyrean territory. Any year might be the one that brought Shade to Suzail. The borders stood, the war wizards kept watch, the military trained, and still, everyone knew, it might not be enough. The Shadovar might ooze out of the dark corners of the city, slipping across the planes to overwhelm Cormyr.

It nearly shook his resolve, but no—Shade wasn't a danger enough to risk everything. "Lead armies yourself, then. You'd make a better general than I would. *Squall* would make a better general than I would."

Constancia sighed. "If this is about that girl—"

"What girl?"

"Please. I saw you and her on the road here." Constancia shook her head. "I told them it was a poor plan to keep you isolated that way. Better to learn 'the way of kings' with suitable maids, than to wait and have you swoon over the first girl you meet in the world."

"It's *not* about Havilar," Brin said firmly.

"Don't let it be," Constancia said. "You can't marry some feral tiefling."

"Who said anything about marriage?" He'd known Havilar all of a few tendays, and maybe . . . maybe he *was* fond of her. He thought she might be fond of him. Fond enough he started to suspect she was teasing him. But even if she were serious, he wouldn't think of marrying her. He didn't think of marrying anyone, if he could help it.

Constancia added, "You get a bastard on her, and it might well be worse."

"Oh holy gods!" Brin cried, certain his face would burst if he blushed any harder. "That's enough. Don't talk about her like that, and don't give me any more advice I don't need."

Constancia chuckled. "It wouldn't be embarrassing if it weren't a little true, now would it? I'm only saying what you need to hear."

"No," Brin said. "You're saying what you think will make me come home. I had good reasons for leaving, and good reasons for not going back. Right now, no one outside the Citadel knows I exist, and everything's fine. Everyone's as safe as they can be. As soon as Aunt Helindra tells the whole world she's reordering the line of succession, that's going to change."

Constancia heaved a great sigh. "You're not going to *die*."

"No, but *you* might!" Brin said, his voice rising. "Did you think of that? Did you think that you might be the first person someone who wanted control of me would assassinate?"

He was suddenly aware of many eyes watching the pair of them. Mehen cleared his throat, and Brin colored. "I'll give you a moment more," the dragonborn said, turning back to his things. "Only do it *quietly*."

Constancia chuckled in a good-natured way, and Brin recalled they hadn't always fought, she hadn't always pressed him to please Aunt Helindra. Once upon a time, Constancia had held him while he cried for his father. She'd even taken the flute his father had carved and carried from out of the midden pile, so Brin could carry it as well.

"I'll be fine, you know," she said. "And so will you. You've painted yourself this horrible scenario where you have to save us from ourselves, but you forget the Crownsilvers have been lords of Cormyr for twelve hundred years. They will survive, and so will you and I because of that. But only if we do our duty."

"I'm more than just a Crownsilver," he said. "And so are you."

Constancia shook her head sadly. "You'll come around to it one day, Aubrin. It's fine to spend your youth pretending you're beholden to no one but yourself, a lone rider on the road of life. But one day you'll realize that you're never really alone. You're a part of something greater. You're a Crownsilver, and you shall always be so."

"All right," Mehen said. "It's best we were on our way." Brin took a step back from Constancia, whose gray eyes narrowed.

"I . . . ," he started. He swallowed. "Mehen, it was good to have met you."

The dragonborn nodded stiffly. "So you're staying behind?" he said. "Probably best." The hard stare made Brin wonder if he'd given Mehen just as bad an impression about Havilar as he had Constancia. Mehen took hold of Constancia's shackles. Constancia pulled away, bent forward so she was close to Brin's ear.

"There's a coinlender in the city, Tannannath and Frynch," she said quickly. "You ask for the Broken Marble safehold. Write the runes A C O atop each other when they ask, and the answer is 'He made the right choice'—although if you need me to tell you that when it comes to it, I'll box your ears. There's plenty to keep you fed and sheltered until you change your mind."

"Constancia—" he started.

"And take some of that coin and buy Squall back," Constancia ordered. "You can ride him home. He'll carry you."

"I'm not coming home."

"Let's go," Mehen said, muscling her toward the doors that led to the hall of the portal.

Brin thought of chasing after him, but the thought of saying good-bye to any of them was more than he could bear. Especially Havilar.

You'll see them again, he told himself. It's not such a big world. He watched Mehen's back as he disappeared into the crowded hallway. You don't have to say good-bye.

Coward, Brin thought.

# CHAPTER TWO

*WATERDEEP*

*28 KYTHORN, THE YEAR OF THE DARK CIRCLE (1478 DR)*

**T**HESE ARE THE STORIES, TAM THOUGHT AS HE STARED UP AT THE SOOTY ceiling, that no one bothers telling.

Down in the market square of Waterdeep, he knew, at least a dozen vendors sold chapbooks filled with the stories of ancient warriors and clever rogues. Of wily adventurers who outsmarted greater evils and freed their true loves, as well as a great deal of treasure. Of the glory and greatness that awaited the hero when the deed was done.

None of those heroes, he was sure, was ever described as having been made to sit for an hour in a windowless hallway, waiting to turn in a report to his superiors who had hurried him back as if the city were on fire.

"Every stlarning time," he muttered.

The Harpers of Waterdeep were certainly not unique in their formalities—a spymaster with no sense of what happened in his or her organization was no one Tam wanted to work for. But they stood out for the sheer inefficiency of all their rules and regulations. It was clearer by the day that they'd once been little more than loosely allied adventurers.

Written reports—which would be read and then destroyed—face-to-face meetings with his handler—who was running late *again*—and to top it off, no system for the dull realities of spies needing to have coin to run around the continent on and safe places to hole up in.

A far cry, he thought, from chapbooks.

Not that he blamed them, not entirely. A hundred years ago, the Harpers had spanned the continent. From the highest houses of Waterdeep to the docksides of fallen Halruaa to the ranks of the gods' own Chosen, they said, the organization had power enough to run itself and keep in check such threats as Shade, the nefarious Red Wizards, and the Black Network, the Zhentarim.

But a hundred years was a long time, and since then the Harpers had fractured, crumbled, collapsed under the weight of a world recovering from the catastrophes of the Spellplague, the return of Abeir, and the loss of whole nations. The Harpers had scattered and the organization had retreated and retreated and what was left curled itself away in the city of Everlund, forgotten by most everyone, except a few chapbook purveyors, who embellished the legendary Harpers into something more akin to mythical heroes.

Those who were left had banded against Netheril's advancement—the worst of the threats facing Faerûn these days. There hadn't been enough of them to do more.

Until recently. The Harpers of Everlund weren't the only ones set against the Empire of Shade, and recent years had brought greater numbers of agents to their cause. That had been what convinced Tam. He'd seen firsthand what the Shadovar were capable of in the name of Shar, the goddess of loss.

But with more agents, it seemed the Harpers were getting overeager. It couldn't just be about Shade and Netheril anymore. And how could any of them refuse to stand against the Hells or the Aboleth Sovereignty, or worse things?

Tam skimmed the carefully inked report he'd laid on the bench beside him without really reading it.

*. . . Shadovar scouts . . .*

The blank-faced man all in black buying supplies, eyeing Tam and—no doubt—the blessings of Selûne that marked him, just as Tam eyed the sliver of shadow that marked Shar's own. Both aware of what they stood for—a battle more ancient than the gods—and both aware that neither was ready to take that field, not there, not yet. A promise of something worse, he thought. Something he would have liked to chase down. If he'd had the chance.

*. . . nest of wererats, curse appears localized . . .*

The night he'd gotten too close to what he was looking for and found himself fighting off half a dozen wererats near the dockside, coming away soaked in blood and fearful he'd been bitten. The blessings had worked, or perhaps he'd avoided their teeth, but the wounds were still raw under the bindings and he'd not found the purpose of the nest. Only that it was prepared for attempts to infiltrate it, and well-armed.

*. . . worshipers of Asmodeus, possibly those of other devils, attacked the House of Knowledge . . .*

He'd left Farideh and Havilar out of that part of the report, written it around the warlock's role in the fight and her wilder assertions. But something fiendish lurked in Neverwinter, no doubt. He'd seen its mark on Havilar the night he returned from the wererats' attack. He'd been close enough to see the remains of the creatures the twins insisted had been called up from the Chasm by a succubus. He'd seen Farideh's single-minded determination bear this out.

*. . . taint of Far Realm magic and suggestions of aboleths near river and Chasm . . .*

Worse and worse and worse. And here were only the bare facts and not the fleshed out dangers of a world that had lost its way and was only starting to come back to it. A world that needed people like the Harpers—people like Tam—to stand against such hidden horrors.

If they would just sort out their bloody payroll, he thought.

The door finally opened, and a man about Tam's age with a sharp beard and a comfortable belly opened the door. Tam's handler smiled cheerily and waved Tam in.

"Shepherd!" Aron Vishter said. "Sorry to keep you waiting."

Tam frowned. "You don't have to call me that."

"Ah, but I want to. A reminder of old times, better times." He took the report from Tam. "Well, more exciting times for me, more comfortable times for you, eh? Viridi never ran you ragged, did she?"

Tam sat in the chair opposite Aron. He'd known the spy as the Fisher when he'd worked for another spymaster, a Turmishan woman called Viridi. In those days, "the Shepherd" had been the cleric in Viridi's house, responsible for healing and occasional resurrections, and "the Fisher" had been a field agent sent specifically into well-to-do merchants' circles. From the look of him, the Fisher still enjoyed the same sort of lifestyle he had in those days—his shirt was made of a linen finer than Tam could have imagined affording, and the brace of rings he wore on his thick fingers all glittered gold.

The Fisher sat behind the desk and perched a pair of spectacles on his nose. He read the report with as much focus as Tam had in the hallway.

"It's a bit of a mire up there, isn't it?" he muttered. "You still advocating we pull out entirely?"

Tam hesitated. "The team you have in the city's not enough. They need reinforcements—double, maybe triple. The Shadovar at least ought to be—"

"Who exactly do you think I have to spare?"

"If you can't reinforce them, then pull out," Tam said. "Recall all of them before they're killed. Neverwinter can't be saved by a half-dozen Harpers."

"We'll leave it to Cymril," the Fisher said. "What about the lycanthropes? Wasn't that what you were sent for?"

Tam sat back in his chair. Not worth it, he thought. Not worth the argument. The Fisher would do as he pleased. "Definitely there. Wererats for certain. Well-organized too. It goes deeper than just some wildlings down from Luskan—"

"Watching Gods," the Fisher swore at the report. He looked at Tam over his spectacles. "You *fought* them? Has someone seen to you?"

"It was over a tenday ago. I'm fine. No symptoms."

"Well, I'm quite sure no one told you to go brawling with wererats. Don't want to see any reimbursement requests for lycanthropy blessings." The Fisher smiled blandly at Tam and set the report to the side. "Seems in order. I'll see what our people in Neverwinter can do about the rest. They won't be happy you didn't sort out those wererats though."

Tam gritted his teeth. "Your coordinator in Neverwinter wasn't too helpful."

"Cymril? Yes, well, she's got her hands full, doesn't she? 'Specially now."

Every stlarning time, Tam thought. He might as well have given his reports to a bare wall. Aron Vishter would do as he pleased and all the better if he could ignore Tam's advice. Better just to get out of the Fisher's offices. Figure something out later. Find a way around the Fisher and Cymril when neither was so angry at him—or wiser still, accept the truth, that the city was doomed, whether the Harpers listened to Tam or not.

Save what you can, he thought. There's too much world at stake.

"Where am I next?"

"Oh, here," the Fisher said, nodding at the chair Tam sat in. Tam frowned.

"Is there something particular happening in Waterdeep?"

"Yes," the Fisher said. "You're having a rest."

Tam waited for the handler to elaborate, to explain the cover. The Fisher said nothing. "You can't be serious," Tam said. "You must need me *somewhere*."

The Fisher leaned back in his chair. "How many missions have you been on of late?"

Tam shrugged. "Enough."

"A pretty answer," the Fisher said. "The *correct* answer is that you've been sent to deal with fifteen different threats and concerns in the last year."

"You're short of agents," Tam said. "It was necessary. And it was fine—I didn't botch any of them, did I? I didn't fail?"

"One could argue Neverwinter was not a success."

Tam gripped the arms of the chair. "One could argue you sent me in there without the faintest idea of what I might find."

"We sent you to assess the city, and ferret out some wererats."

"And it doesn't matter if the place is crawling with Shadovar and aboleths and devils and worse, on top of the lycanthropes—you still don't have the agents to deal with any one of those things. And don't tell me Cymril can handle it."

The Fisher smiled at him in a tolerant sort of way that made Tam's knuckles itch. "I certainly don't have the agents to let you run yourself into the ground pretending you're still a strapping lad of twenty. We've gotten old, Shepherd. There's no denying it."

Tam leaned back in his chair, still clutching the arms. "I know when to cool my heels."

"Do you? Before or after you get yourself tangled up in . . ." The Fisher lifted the top sheet of the report. "A border battle between devils and aboleths? And right after you tangled with those wererats, I see." The Fisher clucked his tongue. "You're really going to tell me that's all fact and argue you don't need some time to . . . gather yourself?"

"You don't have agents to spare," Tam said. "Half efforts will just get people killed."

"Half efforts are better than no efforts."

"Not like this! Pull your agents back. Focus on what they *can* do."

"Don't tell me what my agents can do," the Fisher retorted. He pulled a bottle down from the shelf beside his desk. "And don't take that tone with me. It's not like the old days." The Fisher poured a half inch of amber liquor into a pair of glasses and pushed one across the desk to Tam. "We don't have patrons like Old Viridi to keep our coffers full and the wheels of the world greased."

"You're the bloody Harpers," Tam cried. "*Find* some patrons."

"And what would they patronize? Hmm?" the Fisher said. "A hundred years ago, the Harpers were the peak of it—courageous, clever, brave as they came. Now what do I get, but a half-dozen young peacocks and preening lasses who've read too many godsbedamned chapbooks about Saer Danilo Thann and his magic what-have-you-this-tenday—*none* of which do the man a damned bit of justice." He swigged the liquor. "They show up becloaked and picking off-key tunes on bloody lyres with swords fit for nothing but show and want only a bloody pin that says they, too, are the true article. And those are the ones we've vetted. I shudder to think what would happen if we recruited openly." He studied the dregs at the bottom of his glass a moment, then drained it. "Even *I* wouldn't send those poor young fools into Neverwinter, assuming you have the right of it."

Tam scowled at his own glass. "So they need training. Train them."

"And who can train them?" the Fisher demanded. "All my veterans are out, ridding the plane of evil—because who could possibly stop at Netheril alone?—or here, resting."

"I don't need a rest," Tam protested.

"Fine," the Fisher said, with an unpleasant grin. He shuffled through a stack of parchments beside him. "Then *you* can train up one of my greenlings. Boy's called Dahl. Studied with the Oghmanytes but doesn't seem to have taken to the priesthood. Don't know why. Don't suggest you ask—it seems a sore point. I've had him scouring the city for antiquities the last two tendays, so—"

"Antiquities? You're sending me out shopping?"

"The Harpers have a proud tradition of preserving lore," the Fisher said. "Besides, it gave him something to do—find out if he has an eye for it or not. Make sure he's not spending any coin on useless things."

"All of it is useless," Tam said. "What do you think to find in the Waterdhavian market? The Simbul's spellbook? The last of the Nether Scrolls?"

"Then train him at spycraft," the Fisher said. "I don't care. History, skulking, thievery, the bloody lyre—I don't care. Do what you can to make him a proper Harper."

"I'm not a wizard."

"You're also not a proper Harper," the Fisher said sharply. "So give him what you can and make me the sort of agent I *can* send to Neverwinter." He smiled again, and again Tam wished he could knock the grin off his face. "After all, neither of us is going to live forever, Shepherd."

•:◠:•

Farideh had not been in many temples, but if the hall that housed the portal to Cormyr had not previously been one, the keepers were doing a fine job replicating the spirit of such a place. A long marble pathway guided travelers in between painted columns of warm wood, like supplicants toward an altar. The portal stood behind an ornately carved screen, and flashes of iridescent light threw stars through the cutouts. The high ceiling had been painted with frescos of bucolic countrysides, and throughout there was a cozy sense of peace that it was hard not to settle into, even for Farideh.

Despite the seething anger that all but poured off of Constancia. The knight of Torm had never been a cheerful bounty, but since they reached the portalkeeper—since Brin had left them, Farideh thought—Constancia had grown surlier by the moment. It made Farideh's nerves itch, and the tip of her tail traced an arc over the marble.

Just past the chained woman, Havilar took no notice of Constancia's state, looking past her sister, past the other travelers, at the door leading out to the street.

Farideh frowned, and—holding tightly to Constancia's shackles—followed Havilar's gaze over her shoulder and back to the door. "What are you looking at?"

"Nothing," Havilar said, not breaking her vigil.

They might have been twins, but a lifetime of looking at her sister's face only drew the differences into sharp focus for Farideh. Havilar might have the same cheekbones, the same swell over her brow where her horns budded and swept back in graceful curves. The same tawny skin and the same dark hair. She might have the same jawline and the same nose and the same mouth, but Havilar, with her easy grin and golden eyes, looked only like Havilar.

"Wrong blasted day to be traveling," Mehen said as they edged closer to the portal. Its shimmering light bounced off the polished wood and stone as another traveler passed through.

"Could be worse," Farideh said. "We could be trying to bring that horse through." Constancia gave her an even darker look.

We'll be in Cormyr soon, Farideh reminded herself. And she'll be someone else's problem. Still, she pulled her right hand into her sleeve to hold the etched rod that channeled her powers.

Mehen put an arm around her shoulders and pulled her into a half embrace, rubbing his jaw ridge over her head affectionately. She rested her head against her father's chest a moment, uncomfortably aware of the knight's disgusted expression.

"When we get the bounty settled," Mehen said, releasing her and mussing her dark hair with one massive hand, "first thing, we get you a new cloak."

That caught Havilar's attention. "What? That's not fair!" she said. "If I'd known setting my cloak on fire meant I could have a new one—"

"It's still warm," Farideh said. "I don't *need* a cloak." I don't want a cloak, she thought. I don't want to hide.

I don't want to *want* to hide, she amended.

Mehen looked down his snout at her, puzzled. "You need a cloak," he said a little sternly. He reached over and tugged on Havilar's long braid. "And you need a haircut. Getting to be a damned axe man's handle."

Havilar swatted him away. "I'd rather have a new cloak. And Fari's hair's just as long."

Mehen's expression closed a little more. "Fari stays out of range of axes. At the moment." He cleared his throat. "Here we are."

The group of men ahead of them stepped behind the screen and into the portal, and Mehen stepped up to buy their passage. Havilar bit her lip, her eyes darting once more to the door.

"Truly," Farideh said, "what are you watching for?"

"*Nothing!*" Havilar insisted.

"He's not coming," Constancia interjected. Her gray eyes flicked over Havilar and she sneered. "Not for me and not for you, you silly slut."

Havilar could not have looked more surprised if Constancia had bashed her square in the chest with her shield—which was much how Farideh herself felt. The powers of the Hells shot through Farideh, twining around the knot of embarrassment her chest had contracted into. But seeing her twin's blanched, shamed expression, that embarrassment lit into a white-hot fury.

In one quick motion, she pulled the heavy rod out of her sleeve and pressed the quartz tip of it to the soft underside of Constancia's jaw. Hellish energy burned up through her veins, and they stood out black across the backs of her hands. The knight tensed.

"You hold your tongue," she said, her voice shaking with nerves and anger.

"Fari!" Havilar hissed. "Gods, don't be dramatic. Put it away!"

Constancia chuckled nervously. "Yes, put away your toy, warlock. No one here believes you'll use it. Not where you'll be found out."

She could. She might. A quick spell and she could shatter Constancia's prized armor, just to prove she could. She could burn her. She could make a lot of trouble.

We'll be in Cormyr soon, Farideh thought, replacing the rod in its pocket.

"You utter anything like that again," Farideh said, quietly, "and I won't care who sees."

Havilar gave the door one last, gloomy look before turning back toward the portal and their bounty. "Gods," she sighed. "I hate Cormyr already."

"*How* much?" Mehen roared from the head of the line.

Farideh and Havilar traded glances.

The man standing between them and the arcane circle that led to the city of Suzail, several thousand miles to the east, didn't so much as flinch. His eyes flicked over Farideh, the shackled Constancia, and Havilar, sullenly leaning against her glaive.

"Eighty-five," he repeated, "for the lot of you. Or twenty-five apiece. Gold, please."

"I spoke to your woman two days ago," Mehen said. "She said forty for all of us."

"Big fellow like you? Plus the knight and her armor and those two tall-trees? I can't move you all that cheaply. Maybe if you were halflings, I could do forty."

"You're not *carrying* us," Mehen snarled. "I've been through portals. The size doesn't matter."

"Maybe you're used to plague-battered portals," the man said. "Cheaper 'cause you don't always come through. This one's new and as solid as they come. Verified by the Blackstaff himself."

"You still quoted forty!"

The man shrugged. "Take it up in Suzail."

Mehen let loose another string of invective in his native tongue. Farideh grabbed Mehen by the arm and pulled him away from the man.

"That *henish*!" Mehen started. "He knows well and good—"

"And he's never going to admit it," Farideh said. "You've gotten all the advance on the bounty?"

Mehen glared at Constancia. "Spent what she was carrying on getting here. We've got sixty-five and the purse will be empty after that."

"Then there has to be another portal?"

"It's a portal, not a blacksmith's. If there's another they're keeping it private." He bared his yellowed teeth and tapped his tongue against the roof of his mouth, tasting the air for trouble. "We can't afford eighty-five. We'll have to take the overland route."

The overland route to Cormyr's capital would take tendays—months if the weather didn't hold. They might be able to fund their passage by hiring on with a caravan—assuming they could find a caravan willing to take on tieflings and a dragonborn with a shining knight of Torm as a bounty—but even if everything worked out, it meant tendays in Constancia's company. Farideh traded another look with her sister, who clutched her glaive until her knuckles were white—Havilar might be taking her turn as the good sister, but it wouldn't last long with Brin's awful cousin provoking her.

Farideh bit her lip and studied the portal, the stubborn portalkeeper and his guards all waiting for an answer. "What about fifty?" she said.

"Fifty wouldn't be as good as forty, but it would do."

"So buy passage for yourself and Constancia—that's fifty. Leave Havi and me here."

Mehen looked down his snout at her, as appalled as if she'd suggested they pay the portal fee with his ancestor's eggshells. "Out of the question," he said. "We'll find another way."

"What other way? Overland will take months and cost just as much, maybe more. This way it will be finished in a few days at most." She shrugged. "What can happen in a few days?"

Mehen narrowed his eyes. "Where should I start?"

It would take a shift in the planes, Farideh thought, for Mehen to stop treating her and Havilar like children. She could lead an army across the continent and he'd still try to make her drill with Havilar and then send her to bed. If he wasn't there to watch over them—

"What . . . what if we stay with Tam?" she asked. "We'll keep to the inn he mentioned, make sure he knows where we are, and you'll be back soon enough. Tomorrow, right?" she added. "That's not enough time to get into trouble."

Mehen growled low in his throat, the scaly ridges of his face shifting with annoyance as he warred with reason and fear. The growl cut off abruptly and Mehen stormed across the room to the portalkeeper. "Paper and a quill," he snapped. The portalkeeper demanded a few coins for the favor, and soon Mehen was scribbling a lengthy, hurried note.

"You take this *directly* to Tam," he said when he was finished and the ink had mostly dried. "You're not to go out without each other or without your cloaks—which means Fari, *get a cloak*. Go to sleep at a reasonable hour and, Tiamat pass you by, you keep that boy away from Havilar, understand?"

"Who? Brin?" Farideh said, taking the folded note and the small pouch of coins he offered her.

"Fari," he said in a warning tone. "I mean it."

"I don't think you need to worry about Havi and Brin."

"I hope so," he said, half to himself. He glared down his snout at her, in that fierce way she knew meant he was angry not at his daughters, but at the world they lived in. "Whatever blossoming romance you think is happening, at your age, it's doomed, no matter the sweetness."

Farideh flushed. "I'll keep that in mind should I ever have a 'blossoming romance.' "

Mehen narrowed his eyes. "That devil shows up, your sister *will* tell me. You're better off without him around."

Farideh doubted that. She wasn't Havilar, after all, who took to the glaive like she'd been born with one in her hands. The sword she carried had become mostly for show since she'd taken the pact—a state that was safer, really, for everyone involved. She couldn't lose her grip on a burst of magic.

But without the pact, she had no magic. And without Lorcan, she had no pact.

"What did you *say*?" Havilar marveled after they'd watched Mehen and Constancia pass through the portal, and started heading toward the inn.

"Just the right reasons at the right time."

"Well you'd better tell me the reasons. For future reference." Havilar considered her sister for a moment. "Would you have done it?" She jabbed two fingers toward the underside of her jaw in pantomime.

"No," Farideh said, embarrassed. "Though I wished it had scared her just a bit." They turned and headed out of the hall. "She's horrible, isn't she?"

Havilar shrugged. "I'm sure she has good points. She raised Brin after all."

"Mehen thinks he ought to worry about you and Brin. Isn't that funny?"

"Mehen worries about everything," Havilar said. "What's the note say?" She snatched the note from her sister and unfolded it.

"Gods, he wants Tam to keep us on a short lead. Meal times, *bed times*—is he *mad*? We aren't *twelve*—suggestions for sparring to keep us busy. What does he think we're going to do in a day?"

Farideh looked askance at her sister. In the previous year, Farideh had taken on an infernal pact with Lorcan, gotten them ejected from the village, been accosted by numerous priests and bystanders, and accidentally run afoul of a cult of devil worshipers. And Mehen thought of her as "the quiet one."

" 'No whiskey,' " Havilar read. "Calls that out specifically. Nothing *happened* the last time I drank whiskey. 'No boys' is on here too." She scowled and folded the note up.

Farideh watched Havilar a moment. "Mehen's not right, is he?"

"Of course he's not right," Havilar said. "Don't be stupid. You need to buy a cloak, right? Let's do that. Go back to the inn later."

"Do you think Brin's gone there?"

"I don't care," she said, firmly taking Farideh by the arm and steering her toward the market in the middle of the city. "I think you should get one with ribbons. Or velvet. Something in a nicer color than brown."

"I don't know why everyone's so fussed about you two," Farideh said. "You're just friends."

"Friends keep their promises," Havilar replied. "He said he'd come with us."

"He said he might. And he meant 'no.' "

"Then he should have *said* 'no.' "

They walked in silence until they reached the market. Stalls and tents overflowed with bright apples and crinkled, emerald greens, nuts piled up like treasure, bolts of fabric and smooth pots and all manner of other things—all in the shade of a striking black tower.

Farideh eyed a cart of chickens with jewel-red eyes, all strung together and clucking. "You know he gave me trouble about Lorcan too. It's not just you."

Havilar snorted. "It was for show, then. Mehen doesn't think you can call Lorcan anymore. He just doesn't want you to try."

"I might be able to," Farideh said defensively.

"Well, you haven't," Havilar said. "And that says something." She sighed. "I almost wish you *would* get Lorcan back. Then Mehen would stop bothering me about boys. Come on."

Havilar marched her toward a likely looking storefront. The shopkeeper didn't greet them as they entered, only eyed them with a puzzled stare.

"Well met," Havilar said. "D'you sell cloaks?"

The man blinked at her. "Sell the fabric," he said slowly. "Got a few readymade. Used, all of them." He jerked his head toward the far end of the shop. "Over there."

Havilar dragged her sister over to the shelves of colorful cloth, the rack of shabby clothing. "How long do you think it takes to make a cloak?" she asked.

Farideh looked back over her shoulder at the shopkeeper, who'd moved around his counter to keep a better watch on them. "Awhile, I suspect. We'd need a tailor. And more coin. Just look at the worn ones."

Havilar wrinkled her nose. "These are *hideous*. Better you wear your burned-up one than this." She pulled out a roughspun cloak large enough to cover Mehen.

"Add some ribbons," Farideh said, turning back to the store.

Havilar chuckled. "Not enough on the plane to make it pretty."

The rest of the shop held a jumble of items peculiar to the sorts of wares adventurers and wayfarers sought out. Cheap, sturdy goods alongside the sort of flashy items a person who'd fallen into sudden coin might splurge on. Weapons. Jewelry. Magical implements.

And a shelf of thick, beautifully bound books that shimmered with the suggestion of waiting magic. Ritual books.

Farideh ran a light touch over the buttery leather spines. They were far finer than the book Tam carried. She wondered if the spells were finer, too—the far-speaking one instead shouting to the heavens; the temporary chapel erecting a splendid temple; the binding circle blocking out the very Hells—

She stopped, eyes locked on her tawny fingers pressed to a cream-colored book. "Havi?"

"Hmm?"

"Do you remember the spell you did?" Farideh asked. "The one that called Lorcan from the Hells originally? How did you do that?"

"A scroll," Havilar said. "A ritual thingy. Garago had it shoved behind some books."

Farideh's pulse sped up. "Do you recall what it looked like?"

"Bunch of runes and lists of things to use. A drawing of the circle you were supposed to do alongside it. I didn't get to read it too much. It burned up when I did the spell." Havilar came to stand beside her. "Why?"

"Curious," Farideh said, taking her hand back.

Havilar peered at her. "I was only joking," she said. "You should leave Lorcan be. He's probably dead and if he's still alive, he's still trouble."

"He was more help than trouble in Neverwinter," Farideh said. "Do you really expect me to leave him for dead?"

"It would be smarter," Havilar said. "He might have been a help, but he's still a *henish*."

But not the worst. Farideh thought of Lorcan's wicked, clever sister, of the promise Sairché had left her with in the ruins of Neverwinter. "You will come back eventually," she'd said. "You will accept my offer. It's just best if you decide to do so on your own."

It was Sairché who'd told Farideh that Lorcan had made the pact with her because she was descended from one of the first true, infernally pacted warlocks in Faerûn, Bryseis Kakistos. The heirs of that coven of warlocks were rare, Sairché had said, but none so rare as the heirs of the Brimstone Angel, Bryseis Kakistos. There were only four, she'd told Farideh. Four in all the known world, including her.

Five, Farideh had realized, if you included Havilar.

Lorcan had assured her no one knew about Havilar at the time. Since then, who knew what had changed, what had happened? There might be a veritable auction house of devils vying for the right to corrupt her impulsive, eager sister. Vying for the right to claim Farideh, too. And the only devil in the Hells who would tell her what was going on was Lorcan himself. He might dissemble. He might twist her words around to trap her with a false understanding. But Lorcan, she knew, never lied to her.

**LESSER EVILS**

If I leave him be, Farideh thought, then I don't know what comes next.

Havilar stood, braced as if for an argument, and for a moment, Farideh thought of telling her everything: Bryseis Kakistos and collector devils, Sairché and Lorcan's promise, and what might be on the horizon. She'd have to tell Havilar eventually, she knew.

"I said I was just curious," Farideh told her. "Lorcan can handle himself."

"Go ask the shopkeeper how long a cloak takes," Havilar said. "I don't want to borrow any of these from you."

Normally, Farideh would have begged off. Normally she would have protested she didn't want a cloak anyway, so who cared if it was nice or not. Normally, she would have done everything she could to avoid talking to the unfriendly shopkeeper.

But suddenly, there was a chance she might rescue Lorcan and keep Havilar safe. Heart in her throat Farideh walked straight up to the wary shopkeeper. "How much are the ritual books?" she said quietly.

Again, the man said nothing, his eyes flicking from her horns to her tail to the faint tatters of shadows along her arms.

"It's a simple question," she said, calm and measured as she could. A little haughty maybe. A little sharp. The way Lorcan might have said things. "How much?"

The shopkeeper looked past Farideh, at Havilar holding up a blood-red cloak whose mud-stained hem came only to her calves. She looked up at the two of them. "Can you make this longer, do you think?" she called.

The man looked back at Farideh. "I can't sell you that. You're not of age."

"Of age for what?"

"For magic. You'll not get me into trouble with the Lords. Buy a cloak or go."

Farideh glowered at him. She could feel the powers of the Hells pulsing up through her feet, the curl of shadow blurring her form. Stop it, she thought. Relax.

"My, my," a man's voice said behind her, "you *are* giving this young lady a lot of trouble, Amael." Farideh hadn't heard the man come in, and by the shopkeeper's jolt of surprise, neither had he. The stranger smiled at her through a trim, dark beard studded with jet beads. His tousled hair bore more of the ornaments, and the rich, heavy robes he wore were a rainbow of shadows, making his blue eyes stand out like beacons. His gaze pierced her for a breath, then slid to the startled merchant.

"Master Rhand," the merchant said, and if it were possible, he sounded even warier than when he'd spoken to Farideh. "Didn't see you there. This a friend of yours?"

"Not yet," the man said, and the hairs on Farideh's arms stood on end. "Tell me," Master Rhand continued. "When did the Lords pass a law that placed an age barrier on purchasing ritual books?"

The merchant shifted. "Just seems proper. Ought to be a law, anyhow."

"Show her your wares, Amael."

To Farideh's surprise, after a moment of staring at the man, the shopkeeper snorted and reached under the counting table. He hauled out a thick book bound in rusty-colored cloth and dropped it on the table. The yellow, wrinkled pages exhaled a breath of dust and aging ink.

"Fari!" Havilar called. "Come try this one on. See if it fits over your horns."

"You can have this one," he said. "Came in earlier this morning and I haven't had time to get a wizard to look at it. Sixty-five and you and your double get out of my shop."

Farideh swallowed. "Thirty."

The shopkeeper peered at her again. "It's a proper ritual book," he said in half puzzlement, half protest. "Might look a bit shabby, but that's what you get for such a good price."

Behind her Master Rhand chuckled. "Thirty," she said again.

"You want to spend thirty, I'll sell you a cloak and a pound of sweetmeats," the shopkeeper said. "Fifty and not a nib less, devil-child."

She shook her head. Fifty might as well have been five thousand. She had thirty and not a copper piece more—and Mehen was already going to be furious she was spending what she had on a book and not a cloak. "Thirty or not at all."

The shopkeeper sighed and tucked the book back under the counting table. "Well, for thirty you're not going to get much. Not these days. You *are* mad if you think otherwise." He squinted at the man behind her. "Can I help you, Master Rhand?" he said a little sharply.

"We'll see, won't we?" the man said. "Has my piece come in yet?"

The merchant's expression drew tighter. "Aye. I'll . . ." He eyed Farideh for the barest moment. "I'll be right back." He disappeared into his storerooms.

"I do hope," the man said, "you've come to Waterdeep for more than a cut-rate ritual book. You'll never get Amael down to thirty."

"Yes, well. I suppose I'll try somewhere else." She stepped back, enough to put a more comfortable amount of space between them. It didn't quiet the sense of unease he gave her, as if he might suddenly lunge at her like a snake.

"Allow me to introduce myself," the man said, taking her hand and bowing low over it. "Adolican Rhand."

"Farideh," she said, uncertain of what she was supposed to do in return. Adolican Rhand smiled and held her hand a little too long, before she pulled it away.

"Enchanted," he said. Havilar hurried over. He took her hand too, much to Havilar's puzzlement, but his unsettling gaze stayed on Farideh. It made her wish for a cloak after all.

"If you want a ritual book for a better rate," he said, still eyeing her, "I do know a fellow in Dock Ward who can give you the best deal out there. Goodman Florren, on Dust Alley. Stop by there tomorrow."

It had all the air of an order, and Farideh bristled. "We'll see."

"We're looking for a *cloak*," Havilar said, glaring at Farideh.

"We're looking for both," Farideh said quietly.

"Indeed," Adolican Rhand said. "In the City of Splendors, you can look for anything and find most of it. Such splendid oddities." Farideh's back tightened and her tail flicked, which only made her temper surge. Who was this *henish* to make her nervous?

The shopkeeper returned with a large bundle of canvas, clearly heavier than it looked. He set it on the counter and slid it forward, pushing one side then the other. "Here," he said. "Still owe—"

"Yes, yes," Adolican Rhand said, waving him off. "Send the bill around and my man will pay you the coin." He looked back at the twins. "Would you like to see?"

Not waiting for an answer, Adolican Rhand pulled loose the canvas to reveal a strange and alien sculpture. In the middle, a nude woman twisted, her rib cage stretched and her breasts taut as she reached up toward the monstrous maw above her. The formless creature, a nightmare of teeth and hands and shapeless ooze, surrounded her. Bled into her. Farideh peered a little closer and saw the woman's mouth was full of tiny, sharp teeth of its own, rendered in shell.

" 'Jhaeranna Saelhawk and the Spellplague,' " Adolican Rhand said. "What do you think?"

"It's . . . fascinating," Farideh said. Unsettling was a better word—she'd rather have looked at Adolican Rhand than the strange statue another moment.

Fortunately, he only had eyes for his acquisition. "A wizard at the cusp of her true power. They say she was plaguechanged, but the change took her from the inside. Her body looked as perfect as Mystra's last day. Almost—the back"—he turned the statue to reveal a writhing garden of tentacles sprouting from the woman's shapely back, grasping at the air—"revealed her true nature. The horrors lay within." His blue eyes pierced Farideh, and he gave her a wry smile. "The distortion makes it more beautiful, if you ask my opinion."

"We need to go," Havilar said, grabbing hold of Farideh's arm. *"Now."* They hurried from the shop.

"*What* do you *do* to draw all these . . . creepers?" Havilar demanded. She shuddered visibly. "Gods, it's like your pact is a lodestone for shady codloose winkers. Please tell me you've already forgotten that merchant's name?"

Goodman Florren, she thought, of Dust Alley. "I don't do *anything*," Farideh said. "One random rake in a shop isn't my fault. And there are hundreds of merchants in this city. I don't need his help."

Havilar fumed. "Because you *don't* need a *pothac* book," she said. "You don't need Lorcan."

"You've had your say about that," Farideh said.

"If you run off and go looking again on our *one* night in Waterdeep, I will never forgive you. And," Havilar added after a moment, "you are *not* the pretty one just because some letchy creeper likes your weird eye!"

Farideh sighed. This would go on forever if she didn't stop it, as flustered as Havilar was getting. "No one said that." She slipped her arm through Havilar's. "And I won't run off tonight or any night. We'll stick together. We'll look for a cloak. Maybe some sweetmeats and chapbooks if we've got enough. Sound good?"

Havilar hugged Farideh's arm close. "Do you think Brin likes you better, too?" she murmured after a few moments.

"Of course not," Farideh said, almost laughing. "He likes us both well enough. Why would you . . ." She trailed off as she realized that wasn't what Havilar had meant. She felt a blush creep up her neck—really? How had she missed such a thing? "Oh."

"Don't say 'oh' like that. I'm just *curious*." Havilar sighed. "If Mehen's going to act like I have to be corralled from him, and his stupid cousin's going to call me names, I'd like to know he at least preferred me to you a *little*."

"Right," Farideh said, but she was turning over every little interaction she'd seen between her sister and the runaway lordling. How much of that was true and how much was Havilar saving face? And why—*why*—hadn't Havilar said anything sooner? Gods above, she hoped Brin was far gone . . .

Farideh squeezed her sister's arm, as they turned up Sul Street. "Forget Brin and forget Mehen," she said. And forget Lorcan and Bryseis Kakistos, she added silently. "We'll have whiskey tonight."

# CHAPTER THREE

*WATERDEEP*

*28 KYTHORN, THE YEAR OF THE DARK CIRCLE (1478 DR)*

**D**AHL PEREDUR WAS EARLY TO THE TAPROOM OF THE BLIND FALCON Inn, early enough to order an ale and reconsider his notes once. Was being early good, he wondered, or was it bad? In his days with the Church of Oghma, it would have been counted as an extravagance, a waste of useful time—punctuality was the mark of a finely tuned mind. But the Harpers might have appreciated the fact that Dahl had come ahead, to study the taproom and prepare for his meeting.

Maybe. Dahl finished the ale in front of him and waved to the keghand for another. Or maybe they'd chastise him for being too obvious. Or maybe the lorekeepers in Procampur had been wrong and punctuality was no virtue but the sign of a kind of small thinking that the god of knowledge detested—it was clear enough to Dahl that they didn't know everything.

Besides, his contact—*partner*, he amended—was late.

He pulled out a stack of papers he'd only just tucked away. Reread the list of antiquaries and items to be sure nothing was missing; everything was in order. Skimmed the advertisement—*The Secrets of Attarchammiux, Terror of the Silver Marches*—he'd pulled from a market stall that morning. A lucky catch, that. The runes the seller had painstakingly recreated suggested more than the usual brass-grabbing. He shifted it behind the list and set the stack down, as the keghand brought another dark, thick ale.

He looked at the letter on top of the stack and sighed. His mother's neat writing had the delicate slant of wheat stalks in a breeze off the distant Dragon Reach. To have reached him here in Waterdeep, her letters had to have made a long and tortuous journey down into Harrowdale, across the Sea of Fallen Stars to the overland routes from Westgate up to the City of Splendors. And yet every month, another letter came, full of news that wasn't noteworthy anywhere but at his parents' small farm in the northern Dalelands—whose daughter had married and whose sheep had lambed, whose crops had come in best and whose children had gone off to other Dales, and farther afield.

It was a world Dahl had left behind a decade ago. And while the litany of his parents' lives called up something primal in his heart, in his thoughts he marveled at how alien and unfamiliar those concerns were. He didn't belong in Harrowdale, even if he didn't belong to Oghma either.

His mother knew he wasn't meant for the Dalelands. He suspected that she'd always known. She did not ask why he had left Procampur so suddenly, she never asked him to come home. She just closed every letter in the same fashion.

*We love and miss you,* she wrote, *and hope the world treats you well.*

Dahl folded up the papers and gulped down enough of the ale to quash the swell of homesickness that rose up in him. He'd write her back later. Tomorrow.

The taproom was still all but empty, and Dahl found himself reconsidering each patron, in case one was the elusive Tam Zawad.

" 'The Shepherd,' we used to call him," the spymaster, Aron Vishter, had said. "Priest of Selûne, but don't let that fool you. Might have the peace about him, but he was quite the blade when he was a lad. Middle-aged, Calishite. Thinner than you, but about as tall. Got a beard. You won't miss him."

Dahl doubted that either of the heavyset men in the corner, decked in lush fabrics, was this "Shepherd." The other man was too old, and the last three patrons, playing a hand of cards in the corner, were very much female. He sighed and drank some more ale.

The door swung open again, letting in a flash of late afternoon sunlight and two young women.

No, not women. Tieflings.

Dahl tensed. Descendants of fiends and mortals, tieflings were one thing that never came up in his mother's letters. Dahl hadn't seen one of the horned, blank-eyed creatures until long after he'd left home. Even in Waterdeep, where you could find everything, one had to go looking for tieflings.

Just as well, Dahl thought, keeping his eyes on the two. That fiendish blood didn't just wash itself away after all. Perhaps this wasn't the best place to meet Tam.

The tieflings looked like mirrors of one another. Twins perhaps, or maybe it was just that they weren't human. Maybe that was what all female tieflings looked like. One stood with her arms folded around a battered glaive, her long tail slashing the floor behind her and her gold eyes fixed on the door to the inn's rooms. The other scanned the taproom as if searching for someone. When she came to him, Dahl met her gaze—one eye silver, one gold like the other's—and she turned away with a blush.

"He's not here," he heard her say to the other. "We should wait."

"Fine," the gold-eyed one said. "Whiskey time." She laid the glaive on the floor along the bar, pulled out one of the stools, and hopped onto it, signaling to the tavernkeeper. Her twin settled in beside her. "If he *isn't* here," the gold-eyed one said, "then we can—"

"Do exactly what Mehen told us," the odd-eyed one said more firmly. "A whiskey is one thing. If he comes back and finds out you've run off or spent a load of coin or . . ." She waved a hand vaguely at the taproom. "Started a brawl—"

"I don't start brawls." The gold-eyed one grinned wickedly, displaying sharp white canines. "But I'd finish them."

Her twin snickered. "That's not better. Get me a cup of hot water, would you?" She bent down to pull a small pouch from her bag while her sister spoke to the tavernkeeper. As she righted, she glanced up at Dahl again, and this time he looked away. Not that he ought to have. He could look where he liked, after all.

"Of course it's better. I'd *win*."

"And spend all the bounty repairing the taproom."

"So you say. Anyway, I never said I was going to start a brawl. I just think we ought to take the opportunity to have some fun. Maybe we could go back to the market. Try on some nicer cloaks. Mehen can't argue with that." She drummed her fingers against the bar top. "We're going to be in this inn for ages anyway. Why start too soon?"

Dahl kept watching them from the corner of his eye. Whoever they were waiting for—whoever that "Mehen" was—the tieflings didn't *seem* dangerous. In fact, they seemed a little foolish to his mind—cloaks and whiskey and arguing about brawling. But who hadn't heard the saying? One's a curiosity, two's a conspiracy, three's a curse.

"If we don't do anything Mehen can call trouble," the odd-eyed one said as the keghand set a small cup in front of her sister and a steaming mug in front of her, "then he has to relax a little." She dropped a fat pinch of herbs into the water.

The other snorted. "Right. Tell me how *that* goes." She sniffed at her sister's tea. "How is that? Does it do anything interesting?"

The odd-eyed one shrugged. "Makes my sleep a little quieter for part of the night and tastes like old roots. Three pinches together knocks me out. You're better off with whiskey." She looked up at Dahl and narrowed her eyes. "Can we help you with something?" she said sharply.

"No," he said, but he didn't look away. She should know he was watching.

"*Gods,*" the other said. "Are you listening to yourself? This is probably how you attract such creepers. *One* fellow—one good-looking fellow!—in this whole taproom is giving you notice, and you jump down his throat." She grinned at Dahl. "Excuse my sister. She's better at worrying than enjoying herself, but she's in the market for a good tutor." Her sister turned scarlet and hissed something in an unfamiliar tongue.

"I think I'll decline," Dahl said coldly.

"No one invited you," the blushing sister snapped.

The door opened again to admit a wiry-looking Calishite man, his brown skin crinkled around the eyes and his dark curls threaded silver. He looked exhausted and ferociously annoyed, but he was also wearing a small, unobtrusive broach—pinned from the inside of his cloak.

A Harper, Dahl thought. Here was the elusive Shepherd.

He slid the parchments back into his jerkin and started to stand. But Tam Zawad had spotted the tiefling twins and stopped in his tracks.

"Farideh?" he said. "Havilar? You're supposed to be—"

The odd-eyed one—Farideh—cut him off. "Here," she said curtly, shoving a folded scrap of parchment at him. "Mehen went to Suzail. The prices went up on the portal, so he wants you to watch us."

Tam looked at the paper as if she'd shoved a dead fish into his hand. "What?"

"He'll be back tomorrow," Farideh said. "Maybe in a few days."

"I don't have time to . . ." He unfolded the paper and skimmed it. "What do you need watching for?"

"We don't," Farideh said.

"So *pretend* to watch us," the gold-eyed one—Havilar, Dahl supposed—said. "And we'll pretend you were terribly strict and never let us out of sight. Mehen will be pleased, we'll be pleased—"

"And you can go on doing whatever you were planning to do," Farideh finished.

Tam raised an eyebrow. "You want me to lie to your father."

"We want you to tell Mehen whatever you need to tell him," Farideh said. "Tell him you thought his note was rubbish, if you like. He's already left for Suzail. He won't be back until tomorrow at the soonest. Neither of us has any intention of doing anything that needs a nursemaid."

"I would believe that better," Tam said, folding the note, "had you met me at the gate and not turned up spattered in the gore of unmentionable creatures instead." Farideh blushed again and Dahl had to wonder what the Harper meant.

"We *still* didn't need a nursemaid," Havilar said.

Tam rubbed a hand over his face. "And that by the grace of all the gods." He sighed. "All right: Get a room here. Tell me if you plan to be out all day. Do stay out of trouble—even the mundane sorts—and if you can't help it, send word for me and for the love of the Moon *don't* try and get yourselves out of it if the Watch is involved."

Havilar snorted. "What are you afraid we're going to do?"

"Be seventeen and short of temper," Tam replied. "And I'd hate to explain that *again* to Mehen. Come out of this without being arrested, cursed, grievously wounded, or impregnated, and I think we'll be fine."

Farideh looked as if she'd been slapped, but Dahl could hear her sister snickering. They both thanked the priest and went to find the innkeeper about a room. Tam watched them leave, weariness overtaking his frame as if the twins had stolen something vital from the room. He sighed, shook his head, and started toward a table.

"Master Zawad?" Dahl said, climbing off his stool and stepping into his path. He extended a hand in greeting. "I'm Dahl Peredur. Aron said . . . He should have mentioned *my pin*—"

"Good gods," Tam said, looking Dahl up and down. "You? Where did you get the impression that eavesdropping like a gawping spectator made for good spycraft?"

The rebuke shut Dahl's mouth. "My apologies," he said after a moment. "I didn't mean to intrude on your business."

Tam sighed again. "Get that pin off your cloak. You've never met me—what if someone else had shown up in my place? An agent of Shade or a Zhent or something worse?"

"I suppose I'd question their goals," Dahl said, sharply, removing the harp-shaped pin that marked him. "Searching out antiquities doesn't seem in the best interests of the Zhentarim."

"*Never* assume."

"All right," Dahl said. This was all going to the Abyss's privy and back. Dahl straightened his shoulders and took out the list of antiquities. "I've gone through all the reports that Master Vishter and his friends had," he said. "I've brought together a list of the most likely and mapped out—"

"Is there anything pressing? Anything that will leave someone dead if we don't do something right now?"

Dahl bit his tongue. "They're antiquities," he said. "Not plague-pockets."

"Later then," Tam said. "Tomorrow, preferably. I've had my fill of other people's plans for the day." He stopped and looked back at Dahl. "But I will buy you a drink. We can go over how to present yourself properly."

⁘◠⁘

**ERIN M. EVANS**

The Fisher—fifteen years gone by and still he preferred that epithet to all the others—poured himself a few fingers of Damaran whiskey at the end of the day, intending to read a few more pages of reports and call it a night. But when he turned from the sideboard, he found himself face-to-face with a woman in dark leathers, watching patiently from the shadows of the door.

He stopped himself from crying out—thank the gods—and from tossing the alcohol in her eyes and pulling a dagger. But his disquiet must have shown.

"Did I startle you?" she asked striding into the room. "I couldn't wait."

The Fisher settled himself behind his desk. He knew enough about her to be sure she *hadn't* been trying to surprise him—Mira was simply quiet on her feet, which was far more embarrassing.

Not Mira, he corrected himself. She'd told him another name, like she ought to have, and damned if he was going to breach etiquette that way. Not without a better payoff for the hoarded information. Trouble was he couldn't recall the false name.

"What can I do for you, my dear?" he asked, skirting the issue. "Please sit."

"I've sent messages," she said, standing in front of the desk. "Where's my team?"

Ah, here, *here* was a better payoff, the Fisher thought. "Would you like a drink?"

"No. Thank you." She bit off each word. "Where is my team? We can't wait any longer."

"Ah, well, that," the Fisher said. "You see I can't, as it turns out, spare you so many agents. We're short of hands as it is, and—"

"You promised," she said. There was no plea there; this one was cool as they came.

"I thought I could," the Fisher said. "But don't worry: I've managed something better. A single agent—and perhaps an apprentice if they get along for the first part, you never know."

"What in the Hells am I supposed to do with one agent?"

"A venerable agent," the Fisher said, suppressing a grin. "Tam Zawad. Previously known to a lucky few as the Shepherd, as Brother Nightingale, and briefly, for an unluckier few, as the Culler of the

Fold." The woman's thin lips pursed at the name, tightened with each of the epithets, and the Fisher's grin broke free. "Do you *know* him?"

She stared at him, as if waiting for him to amend his words, as if he would take back what he said and give her a different contact. The Fisher felt the old blood stirring for something more exciting—he'd noticed already she was a quiet one, a calm one, but somewhere in that gaze something dangerous simmered. Too dangerous, likely, for an old spy with a fancy dagger. Or maybe not. He sipped his drink. At least it was more interesting than reports and corralling children playing at being Harpers.

"I understand," she said softly, "that they hold you dear in Waterdeep. A venerable agent, yourself. They respect your expertise, your years of service, to an extent—a cheap extent. It's less than you deserve, isn't it? Makes a man willing to test limits. Seek out other allies."

Her dark eyes pinned him but the Fisher refused to look away. If she thought to cow him, with information he hadn't hidden from her, she was after the wrong man.

"I also understand," her tone a little sharper now, "that you think this assignment is a minor matter. An inconvenient aside to your normal activities. Let me disabuse you of that notion: it is not. You do not accept Maspero of Everlund's coin and then brush him aside. If we fail—"

"You'll not fail," the Fisher interrupted. "You can't. Not without paying the same price."

The woman stared at him again, as if he were a schoolboy speaking out of turn. What she said next came with such venom, such fury, that the Fisher momentarily considered he might have misjudged her.

"Maspero's not one to make unnecessary examples, whatever your reports say. If I fail, it will be because *you* put a man *known* for rushing about to play hero, for trying to make up for past cowardices, for not working well with others—you, Fisher, put him on my watch when I specifically asked for strong-backed greenlings with eyes for antiquities who could follow orders and not ruin my site. This little jape, this game that makes you feel as if you've triumphed—over what, I can only imagine, Fisher; you're a man of so many shortcomings—make no mistake, it's not a mere inconvenience to me. Your games have jeopardized *everything*.

"And on top of that, you've delayed too long." She pulled a folded page from her jerkin and tossed it on the table. "He's selling it."

The Fisher drew the leaflet toward him, avoiding the woman's eyes. *The Secrets of Attarchammiux, Terror of the Silver Marches.* A paragraph of reconstituted history—tales of a wizardly dragon fit for chapbooks. A row of broken Draconic letters. The Fisher cursed to himself.

Sloppy, he thought. Godsdamned sloppy, you.

"You said he'd gladly sell it to us."

"He would have," she agreed. "And then you sat on your hands so you could pull a stupid prank on an old rival instead of moving quickly enough to catch him before he had it appraised by a nib-brained collector who went ahead and decided to tell him we were dealing with a stlarning dragon's hoard. Now it's too valuable to sell for *Harper* coin."

"How high is it likely to go?"

"For clues to a dragon's hoard?" The woman shrugged. "Depends entirely upon the crowd. Worst case: more than one 'lordly adventurer' shows up with their pockets spitting gold and their good opinions of themselves raging, and we have a battle of bidders. Could go very high, very quickly. Ten times the value or more."

The Fisher swallowed more whiskey. "I can't just hand over that sort of coin."

"I'm well aware."

"There'd be questions. They'd want to know what was so important."

"I said, I'm well aware." The woman glared at the city out the window glittering with torches, and bit her upper lip, deep in thought. "The plan will have to change. Your agent will know about the items?"

"He will. The greenling I tasked him with is nothing if not thorough when it comes to antiquities."

She nodded to herself, still thinking. "Then he'll find me. Keep the coin ready. We'll find a use for it."

The Fisher narrowed his eyes at the woman. She stared right back, implacable as ever. Her true identity hadn't been difficult to puzzle out—even if she hadn't told him her name, with those dark eyes he would have suspected. Twenty-five years in the field, missing such a detail would have him reaching for the hemlock.

No place in the world for spies who've slipped.

"They say it speaks, the page," he said. "That it has secrets for mages to hear."

"And?"

"If it's not a dragon's, whose is it?" She didn't answer. "And where'd the stone come from? Your patron never said what it *is* we're dealing with."

"Because it doesn't matter to you," she said simply. "Dragon's hoard, elven ruin, lordling's country mansion's façade—"

"Something . . . darker?" The Fisher studied her expression, but wherever her earlier fury had come from, it released nothing else for the intimation.

"Whatever it is," she said, "you're paid the same."

"Still," the Fisher said, "a man can't help but be curious—what's worth so much?"

She eyed him again, for long moments that seemed to press the very edges of decency.

"A man *can* help but be curious," she said, "if he wants to live very long in the Harpers' good graces."

·:⌒:·

For days and days, there had only been the hollow in the tip of a fingerbone tower, still weeping marrow from the walls. The little room and chains and erinyes after erinyes, a new one each time Lorcan woke, and Sairché beside them, now and again. Chains and erinyes and new sorts of pain. He lost track of the time.

" . . .you'll kill him if you aren't careful," a voice said as he stirred to consciousness.

"*I* didn't do this." Lorcan tried to open his eyes, but a layer of dried blood lacquered them shut. "Bloody Megara let them go completely feral."

"*Is* he dead?"

Every muscle urged Lorcan to stay down. If they thought he was dead they'd stop.

*If they think you're dead, they'll throw you to the layer, idiot,* he thought. *And you don't have the strength to run from that either.* Even being beaten by erinyes was better than being slowly devoured by Malbolge's hungry ground. Someone grabbed him by the chin and tilted his head—a shock of pain went through him and his eyes wrenched open.

His vision swam—three erinyes. One of the *pradixikai* by the door. One of the red-haired ones in the middle distance. A blond missing one eye staring into his face. Sulci. Shit and ashes. He recoiled despite himself.

"Oh good," Sulci said with a horrific smile. "You're up."

Not for long, he thought. After so many hours, his arms were bloodless and numb, his mind was hardly holding on to two thoughts at a time. His resolve was shaken—give him to Glasya, he didn't care anymore—

*I may have need of you and her in the future.*

He shuddered at the memory of that horrible voice crooning in his ear. Of seeing Glasya's punishments meted out to other devils. No—not Glasya. Anything but Glasya.

"There's another," he tried to say. And all he could imagine was Farideh's terrified face—he'd promised her, he'd sworn no one would find out about Havi. And if they took Havilar, Farideh would do something drastic to try and stop it, he was sure. She would leave. She would throw herself to Sairché, or worse.

*If they don't take Havilar,* he thought, *you are* not *going to be fine, and it won't matter what she does.*

"Another heir," he tried again, the words slurring from his broken teeth.

"Aw," Sulci said. "How dear." She uncoiled her whip. "We're all well aware you think you're smarter than us, Little Brother. But don't think we're so stupid as to fall for that. You can't get another heir. Not from here."

"Less talking," the *pradixikai*-shaped blur by the door bellowed.

Sulci looked back over her shoulder. "Lords, Zela, what does it matter? It's not like the worm's rallying where he hangs."

"You have to give him a little credit," the middle one said. "He hasn't broken. He ought to have broken."

"Did you expect some fragile sinner?" Zela said. "Half-mortal or not, he's still Exalted Invadiah's son. So quit waiting for him to break on his own and make it happen."

Sulci didn't move, her eyes still on the larger erinyes. "You mean *Fallen* Invadiah."

Lorcan didn't need eyes to feel the tension in the room. Having spent all his life attuned to the rage of his fifty-eight half sisters, he could likely be a corpse and still know when one of the *pradixikai* was nearby and about to strike.

"And who are you to tell me what I mean?" Zela said, coming closer. Shit and ashes—don't attack her here. One misplaced sword-strike and it wouldn't matter what Sairché, Farideh, or Glasya wanted. "You answer to me, Sulci, don't forget it."

"And we both answer to Baby Sister," Sulci said, not giving an inch. Both devils loomed over Lorcan, giving him as much notice as an imp underfoot. "Since Mother is no more."

Zela's hand shot out and seized Sulci by the throat, but the smaller erinyes was ready and, even choking, pulled an ugly, curved knife and stabbed it into the bare spot between the linked plates of Zela's dress. Zela roared, and twisted Sulci toward Lorcan—

"Zela!" a voice barked. Sairché barked. Lorcan tried to focus and saw only the shape of her, her wings filling the lacuna of the door. "Drop her."

Sulci hit the floor with a spongy thud. Zela turned on her unwanted commander, and the air still bristled with the threat of her rage.

Sairché strode into the room, followed by the shapes of more than one erinyes. Lorcan shut his eyes and didn't bother trying to count the doubling images. More than one. Too many.

"What's the punishment, Sulci," Sairché said, "for disobedience to your fury leader?"

He could hear Sulci panting. "She questioned your authority. I was—"

"What," Sairché said, a little louder, "is the punishment for disobedience?"

Silence. "Eighty lashes."

"Then I think we all know what comes next. Be thorough, Zela."

"Why are you here?" Zela demanded.

Sairché was silent for so long that Lorcan made himself open his eyes again and lift his head. She was glowering at him.

"Unchain him," she spat.

He heard, not felt, the shackles come from his wrists, and without the chains' support he crumpled to the floor. The blood rushed back into his arms and he fainted.

He woke seconds later, his pulse in his ears. Sairché stood over him, looking disgusted. She withdrew a small vial from under her cloak and dropped it beside his head, before turning and walking away, trailed by too many erinyes, into the fuzz of Lorcan's failing vision.

# CHAPTER FOUR

*WATERDEEP*
*1 FLAMERULE, THE YEAR OF THE DARK CIRCLE (1478 DR)*

"Tannannath and Frynch," Brin murmured to himself. "The Broken Marble safehold." He took one last look at himself in the streaky glass beside the door. He'd freshened up his clothes as best he could, combed his ever-lightening hair and washed his face. He still looked like someone's runaway apprentice.

He'd ignored the accounts Constancia had mentioned for days now, and he'd have liked to keep on ignoring them, but he was running short of his own coin. Tam's acquaintance got him a bedroll on the floor of the rooms the priest kept, but Brin wasn't about to ask Tam for board as well. All he had left to sell was his sword, his holy symbol of Torm, and his father's flute.

"Tannannath and Frynch," Brin murmured again, as he left the room. "The Broken Marble safehold." He pulled the door shut behind him and glanced across the hallway. To the room the twins shared.

Coward, he thought.

It might easily be a curse or a blessing that he'd ended up in exactly the same place as the twins. He'd spotted Havilar the day before, arguing with the innkeeper about the futility of peace-binding her glaive, Devilslayer. He'd frozen, like a deer hearing a rustle in the underbrush, and been unable to do so much as say "well met," as she turned and saw him. Her mouth had gone small, her back straight as the polearm, and she'd faltered against the innkeeper, agreeing that perhaps she should retire herself and her weapon to the room upstairs.

He could hear Havilar on the other side of the door, the *thud* and *crack* of her pretending to thrash someone with her glaive. On the road from Neverwinter, he'd watched her and even stepped in to spar with her a time or two. It left him with no doubt at all: this girl was lovely and funny, and she could kill him in the span of a few heartbeats.

And now she was angry at him.

Don't flatter yourself, he thought. As surely, if he apologized to Havilar, she'd wrinkle her brow and ask what in the world he meant by that? Don't even mention it, he told himself.

He hesitated another moment, listening to the rhythm of her feet striking the floor in a complex dance. Dancing, he could have handled, and bladework, well enough, even against Havilar. But no one had given him lessons in dealing with girls, and he felt rather sure it wasn't supposed to be difficult. If you were fond of a girl, you simply told them so or made some grand gesture or gifted her with something—and then you were in love and everything went on as it was meant to. You never worried she was the wrong girl to head down that path with. You never worried she might laugh at you. You certainly never worried about her glaive.

Perhaps it was better to go on avoiding her.

Coward, he thought, and he made himself rap on the door.

Havilar opened it, glaive in hand. The tawny skin above her open collar was beaded with sweat and her breath came hard. Her eyes widened at the sight of him, and he could hear the faint tap of her tail starting to flick against the floor. The sound made Brin's nerves rattle.

"Oh. Brin." She took a step back. "Did you want something?"

He shook his head—just say it, he thought. *I'm glad you didn't go. I would have felt like an utter plinth-head, and . . .* She stared, just stared, at him—angry, surely angry. "How are you?" he said.

"Fine," she said. "All right, anyway." She folded her arms across her stomach. "Farideh's not here."

"I didn't think so," he said, then added hurriedly, "It didn't sound as if she were. I'm impressed you can do any practicing in these little rooms."

"Oh." Havilar blinked at him. "Do you want to come in?"

Yes, yes he did. Constancia wasn't right, but she wasn't entirely wrong either. Havilar wasn't the sort of girl, the sort of woman he was supposed to look twice at. She wasn't human, she wasn't ladylike, and she stood over him by a noticeable amount, even if you didn't count her horns. She was wild and a little silly, and entirely too attached to her polearm.

And yet, despite—or perhaps because of all that—a part of him would be very pleased to be alone with her in a room, with all their weapons set aside.

"No, I just wanted to see you," he said. "To say . . . to see how you were."

Havilar frowned at him, as if she couldn't tell if he was being serious. "I told you already. And you?"

Ye gods, could this go any worse? he thought. Sune's bright face, he *knew* how to talk. He could be a little charming—charming enough for court. Why did it all fall apart when it was Havilar looking down at him? It had been so much easier on the road, when they weren't just *standing* there, looking for things to talk about, when they had things to do to distract them . . .

"I have to go to a counting house," he said, "to see about some coin. Would you . . . you could come along."

Havilar blinked at him. "I haven't got coin to count."

"Oh." Brin looked away. "No. I didn't mean—"

"When did you get coin?" she asked, leaning against the door jamb. "I thought you were sleeping on Tam's floor."

Brin flushed. "Did he tell you that?"

"Well . . . I mean, I asked." She looked down at the point of her glaive, worrying it into a knot in the floor. "*You* weren't going to tell me."

"You didn't ask me," he pointed out. Gods, what a mess. What a total mess. "I wasn't asking if you needed to go as well. I was wondering . . . Look, I'm a little nervous about this and I'd just like some company. Would that be all right?"

"Oh." She considered him a moment. "Do you think you might be robbed on the way back, is that it?"

He started to say that he didn't think that, that he wasn't planning to take much coin at all—if in fact he took any—and anyway, she didn't need to worry about him. But he caught himself—that was worlds better than having her think he was asking her to see his accounts. "Yes," he said. "Oh, that's most definitely a worry."

Her smile grew. "Let me change."

If the previous shops Farideh had encountered had been shabby, Master Florren's might better have been described as only recently crawling up from "midden heap" to "shop." Light struggled through the torn curtains covering the windows, spearing the dusty air where it broke through. A lamp burned behind a cracked shade, casting the array of over-sharpened weapons laid out beside the counter in an oily light. She shut the door behind her gingerly, loath to close herself into the musty shop.

Her eyes adjusting to the shift of light, Farideh edged forward, toward the counting bench. She said a silent apology to Havilar, but Adolican Rhand had been right—no one was going to give her the price she needed. Two more days of furtive searching and she still had no ritual book. Lorcan was still trapped somewhere in the Hells, suffering gods knew what torments, and she still couldn't do anything about it.

"Well met, girly," a voice called out. She startled. A halfling man—the shop owner—stood beside a rack of staffs, watching her, much as every shopkeeper had watched her, with a cautious, appraising eye. Only, Goodman Florren seemed assured that she posed no threat to him. He may have only come to Farideh's hip, but the halfling held himself as if he knew exactly how to bring her down, should it come to that. "You lost?"

"I'm looking for a ritual book," she said. "Someone told me you had them for a fair price."

" 'Someone,' eh?" Goodman Florren's dark gaze swept over her. "Seems I do *excellent* business with Goodsir Someone."

"I'm sorry," Farideh said. "What I meant—"

"Ritual books are on that shelf," he said, waving a hand at the far end of the shop. One of the staffs spit a jagged spark of purple energy. He cursed and turned back to arranging the implements.

The shelf was sagging and the options sorry. Three worn books slouched against each other: the first thick as her fist, but with a binding so worn it might not make it out of the shop; the second better, but full of faded, yellow inks and missing pages that left a hollow, fragile feel to the magic; and the third blooming with mildew and missing any sense of magic around it at all.

"How much are these?" she called.

Goodman Florren came to stand beside her. "Fifty. Forty-three. And . . . Hells, let's call that one twenty-two."

"Gold?" she said. "That one's not even a ritual book."

"I've got better in the back, if you don't like the quality."

"For double the price, I'm sure."

He chuckled. "More like triple."

"That's robbery."

He shrugged, unperturbed, and went back behind his counting table, climbing onto the high stool there. "I'll take a trade. Weapons, scrolls, jewelry. Might make the price more palatable." He gave her a wicked smile. "Mayhaps I can think of something."

"You want me to *steal* for you?"

"Did I say that?" Goodman Florren said, all innocence. "It sounded to me like I was trying to make you a good deal by offering to take what you don't need. For Someone's sake."

Farideh hesitated. The rod tucked into the sleeve of her blouse was probably worth purses—how much, she didn't know. Lorcan had given it to her, called it "the Rod of the Traitor's Reprisal." Dead useful, and she might need it to cast the ritual. *If* she could find the ritual . . .

Instead, she undid her sword belt, said a silent apology to Mehen, and laid it on the counter. "How much for this?"

Goodman Florren reached down, lifted the weapon and shrugged. "Fifteen."

Farideh bit back a curse. "It's a good sword."

"Girly, I can get a sword just as battered for fifteen anywhere in the city. You want easy coin, take yourself down to the dockside. Young thing like you might fetch a copper or two from the sort wanting to play at devil's punishment."

She flushed and he cackled. "Fine," she said. Farideh reached inside her shirt and withdrew the amulet Tam had given her in the ruins of Neverwinter. It was, to the untrained eye, only a medallion of silver, etched on one side with the symbol of Selûne—a pair of eyes in a circle of stars—and shaped on the other into a spiral made bright by the polish of too many worried thumbs. But the weak light reflected threefold off the metal and the halfling's eyes widened. He beckoned her closer.

Better this than the rod. Perhaps. If she could get the book, get the ritual, cast it, and pull Lorcan from the Hells . . . surely she wouldn't need the amulet, enchanted to bind fiends. Surely he'd be grateful. She hoped.

"Very fine," the halfling said. "Let's say . . . eighty."

Farideh closed her hand over the amulet. "Do you think I'm a fool?"

Goodman Florren's dark gaze met hers. "You have a source and a story, we'll talk about . . ." He frowned and peered at her face a moment more. His expression closed. "Son of a barghest."

"What?"

He slid off the stool. "Sun and moon eyes. Tluin and buggering Shar. Should have said something!" he called as he disappeared into a room at the rear of the shop.

"What's that supposed to mean?" Farideh shouted after him. "Hey!"

The bells over the door jangled, startling her. A blaze of sunlight sliced through the gloom.

"This is on your list, then?" a familiar voice said. Tam held the door open, blinking up at the cluttered rafters, the covered windows. Farideh sprinted back behind a shelf before his eyes could adjust to the gloom.

"The last before the showing." She peered between a stack of scrolls and a collection of brass goblets. Trailing Tam was the pale, rude man from the tavern. His gray eyes darted all over the shop, as if he were searching for something. "It's . . . not pleasant, but Goodman Florren has connections with adventuring companies, historians, and the like."

"Hmm. I'll bet." Tam surveyed the rest of the shop with a skeptical eye. "Listen, Dahl, I know that Aron said this was important—"

Dahl's expression tightened. "This isn't important. I know that. This is just the only thing they'll approve me to do. I can read up on antiquities. I can't read up on running down threats. And so I cut my teeth again and again."

Tam hesitated and tried once more. "Sounds as if Aron's not using his resources all that well."

Dahl shrugged, still avoiding Tam's eye. "I'd be happy to take on something more challenging, certainly. But I do what's asked of me."

"Not one of these items has proven out."

"But they might have," Dahl said. "These are the items that had the highest likelihood, the best provenance. I already ruled out six times as many."

Tam sighed and shut his eyes a moment. "What are we here for?"

"Goodman Florren!" Dahl called. "Are you in?"

"A moment, a moment!" the shopkeeper's voice called back. "With a customer!" He came tromping back into the front room with a flat package, wrapped in brown paper. Farideh cursed to herself as he looked around for her.

"Where's she gone?"

"Who?"

"That tiefling wench."

Tam's brow rose, and Farideh cursed to herself. There weren't scads of tieflings in Waterdeep, but there were surely enough that he couldn't assume it was Farideh.

Tam seemed to make the same calculation. "There was no one in the shop when we arrived."

"Godstlarning hrast it," the halfling said. He spat. "'Tis what I get, agreeing to run errands for that . . ." He looked the two men up and down. "And who might you be?"

"Dahl Peredur," the younger said. "And this is my associate, Tam Zawad." Tam sighed and covered his face with one hand. Dahl didn't seem to notice. "A friend of ours says you've got something powerfully valuable."

"Everything I got," the halfling said, "is valuable. So you're going to have to be more specific, boy."

Dahl, to his credit, didn't flinch or fluster. "The Lantan artifact," he said. "We'd like to consider adding it to our . . . collection."

The shopkeeper considered him a moment. He set the package on the counter. "That's no gewgaw. Don't pull it out for sightseers."

"We have coin," Dahl said. "If it's worth it."

Goodman Florren grunted and disappeared into the back again.

"Better," Tam said. "Though, again, don't give them your name. No one knows you here. Keep it that way. And put that pin someplace he can't see."

*That* seemed to fluster the younger man, and Farideh felt a pang of sympathetic shame. Tam certainly had a way of knocking your heels loose.

"My apologies," Dahl said stiffly, fidgeting with something on his cloak. "But I don't see that my name matters in this case. He's just a fence."

"It might not," Tam said. "But it might matter in the next case or the next after that. And the more people who know your name and your face—and those beside your 'associate's' name and face—the faster danger finds you. Don't think one mission at a time. Just put the damned pin in your pocket. Bloody things are more trouble than they're worth."

The shopkeeper came back, toting a heavy-looking bundle of oilcloth, which he heaved onto the counter. A few quick pulls and the bindings came loose, cloth falling aside like a blown flower's petals.

"There you are," he said. "Twelve hundred gold."

Farideh peered between the shelves. On the open oilcloth, glinting in the murky light, lay an assemblage of gears, each leaping over the last as if the mass were alive and running. Its purpose might have been anything—arms and teeth snatched at missing connections—but whatever it was, Farideh thought it was beautiful.

"From the ruins of Lantan," the halfling shopkeeper said. "Preserved from the seawater by the dying magic of its creator, a great and powerful dwarf, blessed by—"

"It's a fake," Dahl sighed. He turned the clockwork on its side and pointed to something on the bottom. "Neverwinter reproduction. From maybe forty or fifty years ago. Before the collapse."

"Well, that's still plenty old!" the shopkeeper protested.

"It's not magical either," Dahl countered.

"Is too! Has a clever little charm to repel dust, since it's meant for display."

Dahl ran a finger over the largest gear and wrinkled his nose. "You might want to have that verified elsewhere."

"Thank you for your time," Tam said. He hustled Dahl from the shop. The door closed, and Farideh sighed in relief.

"Knew you couldn't have gone far," the shopkeeper said. She eased out from behind the shelf, one eye on the door. "Hiding from Harpers, are you?"

"Not especially," she said. "Just that one."

Goodman Florren slapped the paper-wrapped package. "You should have said your Someone was Adolican Rhand," he said, with some distaste. "Can't expect me to remember everything. Could've saved us some time and avoided your Harper."

"How much is that one?" she asked.

"For you? Price is already paid," he said. "Master Rhand sent this over. Said it's for the tiefling girl with the sun-and-moon eyes, 'course he didn't bother explaining, never does, that one. You're *late* though. He said two days ago. Stuck it in the back when I figured you weren't showing—out of sight, out of mind."

Farideh's stomach tightened. "I think there's a mistake. I didn't buy anything from him."

"No one's asking how you earned it," Goodman Florren said. "But you want to tell me there's someone else he means?"

The package was the size of her haversack, square, and heavy. A ritual book, she thought. What else could it be? She untied the twine and pulled the wrappings aside.

The ritual book had been bound in deepnight blue silk, of all things, and gilded with a pattern of leaves and curling vines. Stunned, she ran careful fingers down its cover—she'd never felt anything so fine, except perhaps the crisp, cream-colored pages within. She leafed back through them—someone's sharp, precise handwriting marked the first few pages, the instructions for at least three rituals. Adolican Rhand's instructions. The book fell open to the frontispiece, an etching of the night sky, and an envelope tucked there. She broke the black wax seal.

*I think you will find this to your liking*, the note read in the same handwriting, the same dark ink. *Consider it a welcome to Waterdeep. Should you need assistance filling it, I am ready and willing. Your presence is always welcome at my manor. Adolican Rhand.*

Innocent enough words—provided they were turned the right way. But the memory of the man who wrote them made them, when resolutely read, distressing, and there was no place on the face of

Toril she'd like to avoid so much as Adolican Rhand's manor. Farideh dropped the note and wiped her hands on her breeches, staring at the package as if it might come to life.

"I don't want it," she said.

Goodman Florren gave her a withering look. "Then take it back to Master Rhand. Just make it clear I held up my end." He wrapped his Lantan clockwork back up in its oilcloth. "Besides—it's obvious you do want it if you're coming down to Dust Alley to bargain."

*. . . the erinyes scream and shatter into a dozen enormous wasps; wasps with cunning eyes and swords for arms. The air is full of swords and monsters. Lorcan grabs her arm and shoves her back—Run, darling, run fast and run far—*

She shuddered, and rubbed her arm where the brand was that marked her pact. If she threw the book out, she would go on dreaming and Lorcan would continue to be tortured and one day she would wake with no powers, no protections because he would be dead.

"No one *made* him give it to you, darling," she could almost hear Lorcan say. "Let him come looking for favors—we'll simply make certain he regrets it."

She pointed two fingers at the note and drew the powers of the Hells into herself. *"Assulam."* A *crack* and the parchment burst into a fine cloud of ash. The shopkeeper flinched in surprise.

She watched the ashes float down, and said, "You can tell him I did *that*." She folded the paper back around the book and scooped it up, all her attention on the churn of Hellish powers seething beneath her skin as she left the shop. She looked both ways down Dust Alley—no sign of Tam, no sign of anyone much, other than some coinlasses loitering in front of another shop several doors down, and a woman hanging wash out her window. Farideh slipped out of the safety of the doorway and hurried up the narrow street.

"What happened," she heard Tam call out from behind her, "to staying out of trouble?"

Farideh cursed to herself, stopped, and turned. Tam stepped out of a narrow alleyway. "It's not trouble," she said. "It's . . . shopping."

"At a fence?" He dropped his voice as he reached her side. "What in all the broken planes did you buy from a fence?"

"A ritual book," she said. "And I didn't know he was a fence. I was only told he would be inexpensive."

"Inexpensive is just another way of saying 'illicit,' " Tam said. "You ought to know that."

"With my vast experience bartering for goods?" she said, acidly. "Be fair."

"We need to get going," Dahl said. The younger man watched Farideh and Tam from the shade of the smaller alley. "We'll be late for the viewing."

Farideh glanced from Dahl to Tam. "I'll leave you to it."

"Not necessary," Tam said. "And we can stroll and speak."

"Is that wise?" Dahl murmured. "She's not . . ."

Tam sighed. "Goodman Peredur," he said smoothly, "have you met Farideh? I assure you she isn't going to rush off with the secrets of where Waterdeep's most plausible fake artifacts lie and sell them to Shade. Although if she would, I think we'd be a little grateful for giving them the distraction. Come along," he said, and he started toward the market, Farideh and the now-scowling Dahl Peredur following behind.

"I suppose," Tam said, when she fell into step beside him again, "you'd prefer I not tell Mehen about this?"

"What's there to tell? I went into a shop. I bought a perfectly respectable item. He should be pleased, really," she added, although he would be no such thing.

"Farideh, this city is no mountain village. There are places a young lady really shouldn't be wandering."

"I can take care of myself," she said.

"Oh, believe me," Tam replied, "I've forgotten nothing of Neverwinter. Not even the parts where you *did* need help." Farideh locked her eyes on the cobblestones. "But I also seem to recall that if you were to come into a bad way, it's me that your father will blame."

She pursed her lips. "You haven't heard from Mehen, have you?"

"No," Tam said. "But having been to Suzail, I can tell you that getting paid for a bounty was never going to take less than a tenday. I'm certain he's fine."

And Farideh felt certain that Mehen would have sent a message if it turned out to take more than a day, let alone the three days that had passed since he'd left.

"You don't need a fence for a ritual book. What were you really doing?"

"They're expensive," she protested. "I tried plenty of . . . normal sellers, and it was always three and four times what I could spare." She thrust the package at him. "Do you want to check it?" Tam waved her away.

"What is it you want a ritual book for?"

Gods, Farideh thought, for all Tam's insistence that he wouldn't be a nursemaid, he could certainly play the part. She glanced over at Dahl. If he weren't there, she might tell Tam the truth—she'd told him a great deal of it already, of Lorcan and the security and danger of the pact. But not in front of Dahl, not after the way he'd acted in the taproom. She wasn't ashamed of being what she was, but she wasn't about to open the gates and let his revulsion wash over her.

"Is it so unlikely I want to learn rituals?" she said. "You made that temple in Neverwinter from a ritual. That was impressive. And helpful." The temporary shrine to Selûne had provided a safe place to hide from the fiends infesting Neverwinter.

Including Lorcan.

Tam looked unconvinced. "That ritual's no trifle. Are you planning something that might require a temple again?"

"Not if I can help it," she said. "What is it you two were doing at a fence?"

Tam smiled that thin smile she'd come to expect when the priest wasn't telling the whole truth. "Scouting artifacts for a buyer, you could say. What are we up for next?" he asked Dahl.

"A pair of artifacts," Dahl said, holding out a leaflet to Tam. "The main one's a page torn from an ancient book. A magic book. Draconic writing. Same writing on the granite facing that accompanies it."

"Oh, stlarning Hells," Tam said. "The dragon's secret page?"

"So you know it?"

"The streets of Waterdeep have been fairly buzzing with talk of it—claiming it's everything from a treasure map to the cursed testament of a plaguechanged wizard." He ran a hand through his hair. "Gods above, this will be a sty's pile. Did anyone approach the seller ahead of time? Try to get him to give it up?"

Dahl lowered the paper. "I tried. He wouldn't see me without a serious bid in hand. Master Vishter told me to stand back. That we'd sort it out once we see what we're in for. That he had an eye and a hand ready for that."

"So you haven't got any idea of what you have to bid with?"

"This is just a viewing for potential buyers." He folded up the paper with exaggerated neatness. "We still have time."

Tam sighed. "Well, shall we see what the city is fussing about?"

It didn't take long before they hit the crowds. Hungry-eyed merchants and adventurers in scarred armor rubbed elbows with urchins and Watchmen. Waterdhavians trying to finish up their market day struggled past with baskets, or just gave in and followed the eyes of the crowd up to the covered dais where the merchant had set up his treasure.

Faded ink skipped and shifted over the yellowed surface, changing from lines of text to detailed drawings, always ebbing away from the torn, jagged edge. Held up by the invisible strings of a spell, the page seemed to shiver with the changes, as if it were alive. Something about it made the air hum, and Farideh's brand started to itch. The hum broke into a low string of whispered words, a language Farideh couldn't place.

The page was speaking.

"This," Dahl murmured, "is more promising."

Behind the spell's shimmer and to one side of the page, there was a piece of granite leaning against a small chest. The size of a charger, it had been polished once, but years and weather and gods knew what else had dulled its surface and softened the edges of the runes that spattered the blue-gray surface. The edges were broken and jagged, all but on the right side, which ended in a smooth, straight lip, as if it had once fitted against something else.

On either side of the dais were two guards—a lean half-orc man and a human woman with dark eyes and darker hair bundled up on top of her head. She looked down at the crowd, at Tam and Farideh and Dahl, and her mouth went small. She whispered to the half-orc and slipped away. Farideh frowned and glanced at the crowd around her—not a few people were eyeing her the same way.

"*Henish*," she muttered. What did they think Farideh would do? Steal the page from thirty feet away in a thick crowd?

"Mother of the moon," Tam swore looking around at the crowd. "No. It's too many people. The price is going to get too expensive too fast."

"If there's anything in this city that the Harpers ought to protect," Dahl said, "any artifact worth watching over, it's this."

Dahl pressed the sheet of paper against the wall of a nearby stall and tapped the line of runes reprinted there. Draconic letters scratched their way across the paper like a line of claw marks, each dripping tails and serifs. Farideh peered at the runes.

"So the page keeps changing," he said. "Faster, the more people that get near it. The same Draconic letters as the stone, but more, too—Dethek, Elvish, all sorts of things in bits and pieces. The merchant's not repeating any of that. This replica is of the text on the stone."

"What does it say?" Tam asked.

Farideh frowned. "It—"

"I haven't translated it yet," Dahl said over her. "But the style is old. Absolutely pre-Spellplague." He traced the curve of a rune, a hard glottal sound, with the tip of his smallest finger. "Modern Draconic doesn't make this line curve so much. The serifs are shortened too. It's a strong indicator that whatever it came from is older than they're saying. Considering how slowly Draconic changes, it could be as old as Waterdeep. Even if it's just some dragon's laundry bill, if it's that old, it has to have value."

"But it's not Draconic," Farideh said.

Dahl startled, as if he hadn't expected her to know how to speak. "Of course it's Draconic," he said sharply. "I know what Draconic looks like, and I'm sure the merchant does too."

"And I can *read* Draconic," she countered. "It's not Draconic."

"What is it if it's not Draconic?" Tam asked her.

"The letters are," Farideh said. "But they just make gibberish. It doesn't say a thing. Here"—Farideh reached over and drew a finger beneath the cluster of runes recreated on the leaflet. "*Ah-nuh-jach nuh-thay-rell*," she read. "Even if you suppose the merchant got some letters wrong in the copy—"

"What did you say?" Tam demanded, his eyes suddenly wide.

Farideh blinked at him. "It's . . . gibberish?"

**LESSER EVILS**

"The runes, Fari, what does it say?"

"*Ah . . . ah-nuh-jach*," she repeated, carefully rechecking the letters. "*Nuh-thay-rell.* The vowels . . . it might be a little different, that's mostly where things change. The 'ch' is harder in true Draconic. But not much."

"Nuh-thay-rell," he repeated. Tam ran his hands through his hair and cursed. "Loross."

"Netherese?" Dahl said. He looked back at the letters and cursed.

"Is that what it's speaking?" she asked. "It doesn't sound like Draconic spoken."

"*Speaking?*" Dahl said. "What speaking?"

Farideh narrowed her eyes. "The mumbling noise. It sounds like speech. Like an old man muttering."

"What's it saying?" Tam asked, urgently. Farideh shrugged.

"Gibberish," she said. She closed her eyes, concentrating on the fine, whispery syllables. "*Ashenath . . . enjareen . . . nether pendarthis . . .*" She shook her head and opened her eyes. "You can't hear it?"

"Only a hum." Tam pursed his lips, staring at the page. "Right," he said after a moment. "Dahl, I'm assuming you can cast a language ritual?"

"Not here," Dahl said. "I need—"

"Of course not here," Tam said. "You have the components?"

Dahl bit off whatever he'd been saying. "Yes."

"Good." Tam steered Farideh toward the dais and pressed her through the crowd, close enough that she had to force people aside. "Study that stone," he implored, low and in her ear, "and remember as much as you can. Every letter you can manage. I'm going to need you to redraw it for Dahl."

"Why?" she asked.

"Because," he said, "you're right and he's right: it's older than the mountains, and it's *not* Draconic. It's from ancient Netheril."

At least, Dahl thought, something useful came of all that antiquary hunting. Even if it wasn't entirely clear what it was.

Dahl laid out the components for the ritual that would let him understand the ancient language on one side of a square table. On the opposite side, the tiefling woman drew the remembered runes onto the back of Dahl's list of artifacts with ponderous care, a strand of purplish-black hair trailing in the ink.

Gods, he'd like to have died then and there when she'd shown him up. There were dozens of languages that used Draconic letters—he knew that. Why had he just gone along and assumed they spelled out true Draconic?

This is why Oghma has no need of you, he thought. Because you're stupider than some tiefling girl out of the mountains.

Tam paced between his bed and the fireplace, his expression drawn and distant. When Dahl had asked what his plan was, Tam had merely shaken his head and said nothing. Dahl set down the last of the components, an ink imbued with salts of copper. No room for error, now—if he miscast the ritual, the Harpers would never have him doing anything more than scouring the markets for goods.

"That should do it," he said. He hefted his ritual book onto the table, a thick volume bound in crimson leather and embossed with the golden harp of Oghma in the center of the cover. Once upon a time, ritual magic had been a specialty of his, a focus among many dazzling and precious forms of the Art and the magic of the divine. The tome was nearly filled now, most of its pages inscribed with magic obtained after Oghma had left Dahl and Dahl had left Procampur.

Farideh stared at the heavy tome as he flipped to the proper page. "That's . . . quite a lot of spells. Did it take you long to learn them all?"

"Years," he said tersely. He paused—calm down, he thought, she's not picking at you. "It's . . . an interest of mine."

Thankfully, she was quiet after that, as was Tam, and Dahl could put the both of them, the Harpers and the Oghmanytes, Netheril and dragons and the wheat waving in the sea breeze, well out of mind as began the quiet chant of the ritual.

He poured a thin line of ground silver into a rectangle around the ink bottle, added the cross-line of powdered bluefoot mushrooms, and dipped the end of a bone-white feather into the prepared ink. He brushed the mixture over his eyes. The liquid turned icy and he flinched.

"Give me the paper," he told Farideh.

Dahl felt the magic of the Weave settle over him, broken strands of magic knitting themselves around his eyes. He opened them and looked down at the sheet she slid across the table. The tapered strokes of the runes seemed to shiver and reset themselves, forming letters and then words and then phrases his eyes recognized, and his thoughts parsed out. His mind began to move more quickly, skimming along like a fleet skiff on a calm sea.

" '. . . the final secrets of . . . Tarchamus," he read. "Whose name is the Unyielding, whose strength is mighty. Who tears out the *ssheratith*"—some organ, he thought, drawing a line to mark it—"of the volcano. The heart of the world *faljar anaresh*"—misremembered, he thought, or some damned ancient turn of phrase?—"against the light of day . . ."

A gap there where she'd forgotten the letters. "Look upon *halaris enjar* despair of unminded fellows. Such comes peril to Netheril," he finished. "And peril to the Weave. All contained within.' That's all of it."

Dahl frowned at the transcription. "That's enough to be interesting. Parts of it don't really translate. But it's angry and it's definitely talking about a wizard."

"Arcanist," Tam said mildly, his eyes on the transcription. "So it's Tarchamus the Unyielding, not Attarchammiux, the Terror of the Silver Marches."

Dahl shook his head. "Draconic implies some vowels. Loross doesn't."

"So that's the author of the page? Heard of him?"

"Never," Dahl said. "But then Shade's not exactly sharing all its historical documents." He pointed at the last untranslatable bit, which was coming clearer by the moment. "This means something like 'his works of power.' Spells, maybe. Or enchanted items."

"Or weapons?" Tam said. "Is that what the page shows?"

Dahl shook his head. "No way to know. Not without watching the changes."

"*Ashenath,*" Farideh said, and Dahl startled. "*Enjareen nether pendarthis.* That's what it's saying. What's that mean?"

Dahl bit back a curse. He should have remembered that. "Say it again." She repeated the string of Loross. " 'Brought through rock and flood . . .' and something like 'and this is what we get.' Maybe 'Brought through rock and flood to *this*?' Are you sure you're remembering it properly?" Farideh shrugged, but didn't answer.

"The runes were broken," Tam said. "It's a piece of something larger. Something that's sealed away a peril to Netheril. And there's a fair chance half the people in that square read it too."

"They'd have to speak Loross," Dahl pointed out.

"Many Netherese do," Tam said dryly. "And the page is just a part, a piece of some larger text." He cursed again and straightened.

"Stay here," he told Dahl. "I'll be back as soon as I can." He scooped up his cloak and the chain that hung on the chair. Farideh looked up at him.

"Where are you going?"

"If I wanted you to know," Tam said, pulling open the door, "I'd have told you. Stay here. Don't follow. *Either* of you."

The Fisher's not the only one who doesn't use his resources well, Dahl thought.

Whatever he'd hoped would be true of the Harper priest, they weren't partners. Dahl might have found the fragment, might have done the hard work of translating, but he wasn't even on Tam's mind when it came to sorting out the looming threat associated with it.

After all, why else would the priest have taken the chain?

He glanced over at Farideh, still sitting in the opposite chair, staring at the door. At least Tam hadn't taken her along instead.

It isn't her fault she speaks Draconic, he reminded himself. But she could have been a little less rude about it. How was he supposed to know, anyway?

She turned and eyed him for a moment, before she raised her face . . . and he realized she'd been staring at his ritual book with those odd, focusless eyes and not at him.

"Have you been casting rituals for long?" she asked.

"Some years," he said. Seven to be exact—when Dahl had sworn himself to Oghma in Procampur, they'd started him on rituals almost immediately, seeing as he had a knack for magic. *Had* is the important word, he thought glumly.

"Where did you learn them?" she asked.

"In another life."

"Have . . . have you ever taught anyone? How to do them?"

"No." He wished she'd leave, stop asking these questions. Bad enough Tam had left him behind, he didn't need to be reminded of Procampur. "I have to write a letter, if you don't mind . . ."

"Sorry," she said. "Yes. But . . . could you? Would it be too hard?"

Dahl scowled. She probably didn't even know what it took to cast rituals. What was involved. It *was* serious magic, whatever she or others might think. "It's not simple," he said.

"I need someone to teach me," she went on. She pulled the loosely wrapped package she'd carried out from under her chair, and took out an expensive-looking ritual book. "I've got this. Someone . . . That is, it came with some spells already in it. But I don't know—"

"You should ask Master Zawad," Dahl said.

"Master Zawad doesn't have any more time for me than he does for you." She fell quiet a moment. "Besides, it seems as if you're better at this than he is."

Dahl shut his ritual book and ran a thumb over the worn bottom edge of the cover. "You said you had a few already? What are they?"

She handed over the silk-bound tome. Gods' books, it was a good quality—heavy pages, tight binding, crisp printing on the frontispiece. He frowned at the depiction of a moonless sky over bucolic hills. He leafed forward to the rituals, and skimmed what was written there. Oghma, Mystra, and lost Deneir, he swore.

"Where," he asked after a moment, "did you get this?"

She didn't answer right away, but pursed her lips, and try as he might, he couldn't divine if she was annoyed or embarrassed or worried.

"Does it matter?" she finally said.

"A great deal." He turned the book around. "This first spell is fairly minor. Puts all the lights out."

She wrinkled her nose. "That doesn't seem like much use. Why not blow out the candles?"

"You can set it to finish at a later point. If you're preoccupied," he said dryly, and she flushed at the implication. "It's used more often by people calling creatures that can pass through the shadows," Dahl said. "It's not difficult, but it takes some . . . uncommon components. Unpleasant components.

"The other two," he said, "aren't better. This one makes phantom restraints. The other . . ." Despite himself, he blushed as well. "I don't know you well enough to tell you what it does," he said stiffly.

"Oh."

"And they are all rituals sourced from casters *I* don't want to associate with."

She wrapped her arms around her chest and made a noise under her breath that might have been a curse. "The book's ruined then?"

"No. Of course not. That isn't the point. Who gave it to you?"

"A man," she said after a moment. "I met him in a shop and"—she rolled her shoulder as if trying to shake something loose—"he's just . . . he decided to help me."

Dahl shut the silk-covered tome. "Does he have a name?"

"Adolican Rhand."

Dahl studied her face for some sign of what in the world she could possibly be thinking. "Adolican Rhand," he repeated. "Are you *mad*?"

"No," she said sharply. "I told you, he's the one sending me books. *I* haven't had much choice in all this. Who is he?"

Dahl pushed the book back across the table, shaking his head. "You got it off a Netherese informer, and you ask for my help, not Master Zawad. Gods. What are you trying to hide from him?"

"Nothing." Farideh leaned back away from the table. "Are *you* really going to tell me it's better to be lectured by Tam?"

Dahl bit his tongue. What did she know, anyhow? "Maybe he needs to lecture you if you're flirting with shady merchants and collecting their love tokens."

She turned absolutely scarlet. "What would you have had me do?" she asked. "Take it back to his manor to say 'no thank you,' and be caught there? I might not know his business, but I'm not a rabbit tumbling into a snare." She snatched the book off the table. "If you're going to say no, just say it and stop dragging me through the mud behind you. I'll manage fine on my own."

Dahl scowled. "Of course. *You* don't need a master or years of study or dedication or any of that." He had, and what good had it done him? "You probably think you'll just smile sweetly at the first person you see with a ritual book in hand, and he'll be a bloody warlock ready to train you to be his heir. Is that how it happened with Master Rhand?"

Farideh whirled on him, still flushing like a maid, but with fire in her eyes and shadows—yes, shadows, he was sure—seething from her skin. *"Karshoj ardahlominak,"* she hissed, and suddenly the shadows surged around her as she stepped toward the door. There was a burst of light, a gust of air hot enough make Dahl turn aside, and a *crack* as a vent tore in the skin of the plane, and Farideh vanished.

Dahl sat, blinking back tears for a moment as the scorching air cooled. Ah, Hells and farther realms, he realized. He ought to have seen it. He ought to have known. She didn't need a warlock to swoop in with ritual lessons. She was a warlock herself.

.:⌢:.

Her hair combed and her armor wiped clean, Havilar did sort of look like she might be Brin's bodyguard. Particularly, he thought, since she'd insisted on bringing along her glaive.

"If you *are* robbed," she'd said, "this will put a stop to it much quicker than if I have to fight hand to hand."

"You *do* know I can defend myself?"

She regarded him as if he'd made a half-hearted joke. "Of course. But if you're robbed, you'll have to get the coin and run off somewhere safe. One of us has to."

"*You* could."

Havilar had wrinkled her nose. "Well, yes. But I think you'd be better. You're clever."

As they made their way through the streets of Waterdeep, he still wasn't sure what she'd said was a compliment. He felt fairly sure that girls preferred the kind of fellows that didn't need rescuing.

And he was fairly sure that he'd prefer a girl who didn't always have the upper hand.

It hadn't ever mattered what he preferred. Helindra would choose a bride for him, and he was meant to be grateful for the opportunity to further the family's influence. But if he didn't go home . . .

He gave Havilar a sideways glance. When he'd first met her, he thought she might be a little simple, or maybe a little cruel. The sort of person who could tear into a battle and come out with a slew of kills to her credit, and only worry if she'd looked good doing so.

But it hadn't taken long to realize Havilar wasn't angry and she wasn't cruel. Competitive, to be certain; vain, a little. But never cruel. And not as simple as she seemed on first flush, just . . . *light*.

A good person to be friends with, he thought. I'm making everything too complicated.

Tannannath and Frynch was exactly as stern and fussy an edifice as Brin had been expecting. It only took a moment for him and Havilar—and Havilar's glaive—standing at the enormous doors and looking up at the elaborate stonework before a guard appeared.

"May I help you?" he said, in a tone of voice that made it clear he did not expect to do any such thing. Brin narrowed his eyes.

"I'm here to see about the Broken Marble safehold," he said. "Do be quick about it." The guard's brows went up, but he opened the doors, took Havilar's weapon, and escorted the two of them down a long, dimly lit corridor, ringing with the phantom sounds of a flute and a lyre. The guard held one of the half-dozen doors lining the hall, and waved them in.

Within, a half-elf woman wearing an emerald lens over one eye waited. "Sit, please," she said, and she pulled out a tray of sand. "In or out?"

"Beg pardon?"

"Do you wish to put coin in," she asked, "or take it out?"

"Oh. Out, I suppose."

"Your mark, then."

Brin took up the stylus and traced the runes as Constancia had ordered. The coinlender pulled out an enormous codex and started flipping through the pages. "Broken Marble?" she said. "Rhiiman."

Brin frowned. "I'm sorry?"

The woman looked at him through the emerald lens. "Rhiiman," she said, enunciating.

It was the name of the man who had founded the Crownsilver family, a younger brother of the first king of Cormyr, if he was remembering right, who married a daughter of the Silver line—whose name was escaping him . . . Constancia would box your ears, he thought.

"Oh," he said. "Made the right choice."

The woman dipped her head to consider the codex once more. "Welcome, goodsir. The account is equivalent to two hundred eighty thousand, nine hundred and seventy-four Waterdhavian dragons." She looked up. "If you'd like to withdraw the full amount, I'm afraid you'll have to accept trade bars and give us a day to collect them."

Brin very deliberately closed his mouth. "No, no, that's all right." He was glad for the chair she'd offered him. "May I ask if anyone else is accessing the coin? I'd . . . I'd hate to take funds some cousin was relying on." Or to find out Helindra was keeping a close eye on the account's activities.

The coinlender's eyes flicked over his head to where Havilar stood, before returning to consider him carefully. He passed whatever threshold she'd decided on for frauds and thieves, but by her tight expression, only just.

"The last business with the account was . . . three tendays ago. A withdrawal of one hundred dragons. Before that it's only been maintenance, so far as my records stand."

"You have that much coin just *sitting*?" Havilar hissed at him after he'd withdrawn a small sum, enough to cover a room of his own, board, and a little extra. "What does your family *do*?"

"Meddle," Brin said, frowning at the bag of coins. "And it's not my coin. It's theirs. I've certainly never seen that kind of coin."

It would be enough, he thought. Enough to buy passage to any city in Faerûn. Enough to buy a new name, a new life. Enough to get far, far ahead of the Crownsilvers before they did something rash.

The temptation of the coin on the ledger was bad enough. But there, too, was the reminder that the Crownsilvers commanded vast resources. The coin in the bank was a pittance—a forgettable amount, likely, comparable to funds in cities like Athkatla and Baldur's Gate and Westgate, where a family member might need easy access to coin. It was nothing compared to what Helindra commanded in Cormyr.

And no vault could contain all the Crownsilvers' connections.

"Is that why you didn't say?" Havilar said as they crossed the market. It was late and the stallkeepers were closing up. "About being His Grace and . . . what are you, anyway? A prince? A king? A . . . *nentyarch*?"

"Nentyarch?"

Havilar shrugged, her eyes on the cobbles. "It's some sort of frozen war prince," she said. "Read it in a book." She looked up at him. "Why didn't you tell me?"

Brin sighed. "It's complicated, and it would get far, far more complicated if I put any stock in it. Look, I didn't tell you—but I didn't tell *anyone*. I don't want to be a prince or a king or a nentyarch." He smiled at her. "I told you a lot more than anyone else. I told you about Constancia and Helindra."

She nodded absently. "I would have understood."

"I hardly understand it." He opened the door to the inn. "I would have to draw charts."

She didn't laugh. "Are you hungry?"

"Yes," he said. "Sorry. Let me buy you evenfeast. You and Farideh."

They'd no more than reached the top of the stairs when Farideh stepped out of the air, forcing them both to leap back. Flushed and furious-looking and seething that strange, wispy shadowstuff that stung his eyes like burning brimstone—it was a stark reminder that Havilar wasn't really the scary one. Usually, Brin amended.

"Hells, but you look terrible," Havilar said. "What are you doing, jumping around corridors?"

"I've met Brother Tam's new apprentice," Farideh said sharply. "That fellow from the taproom."

"The tall, good-looking one?" Havilar asked.

Brin had to admit it was a bit like being hit in the stomach by the shaft of her glaive. "When did you meet him?" he asked.

"The first day we were here." Havilar smirked at her sister. "Did you get him to loosen up?"

Farideh shot her twin a dark look. "No. Though if you'd like to knock his jaw free to help him with that, I'd thank you for it. He's very skilled at needling my last nerve."

"Who isn't?" Havilar said. "We've just been to see about Brin's sudden fortune."

"Not sudden," Brin said. "It's not mine, either."

"Oh, just be pleased," Havilar said, nudging him with her elbow. "Even if you let it all sit in that vault, you've got *piles* of sudden fortune. Anyway, now we're going to have a drink and some food. Do you want to come?"

Farideh drew a long breath, the tendrils of smoke retreating. "No," she said. "I'd rather just sleep."

"Come on," Havilar cajoled. "It will cheer you up."

"And then I'll see that *henish* and I'll be unbearable for another day," Farideh said too lightly. "No." Her tail started flicking against the wooden floor. "Come up soon."

"When we do," Havilar said with a wave of her hand.

"What were you doing with Tam and his apprentice?" Brin asked.

Farideh shook her head. "There's an artifact for sale. A page from a book of some kind and a piece of a door or something. I was helping them do the translation." She hesitated. "It's a Netherese language."

A feeling like icy water poured down Brin's back and drove every thought about his own petty problems out of his head. Constancia's warnings about encroaching Shadovar armies echoed after them.

"Ye gods," he said. "Where's Tam?"

Farideh shook her head. "He ran off—but he didn't say where to. He took his chain."

"Well, that's good," Brin said with forced cheer. "He's likely taking care of things."

"There were guards around the treasure," Farideh said. "Sharp-eyed ones."

"He's pretty sharp himself," Havilar said. "And I thought silverstars could"—she waved a hand in the air—"you know, go all invisible and things?"

Farideh stared at her sister. "Where in the world did you hear that?"

"Everyone knows that. Why else would you worship the moon goddess?"

Brin took a deep breath—*slain down to a soul*—and calmed himself. Tam knew better than any of them what Netheril might do, and he was taking care of things. What was one moldy old page anyhow? "Did he have a guess as to what sort of book it was from?"

Farideh bit her lip, tenser and more uneasy. "It belonged to an arcanist, from the sound of things. A powerful one."

# CHAPTER FIVE

## WATERDEEP

*1 FLAMERULE, THE YEAR OF THE DARK CIRCLE (1478 DR)*

**T**HE SMALLWYRM INN, THOUGH LESS GRAND AND LESS CAPACIOUS THAN its cousin, the Greatwyrm, had gotten a reputation among Waterdeep's moderately well-heeled as an excellent place for a meal, a draft, and perhaps a few stronger substances. It was pleasant enough that the merchant, his guards, and the treasure they guarded had taken rooms on the third floor.

*You are too old for this,* Tam thought as he slipped through the packed taproom toward the entrance to the inn. *You have been too old for this for well on fifteen years.*

But what else could he do? Send Dahl in to steal the page? Send Farideh? Beg the Fisher for the thousands upon thousands of gold pieces it was likely go for?

No, he'd have to take care of matters himself.

There was a guard at the door to the guests' rooms, the burly fellow who'd been beside the stone at the auction viewing. Tam watched him from the corner of his eye as he eased past. The guard's eyes never left Tam. No slipping by that one.

He kept walking. Fortunately, inns were notably insecure. There would be another way to the treasure of Tarchamus.

The merchant running the auction, a man called Artur Chansom, wasn't that way. Chansom had held out, despite—Tam had discovered—already receiving multiple offers to buy the piece. There was too much coin to be made. Far too much to hope that his sense of duty could overwhelm his sense of profit. Even if it could mean leaving a path to the sort of powers that Netheril spent ages acquiring.

Even without knowing what the page and stone had once belonged to, even without being sure what the arcanist's works of power entailed, Tam knew enough about the heights of power that ancient Netheril had reached to know the artifacts couldn't just be left to fall into anyone's hands. Works of magic like none the world had seen, yes, but Netheril's arcanists had also destroyed or decimated the surrounding civilizations in their quest for an empire, flouted the gods themselves, and reached for powers that ended in the First Death of the goddess of magic and the ultimate collapse of ancient Netheril. Not treasures, he thought, one left for the taking.

Tam passed through the side door and in through the kitchen entrance, his thoughts echoing back to the night when he and his comrades had run afoul of the Shadovar scouting party. It was before he had gone into Viridi's service, before he had even taken vows as one of Selûne's silverstar, when he was just a headstrong lad with no sense at all of what he could lose. And then they'd died—dear Ariya, brave Seris, wide-eyed Myk, that blessed bastard Payel—and the Lady of Loss had made it clear how much could be taken away.

Slipping into the Smallwyrm's stairwell, he shuddered. He'd pledged himself to the Moonmaiden, the eternal enemy of Shar, shortly after. If what he'd seen were the predations of a minor scouting party, Faerûn would need all the help it could get to stand against the city that sent them, and he'd been young, idealistic, full of spleen and holy fire.

Which is exactly how Viridi had caught him and brought him into her service.

A far more orderly one than he served now. He settled down in front of the keyhole to the second floor with a grunt for his achy knee. Did Dahl even *know* how to pick a lock if pressed? he wondered. Or what to say if someone caught him at it? How to disarm a pressure plate or a trip wire? How to pass as a wealthy merchant or a copperless beggar? How to get up off the floor and bring down an attacker in one swift movement? Tam couldn't have said, and what's worse, he doubted the Fisher could have either.

His lockpick snapped with a sudden *ping*, and Tam cursed. The metal spine protruded hardly a hairsbreadth from the edge of the keyhole. He pulled his head back to see better, scraped at it with his fingernails. The damned thing slipped deeper.

Beyond the door, he heard footsteps.

Tam leaped to his feet and hurried up to the next landing just in time to see one of the potjacks come through the door laden with chamberpots. The boy trundled down the stairs, and did not notice Tam catch the door just as it started to close and duck inside. He bent and rubbed his knee.

*After this*, he thought, catching his breath, *I need to do a healing on that stlarning knee.* It wouldn't last long—it never did—but it would take the edge away, keep him flexible.

He peered down the hallway of the inn, remembering that night twenty-seven years ago, when he—an overeager silverstar—had stumbled on a representative of Netheril, rooming in an inn in Athkatla, and killed him. He was damned lucky—he knew it now and he knew it then. He was doubly lucky that when Viridi's assassins had broken in and found him there—unsure of how to escape while covered in another man's blood—they'd nabbed him and returned him to Viridi instead of leaving him to take the blame.

He'd come to in a lavish study, bound with bent knees and lying on a plush Amnian rug, a roaring fire behind him, and an enormous wooden desk in front of him. The dark-skinned woman behind the desk, her crinkled hair the color of tarnished silver, marked the balance of a pair of brass scales, made a note in her ledger, and said nothing as Tam pulled himself onto his knees.

"I find it interesting," she said, "that what took two months of planning on my people's part apparently took you an afternoon and a bottle's worth of courage."

Tam didn't reply. "You bound my wounds," he said.

"What did you think?" Viridi said. "That I'd leave you bleeding on my silk rug? Come now, priest." A trickle of gold coins fell from her fist into the scale's tray, bringing it nearer to level. "My people say you're a mercenary as well. That's an odd combination, Brother Nightingale." She clucked her tongue and turned to face him. "A bit melodramatic for a cryptonym, don't you think?"

"What do you want?" he asked. "Vengeance for your man?"

"Not my man. It so happens," Viridi said, "that we're on the same side." She peered at the scales and wrote something. "More or less. I'll take coin from a lot of people, but I don't want Shade owing me any favors. But you," she said thoughtfully, "we could owe each other quite a few favors, I think."

For more than a decade, Tam had been her Shepherd, her cleric in the house—healing and resurrecting her spies—and her field agent among the faithful. And here and there, she put him on teams set against Shade. She kept his secrets and he kept hers, more loyal than he would have ever imagined, as a headstrong lad. For more than a decade, the Shepherd had been his purpose and his focus.

And then Viridi had died, and it all came unraveled.

He knew a handful of her agents who'd been killed for the mistake of seeking employment with Viridi's prior clients. He knew half a dozen more who'd died because they ran afoul of her prior targets. And one who died to save Viridi, the agent known to her only as the Shepherd, and his dearest secret. And he hadn't been able to stop any of it.

The Harpers needed a Viridi. Several Viridis, he thought, coming to the merchant's chambers. People who could keep things together and running smoothly, who could gather the sort of patrons that made field work possible and the sort of agents that made it sensible. He listened for a moment, then slipped the lockpicks into the keyhole.

But the Fisher was right—it was a different world. Even if there had been spymasters on every corner, there were a thousand other, smaller organizations ready to claim them. He picked the lock more smoothly this time and eased the door open without leaving any of the pick behind.

The room wasn't empty. The locked chest that held the page and stone sat on a table pushed against one wall, and a woman—a guard, by her look—leaned against the table. Dressed in leather armor with her dark hair bound loosely off her neck, she seemed far more interested in the book she held open in one hand than the fact that she was being robbed.

She looked up, her dark eyes momentarily surprised, and Tam felt as if the world had shifted to one side and left him behind as the one secret he kept above all others lay bare to the world.

"Good evening," she said. Then, almost as an afterthought, "Da."

**Lesser Evils**

"Mira?" He stepped into the room and closed the door. It was still his daughter standing there in front of the chest. Still his little girl, armed and armored and bristling. "What . . . Why aren't you in Baldur's Gate?" he asked dumbly.

"My employer wouldn't appreciate that," she said. "And it's lovely to see you, too."

He shook his head. "I . . . Apologies, Mira. I just didn't expect . . . Well, you understand. How could I expect?" His only daughter regarded him coolly.

Selûne and her tears, why was he always startled to see she wasn't eight years old anymore? He crossed the room and pulled his daughter into a stiff embrace. "It's lovely to see you. What are you doing in Waterdeep?"

"Guarding Master Chansom's treasures," she said, stepping back. "From you, apparently."

He chuckled. "Yes. Well. It's rather complicated."

"Try me," she said.

"I need what's in that chest."

She smiled. "You and half of Waterdeep."

"Half of Waterdeep isn't your father," he said, and her smile faltered. She folded her arms across her chest like a barrier.

"What?" she said. "Are you planning to have Mother restrict my sweets if I don't stand aside?"

"Mira, that's not what I meant," he chided. "Listen to me. If you knew what you were guarding—"

"I know what I'm guarding."

"No. That writing isn't Draconic," he said. "It's—"

"It's Loross," she interrupted. "It's Silver Age, well older than Chansom thinks it is. Chansom bought both from a farmer in the Silver Marches who found the page wrapped up in the bottom of a trunk his great-grandfather carted home after adventuring—he retired after his comrades didn't make it back. Judging by the stone type, I'd say he found it somewhere in the Nether Mountains, and I'd wager well it wasn't all he found. I know it's speaking. Chansom doesn't, and none of the wizards who want to buy the thing have mentioned it to him, but I'm pretty sure they've heard it. too. I know both pieces claim to be the property of 'Tarchamus,' the same name as an arcanist of Netheril who disappeared two thousand years ago, so far as anyone knows. It's not a map to a hoard. In fact I'm willing to bet no dragon has come within leagues of these things." She looked away, as if the outburst of knowledge embarrassed her. "So, *yes*," she added. "I do know what I'm guarding."

Ah, Lady, he thought, what a terrible time to have this argument. She'd always had a head for history, an eye for details, and he ought to have remembered that. She'd gone off to Baldur's Gate when she was seventeen to apprentice to antiquarians hunting in the Werewoods for ruins. By now, she likely knew far better than he did what was a Netherese artifact and what was a forgery.

"My apologies," Tam said after a moment. "I suppose, I'd forgotten—"

"How long have you been in Waterdeep?" she interrupted.

"A few days," he said. The window rattled against its latch—Tam's attention jumped to it. Just a breeze, he thought. Pay attention to her.

"I didn't know to look for you," he said. "Or that you were working as a guard. What happened to your studies?"

Mira's mouth quirked in a sad, little smile. "There's little enough coin in ancient history," she said. "At least this way I can eat while I examine other people's artifacts."

Tam wanted to speak, to tell her this was not the life she wanted—trust him, he knew. "What does your mother think of all this?" he asked, rubbing his aching eyes. The window latch clattered with the breeze, tapping out an alarm he forced himself to ignore.

Mira shrugged. "She doesn't much mind. Sends letters regularly. I'm to visit for . . ." Mira narrowed her eyes at the door. The soft *click* of a lockpick against a loose tumbler.

Tam stiffened. "Hrast."

"We have company," she said calmly.

As if they'd heard her, the intruders burst into the room: a Turmishan man by the window, sleek as a shadow and carrying two hooked scythes; a pale-skinned woman by the door, her face a mess of scars around bright black eyes. She reached back and drew her sword.

"Get out of here!" he shouted to Mira, as he moved between them and the chest, pulling at the chain he wore wrapped around his waist from the center. The spiked links unhooked and fell loose. He whispered to Selûne and felt her blessing pour over his skin and light every link of the chain.

He'd expected Shadovar. He'd been waiting for echoes of the shadar-kai he'd seen in his youth. But no— a gray skull on a background of brown rays, displayed as the woman drew her sword and turned her shoulder toward him. Zhentarim. Mercenaries of the Black Network.

They might not have expected him, but that gave the thieves no pause—the pair moved at him so quickly, he only saw blades. The chain lashed out, tangling the man's wrists and scythes together. Tam pulled, and the assassin tripped forward, crashing to his knees.

The woman with the sword took the chance to slash Tam's forearm, leaving behind a sudden line of red. Sharp, stinging—not enough to stop him from directing a burst of holy fire at her midsection, shoving her back. The sword screamed past him once more, close enough to tear the fabric of his shirt. Tam yanked his chain back from the prone man and slung it toward his companion, the light of the moon goddess building along the links until it burst out the end with a low *whoosh*.

The man was on his feet again, one scythe slicing toward Tam's throat. He threw an elbow up into the man's forearm, pushing the blade, up, away. It nicked his cheek. The assassin's arm shifted, hooked up under Tam's arm, as if to pull the priest into the other scythe.

The man jerked back. Tam broke away.

There was Mira, one knife sunk in the Turmishan man's side. The other up, high, drawing across the assassin's throat in a sharp, swift cut. Blood poured out of the wound, blood bubbling with the assassin's desperate breaths, and still Mira held him up on her knife's blade.

Get her out of here! a voice shouted in Tam's thoughts, over and over. Get her out of here! Threatening to overwhelm the focus of the Moonmaiden's powers, threatening to take his thoughts away from the battle at hand. Mira dropped the body as the man stopped trying to breathe through the wound in his neck.

Dead, he thought forcefully. He didn't need to save Mira from the dark-skinned man. The man was dead.

He faced the woman, back on her feet, despite the blood that poured from her wounds and between her teeth, and slashing at him with that black-bladed sword. He jerked the chain up and caught the blade between its spiked links. Too quick, she slipped it free and struck a glancing blow off the heavy leather covering his left shoulder, hard enough to bruise and he cried out with the shock of it and loosed his grip on the chain.

Mira moved toward the assassin, knives ready and he fought to speak, to tell her to get out of the way, to run from the room. His heart turned inside out as the assassin's attention shifted, took in Mira—little Mira.

The sword sliced through the air, carving a path toward Mira's shoulder. Tam raised a hand, the force of the moon swelling through him like a tide on his blood. Powerful, but not powerful enough—time slowed as the assassin went after his daughter.

"Lady aid me," he cried, the prayer taking hold, rage chasing the fear.

Mira dropped, straight down, as if her legs had given out, and landed flat on her back, well out of the sword's attack. But now an easy mark for the bleeding assassin. The assassin raised her blade.

Holy fire, bright as a full moon, streamed from Tam's open palm and crashed over the assassin, throwing her into the far wall. The wave caught her, then she hit the wall and lay silent, dancing with the residual magic of the silverstar.

What remnants of Selûne's peace he'd held tight to now fled. Tam was on the Zhentarim woman in an instant, his chain dropped and a dagger drawn. He cut the assassin's throat, savage and quick—make certain she's dead, he thought, the image of her standing over Mira's prone body hammering at his thoughts.

Panting, Tam turned a slow circle, scanning the darkened corners of the room. Nothing. Mira came to her feet, her knives still gripped in both hands. He jumped at the sudden movement.

"Are you all right?" he all but shouted, his pulse in his ears. He reached for her, to comfort her, perhaps, but also to comfort himself, to be certain she was all right and not cut to ribbons for merely being in the way of one of his missions.

Mira stiffened and sheathed her knives. "Fine," she said, though she was pale-faced and out of breath. She looked down at the bodies, her eyes distant. "Fine for the moment."

"You're not hurt," he said, looking her over. All the blood was the Zhents,' but still, she was splattered with it. Like his worst nightmares given flesh. "You're not hurt," he said again. "Gods." He looked around at the carnage. "Gods, if I weren't here, you could have been killed."

Mira's mouth went small. "Possibly. But if you weren't here, then this fellow wouldn't have come so close to stabbing you in the ribs."

He ran a hand over his beard. Never, he'd sworn the last time his duties brought danger so close to his daughter, never again. But now, here Mira stood, looking down at the bodies, calm as the waters of a sacred pool. She always was a calm one, he thought. Even as a babe in the cradle.

Not a babe anymore, he thought. A woman with very sharp knives.

"We still have time," Mira said. "Though not much. Word's traveled fast, but not accurately." She looked up at him. "How much coin can you get together?"

Tam shook his head. "You can't imagine your patron will go ahead with his bidding. These are *Zhentarim* assassins."

"And they only sent two," she pointed out. "Which means they haven't figured out what the page and stone point to. They might still think they're clues to a hoard. They don't know about Tarchamus."

Tam started to protest—if they didn't know, they wouldn't have sent any assassins, and now that they'd sent two, they *would* send more. And Shade was still a die unthrown. Now wasn't the time to be complacent.

But Mira's expression didn't suggest she was relieved. She chewed her upper lip, and stared at the body of the male assassin, as if she were trying to spy the fragments of clues scattered over his skin. There was more here.

Stop thinking like a worried parent, he told himself. Think like a Harper.

"You said you know where it came from," he said. "Where? Or rather, where do you think Shade and the Zhentarim think it came from?"

ERIN M. EVANS

She looked up at him and blinked. "Getting artifacts from ancient Netheril isn't easy. What exists is largely in Shade's hands and they're particular about what they share. But there are two references to the arcanist Tarchamus. Both are fragmented. Both are widely considered to be apocryphal, or at least exaggerated. But both make it clear that Tarchamus was a formidable arcanist, an expert at tapping into the powers of other planes without traveling to them, capable of crafting weapons that could level cities and *mythallars* that could stop the stars in their courses."

Tam raised an eyebrow and she rolled her eyes. "I told you. They exaggerate. But even as such, it's clear he was no dabbler."

"If he existed," Tam added.

"Someone made the book the page was torn from." She laid a hand on the chest. "It's possible his spells or the artifacts imbued with his magic still exist somewhere—wherever this came from. And I think the stone is a piece of the door that sealed it. If Shade knew this page might be a clue to the location of Tarchamus's lost enclave, they would have sent an army by now."

"And the Zhentarim?"

She cast a skeptical eye down at the dead mercenaries. "They know it's valuable. I doubt these two's masters have worked out how valuable. As it stands?" She shrugged. "The Netherese probably know Chansom's selling something Netherese and would rather it remained in the princes' treasury. And the Zhentarim probably know Shade wants it."

"For now," Tam said. "If word of the page traveled that quickly, word of its secrets can't be far behind." He shook his head. "We need to destroy both pieces."

Mira didn't move. "If you destroy them," she said, "then you destroy the key to finding the source. But the lost enclave will still be out there. The stockpile of magic weapons might still exist. The secrets of Tarchamus haven't been destroyed—they're waiting for Shade to come and excavate them.

"We have to get there first," she said.

Before Tam could respond, the door opened, admitting the stout and slightly tipsy Artur Chansom, and another man, a lean fellow all dressed in dark velvets.

At the sight of Tam, Artur Chansom startled. At the sight of the two dead mercenaries slowly soaking the rug with blood, he threw himself back against the wall.

"Waukeen rob me blind!" he cried. "What happened?"

Mira looked down at the dead Zhentarim. "It seems someone wanted to circumvent his competitors."

"Indeed," the other man said. He looked up at Tam, curiously, with piercing blue eyes. The hairs on the back of Tam's neck stood on end. "Artur, I must commend your guards."

"Beshaba spit on the day I took this on," the merchant muttered. He ran his fingers through his forked beard and glared at Tam. "That one's not mine. Who in the Hells are you?"

"Ah, yes," Tam said, reaching for the merchant's hand. "I'm Mira's father—"

The merchant squinted at him. *"Who?"*

"Pet name," Mira supplied. "Means 'little dove' in Old Calishite." She squeezed Tam's arm. "You'll have to forgive him. Can't help embarrassing me."

"My apologies," Tam said, catching on. She'd used another name? Why? He smiled at the merchant. "They grow up so fast, don't they? One day she's my *mira*, the next she's . . . well, killing robbers for you, it seems."

"Yes," Chansom said, pointedly not looking at the corpses. "Unacceptable—not you, my dear, nor your father. You've done plenty well. I'll reflect it in your pay. Although I would rather have had them alive."

"Wasn't an option," Mira supplied.

"But this"—he waved his hands at the room—"this won't do. Clearly these walls might as well be spidersilk for all they keep out thieves. No, it won't suit." He combed his fingers through his beard again. "Going to kill me in my sleep. Run off with all the gold."

"I'd be happy to accommodate you," the other man said. "I have plenty of room for you and your employees." He smiled, and Tam could not shake the sense that something was decidedly off about the man. "You can bring your things along with the chest."

"That's kind of you indeed, Saer Rhand," Chansom said. "But I've got appearances to see to. You and I know your bid's far better than what the rest of them will offer—but I have agreements to keep. Another showing—an exclusive one. Even if they can't own it, plenty have paid coin to clap eyes on it. You understand?"

Saer Rhand's smile had a brittle, vicious quality, as if it were shielding something furious and fearsome. "And the street was not good enough for them?"

Chansom gave the man a skeptical look. "It's Waterdeep. There's folks enough with more coin than sense, and I'd be a poor man if I told them how to spend it. They want a revel around the thing—to gawk at it and gawk at one another—and I want the coin for tickets—nay, at this point, I don't want to give the coin back!"

"Of course," Rhand said. He hesitated for the barest moment. "Perhaps, though, you could indulge me: I'm very eager to lay hands on my treasure. Let me hold the revel. The day after tomorrow, let's say. All your former bidders, your . . . gawking nobles, are welcome to attend, and I promise it will be well worth the coin they've given over." He looked up at Tam and Mira. "And do let me lend you some of my guards. I'm sure this lovely lady would like to be spelled."

Mira regarded him mildly. "This is my livelihood, goodsir. I'm fresh for the rest of my shift."

"Well, fresh or not," Chansom said, "I'm not staying here. Pack it up and let's head for Cloudcroft's manor. At least then he'll stop prattling on about me refusing his hospitality. Late wife's cousin," he explained to Rhand. "Better beds than this tick-and-roughcloth nonsense at least, and he doesn't want the battered thing. Send your guards over there at first light. But be discreet, would you? I don't need any more attention than we've already got."

Mira's dark eyes flicked to her father's. "It will be a happy day when you take this thing off our hands," she said to Rhand.

"Sooner than you think," Rhand said lightly.

Chansom excused himself and his guest to gather Dankon, presumably the half-orc guard from before, and call the Watch to come deal with the bodies. Rhand's piercing eyes watched Tam the whole while. He nodded back, pleasantly, while inside he cursed—he didn't need another mystery.

"Give it to me," Tam said once the door closed. "If half of what you say is true, at the very least they need to be locked away."

Mira didn't budge. "Chansom knows who you are," she said. "You *or* I run off with those artifacts now, he'll know how to track us down." She chewed her upper lip, staring at the chest. "You have to steal them from their new owner. If they're stolen *before* the transfer, you're the first person Chansom will finger—certainly he's stunned now, not thinking straight. But he's a shrewd one; he'll work out that you shouldn't have been here. What's he going to find when he tracks you down?" Tam didn't answer.

"But after," she went on, "well, our Master Rhand seems like the sort of man to have a lot of enemies. Wouldn't you say so?"

·:⌒:·

There were worse places in Malbolge than the little room at the tip of the farthest fingerbone tower, but at the moment, Lorcan was hard-pressed to think of any. He sat with his back to the curved and oozing wall, watching the membrane over the lacuna of the door and waiting.

Sairché's healing potion had been enough to mend his bones and restore his lost blood, but there hadn't been power left to resolve the bruises that mottled his red skin, nor repair the scars that now marred his chest and hands. He dreaded what he'd see in the mirror. But as the days passed and no more erinyes came to torment him, the pain had started to fade and he merely ached. And wondered.

"What are you playing at?" he whispered to the door, to his sister beyond it, somewhere in the plane of Malbolge. He was not such a fool to think the potion was a peace offering, a sign that Sairché was through with him. If she were through, she would have killed him. Something had changed. Something had complicated Sairché's plans.

And it remained to be seen how it would affect him.

He had not untangled the puzzle before the door unsealed to admit Sairché and two erinyes carrying a bundled rectangle nearly two-thirds their enormous heights.

"Against the wall," Sairché directed, not taking her eyes off of Lorcan while their half sisters settled the mysterious package beside the door. "I've brought you a gift," she said.

"It's not a gift if you want something in return."

"Then we shouldn't call your continued existence a gift either? What would you prefer?"

"That we be plain," Lorcan said. "You're holding me prisoner like I'm some sort of prize to lord over the Hells, but the longer you go without killing me, the more that everyone is going to wonder if you've lost your wits. The more they're going to notice that you're *not* Invadiah—because we both know Mother would have killed me the moment we left Glasya's sight—and think they might be able to bring you down. Why?"

Sairché scowled and flexed her wings again. She waved the erinyes out. "If you want to die so badly, there's the window. Or if you can't manage it yourself, I'm sure Bibracte would be *delighted* to assist."

"Of course she would," Lorcan said. "That's hardly worth mentioning." He squinted. "You can't find her."

Sairché matched his false and feral smile. "Why are you protecting her?"

"For one thing, it amuses me to keep you from getting your way."

"Enough to die for it?"

"Are you going to pretend you aren't going to kill me anyway?" He clucked his tongue. "Don't be tedious, Sairché."

"You're hiding something."

Lorcan kept his smile, but his thoughts went to Glasya, to the terrible voice whispering in his ear as he was led from the palace to be lost in the little room. It amused him much more not to cross the archduchess.

"Aren't we all?" he said instead. "For instance . . . why is it you want my Brimstone Angel so badly? You don't collect warlocks. So you must have a buyer in mind. But I can say with fair certainty that there are no devils in Malbolge who want her and would be willing to deal with you. So you're crossing the layers."

Sairché shrugged. "Simple enough to figure out. I never hid it. I'm more interested to know why you're being so coy. So careful. I thought you might do better to have a little more . . . slack in your lead." She pulled the drape of linen aside to reveal a heavy iron-framed mirror leaning against the curved wall. Its surface stirred gently, as if a sheen of oil marred the glass. A scrying mirror, for viewing the plane of Toril, the world of Faerûn.

Lorcan smiled to himself, though his stomach started to churn. "You really do think I'm a fool."

Sairché ran a finger across the surface of the mirror, swirling the sickly colors and distorting the reflection. "Twelve of your pacts have very distinct signatures. I found the five whose souls you'd laid claim to almost before I started looking. Tracing the lines of power from the Hells to the rest was bothersome, but not difficult."

"Yes, yes," Lorcan said, dismissively. "You're very clever."

"The thirteenth . . . well, you know perfectly well there is no such signature for her, no line of power—at least, not one I can find. It's as if it dissolves into nothing." She stared at her brother's reflection in the mirror, her golden eyes burning. "It's as if she doesn't exist."

"And yet she does," he said. "Sounds like you're not as clever as you think." He watched her reflection beside his, searching for some sign of her intentions in the shared shape of their eyes, the shared curve of their smirk.

"Who's got you trapped?" he asked again.

"I'm not discussing my business with you."

"I don't know that you have to," Lorcan said. There was nothing she could have said that would have taken away the clear desperation in Sairché's actions. She didn't want Farideh. She *needed* her. Someone thought Sairché could get them a Brimstone Angel, and the price for failure was too high.

But then . . . why was Lorcan not writhing in a dungeon bleeding out of his eyes?

"Is it Glasya?" he asked.

Sairché smirked back. "Wouldn't you like to know. Enjoy the mirror."

"And distract myself from my window?" he asked. "I might miss another succubus scuffle."

She crossed to the door, chuckling to herself. "You think you know me? I know you, too, Lorcan. I know it's taking everything you have not to push me aside and check on your warlocks—I'd lay good coin on my being no more than ten steps out the door before you're checking up on *her* in particular." Her gaze flicked over him. "Five, if the erinyes broke you as much as it looks. Good day."

He'd prove her wrong. Lorcan waited until she'd left, until the door had shut and merged back into the still-living marrow of the walls, until he glimpsed the troop of erinyes passing into the distance, before dropping to his knees in front of the scrying mirror.

It would be swaddled in protections and magic to trace its use—even if he couldn't sense the spells' presence, he knew Sairché wouldn't forget such a simple precaution. He called up the mark of his Phrenike heir. The reflection shivered and blurred and changed to reflect a young man with horns, bloodless skin, and a tail that lashed the frame of the bed he lay snoring in. Lorcan sneered. Even to thwart her brother, Sairché wouldn't take that one.

He called, again and again, each of the heirs of the Toril Thirteen, the circle of warlocks who'd aided Asmodeus in his ascension. The Nicodemus heir shimmered with the mark of a rival from another layer. So did the heir of Caisys the Vicelord. The Elyria heir lay dead in a puddle of her own viscera. Lorcan scowled. He'd been fond of that one.

Four were lost altogether—stolen by other collectors of warlocks or dead of refusing them. The other eight might well have never known he was gone, as little as their routines had changed. None seemed to be focusing on the sorts of rituals that might rescue Lorcan from his captivity.

Bastards, he thought. Couldn't count on a one of them.

Lorcan held the pendant he wore, a piece of leather shaped in the form of Glasya's copper scourge—the one piece of ornament he'd been left, since it was the only one without a clear enchantment—and worried it with one thumb.

He drew a steady finger down the center of the mirror—pointedly did not think of Farideh, the heir of Bryseis Kakistos, the Brimstone Angel, rarest of the Toril Thirteen—and pretended it wasn't such a hard thing to do.

# CHAPTER SIX

## WATERDEEP

*2 FLAMERULE, THE YEAR OF THE DARK CIRCLE (1478 DR)*

**M**IRA FOUND THE NOTE FROM HER FATHER TUCKED INTO A CRACK IN the window frame of her room, after she and Dankon returned from moving the artifact to the manor grounds. Cloudcroft had as many guards in his manor as he had vulgar works of art, and Chansom had given his guards the morning to themselves.

Dankon nodded at the little scroll as she reached to palm it, shedding armor pieces and weaponry. "Who's that for?"

Mira unrolled it. "You have a brightbird you're expecting love notes from?"

The half-orc chuckled. "Do *you*, Lady Ice Storm?"

*Plans are in place and the way is clear,* the note read in a simple code she could have managed in the cradle. *Meet me at the statue's head in North Ward, once your duties are discharged. Be prepared to leave.* She sighed—a less obvious message with the innkeeper would have sufficed.

"What's your paramour have to say then?"

"Nothing I want to hear," she said. "I need to go out."

Dankon heaved his chestplate over his head and onto the floor. "Well, come in quietly. I intend to sleep every heartbeat we're given."

Mira slipped down the stairs and out the rear door of the inn. She sighed again—she could only hope that by leaving he meant to go to Everlund, the city that held the Harpers' stronghold in the north, but even then the portal meant that none of her prior plans were going to be of use. You make Beshaba proud, Fisher, she thought.

She'd have to make tentative arrangements for supplies in Everlund, and send word to her own contacts that their plans had changed.

The Fisher had wanted her unsettled, but she wouldn't give him that pleasure. She could keep a calm face and a calmer tongue. She could ride alongside her father and not rise to the myriad reminders that he didn't trust her, didn't expect enough of her. That he thought things could be simple between them because here and there in her life he'd stopped in and dropped advice on her like a sudden hailstorm, nothing but puzzled when she had ideas of her own. She would show the Fisher he'd made no roadblock, but only a side path. She was clever enough to get through this, she thought, leaving the inn in the pale hours of dawn to find a more private place to contact Maspero.

Nothing would ruin her discovery.

Tarchamus the Unyielding. A figure so vague and difficult to pin down that most insisted he was only a legend, or some error of translation—several arcanists of Old Netheril spliced together in the intervening centuries like one of those wizards' terrifying creations. It was said he'd crafted a spell so powerful, it burned the floating city of Tenish right out of the air, stone and citizens and all. It was said he had done so while spurning the *mythallars,* the concentrations of magic that the Netherese arcanists had perfected. If the fragment led to the lost enclave—or tomb or hoard or even midden heap— of Tarchamus the Unyielding, Mira thought, she could make her name—her *own* name—as a historian. She could get out from under petty patrons and other people's conflicts.

She could spend a whole lifetime studying the secrets of Tarchamus.

Mira sighed, and imagined what Tam would say. "Do you really want to study the secrets of someone who destroyed whole cities?" Fury squeezed at her chest and throat even at that imagined comment. He would, he would say something exactly like that—he knew best, after all. Her life was precisely like his, wasn't it?

Enough, she told herself, with another great sigh. At least her father was predictable. She could manage this.

She stepped into the alleyway and withdrew from the pouch around her neck, one of the small glass eggs she carried there. Looking around to be sure she hadn't been followed, she shook the egg and sent a swirl of white smoke spinning through the center. She smashed it against the wall.

"Plans changed," she said quickly, as the smoke eddied over the brickwork. "We'll need supplies in Everlund. Extra hands too. Be there quicker than expected. Should have location deciphered before you arrive." She hesitated. "Harpers involved."

The smoke whirled around one more time before catching a breeze and streaking eastward, and Mira heard the faint echo of her words hissing along with it. She brushed the broken glass off the edges of the brick, wondering if she should have mentioned that the Harper involved was her storied father and not the untrained young hirelings they were promised.

No, she thought, stepping from the alley. Maspero might well have called off the whole endeavor. And she could manage her father.

She was within sight of the inn when a pair of wiry men stepped into her path. Mira stopped and looked the two of them over, hands resting on the hilts of her knives. "May I help you?" she said dryly.

"Master Rhand would like to speak with you," the one on the left said, jerking his head toward a carriage waiting across the road. "At once."

Mira peered at him for a long moment, long enough so that the man started to tense. There was something about his face. Something . . . off. A disguise, she decided. Interesting. She smiled, "Lead on."

The man in the carriage did not descend, but beckoned her into the plush, dark space. He watched her settle with piercing eyes.

"You are Goodman Chansom's guard, yes?" he said, both hands resting on the silver knob of a cane. "The one who killed those thieves."

"I am. Are you looking for a guard?"

"No," he said. "I'm looking to . . . clarify some things. Does your Goodman Chansom know you have more than one allegiance?"

Mira kept smiling and shook her head. "He knows so long as he's paying me, my allegiances are all his."

"Truly?" Master Rhand smiled back at her and she found herself wishing he wouldn't. "I find myself unconvinced. Your thieves were Zhentarim, my sources say. Cyricist Zhentarim. And so I must ask how it is that the Black Network has found out about my little treasure. How they have come to decide it's dear enough to go toe-to-toe with such a pair as was guarding it."

Mira knew none of her surprise would show—not even for Master Rhand. She was too practiced for that. "My, Master Rhand, your sources are quick. But my father's presence was a happy accident. As for me, you can well imagine the likes of the Zhentarim . . . they would be inclined to underestimate a mere guard."

He chuckled. "As the bodies prove, yes? Convenient, that. I suppose you'll tell me I'm being overcautious. Paranoid."

She gave him a patient look. "My livelihood, goodsir, is based entirely on meeting a need for caution. I would never gainsay it. But in this case, it seems I cannot do much for you but offer my unneeded services and assure you, on my word, I had nothing to do with the thieves."

"I suppose that's all I can ask for," Master Rhand said. She started to excuse herself. "But," he added, "should you *know* anyone who might have had something to do with those thieves—who might have anything to do with future thieves, future attempts to take the artifacts—let me give you a word of caution. To pass along."

Rhand beckoned the guard who'd stared down Mira earlier to the carriage door. He pulled an amulet from inside his robes and held it up near the man's face. The mask of magic that had obscured the man's face shivered and dissolved. He looked over at Mira with cold, black eyes and a wicked sneer, twisted by a row of rings in his lips chained to larger rings in the cords of his neck.

It took a great deal more effort to master her surprise this time. "Your guards are shadar-kai," she said, naming it to nail it down, to make the fact more palatable. It didn't work.

Rhand lowered the amulet, and the man's disguise returned. "Mortals born infused with the promise and peril of shadow—isn't that what they say? So poetic. I assure you, though, anyone who crosses me will not enjoy the sorts of things they find poetry in."

"So I've heard." Mira didn't have to have fought shadar-kai to know they'd relish every strike they took, shocked by the pain away from fading into the Shadowfell. Gods knew what he sent them to do to sate that need when people weren't stealing his things. She thought back to her father's note, his half-cobbled plan. Piss and hrast. "I see why you say you don't need guards," she said as pleasantly as she could.

Master Rhand leaned forward, the cane in his hands more of a staff, a bludgeon perhaps. "You'll be sure, I trust, to let anyone who might require such information know that Garek isn't alone. That I'm well protected, and—if need be—that my . . . betters are keen to keep hold of this pair of artifacts."

He didn't have to say Shade. With shadar-kai guards he could mean no one else. Mira nodded, shaken—let him see you're shaken, she thought, he wants you shaken—and scrambling for a new plan.

Leaving the artifacts—and the possible treasures of Tarchamus—to Rhand and Shade was not an option, not in her father's eyes and not in Maspero's. She'd sold them both on the promise of precious history and of thwarting Shade: they'd both be prepared to deal with the pressures of Adolican Rhand. But to get the page and stone in the first place . . . that would require far more than her father's quick thinking and lockpicks. She needed time to reconsider her options.

"I'll do what I can," she said as she stepped from the carriage.

⁙⁚⌒⁚⁙

The next day, Farideh slipped out after an early morningfeast and returned to the inn just before midday, footsore and frustrated, with no better idea of where she could learn the rituals she needed. Waterdeep seemed to grow daily, sprouting all manner of shops which sold rituals to copy for more coin than she had, and offered to buy the few things she owned for far less than they were worth. But at least she was one tattered cloak richer. Mehen wouldn't be able to scold her over that.

She refolded it nervously as she crossed the empty taproom and approached the innkeeper. "Have there been any messages?" she asked. "Anything from a Mehen?" And she braced for the inevitable brief chuckle and "Not today," only slowing as she passed him.

But the innkeeper reached under the bar and took out a thick envelope that he slapped down on its surface. "There," he said with a grin. "Not Mehen, but for you all the same."

"Are you sure?" she asked, reaching for the envelope. "He's the only one who knows where—" She turned the note over and saw the black wax seal. The same as the one on the note with the ritual book. She set it on the bar, her blood running cold.

"That's not for me," she said.

"I'd say it is," the innkeeper replied. "Fellow in livery, of all things, left it here. Said it was for the tiefling with the sun-and-moon eyes."

The description made her stomach flip. "How did he know I was here?"

"Am I supposed to know that?" the innkeeper chuckled.

She picked the note back up. "Would you tell me if he comes back? Or anyone like him?"

"As long as you keep that sister of yours from leaving more gouges in my floor."

Farideh nodded absently, tucking the concern for Havilar's damages behind the nature of Master Rhand's note. It was likely nothing: A letter to see if she'd gotten the book. Maybe another offer to show her the rituals she needed. A more forward request that she reply.

But, Farideh thought, climbing the stairs, no matter how innocuous it might be, it should not have found her here, and that knowledge made her stomach churn. She pushed open the door to her room. "Havi," she started, "the innkeeper . . ." She looked up from the black seal. The room was empty. Havilar's glaive leaned against the corner.

"Havi!" she cried, tearing back out into the hallway. She wouldn't go anywhere without the glaive—she *never* did. Could Sairché have found them? Could she have lured Havilar away, or worse? She looked down at the envelope—*karshoj*, it couldn't be about *Havi*, could it?

She met Tam coming up the top of the stairs, looking exhausted and rumpled. "I can't find Havilar," she said in a rush. "She's left her glaive and—"

"Hang on," Tam said, holding up a hand to stop her. "Have you checked with Brin?"

"No," Farideh said, "but you don't understand, if she's *left*—"

"Check the room first," Tam advised, maneuvering past her. "They've been in there most days when I come back."

Farideh blinked at him. "In your room?"

Tam laughed at her. "Nothing so brazen. But what do you think she does while you're out roaming the city looking for things your father doesn't want you to buy?"

"He *told* me to buy a cloak," she started. But a trill of laughter—Havilar's laughter—cut her off and her attention turned toward the noise, from behind the door across the hallway.

"Well there you are," Tam said. "Come find me if I'm wrong. Heavens know there's a good enough chance she's gotten into something."

Farideh straightened as he passed her, feeling as if she'd been tossed into the wrong day. What did she think Havilar did? Drilled, mostly. Bothered the innkeeper. Went on errands with Brin. Or wandered herself, she thought.

Mehen was going to be furious she hadn't kept them apart. Farideh went to the door—there were definitely voices beyond—and tapped gently on it.

"Come in!" Havilar's voice called out. Farideh nudged the door open. Her sister sat on the floor in the narrow space between the wall and the bed, her pointed toes resting on the bedrails. Brin was crosslegged above her on the bed.

"Well met," he said.

Havilar gave her a look that was somehow equal parts irritation and self-satisfaction. *Good, you're here to see this* and *When are you going to leave?* Farideh bit back a reply to the unasked question. "I couldn't find you," she said.

"*You* were gone," Havilar said, just shy of accusatory. "Where did you go?"

"Hey, you found a cloak," Brin said. Farideh held it open: a plain, brown stormcloak, its half-dozen rents mended in dark thick thread like brutal scars.

Havilar winced. "That's all you could find?"

"It was cheap," Farideh said, bundling the cloak back up. "And it's long enough. What are you two doing?"

Brin held up a fan of parchment. "Reading chapbooks."

"Brin bought one of just about every title." Havilar giggled. "Do the lonely widow's voice again."

"I said no," Brin said, but he chuckled when he said it. He looked up at Farideh. "Did you need something?"

"No," she said, "I just . . . I couldn't find Havi."

Havilar shook her head, as if that were such a strange thing to worry over. "I was right here. Better than sitting among Tam's things, pretending we're not curious."

"Has he come back?" Brin asked. "I need to tell him I've moved over."

"Oh, yes." Farideh gestured at the open door and the hallway beyond with the envelope. "He's just come in, I . . . ran into him," she finished awkwardly. "He's here."

"What's that?" Havilar asked, pointing to the envelope with her chin.

Farideh looked down at it. Whatever it was, she didn't feel like opening it in front of Havi and Brin anymore. "Nothing," she said. "Are you coming down to eat?"

"In a bit," Havilar said. "We'll see you there."

Farideh slipped out and closed the door behind her, hardly sure what to think, but certain she wasn't wanted in there. Hells, how long had she been in their way?

And how mad would Mehen be if she didn't *stay* in their way?

Farideh sat down on the stairs to the taproom, considering the envelope again. With any luck, Mehen would be back soon and both her problems would be solved. They'd leave Waterdeep, and what to do about Master Rhand would be a question she didn't need to answer. Mehen would see what was going on with Brin and Havilar and she wouldn't be responsible for being his proxy—or better yet, Mehen would whisk them away after some new bounty, and *no one* would have to convince Havilar of anything before . . .

They're just reading chapbooks, she thought. Even if she's fond of him, it's nothing she can't walk away from.

Farideh shook her head—it wasn't her problem anymore than the envelope was Havilar's. She broke the seal and skimmed the note as quickly as she could, as if any word might be like a pressure trap, triggering if her eyes rested on it too long.

**LESSER EVILS**

An invitation. But not, thank the gods, to come alone. A revel. A viewing for some new treasures. The statue from before. Some sort of painting. An artifact he was particularly proud to show off. And she should come and let him know how the ritual book was suiting her.

All innocent enough. But she couldn't help but sense the vaguest menace in the way these things were phrased. He seemed, she thought, annoyed that she hadn't sought him out to say thank you. Insistent that she should. And every word was laced with double meanings.

And now Master Rhand knew where she slept. Farideh folded the note back up, wishing even harder for Mehen to return so they could leave Waterdeep.

She called up enough of her Hellish powers to tint the veins on the backs of her hands, considering all the consequences of the alternative, should Master Rhand press his interests.

⁘⌒⁘

The sound of the door opening jerked Dahl out of a shallow sleep, spent hunched over the small table. He blinked, orienting himself. Then he focused on Tam, frozen beside the open door and looking at Dahl with open surprise.

"Good morning," he said. "Have you been waiting long?"

Dahl swallowed a yawn. "All night. Where have you been?"

Tam unfastened his cloak and chuckled. "Whatever were you waiting for?"

"For my partner to tell me what by all the gods' books is going on," Dahl retorted. "Have you got the page?"

"No," Tam said, piling the slender spiked chain on the floor. "I found it, but it's been sold already."

Dahl waited a moment for more information. "And so? You're just letting it go?"

"Of course not."

"So what's the plan?"

Tam considered him a moment, as if he were trying to decide how best to get a sick bull into a cart bed. "I think it's best," he said carefully, "if I do this alone."

Dahl bit back a curse. "Are you at least going to tell me what 'this' is?"

Tam shook his head. "Better not to involve you."

"What is it you think I'm here for?" Dahl asked tightly. "At the very least tell me what you're doing so I can tell Master Vishter what happened if you don't come back."

Tam gave him a thin smile. "I always come back."

"Until you don't."

That made him chuckle again, like an amused uncle. Like he found Dahl's concerns an adorable approximation of a *real* Harper. Dahl balled his fists.

But amused or not, Tam took the borrowed leaflet from the pocket sewn into the lining of his cloak and spread it face down on the table. Sketchy lines of charcoal—the tip of a burnt sliver of wood, perhaps—traced the suggestion of a large building's floor plan.

"The viewing's in this North Ward manor," Tam said. "The page will be placed in the ballroom, about here." He tapped the largest room in the building, toward the back of the house. "Eight windows face the rear gardens, which are walled in by seven feet of stone. Everyone enters through the front gate, and exits in the same fashion, if the guards have anything to say about it. He's expecting around seventy guests."

"You found all this in a night?"

"I am very good at what I do," Tam answered. "Now the festivities start at sundown tomorrow, an hour after the page is brought in and placed. A friend is getting me in."

Dahl frowned at the drawing. "You mean to steal it from him at the viewing?"

"Well," Tam said, straightening, "I think it unlikely Master Rhand will sell it after he's just bought it."

"Rhand?" Dahl looked up. "*Adolican* Rhand?"

"Do you know him?"

"I've heard of him," Dahl said dryly. "The Harpers think he's got ties to Netheril. He runs caravans up north, to points that make no sense, and he profits a great deal from it. We're fairly sure he's smuggling goods to Shade. Possibly information too." Tam raised an eyebrow and Dahl folded his arms. "People talk."

"Indeed. All the more reason to keep the page out of his hands."

Farideh's dealings with the wizard were on the tip of Dahl's tongue, but Tam's dismissal made him set that revelation aside. "All the more reason," he said, "not to go into this lightly. You can't rob him on your own."

"It's better I do," Tam said. "The fewer people involved, the fewer chances someone gets hurt. I have a contact inside—I don't need anyone else."

"And if that manor's full of Netherese guards? Or worse? There are rumors he's got access to shadar-kai—"

"I'll manage," Tam said, in a voice that sounded so much like Dahl's old enchantments teacher that he bristled. "This is the best option."

"Have you explored *any* of the other options? 'Cause I'm fairly certain having agents as backup or distractions or cover would prove useful. Have you asked Master Vishter to assign more Harpers?"

"He won't," Tam said, as if Dahl were asking why the sky was blue or why the moon didn't fall down on their heads as she crossed the sky: it was an immutable fact of nature. Aron Vishter wouldn't help them.

Dahl drew another long breath, and counted to himself.

"Don't you think," he said, as civilly as he could, "that it would be safer and simpler to take the page *before* viewing? Or before it's transferred?"

"No," Tam said.

Dahl waited for some explanation, but Tam was already folding up his map. "Because," Dahl said, "it seems there will be even *fewer* people involved if we just knock aside some guards."

"It's too dangerous."

"For whom?"

"For all of us," Tam said sternly. "Trust me, I have been doing this for some time."

"I'm well aware," Dahl replied.

Every moment of this assignment made it clearer and clearer that Tam didn't think of Dahl as a partner, nor truly even as an assistant.

Him, Dahl thought bitterly, and everyone else. A millstone, perhaps. A nuisance to be worked around.

Jedik had put Dahl in contact with the Harpers just a year before, hoping no doubt that the opportunity would clear Dahl's mind, give his thoughts somewhere to focus and his hands something to do besides pick up another bottle. It didn't matter. The Harpers hardly needed him either.

"At least put me somewhere I can be useful," Dahl said bitterly. "Give me that if nothing else. A lookout—put me near the doors."

Tam smiled, but it was that slick, outward smile Dahl had begun to notice and hate. Unimpeachable on the surface, but gods above, Dahl knew he didn't mean it. "I can handle a good deal more than you give me credit for," Tam said.

"I'm not doubting you. I'm saying there are too many things that can go wrong."

"A good reason for you to stay out of the thick of it."

Oghma's bloody papercuts, Dahl though, I'd like to hit him. "So my *entire* purpose is to tell Master Vishter how you died?" Dahl fumed. "You do know I can swing a godsbedamned sword?"

"No one needs to swing swords," Tam said more firmly. "We want everyone to walk away from this."

"Good luck to you when there's a room full of shadar-kai on you."

Tam looked as if he'd like to hit Dahl too. "Watch your tongue."

There was a tentative tap on the door, and a slight, pale young man with streaky blond hair pushed in. His eyes darted from Tam to Dahl, and back again.

"Good morning," he said. "Are you just getting in?"

"Ah, gods, Brin!" Tam said. "My apologies." He turned back to Dahl. "You might have answered the door, seeing as you were using my rooms."

"No, no," the young man said. "I took a room of my own. Farideh said you'd gone out and when I didn't see you return . . . well, why come knocking?" He looked over at Dahl. "Is this your new apprentice?" he said, a hint of a chill in his tone.

"I'm working with him," Dahl said, too furious to be more articulate. He was *years* out of apprenticeship. "Dahl Peredur."

The young man's expression took on a certain steeliness as he clasped the proffered hand. "Brin. Brin Crownsilver."

Dahl's surprise must have shown; the young man smirked. The Crownsilvers were well-heeled and influential in Cormyr, enough that even a farmer's son out of the Dalelands recognized his name.

"I thought you were fresh out of coin," Tam said, "Goodsir Crownsilver."

Brin turned back to him. "Yes, well, I've . . . come in to some. Quite a bit, actually. I was hoping . . . I'm not sure I ought to be using it. It's . . . family coin."

"Presumably your family is the one who gave you access to it," Tam said, "so I should think they don't mind."

"*I* mind," Brin said. "If I'm taking it, I feel as if I ought to be putting it to some better use than room and board."

"I think you'll find surviving is a very good use for coin," Tam said. "Start there. Now, if you'll excuse us?"

Brin looked over at Dahl again. "Are you two working on that page Farideh mentioned?"

"This isn't open business," Dahl said.

"It's more open than you think," Brin replied. "I know what Tam does outside of his goddess's dictums. I'm going to assume you do the same?"

Tam held the door open. "What he does or does not do isn't a point of discussion. Now, if you don't mind—"

"She seemed to think you were going to steal it," Brin went on. "But you haven't got it, have you?" He looked back at Dahl. "You wouldn't be arguing if you had." Dahl scowled—he hadn't meant to be loud enough to be heard, and now Tam would surely point out his indiscretion.

"Enough, Brin," Tam said, pulling the younger man toward the door. "We're not playing at courtly intrigue. Remind Farideh of that as well, if you please." He did not shut the door behind Brin.

"Well," Tam said, in a voice that brooked no argument. "We'd best prepare."

Dahl squeezed his fists even tighter and counted to ten the way Jedik always insisted. Dahl's patience broke anyway.

"I see now why they say the Harpers are a dying breed," he said acidly. Tam's expression shifted, as fierce as a dire wolf, and he shut the door, the only way out of this. But it had been too much already. Let's do this, Dahl thought. "The answer was right there before you—"

"Brin is not the answer," Tam said. "I already have a plan."

"It's not much of a plan."

"If you want to play adventurer," the silverstar said, "and run about with foolish ideas that don't account for reality in the slightest, then get down to the Fisher and hand him your bloody pin. But if you're assigned to me, you'll have a little godsbedamned sense and *listen*."

"I *have* been listening!" Dahl shouted. "I've done nothing *but* listen to you, and you're wrong. He was standing there, all but *offering* you the funds to cover a competing bid. If we'd asked for the coin—"

"We'd have doomed the scion of a very wealthy family to the tender ministrations of the Shadovar."

"If you go in alone—"

"Then I have only myself to manage. Which seems a good sight better than the alternative."

"So you'd rather doom yourself and this mission than tell me what to do?" Dahl shouted. "You're not the only person involved! You're not the only one who can do anything."

"This isn't a discussion!" Tam snapped. "Go back to Aron and tell him you're free for more antiquity hunting."

Dahl stormed from the room, cursing Tam in a dozen different tongues. How could he act like Dahl couldn't do anything, like he couldn't help? He wasn't broken. He wasn't useless just because he'd fallen, and yet there was Jedik tossing him aside—

Tam. Not Jedik. The thought stopped him in his tracks. Gods, if ever there was a time for a drink. He headed down the stairs.

At the foot of them, Farideh stood, staring down at a note as if it were a slowly opening portal to the Abyss. Dahl's temper flared.

"What is *wrong* with you?" he demanded in a low voice. "Did you just flit out of there and start telling anyone who'd listen?"

Farideh looked up at him as if he'd gone a little mad. "What?"

"Your Crownsilver friend knew about the page," he said. "About what it was."

"Oh." She looked back down at the note, turning it in her hands as if she weren't sure whether to crumple it or handle it like it was made of crystal or read it over again. "He's no one to worry about."

**Lesser Evils**

"Considering your other 'friends,' you'll forgive my skepticism. Any more gifts from your dear Master Rhand?"

The look she turned on him could have melted steel. She shoved the note at him, crumpling it against his chest. "He sent that," she said, a tremor of anger in her voice. "He *knows* where I am."

Dahl caught the note and opened it: an invitation to the viewing.

An invitation to come right into the room where the page and stone would be, whether Tam appreciated it or not. His thoughts started spinning. He could salvage this . . .

"Would you consider going?" Dahl asked.

She looked at him as if he'd gone *completely* mad. "I know you don't like me, but *karshoj*—why would you even suggest such a thing?"

He considered the note, the spiky handwriting and the subtle suggestions. He could spin a story, try and convince her it was in her best interests—Hells, maybe it *was* in her best interests to show up and tell Adolican Rhand to leave her be.

But she'd never trust a word of it. And then he'd be as bad as Tam.

"I need to get into this revel," he told her quietly. "He's bought the page and he's putting it on display. Master Zawad intends to steal it." Dahl handed back the invitation. "I think he's underprepared and I want to be there to help."

"To help," she asked, "or to catch him in his mistake?"

"With luck there is no mistake, and he can lecture me on my lack of trust," Dahl said. "But if I can save his neck—and I'm willing to bet I will . . . I'm not going to promise I won't ask for his thanks."

"I wouldn't believe you if you did."

He bit back a retort. "You know we have to get that page," Dahl said. "And . . . what I said before, I was only repeating what I'd heard. For all you or I truly know, Master Rhand is just . . ." He hesitated, trying to think of the most innocuous way to phrase it. "An overly wealthy gentleman with poor conversational skills and unfortunate dress sense."

"That's plenty for me." Farideh bit her lip. "Maybe you could just take the invitation," she said. "I don't want to wind up in any trouble, and—"

"I'll teach you rituals," Dahl interrupted. "Five. Fair?"

She hesitated. "I don't know if you know the ritual I need."

"As long as it's not along Master Rhand's lines, I can all but guarantee I do know it. Common or obscure—I have a *lot* of rituals. Ones you won't find outside of Oghma's faithful." She looked unconvinced. "Ten," he said. "One a day for a tenday. You can choose half of them. Once we've got the basics. And I'll set up a safehouse for you," he added. "And your sister. Somewhere Rhand can't bother you."

She seemed to consider the invitation in her hands, and sighed. "I might not *be* here in a tenday."

"Then as many days as you are here," he said. "I can't take the chance they won't let me in, and we have to be *sure* Netheril doesn't tease any information out of that page. It could spell war." Still she hesitated. "I'll get you a dress," he said in a wheedling tone. "Something to wear to the revel."

She scowled at him. "Do you think I'm an idiot? Get me a knife. I'll need that more."

"A knife *and* a dress. You'll look out of place in leathers."

"Then get one for Havi too," she said. "I'm not going in there without someone at my back, and she'll be a terror if she doesn't get to wear something frilly."

Dahl winced. "No. You'll stand out as it is. Add your sister and all the guards will be eyeing us."

Farideh folded her arms across her chest. "You'll be watching Tam's back. Which means I'll be left alone . . . And if we're moving to another place, I want to be sure we aren't separated. I want Havilar with me."

"If anything happens I can't promise I can get both of you out of danger."

Farideh laughed to herself. "If anything happens, Havi will be happy to clear a path twice as wide as you need."

# CHAPTER SEVEN

*WATERDEEP*

*4 FLAMERULE, THE YEAR OF THE DARK CIRCLE (1478 DR)*

His prayers ended, Tam opened his eyes to the waxing moon and the sure sensation of Selûne's blessing coursing through his veins. He lay on the roof tiles a few moments more, letting the powers quiet and settle. If his life had followed a different course, such nights might have been the center of his existence. Channeling the moon goddess's powers to the people in the world below, a vessel for her quiet power.

Some days it seemed as if it would suit him far, far better than being her weapon, most often after a night where he gathered his powers from Selûne without haste, the gift of powers as familiar and easy and untouched by time as sitting with an old friend. Other times it felt more like a rush, powers pouring into him before he could ask for them—Selûne knew what he needed.

And now and again, there were nights where the communion made clear the extent of the goddess's powers.

Mira, he thought, staring up at the moon poised among the shining fragments they called her Tears. The night Mira was born he'd been away and racing back, knowing he would be too late the moment the midwife's sending faded. Truly, knowing from the moment he'd left Athkatla, but he'd agreed months before to accompany Viridi into Tethyr. He wasn't supposed to have a child, her mother, Laeyla, wasn't supposed to know how to contact him, and he wasn't supposed to know how to contact her. He wasn't supposed to be entangled with the rest of the world—for their safety and his own.

But a rash night led to an accident led to Mira's mother deciding she wanted to be Mira's mother, led to Tam realizing he didn't want to cut out all entanglements.

"Something's bothering you," Viridi had noted almost immediately. And he'd denied it and denied it and denied it—but once the sending came, he admitted everything.

"I don't know what I'm doing," he said. "I knew the rules. I know why they're there." He shook his head. "I'm no one's father."

Viridi sighed in that way she had, that said he was so painfully young and if she remembered feeling as lost and unsure, she knew better than to try and explain it. She'd pointed out the fastest horse to him and told him not to come back to her compound in Athkatla for a month.

"At least," she said. "But once you've sorted yourself out, I expect you to return."

Near deepnight, he'd had to stop and change horses again, and he made his vespers to Selûne, going through the prayers as carefully and quickly as he could, as if a single misspoken word would make everything fall apart. But when he'd finished, he'd sat there, alone in the grove. Listening to the sound of his horse clipping the spring grass. Afraid to move.

Please, he prayed, let it look a little like me.

He trusted Laeyla—the babe was his—but somewhere in the frightened center of his heart, he was sure she would be only Laeyla's. She would have her mother's eyes and nose and chin and cheeks, her mother's barking laugh and her mother's calculating mind. Her pointed feet, her tapered fingers, and nothing at all of Tam Zawad.

Please, he prayed, because it seemed as if it would make everything turn out all right.

Please, and I will never ask for another selfish thing again.

Please.

And the moon goddess's regard fell fully on him.

For a moment, it felt as if there was no Tam, no Laeyla, no babe. There was no grove or horse or time or place—nothing except the silvery light and a sureness he had never felt in himself. Instead of his shut eyelids, he saw a face of Selûne, a kind-faced elf woman with silvery hair. She smiled gently at him.

*Go.* The thought might have been his, and it might have been the voice of the god, and it might have been both. *Go.* Because this is happening whether you're ready or not. *Go.* Because you will be more ready by the moment and sitting here won't change that. *Go.* Because you'll quickly realize now that you have a daughter that there are a thousand more prayers in you that you would have called selfish—for her safety, for yours, for her happiness, for yours. *Go.*

Because she'd already been born and she already had his eyes.

On the rooftop, Tam sighed and sat up. He climbed back into the room he was keeping by the window and changed into a suit of dark grays and blacks, perfect for blending into the shadows. He took his chain and the haversack with his lockpicks and a variety of deterrents in case he was cornered. Secured the daggers in his boot and belt. Pinned the holy symbol to his chest where he could reach it easily. Cast a quick healing on his achy knee. Ready.

He slid by rope out the window into the alley below. And found himself facing a waiting Mira. Despite himself, he startled.

"What are you doing here?" he asked. "You're supposed to be with the chest."

"There's a problem," Mira said. "Rhand knows you're going to try and steal it. He pulled me aside and made some . . . insinuations."

"Insinuations?"

"His guards are all shadar-kai," she admitted. "*Loyal* shadar-kai. And bored, too."

Without warning, Tam's thoughts flitted back to that night in the Akanamere, to the shadar-kai and their brutal blades and the sheer, horrible range of sounds a tortured body could be made to make. He shut his eyes. "Shar and hrast."

Mira hesitated. "Are you going to let it go?"

"How can I do that?" he demanded. "If you're right, and this page is the key to untold dangers? We don't have a choice—we have to get it free." He ran a hand over his beard. "But out of a nest of shadar-kai."

She nodded. "But I've had a thought," she said. "If you try and steal it beforehand, they'll be ready for you. If you wait . . ."

"For what? For the middle of the revel? For a score of innocents to screen me? No, many thanks."

"For a moment during which no one thinks you'd be mad enough to strike," Mira said. "Rhand thinks there are other players—those Zhentarim."

Tam shook his head. "And I should pretend to be one?"

"I think they may return," Mira said. "We just have to watch and wait."

"It's too risky," Tam said. "What if they don't come?"

Mira pursed her lips. "Then we are exactly where we are now—debating the merits of rolling against Beshaba with a score of shadar-kai." She took him by the arm. "But as it stands, I did get you invited to the revel. So we'll be able to decide in the moment which die we ought to throw."

·:⌒:·

I do not want to be here, Farideh thought, looking up at the brown stone manse looming just behind a pair of ivory-spangled gates.

If you don't do this, a little voice replied, then Lorcan is doomed.

I don't want to be here.

If you don't do this, then Lorcan is doomed.

The two thoughts chased each other into a maelstrom of competing worries, each as forceful as the other, each as heavy. I do not want to be here. If you don't do this, then Lorcan is doomed. Each had all of her attention, all of her heart tangled in them. They twisted together, fighting to shove the other out. It squeezed the breath from her lungs.

It took all her concentration just to get herself into the too-short green gown Dahl had found her and out the door.

"If your hem had to be so short," Havilar said, "he could have at least found you slippers. Everyone can see your boots."

"I don't care."

"You should care a little." Havilar's borrowed gown was murky blue and too loose in the bodice. She'd pinned it haphazardly snugger, and left her unbraided hair hanging in loose waves. "How often do we get to go to a revel in *dresses*?"

"I don't know," Farideh said, concentrating on the fear her dream of Lorcan left with her so she wouldn't think of what lay inside the manor doors. "I hope not too often."

"Don't even *say* that! Even if your dress is ugly . . . Wait, are you wearing your armor underneath?"

Farideh wrapped her arms around her chest. "The dress was too big. And you took all the pins." And the brigandine gave her an extra layer between herself and anyone else—a small difference, but she would take anything she could get. Especially when she couldn't be sure of her promised guards.

Ahead of them, Dahl pressed forward, as if Farideh's purpose were already served. The idea of perhaps turning around, going back to the inn and letting him storm Adolican Rhand's manor on his own kept surfacing in Farideh's thoughts. But he'd never hold up his end of the deal if she didn't make certain to get him inside.

Which meant she had to go inside too.

"Well at least it makes your figure look better." Havilar said, which had Farideh wishing for her new cloak. Brin came up behind them. A new suit of a cream-colored fabric hung off Brin's shoulders a little loose—when Havilar had insisted Brin come too, Dahl had pointed out Brin dressed like someone's apprentice playing truant; at which point Brin had stormed off and reappeared with a new-bought outfit that he hadn't had time to have tailored.

"Crowded," he commented.

Havilar watched him from the corner of her eye. Brin, for his part, looked past Havilar, scowling at Dahl's back.

"I don't want to be here," Farideh murmured.

"There's nothing to worry about," Havilar said to her. "Just stop being nervous. Have fun."

Stop being a nuisance, Farideh thought, so she can make time with a boy more interested in sniping at a rival. "You *cannot* leave me alone."

"No one's going to leave you alone," Havilar said. "Calm down. And stop doing *that*." She dusted off Farideh's sleeve, as if she could brush away the smoky blur of shadows that seeped from her skin and through the fabric. "Bad enough your dress doesn't fit. You look like you've caught fire or something."

Farideh blushed and swatted her sister away. People milling around the entrance were staring. "Stop it. You're making it worse."

The groom at the door, a tall, sinewy man with almond eyes, took her invitation, casting a jaundiced eye over their group. Farideh found herself staring at her boots. None of them looked fit to mingle with the glittering Waterdhavians beyond the door. Maybe he would shoo them off.

*. . . The cambion pinned to the wall cannot answer—the hellwasps have smashed his teeth and torn out his tongue. He is screaming, wordless, and so is Farideh . . .*

I do not want to be here, she thought. If I don't do this, Lorcan is doomed.

She drew a deep breath and met the groom's gaze. "Is there a problem?"

Recognition dawned on his face, and a little part of her cursed. Rhand had told him to keep an eye out for her. He hadn't forgotten. "I beg your pardon," he said. "I suppose Master Rhand wasn't expecting you to have guests."

Brin gave a sharp laugh and when he spoke his fancy suit seemed a little less out of place. "Do you *really* suppose Master Rhand would invite the sort of young lady who has no one to accompany her out?" He took Havilar's arm and led her in, adding as he passed, "Give your man a little more credit." Havilar tossed a giddy look over her shoulder.

"He shouldn't have come," Dahl said.

Farideh said nothing, her eyes locked on the long hallway that led to the ballroom. I do not want to be here, she thought. If I don't do this, Lorcan is doomed.

"What's the matter with you?" Dahl said. "You aren't going to be sick are you?"

"I don't know," she said. She looked up at him, wishing he were Lorcan. "Don't leave me, all right?"

Dahl sighed and offered her an arm. "I'll make sure you're with your sister and Saer Crownsilver when I do. Just don't faint or anything."

"I don't faint," she snapped. She took his arm reluctantly, as if it were a shackle that would keep her from running. There's nothing to be afraid of, she told herself. You can handle yourself. They made their way through a swirl of young men and women in jewel-colored velvets and silks, their stares open and their whispers mocking. Farideh felt the shadows surge a little.

"Is that . . ." Dahl was looking down at her arm, at the blur of magic coming off her. "It's warlock magic," he said softly.

"It doesn't do anything to you, if that's it."

Dahl's arm stiffened under hers. "Is it strictly necessary?"

"I can't help it," she said, as they came into the ballroom. "If it bothers you so much, you'll have to see me out of here to make it stop."

The ballroom stretched as long as two trade-ships, and teemed with people, all decked in finery and passing pleasantries over the wine and cordials that passed on circling trays. Their happiness at seeing one another was as aggressive as dagger stabs in a dark alley, and the undercurrent of competition was palpable.

Three stands had been set up—the unsettling statue waited on the left under a downpour of cold, silvery light; the painting, a portrait of a sad-eyed woman in a bloody gown, hung on the back wall; and the page and fragment had been arranged off to the right.

"Can you hear it?" Dahl asked.

The drone of the page was quieter here, dampened perhaps by the shimmer of magic that walled off the artifacts or perhaps by the much louder buzz of Waterdeep's elite. But she could still make out the unfamiliar words in the pulse of the hum. *Ashenath enjareen nether pendarthis.* "It's the same," she said.

He cursed. "Then Master Zawad's plans *aren't* unfolding. Wait here," he said depositing her beside Havilar and Brin. "I'll be right back." He vanished into the crowd before Farideh could stop him. She cursed under her breath, and turned back to Brin and Havilar.

"I'm going to go try and catch some wine," Brin said after a moment. "I'll bring you a glass."

"That's all right," Farideh said.

"Bring her two," Havilar said. He slipped past a pair of women in long gowns of something rich and soft, punctuated with lace-covered cut-outs that showed their skin beneath, one deep as wood char, one bright as gold. They both stared at the twins as if they'd never seen anything as peculiar.

Farideh looked away, out at the crowd again, searching for Dahl or Tam or Master Rhand. Here and there, the sea of aristocrats broke around a body who had been invited for something other than his or her status—adventurers in scarred armor looking bare and antsy without their weapons as they entertained the other guests. But none were the Harpers. Most of the guests were just rich, with manners of satin and expressions of thick velvet, that softened anything sharp and hid it away under surcoats and skirts and jewels. Black was a favorite shade that evening. It would make it hard to spot Master Rhand. "I don't want to be here," Farideh murmured again.

"Why?" Havilar asked, staring back at the women. "Gods, what do you think a dress like that costs?"

"Piles," Farideh said, scanning the crowd. "And where would you wear it?"

"If I had a dress like that, I'd wear it *everywhere*." She turned back to her sister. "You really don't need me to mind you, do you?"

"It's not minding. I just want someone by my side when Master Rhand turns up. Someone to get me away if need be."

"I don't even see him," Havilar said. "What are you so worried about anyway? Even if this fellow's creepy, so's Lorcan. I thought you liked creepy."

Farideh's cheeks burned. "I can't believe you'd *say* that," she whispered. "They are *not* the same."

Havilar snorted. "He's practically Lorcan without the devil-magic and wings. Also, he's not nearly as good-looking, but still. All teeth and hands and—"

"*Thrik,*" Farideh hissed. "Were you paying any attention before?" She'd shown Havilar the rituals and the notes before they left, reminded her of the interaction in the shop. "What happened to 'shady codloose winkers'?"

"I'm just saying you don't need me. You have plenty of *experience* with shady codloose winkers."

"I have not, they are *not* the same, and anyway, I don't . . . I'm *not* fond of Lorcan." Havilar snorted again, and Farideh cut her off. "Oh, go bother Brin."

"*I* don't bother him," Havilar retorted. "You're just mad you're *wrong* about—" She broke off as Brin came to stand beside her, a wineglass in each hand.

"Bad news," he said, handing a glass to Havilar. "I can only carry two glasses." He held the other out for Farideh, but she waved him off.

"I'm going to find Dahl," she lied, and she turned back the way they'd come before Havilar could get another word out. Dahl was in, he had his half of the bargain, and she didn't see any reason she couldn't leave. After all, he'd abandoned her straightaway. Havilar had made it clear she wasn't welcome by her side, so long as Brin was around. No one could say she hadn't tried.

Rhand and Lorcan were *not* the same, she told herself. Even if Havilar thought so, even if half of Waterdeep thought so.

And even if she was wrong, she thought, heading down the hallway, being alike didn't mean she was bound to tolerate both of them. *Karshoj* to Havi, for implying so.

On a pillar at the middle of the hallway, a woman in a garb of sleek, deepnight blue so snug and seamless it seemed to be a second skin, posed contorted into a knot—resting on her forearms with her feet curled over and pointed down.

"Astonishing isn't she?" a voice said beside her cheek. Farideh jerked away and saw Adolican Rhand standing beside her. "She assures me it's quite uncomfortable."

"It looks so," Farideh said, taking a step back. Rhand handed her a tiny glass of bubbly gold wine—pressed it into her hand in such a way that she had to take it or let it smash on the floor. He toasted her with his own glass.

*"Zzar,"* he explained. "Have you had it?"

She shook her head and took a tentative sip. It tasted more like a sweet cake than anything else—until the burn of alcohol exploded in her mouth. She swallowed a cough. "Almonds," she managed.

"Yes, quite a bit," he said, staring into her. "It's fortified with almond liquor, but the base is a rather nuanced elven wine. People say it tastes of summer. Honey and sweet hay. Violets."

Farideh took another sip. All she could taste was almonds and alcohol. She held the glass back out to him. "Thank you. I was just leaving."

"Now, that doesn't sound right," Rhand said, not taking the glass. "My doorjack says you've only just arrived. Not even time to have a glass of wine and see my new collection." He gave her a sharp grin. "Not time enough to say well met and thank you for the gift."

Farideh took another sip, another second to think of what to say. Already her cheeks were flushing and her thoughts looser—a good thing the *zzar* came in such small quantities. "It's . . . Thank you. It's too much." And worse, it made her mouth dry. "But I worry I've given you the wrong idea. I . . ."

Farideh trailed off. The acrobat had lowered herself down onto the pillar and brought both feet to rest on either side of her face. She looked between her feet at Farideh with golden eyes, fringed with needle-sharp lashes of silver, and gave her a mirthless smile.

Farideh's heart skipped. Sairché.

Sairché, and here Farideh was, alone and unprepared. Sairché, and Havilar was here, unaware and unprotected. Sairché, and what did that mean for Lorcan? If she had found Farideh, was Lorcan dead? Was she here to claim her own Brimstone Angel? All this time worrying about the Netherese and the Harpers and Farideh had let herself become complacent about the very real threat of the Hells. Of Sairché, and the danger of the Toril Thirteen.

Try it, Farideh thought, drawing up the powers of her pact, what else could she do? Try it, she dared the cambion in the woman's skin. I'm ready.

"Are you well?" Master Rhand said, sounding distant. "Do you need to lie down?"

The woman settled her feet on top of the pillar and flipped herself upright, and Farideh could see, now, her eyes were only a lovely hazel and perfectly human, the lashes pasted on. The smile was still cold and empty, but now it wasn't for Farideh but for the man beside her.

Not Sairché. Just an acrobat.

She cursed at her fancy. Were the dreams bleeding through after so many nights of broken sleep? She'd drunk twice as much tea the night before and dreamed only fitfully—perhaps she was paying for it now.

Master Rhand stood too close, waiting for an answer. "No," she said. "I need to go."

"Oh, you can manage a little longer surely," he said, folding his arm around hers and holding it there. He led her back toward the ballroom, keeping her drawn close. "Come see my latest acquisitions and tell me how you've enjoyed your gift. Shall I assume you've been sequestered, learning new skills?"

"No," Faridah said. She tried to disentangle her arm from his, without resorting to striking him, but her thoughts couldn't sort which way to pull. He held her firm. "I mean . . . thank you, it's very nice. But those rituals—"

"Not at all," he said. "You ought to bring the book by again. I have several more rituals in mind that will suit you very well."

This was going all wrong. "You hardly know me," she said, trying to sound sharp. "What do you think will suit me so well?"

Rhand regarded her, amused. "You'll find, Faridah, that you are not unique in so many ways as you believe. Though"—he drew a strand of hair between his fingers—"still unique in the important ways."

Such a strange comment—Faridah found herself unsure of how to answer it. But it struck her in that moment it was very much the sort of thing Lorcan might have said to her once, if only Lorcan were not quite so clever.

The thought crossed her mind so knotted and complex she could hardly unravel it once it had. She frowned at the empty *zzar* glass she was still holding, and tried to remember emptying it.

Rhand steered her through the sea of staring guests, toward the display that held the shifting page and ancient stone. As they passed, Faridah picked out faces in the crowd—cruel glowing eyes, sly smiles, crowns of horns. Devils. Her heart started to race. No one else was noticing. No one else seemed to find anything to stare at but her.

Her arm started to ache where it pressed against Rhand, where her brand had etched her skin, and the ache became a burn. Her breath was getting harder to draw by the time they stopped before the display. His guests seemed to give him a wide berth—because the devils fear him, a voice in her thoughts seemed to say, or because he's one of them?

"My latest acquisition," Rhand said. "Perhaps you've heard about it?"

The murmuring voice was louder here, clearer. *Ashenath enjareen nether pendarthis.* Brought through rock and flood to this? She kept her eyes locked on the shifting page. The rest of the room seemed to shift too.

" 'The treasures of Tarchamus,' " she said. "Yes, a time or too."

Rhand chuckled. "Little minx—who knew you read Netherese? Most of this lot still believes it's the remnants of a dragon's hoard. I've had four fools try to buy it off of me already." The page's text swirled into a fluid calligraphy, trailing dots that wafted away like spring blossoms. Farideh blinked heavily. "Are you sure you're well?"

"Fine," she said, automatically. The wine might have gone to her head, but the Hells were boiling up into her veins, ready in case Sairché tried anything. Ready. Except . . . she was forgetting something.

Rhand's arm went around her waist, but she only noted it—too distracted by the shifting text and the nagging sense her plans weren't going to work. "He was quite the power, it seems. Even among the arcanists of ancient Netheril. Stories say he managed to work around the Weave. To harness the powers of wild magic and the planes beyond. They say he tore a portal to the Hells, for example, to destroy a rival's floating city." He chuckled and the sound made Malbolge's energy suddenly surge in her. "Not a fellow to make angry."

"A portal to the Hells?" she repeated. Suddenly the ink turned rust red and skittered across the parchment like insects, leaving a spiral of sharp-edged letters that seemed to smolder and burn the parchment. The page's muttering changed. A rune formed in the midst of the smaller letters. A rune she knew.

*Lorcan crouched a distance away and scratched a rune into the layer of frost and dead moss: a sinuous thing of smoothly angling lines that seemed to suggest a much more complex symbol, as if there were lines to it that Farideh couldn't perceive.*

"Draw the rune," she heard Lorcan say. "Say *laesurach*."

She looked up from the page, through the shimmer of magic, to the other side of the display. He was standing there, just on the edge of the light that poured down on the artifacts, watching her. "Say *laesurach*," he repeated.

Farideh shook her head, not here, not now. He smiled at her and shook his head gently, as if she were being willful. As if she'd change her mind. A line of blood ran down from one of his nostrils, black as ink.

"No," she said. "No."

"Oh, it's safe," Rhand said beside her. "Are you sure you feel well? Why don't you come lie down?" She blinked and it wasn't Lorcan standing there, but a young man giving her a hard stare. She shook her head a little and looked over at Rhand. He was smiling at her in that unpleasant way, and she realized something was very wrong.

*You could kill him,* a voice in her thoughts said, and it occurred to her dimly that it didn't sound like herself at all. *Make it clear who he's toying with.*

"Don't touch me," she said. Then, with hardly a thought, "Do you *know* who I am?" A Brimstone Angel, she thought, but the thought came after as if buoying the demand. Rarest of the Toril Thirteen. Her head was spinning. Flames licked the spaces between her fingers.

Rhand's blue eyes pierced her, surely as swords, and he said, quite simply, cruelly, "My latest acquisition."

*No*—and whether it was her voice or the Hells', she let the flames fill her hands. Her brand felt as if it were on fire.

"Don't touch—" Someone bumped her from behind, and she startled. There were so many people. There was no keeping an eye on them all. She looked back the way they'd come, but Brin and Havilar were lost in a sea of skirts and surcoats.

"Havilar," she murmured. That was what she'd forgotten—if there were devils, they would certainly be after Havilar. She took a step toward the door. Her knee buckled and Rhand held her firm. She was shaking her head again, the Hells surging up into her blood and her nerves with every quickening heartbeat, every extra breath. She could burn him. She could make him stay away. She had to get loose, to get back to Havilar.

"There you are," a voice said, and someone yanked on the back of her brigandine sharply enough to break her free. She stumbled backward, fists up and burning. People were staring—let them stare. Dahl turned her so she faced him. "We need to go," he said.

"Your pardon," she heard Rhand say, "but she and I aren't through—"

"Another time then," Dahl said, and he pulled her out of the quicksand conversation and out through the crowds. The flames sputtered out. She clutched his arm, for fear of falling, and her own arm in hopes of feeling the brand burn again.

"I leave you alone for all of a song," he said, "and suddenly you're exactly where you said you didn't want to be. Are you a fool or do you take me for one?"

She shook her head, still clasping her arm. Her breath didn't seem to be willing to make its way into her lungs and her throat was squeezing tight. If she spoke again, she thought she might scream.

"I don't want to be there," she managed. "I . . . Where's Havilar? I can't . . ."

Dahl stopped and looked back at her. "Are you drunk?" he demanded.

"I don't . . . I'm not . . . I just had a little glass. Almonds. *Zzar*." Her face was prickling with the heat, but she didn't dare touch it, the flames were already in her hands. She tried to shake them out. "He gave me just a little glass. And then the room's full of devils—Dahl, I can't figure out which ones to stop. I don't know what's . . ."

Dahl's eyes widened. One moment he was glancing around, the next he was pulling her behind a settee. She managed to keep the flames away from him, but only just. "You have to vomit," he said urgently. He grabbed her hand and yelped as the fire burned him. She kept shaking.

He pointed two fingers—*Draw the rune, Lorcan says, say lae-surach*—toward his mouth. "Do it yourself, or I'll do it for you," Dahl said, panic in his voice. "He gave you something. You have to get it out."

Farideh stared at her burning hands. The powers kept flowing, kept searching for an outlet. "Even I'll burn," she murmured.

"Stlarn it," Dahl cursed. One hand went behind her head, under her horns, and before she could ask what he was doing, the other slipped two fingers past her lips and suddenly she was sick, vomiting hard enough to see stars.

"All of it," he said, his voice shaking. "Completely empty. I haven't found Tam."

She tasted bile amid the almonds and leaned on him hard. "I need to find Havilar," she croaked.

"You need to find Tam," he said. "You need a healing. And water, lots of water." He kept looking around the room, fierce as a hunting hawk. "There's a fountain in the garden. Come on."

Eyes and eyes and eyes watched her careen across the floor. A layer's worth of watchers, she thought. "I have to find Havilar," she said, a little surer. "I have to find Lorcan."

If Dahl heard her, he made no sign as, still holding her under her arms, he pulled her through the sea of people, to the revel's edges, and up a short flight of stairs. The air cooled noticeably as they broke free of the crush of bodies, and Dahl glanced back once, then pulled her through an arched doorway into the night.

Moonlight swamped the garden, gilding the lashes of water spraying out of a fountain shaped like a pair of monstrous dryads and making deep shadows among the trees.

*In the shadows, something watches . . .*

Farideh dug her heels in—*cast, cast something, anything*. But there were people here too, watching her, and she couldn't tell who was a devil and who wasn't. If she cast fire into the shadows, she'd surely hit someone.

*Maybe you should.*

Dahl leaned her over the fountain's edge. "Drink it, as much as you can," he said. "If you hark up again all the better." He cupped a handful of water and held it to her face. It smelled stale and tasted faintly of stone and dirt, but she swallowed, and took another cupped handful of her own. It made her sick again, all over the stone patio.

"What possessed you to just *drink* something he gave you?" Dahl demanded.

"I'm not a Harper," she said. She wiped her mouth and leaned back over the fountain. "Where I come from people don't suddenly poison you. Not even the devils."

Dahl shook his head, as if she wasn't making sense. "At least you sound a little better. Can you walk all right?"

She cupped more of the foul water—its taste was nothing compared to the burn of bile in her throat. "I don't want to, but I can. I think." Her head was pounding, and her veins found the same pulse in the powers of Malbolge.

"You need a healer," Dahl said. "And a safe place to lie down."

"I need to find Havilar," Farideh said. She stood and looked down at her arms, the veins were as black as she'd ever seen them, and seemed to swirl under her skin. "It's doing something . . . I have to cast, I think . . . it's like a volcano. It's going to vent." She thought of Neverwinter, crisscrossed by ancient streams of lava—her arms like the ruined roads. She shut her eyes. "I'll vent it at him."

"I have no idea what you're talking about," Dahl said, propping her up. "You should have told Master Zawad that Rhand had taken a shine to you."

Farideh leaned back on the fountain's lip. "I can handle it."

"Words, Master Zawad," a voice behind them said, "is entirely too familiar with." Farideh didn't know whether to smile or curse, but she opened her eyes to find Tam striding out of the shadows. The silverstar was dressed in unobtrusive grays—he *might* turn invisible like that, she thought. "You made quite the scene plowing through the crowd," he said. "What are you two doing here?"

"Four," Farideh said. "Havi and Brin. I need to find Havilar. She's in trouble. I know it."

"She's been poisoned," Dahl said. "Rhand slipped her something."

"Hrast," Tam said. He glanced around the garden. "There's a bench. Have his guards come after you?" he asked as the two Harpers helped Farideh over to the stone bench.

"Not yet, but he was mad enough. I can't imagine they'll happily let us leave. She's vomited. Twice. And I got some water into her."

"Not going to do much good since it's already running its course." Tam dropped down to his knees and took her face in his hands. "Look at me, Fari."

The blessing rushed over her like a cold breeze that swept right through her skin and whistled through the spaces in her skull to blow the almond-scented toxin from where it had settled in her mind. Her eyes rolled back in their sockets, and the sound of a woman singing, far away, filled her ears. As it faded, she sighed.

"Better?" Tam asked.

"Some," she said. But the thrum of the Hells still beat in her veins, and each moment made the remnants of the poison surge up. "No. It comes back."

"She's seeing things," Dahl reported. "She says there's devils."

"I have to save Havilar," she said. "The Hells . . ." She held up her arms—could they even see what was happening? Did they even care if Sairché caught Havi?

Tam's eyes widened, and he cursed again. "You've been drinking the tea, haven't you? The tea's complicating the poison," he said to Dahl. "You have to get her out of here and back to a safe location. Thort's. If he has anything to cure it, give it to her and quickly. I'll be there quickly as I can."

Dahl helped her to her feet, but at least now she could feel her legs and keep her knees straight. "What about your other plans?"

"Later," Tam said, ushering them back into the ballroom.

Back toward a pair of lean guards, whose eyes were locked on Dahl and Farideh. Rhand's or Sairché's? she thought. Or Lorcan's terrible lady's?

Does it matter? part of her asked. They're here to take you. And Havilar, too. She scanned the crowd—no Havilar, no Brin—but there, thirty feet from the foot of the stairs, halfway between her and the display of artifacts and square in the path to the exit, waited Adolican Rhand. She brought one hand up, curling her hand around the energy that built there.

"Fari, don't!" Tam said quietly. "Not here. Back out into the garden, both of you, and—"

The crash of glass broke his order, and was itself rapidly drowned out by screams as a score of black-clad men and women forced their way into the ballroom, through nearly every entrance. Rhand jerked to attention, and with a quick gesture, four gouts of shimmering darkness streaked out to the four guardsmen near him, dancing down their frames. They drew weapons, ready to defend. Down from the balconies, half a dozen gray-skinned assassins dropped out of the shadows like spiders into the panicking mass of beautiful people.

"Havi!" Farideh shouted.

"Get her out," Tam ordered Dahl. "However you can. Back to the muster point. I'll—"

Farideh vaulted over the balustrade down to the ballroom floor, her joints shocked by the sudden drop. Behind her, she heard Tam shout her name and curse, but she ignored him. The crowd fleeing the strange assassins broke on her like a wave, carrying her away from where she'd left Havilar.

Be alive, she thought of Lorcan. She drew the powers of the Hells up into her form and with a gasp of Infernal, slit the plane wide enough to step through and reappear on the other side of the crush of bodies.

The strange pain in her arm was screaming again and her head was pounding, but gods, she could have laughed with joy. The pact remained.

But she'd appeared between the dais holding the horrible statue and the advancing attackers. She'd no more than regained her feet when a pair of men, their faces covered with faded scarves, pounced on her with bare blades.

Her hands came up, all instinct, as if the engines of Malbolge moved them for her. A quick, ugly word and a gust of caustic smoke brought them up short as the miasma burned away the scarves and bit into their faces.

Farideh's fist lashed out and struck the nearer man in the center of his chest as he clawed at his face, one handed. He dropped his sword and stumbled back. Flames billowed out from her hands, lighting his hair and his compatriot's linen shirt afire. Her arms and chest ached with the churning, slick power—another burst of energy built in her palms, ready to cast—

One of the assassins who'd dropped from the roof—a gray-skinned woman glittering with piercings and blades—appeared behind the men, and suddenly they were both falling to the ground, each clutching at a dagger and the gout of blood that had been his throat. The woman drew a sword and started toward Farideh.

Farideh scrambled back and out of her path. The woman's jagged blade looked more like a butcher's tool than a weapon, made for hacking apart bone and muscle.

*. . . the erinyes are a thunderstorm, unstoppable and rolling toward them out of nothing. Their hooves crack the cobbles, shatter the rune. Their crowns of horns threaten to spear the moon. Their swords are fire. Their swords are hungry . . .*

Run, her every muscle urged. Run, run, run.

She fought it. She had to find Havilar. She looked down at her hands, recognized the dancing, bruised-looking energy that she'd gathered to attack the men with. Hands shaking, she pointed them at the assassin.

*"Adaestuo."* The woman rolled out of the burst's path, but when she came up, Farideh had another ready and sent it screaming across the distance. The purplish magic seared her exposed skin. But when it burned away, there the assassin stood, more eager and wild-eyed than before.

*. . . the erinyes are a thunderstorm, unstoppable and rolling toward them out of nothing . . .*

She's not an erinyes, Farideh thought, fighting the poison still distorting her judgment. Gods damn it, concentrate. The woman lunged, her heavy blade cleaving down and nearly taking off Farideh's foot. She stumbled aside, so full of the Hells' magic she thought she might catch fire herself. The blademistress heaved her weapon up.

*. . . Lorcan's burning hands mold her fingers—smaller two wrapped around the implement, longer two extended, thumb curled over . . .*

*"Laesurach,"* she hissed, as she quickly made the sign of the infernal rune. The marble under the gray-skinned woman's feet cracked and a surge of magma welled up beneath her as the Hells peeked through to the greater world.

The assassin dropped her cruel blade as she caught fire, screaming and laughing with the most terrible sound Farideh had ever heard. Gods, she thought, backing into the dais, gods—

The silvery slash of Tam's magic struck the man creeping up on her left, and instinctively she ducked. The silverstar carried one of the black-clad attackers' dropped blades. With his free hand, he pushed her away from the assassin. "Stop casting!" he said. "Follow Dahl."

Farideh cast another burst of magic past him and into the encroaching assassin. Tam leaped aside and cursed. "Farideh, go!"

All over again, Dahl was grabbing her by the arm and pulling her through the crowd. She glimpsed Havilar through the riot of fighting, and then she was gone. Bodies blocked her sight. They came past the settee Farideh had been sick behind. There was Master Rhand, surrounded by the wild-eyed attackers, clinging to the page and stone and flinging streams of dark magic. *Ashenath enjareen nether pendarthis*—the page's murmur had become manic, wild. Thrilled.

Suddenly one of the attackers, a man built like a bear, slammed into the Netherese wizard, knocking him off his feet and into the blade of another man. It speared him through the shoulder. Adolican Rhand gasped, and in his shock, threw wide the arm clutching the page and stone. The stone, he kept his grip on.

The page, he loosed. It flew between the attackers and slid across the tiled floor to rest under the settee.

His attacker didn't have long to gloat—one of Rhand's wild-eyed guards broke the circle of black-clad fighters. With a terrible cry, he lunged forward with two blades—one needle-sharp, which he buried in one of the fighter's kidneys, one edged, which he sliced across his throat. Hardly stopping, he caught the bleeding Master Rhand up around the middle, and seizing the charm around his neck, broke it. Both vanished in a burst of black vapors, taking the precious stone with them.

The page still lay beneath the settee. *Ashenath enjareen nether pendarthis.*

"Stay here," Dahl said. Farideh swayed on her feet as he dropped close to the floor and fished the page free. He twisted, trying to right himself quickly as he'd made it under, and ended up with his back to the fight.

A ruddy, scruffy man with an enormous tattoo of a skull on a black sun radiating around the hollow of his throat was on them. Blood flowed from a cut on his cheek and soaked the shoulder of his shirt, but he looked nothing but gleeful as he closed on the Harper and his treasure.

She tried to shout. The poison surged again, boiling up her arms and slowing her tongue. Tricking her eyes. The skull's sockets seemed to glow, and the whisper of shadows seemed to surround him.

The man's boot came up and stamped into the center of Dahl's chest as he turned, throwing him backward onto the floor. He crushed the page in his fist and Farideh heard the cough of the air going out of him even at her distance. He lay there, stunned and breathless as a caught fish, as the man leaped down, raised his sword to make the final stroke—

It hardly felt real, Farideh would later think. Like a dream, perhaps, thin and slow. The poison tried to pull her down into the darkness and the man moved as if he had taken no notice of her, grinning wide enough at Dahl's weakness to display the gap of a missing eyetooth. All around there were screams and flashes of magic and the clang of blades, but here, it was as if there were no one else in the world but Dahl and the assassin.

A blaze of fire caught the man in the middle of his chest and set him crashing backward into the wall. The world refocused. Dahl gasped air. Farideh looked down at her hands, and the lingering flames licking the spaces between her fingers. More, so much more, they promised. *Cast, cast, cast.*

Dahl eyed her as she hauled him to his feet, somehow both grateful and furious. He shoved the crumpled page under his jerkin—*Ashenath enjareen nether pendarthis.* "To the door."

There were a score of bodies between them and the exit—all bladed, all eagerly watching them. They want the page, too, she thought. They want the stone. Dahl picked up the fallen man's sword and started grimly toward them, but Farideh seized him by the arm. With a soft gasp, she stepped into the split between worlds and pulled him with her, out to the other side. No sooner did they step free of the portal, but she cast it again.

*Run, run, run,* the pulse of her heart shouted, even if the pull of the Hells wanted to drag her back, to make the black-clad assassins suffer. To burn off all the poison in the process.

The effort of the spells and the effects of the poison hit her at once, and she stepped free of the split into the entryway, dizzy and panting and off-balance. She crashed into the wall, nearly taking Dahl with her.

"Hrast," he swore, and he caught the blade of a very surprised-looking woman on his own. He ran her through, and it was his turn to pull Farideh on, urging her to run out into the dark night.

She lost track of where they went—her head was spinning and every turn was surely the one that would bring her back to the terrible erinyes of her dreams. Every shadow was full of the strange assassins. Every panting breath thrumming with the page's maddened song. *Ashenath enjareen nether pendarthis.* When Dahl halted at a street corner, considering both directions, she was sick again.

"Havilar," she gasped. "We've left her. We have to go back. We have to go back now."

He shushed her. "Master Zawad has her. You need to calm down. We're nearly there." She followed after as they moved quickly down one street, then another. The smell of the docks, wet and fishy, rose in the air. Her stomach turned. A voice in her thoughts screamed at her to go back, Dahl was wrong, Havilar was still back in the middle of all those blades. But even if she'd wanted to listen, she couldn't have found her way through sprawling Waterdeep, and so she could only follow Dahl and fight the rising sense of panic, the farther they went.

They turned up a wide street, and for a moment, Farideh was certain she was losing her mind as an enormous stone face appeared at the end of the street. Shining white, even under the cloudy sky, the fierce visage of a helmed warrior, seemingly sunk to his neck in the pavement, scowled across the distance at them, his mouth a dark portal.

Gods, she thought, it's getting worse.

Dahl strode straight up to the mouth and rapped on the door. It whipped open and they were rushed inside by a wizened old man leaning on a cane. One wild eye fixed Farideh with a penetrating stare.

"Two of 'em, eh?" he said. "Someone having a sale?" He chortled to himself.

Dahl made a face. "Thank you, Goodman Thort. We need a cure—"

"Oh calm yourself, boy. The priest's already told me. Come along." The old man beckoned Dahl and Farideh through the jumbled shop that took up the entirety of the head's interior. Down a dark and narrow flight of stairs. Through a door, and into a crowded little room where Havilar, Brin, Tam, and a dark-haired woman were waiting. All of Farideh's panic came unraveled and she rushed across the room to Havilar.

"Shar and stlarning hrast!" Tam shouted. "Where in the Hells have you been? You," he said to Farideh, "lie down. They're hunting down an antidote." She sat on the narrow cot he indicated and pulled her feet up.

"I took the longer route," Dahl said. "I wanted to be sure none of them followed."

"Are you all right?" Havilar asked her, as she sat beside her. Farideh nodded—but no, no she was not all right. She wanted to scream or throw up or at the very least vent the churning, sickly magic from her. "They said you were *poisoned*."

There were no devils. Sairché hadn't found Havilar. Her arms ached and her stomach twisted but the world wasn't trying to upend itself anymore and it was all right for her to lie down, even if there wasn't a single inch of her not vibrating with energy. "I'm all right now," she said instead. "You?"

"Fine," Brin said. "We ducked the worst of it."

"I," Havilar announced, "beat the *aithyas* out of one of those pissers with a tray and a bottle of *zzar*. It should count for two at least. Then Mira threw me a sword and I helped get us out." Farideh looked up at the woman with the angular face and eyes that glittered darkly. She was a little older and a little shorter than the twins, her armor was a great deal better, and her expression was a great deal sterner. She looked familiar . . .

"A pleasure," she said, and Farideh couldn't have said if it was or it wasn't.

"Well met," she said.

"They should have had no one to follow," Tam was saying. "Thank the *gods* none of you are dead! What part of our plan did you misunderstand?"

"*Your* plan," Dahl said.

"And what? You were so set against something you did not author that you decided to throw together this ill-prepared mess? By all rights your entire team shouldn't have made it out alive."

"I *was* prepared," Dahl said hotly. "I had Master Vishter arrange a safehouse, and all of their things are stored there with enough for a few days. I was only coming to provide support."

"And be seen by Shadovar agents," Tam fumed. "If it was too dangerous for me, it was too dangerous to bring in inexperienced—"

"I wasn't expecting stlarning assassins to fall out of the windows! Were you?"

"We are *not* having this discussion here," Tam hissed. To Mira, he said, "Do you have any idea of where Rhand would go? Of where those artifacts would lead him?"

"An idea," Mira said. "I spent time enough with both to make guesses—but nothing certain. Netheril stretched across most of the north once. It could be a lot of places. We need those artifacts as much as he does."

The guard, Farideh thought. That's where she'd seen Mira before. That's why she looked familiar.

"I think we *are* having this conversation," Dahl said. He took the page from under his jacket and smoothed it out for Tam to see. "A lucky thing I was there after all. Rhand vanished with the stone, but he dropped this."

Tam took the page from him. The ink swirled purple, catching on the creases before straightening itself into neat lines of runes. For a long moment, the Harper said nothing and the air hummed with the page's mutterings.

"A stroke of luck doesn't absolve you of putting people in danger," Tam said. "But well done."

"I hope you're not going to blame me for not realizing exactly how depraved Adolican Rhand is," Dahl said. "You cannot hold me accountable for an army of assassins appearing to brutalize the guests, either."

Tam looked up at him, as if he certainly could. "I can hold you accountable for forgetting the Shadovar, yes. The Cyricists . . . are a complication I think we can all be forgiven for not expecting."

"What's a Cyricist?" Havilar whispered.

Farideh shook her head. "Worshipers of someone?"

"Madmen," Brin supplied grimly. "They follow the god of strife."

"The Church of Cyric probably doesn't want it," Dahl said. "The Zhentarim probably *do*."

"What's a Zhent—"

"Mercenaries," Mira interrupted before Havilar could finish. "And I'm sure it's more a matter for the Church."

"More than mercenaries," Dahl said. "An organization that has its fingers in a dozen governments and a hundred cults—including Mad Cyric's."

"So Rhand was right," Tam asked. "They must want it badly to attack him in his home. Why?"

"Doesn't matter," Mira said swiftly. "What matters is that you and I"—she turned to Tam—"very much need to get out of

Waterdeep. Master Rhand won't be pleased at all with my guardwork, and he'll no doubt be curious where you might have gotten to. So—"

"Plans have changed," Tam said. He looked as if he could chew iron and spit nails. "All of you are going to have to come along to Everlund."

"Can we?" Havilar asked. She tucked an arm around Farideh's shoulders. "I mean, Fari's not well and Mehen's not back yet." She fidgeted. "But *can* we?"

"If you stay here every eye in that revel who saw the twin tieflings and the Cormyrean lordling will be ready to recognize you," Tam said. "Especially when one fought free of the brawl with a bottle and a tray, and one made a Waterdhavian brightcoin's floor spew lava. You're coming, and don't think there's an argument to change that."

He said the last part to Farideh, but all she could think of was Adolican Rhand saying, *They say he tore a portal to the Hells to destroy a rival's floating city.*

"He grabbed the page and stone when they broke in," she said hoarsely. "Nothing else. It's important isn't it? You think there's something still there."

"Clever, clever," Mira said.

Tam's mouth made an even harder line, as if he heard the request she wasn't making. "You will stay in the tower in Everlund and *wait*. I'll arrange things so that word is sent when Mehen returns, and he can come collect you two. You," he said to Brin, "gods, I thought you were more cautious than this. You're coming too, if you know what's best. Pray to every god they didn't recognize you."

"They didn't," Brin said. "You can be sure of that."

Tam didn't reply, but turned on his assistant. "And you," he said to Dahl. "Since you've decided to play the leader of this little band, you can take charge of their well-being in Everlund. You're on defender duty." He looked up at Mira. "Until we sort out this mystery."

# CHAPTER EIGHT

*EVERLUND*

*7 FLAMERULE, THE YEAR OF THE DARK CIRCLE (1478 DR)*

**T**HE SUMMER SKY IS BLOOD RED AND THE MONSTERS OF NEVERWINTER *swarm through it, but the air's so cold that steam wafts off Lorcan's skin. He looks like sin. He looks like want. He looks like Farideh's doom, and she knows it.*

*It's your doom too, she says, but he ignores her, pulls her hard against him. One burning hand strokes her cheek and she tilts her head away from him. He twists a lock of her hair around one finger and pulls, and the sudden pain steals her breath.*

*Say it, he says roughly.*

*Say what? she asks, but she knows, when he holds her like this, she is likely to say anything he tells her. He is dangerous, but she is helpless here.*

*Laesurach, he whispers. The tip of his tongue flicks over her ear, and she looks past his shoulder. Sairché's standing there, a wicked smile on her lips.*

*Laesurach, Farideh repeats, and the fire surges up around Sairché—but the cambion doesn't flinch as her skin burns away. And suddenly, it's not Sairché standing in the volcano's mouth but Havilar, and her leathers are flowing robes of red and black, her glaive a staff that weeps blood.*

*There are five, she says, but it's the archdevil's voice. That was the surprise.*

*Lorcan's arms are suddenly gone—he doesn't hold her, he stands between her and Havilar—and the lack of him frees her, but it leaves her moorless.*

*Run, darling, Lorcan says as the erinyes rise out of the ground. Run fast and run far.*

*Havilar—who is not Havilar, who is not Sairché, who is not the archdevil—points her staff at Lorcan and a stream of hellwasps pours out of it. Their sword-arms and stingers pierce every inch of him. They tear out his eyes and he screams, and she screams, and over it all Havilar laughs . . .*

Farideh sat up in a spare bunk in the Harpers' tower, her pulse hard and her breath harder. No hellwasps, no erinyes, no Lorcan—but still her stomach churned and she bolted for the window to vomit bile into the alley below.

"Fari?" Havilar said sleepily. "Are you all right?"

Shivering, Farideh crouched beside the window, her forehead resting on the sill between her shaking hands. Her tail rasped against the floorboards. How many nights of this? How many more nightmares before she went mad of them?

"No more tea," Tam had said, not until the very last of the poison's effects had faded. No tea, and no tapping into the Hells. Between the two, her nightmares grew worse and worse.

She heard Havilar pad toward her and felt her sister's hand on her shoulder. She tensed—afraid to turn and see the strange robes.

"Nightmare," she said lightly. "It's nothing."

"It was nothing last night," Havilar said, dropping down beside her. "And it was nothing three nights ago. What're you really dreaming about?"

Farideh turned her head side to side against the sill, the wood rubbing against the ridges of her horns. "Nothing. It's just a dream."

"A dream that makes you hark up." Havilar dabbed a corner of her sleeve to Farideh's chin. "Tell me." Farideh kept her silence—the dreams were horrible enough, she didn't want to argue over them too.

"All right, I *heard* you saying his name. You practically *screamed* it before you woke. So quit lying. What is it?" She ducked her head closer to Farideh's. "Mehen's not here," she said. "You can tell me if it's indelicate—"

"They're torturing him," Farideh said quietly. She turned her head. "That's what I dream about. Devils cutting up Lorcan. And I can't stop it, and when I try to, they capture you too."

"That does sound more like something you'd vomit about," Havilar said after a moment. "You're right, though, it's just a dream. Why would a devil want me anyhow?"

Farideh shut her eyes. Tell her, she thought. Tell her, tell her now.

"Havi . . . what would you do if a devil offered you a pact?"

"What, like Lorcan?"

"Another devil," she said. "One you didn't know. One who offered you anything you wanted. What would you do?"

Havilar's eyes flicked over Farideh's face, as if she were gauging the seriousness of the question. As if she were trying to decide what her answer ought to be and not what it truly was, Farideh noted.

"Tell them to heave off," Havilar said finally. "I don't want to be a warlock, and I don't want to be indebted to a devil." She slipped an arm around Farideh and hugged her tightly. "I don't want you to be either. Do you think he's making you dream that? Like if he wanted you back?"

"Not his style." Lorcan's attention made the lines of her brand ache—but no matter how shaken or ill she woke, her arm and shoulder were fine. If he wanted to lure her back, he would have started by needling at the brand. If he wanted to get her back, he would have let her know he was alive.

Besides, he still has me, Farideh thought, shutting her eyes. For the moment.

Havilar rested her head on Farideh's. "Lorcan's not better than nightmares."

Farideh said nothing, but clung to her sister, listening to the wind streaking down the mountains and trying to drive away the fabricated memory of Lorcan's bleeding eyes.

.:⌒:.

"If you aren't going to pay attention," Dahl said, "then why did you bother bargaining with me in the first place?"

Farideh turned from the window back to the open ritual book in her lap. She had been paying attention—half a *day's* worth of attention—and it was only as she felt certain she'd grasped the magic of the ritual that she'd turned to the sound of sparring in the courtyard of the tower in Everlund, and the pine-scented breeze coming down off the mountain.

Farideh looked down at her careful copying of the spell, the rusty-colored ink laid down stroke by careful stroke. She wasn't used to script and her hands were cramping after three days of it. But since Dahl had seized on it as a sign she wasn't well enough to continue the day before, she kept silent. She wasn't interested in hearing all the ways she wasn't suited to this, and she'd be damned if she'd let him off his end of their bargain just because Tam had torn into him over it and he was embarrassed.

"I've finished." Three days of Dahl's lessons, and she'd learned a ritual for reading unfamiliar languages, one that made the cold and heat more bearable, and one that put broken things back together.

She traced the last lines of that one with her eyes, thinking of the spell Lorcan had shown her that shattered objects with a word. They fit together nicely.

Tam had allowed the lessons, once the worst of the poison's effects had past and she could eat without being sick and walk without losing her balance. The magic of the Hells still pulsed somewhere far along the connection of her brand, waiting to be called up again and pulled through her like a pump pulling water. The rituals' magic had an entirely different feel—almost like laying pieces of fabric on top of one another so that the light shined through the right shade.

She'd tried to explain this to Dahl and had gotten a funny look in return.

"Give me another," she said. "There's day enough left."

"No," he said. "You're too tired to focus anymore. And Master Zawad said you're not to be taxed. Besides, I'm too tired to try and make you concentrate."

Three days of nonstop study wasn't making him any more pleasant toward her. He stood and pulled a rope beside the door and said no more. Farideh took the opportunity to shut her eyes and rest her head against her open palm. She knew better than to say it aloud, but if she never read another word again, she could be quite content.

Except she still needed the ritual that would free Lorcan.

A servant came into the room, carrying a tray of raisin-studded rolls and a pitcher of watered cordial that she poured into two narrow, blue glasses before slipping back out of the room. The cordial was sweet and mild, and tasted of rosemary and oranges. Farideh took it in tiny sips—Tam might well have forbidden the stuff. Dahl drained his glass.

And smashed it against the floor. Farideh jumped from her seat. "What in the Hells are you doing?"

"Testing you," he said. "Do the ritual. Prove you've learned it."

Shards of blue glass littered the floorboards and scattered over the rug. "Are you mad? I haven't got the ingredients."

"Components. It's not a recipe for stew." Dahl hauled his haversack up from the floor beside him. "Use mine." His gray eyes were positively dancing. *Ready to prove I was distracted*, Farideh thought. *Henish*.

Bottles of colorful liquids, packets of powders that gave off a bitter odor, little jars of paste whose lids seemed to be cemented on—the sack was heavy with a clutter of components.

"Do you use all of these?" Farideh asked, picking through them for the needed elements—beeswax, powdered sap, and salts of mithral.

"I can," Dahl said. He straightened the pitcher on the tray, avoiding her eyes. "I like to be prepared."

She found all three components to the spell and crouched down on the floor with them. Careful not to cut herself on the shards, she copied the rune from the ritual book, drawing it onto the wood with the square of beeswax. She bit her lip—was that straight enough? It was too hard to see. The sap and the salts she mixed in the palm of her hand and sprinkled over the floor, making sure to dust each splinter of blue glass.

The air started humming. It seemed to pull on her throat and made it difficult to breathe in—that was probably good. Farideh glanced up at Dahl. He made no sign one way or the other.

She held her hands out over the mess and the thrumming air seemed to yank the words of the ritual out of her mouth, shifting the magic and drawing the fibers of the Weave tight.

The pieces of blue glass surged up from the floor like a swarm of insects. Fragment met fragment with an audible *clink* as the edges touched, and fused—then again and again, faster and faster until the room was filled with the chimes of glass hitting glass. A flash of light, and the unbroken flute hung motionless in the air for a moment, long enough for Farideh to snatch it before it fell again. Her head was spinning.

Dahl took the glass from her and held it to the light. Despite herself, Farideh watched his expression carefully, as she eased back into her chair.

"You aren't," Dahl said, after a moment, "terrible at this. One's missing." He tapped a chip in the lip of the glass. Farideh scowled.

"Drink carefully."

She looked out the window, down into the yard. Havilar was sparring with one of the mercenaries Mira had hired on, a wiry woman named Pernika, with a mass of blond braids and tilted eyes that suggested she might have ancestors in the Feywild. The mercenary's bastard sword moved like a striking serpent, but she wasn't quick enough to get past Havilar's glaive easily. Beyond them, a second mercenary—a man called Maspero—stood scowling at the fight, his arms folded over his chest, his biceps like hams. Brin sat in his shadow. She sipped her drink.

"If you want to go out there with your sword," Dahl said, "you should. I mean it: you're not good for another lesson today."

Farideh laughed and nearly choked on the cordial. "Hardly. The sword . . . I'm not all that suited to it." She took a roll and smiled wryly to herself. "In our village, everyone capable of handling a weapon was sent on patrol by turns. They excused me, because I nearly took off the blacksmith's foot when a marten ran across the path."

Dahl didn't laugh, but a small smile tugged at his mouth. "Who taught your sister the glaive?"

Farideh shrugged. "Everyone. Our father, to start. A . . . friend of his honed her. Some of the people in the village where we grew up knew a thing or two. They showed her what they knew, and she picked up the rest by watching."

He looked down at Havilar in the yard. "I'm surprised she listened that well. She doesn't strike me as an easy pupil."

Farideh shrugged. "Not at everything. Not at much else, really. It's how her thoughts flow. She can watch you fight with a chain or a broadsword or just a pair of daggers, and come back knowing something more about her glaive." She sipped the cordial, watching Havilar leap past Pernika's jab as though she had wings. "I'll bet if you gave *her* ritual lessons, all she'd get from it would be how best to block magic with a glaive."

"You don't fight with rituals," Dahl said.

Farideh looked up at him. He was still staring out the window, the smile gone, his expression closed. "I know that," she said. "You've mentioned it several times."

"And you can't block magic with a glaive," he added.

"Well, good thing I was joking," she said, flushing. "You needn't take everything so seriously."

"It's *serious* magic," he said, and Farideh got the distinct impression it wasn't her that he was talking to so much, but that she was answering for it nonetheless. "Rituals still take years of study and a knack for the Art. It's not just some . . . feather in your cap."

"No one's saying otherwise," she said hotly.

Dahl fidgeted with his glass, still staring down at the practice yard. "Will you tell me what you're after?" he said a moment later. "Because I don't believe you'd be so eager to learn for learning's sake."

"Because I'm just some tiefling out of the mountains?" she said bitterly, and he had the decency to look embarrassed. She'd overheard him talking to one of the local Harpers.

"Because you want something," he said. "And we both know it. I owe you ten rituals. But tell me what you want so we don't have to argue over ten more."

Farideh took another roll and picked at the raisins. It would look exactly like the ritual Havilar's scroll had performed, the one that had called Lorcan forth in the first place. But unlike spells to mend broken glasses and translate strange languages, there was no disguising the purpose of such rituals.

What ill luck had fallen on her that Dahl Peredur was the surest source of such a spell? Even with the ritual book in hand, even with his promise to teach her, and his pride in his talents, the chances he would teach her the ritual that made the passage between the worlds and the circle of protection were small. Smaller, she suspected, if he found out why she wanted them . . .

But if she didn't ask, she would surely end up learning the ten simplest rituals he knew.

"Tam made a circle once," she said finally. "A ring of runes meant to protect—"

"A magic circle," he interrupted. "I know."

"So you'll teach me that next?"

"Perhaps." He pinched off a piece of the bread's crumb and rolled it between two fingers. "What do you need protection from?"

"Shady codloose winkers," she said bitterly.

Dahl scowled and mashed the bread-ball flat. "You seemed awfully concerned before about devils."

She regarded him evenly. "Are you saying you *wouldn't* appreciate protection from devils?"

"I'm saying most people don't need it," he replied. "And Master Zawad could have taught you that. What else?"

Farideh shook her head. She'd have to tell him eventually. "I need a portal," she admitted. "A way to get someone from another plane."

Dahl started laughing. "Are you quite serious? Do you think I can—or *would*—teach you that?"

She felt her cheeks burn. "I'd hoped."

"Portal magic is well beyond you," he said. "It's well beyond *me*. Short of finding a master wizard to help you build a scroll, you're not getting that ritual."

"You said all sorts of things are possible—"

"Well, breaching the Hells is right out," he said. "If there's a way to work around the difficulty of it, I'm not doing it for you."

"Did I *say* the Hells?"

"You didn't have to," he said. "Tell your devil to find its own way out."

Farideh stood. "Then I will see you tomorrow," she said tightly, "and you can show me how to cast the protective circle instead." She stormed from the room before he could start after her again. If he thought he was going to put her off by being rude and unpleasant, he had no idea how very stubborn she could be.

*Portal magic is well beyond you*, she thought rubbing her hands over her face. She stopped and leaned against the wall near the end of the hallway. Gods, ah, gods—there had to be a way. Maybe he was lying. Maybe he was just refusing to try.

She rubbed her bare arm, the brand that marked it. It had been bad enough in the days and tendays after fleeing Neverwinter to know that Lorcan was in danger, to know she had to do something, and soon. But nearly a month had passed and the constant alarm had grown into its own entity, like a second head settled into her own, whose constant thoughts were of finding the means to breach the Hells. Before Lorcan died and whatever protection he provided was gone.

Farideh sighed. *Even your daydreams have gone mad*, she thought.

The hallway ended at a larger room that overlooked the river valley down below. Mira and Tam stood over a great stone table, beside the open windows. Half a dozen maps were spread over the table, small marks and notes littering the reproduced landscape. *Granite quarries here*, Farideh read as she drew nearer. *Water flows up from aquifer here.*

The page lay flat on the table, all on its own. Tam was watching the subdued swirl of its ink.

"Well met," Tam said looking up. "Feeling better?"

Mira kept her head down and her eyes on the distance marked by a pair of brass calipers. Farideh hesitated, but the guard didn't look up or greet her. She still wasn't sure how Mira fit into all of this, only that Tam knew her somehow and that Mira knew about the page and its origins.

"Well met," Farideh said. "And yes, very well. Have you had any word from Mehen?"

"Not yet. But keep in mind," he said when she frowned, "Cormyr has quite a reputation for protocol. You can hardly carry a weapon through the wilds without a proper writ."

"It's been nine days," she said.

"I once spent a month waiting for the charter to travel armed through the forest." Tam shrugged. "I'm sure we'll hear something soon. Take it as a sign of how well he trusts you."

Farideh bit her tongue. It didn't sound like Mehen. Before Neverwinter, certainly, he would have sent a dozen messages by now, and demanded a dozen back. Assuming he'd even left them behind. Even if Neverwinter had made him reconsider his daughters' capabilities, she couldn't see him changing *that* much. She wanted to tell Tam so, to enumerate all the ways he'd miscounted Mehen.

But then Tam was inclined to be as overcautious as Mehen. And he wasn't worried.

"Are you having any luck finding your way?" she asked instead.

"It's not luck," Mira said without looking up. "It's deduction. This"—she planted a finger on a point in the middle of a mountain range—"is the Caverns of Xammux, without a doubt our most likely location. There's the name, foremost, easily a corruption of Tarchamus or Attarchammiux. 'Through rock and flood I've come to this'—so we're looking for some place buried, then, some place with plenty of water. I've managed, too, to coerce the page into displaying a schema of a huge dome—let's assume that's our ruin, and so we need a mountain to cover it. Otherwise, every adventurer in the Silver Marches would have tramped through it already.

"The caverns are at the source of a stream that flows into the River Rauvin. According to the locals, the stream's fed by some sort of river in the Underdark—it floods every so often, and when it does, it sends a great deal of debris into the Rauvin. Including, according to my sources, finished stone with the same circular patterns as Rhand's fragment."

"Your arcanist is buried in the Underdark," Tam said flatly.

"No," Mira said, "the *stream* originates in the Underdark. The cavern's deep into the mountain, but it doesn't go down that far, as well as anyone knows."

"Who goes in and out of a flooded cavern?" Farideh asked. Mira pursed her mouth, as if she had been hoping no one would ask that.

"Cultists," she admitted. "At least that's the tale the locals are telling. But it's highly unlikely they're much of a presence. As I said, the cavern floods. Besides . . . there's a goodly sized population of funguses."

Tam didn't speak for a moment. "Tell me," he said, "that you mean mushrooms."

"Ah, no. The monstrous sort."

"Excellent. Well, I wasn't convinced there were enough of us to uncover a lost ruin. I'm certainly unconvinced we've enough forces to fight our way through cave monsters that blend into the walls and *then* uncover a lost ruin." He drew a hand over his sparse beard. "We need more help."

Mira shrugged, as if he had suggested they needed to pack more waybread. "Surely that would be better—but we don't have the time to seek that out. Pernika and Maspero were dear enough to come by—what do you think we can do before our friend, Master Rhand, starts trailing us? If he hasn't already." She gave Farideh a significant look. Farideh looked away.

"He doesn't have the page," Tam said. "He hasn't seen the schema."

"But he has the stone," Mira said. "And so he can match the rock where we cannot. And we cannot be sure of what he's seen or not seen."

"All the more reason to gather more reinforcements."

"If we wait," she said, "then we leave the cavern open for Shade to find. The more we delay, the more likely it is that Rhand will coax information from the resources he *does* have and beat us there. Maybe even track us down here in Everlund. And which is more dangerous?

"Besides," Mira said more gently, "all we're doing is assessing the site. If it turns out to be full of phantom funguses and mad cultists or Shadovar historians, of course we'll come right back and call for those reinforcements. But if we don't look into it, we'll have no idea how to prepare."

Tam said nothing, but glowered at the map-covered table for several moments. "I need to speak with someone," he said. "Farideh, go lie down." He left the room, Mira watching after him.

Perhaps she's a Harper too, Farideh thought. Surveying skills might serve a guard well, perhaps even a little knowledge of ancient history—but Mira seemed to have more of both than strictly necessary. And a skill for influence she didn't bother hiding.

Farideh had not yet broached to Tam the topic of her coming along, already too certain he would refuse. She needed to stay, he'd undoubtedly say, where she could rest. Where there was little chance of cultists, funguses, and mad-eyed Shadovar breaking his promise to Mehen, however coerced that had been.

But Mira . . .

"That was clever," Farideh ventured. "How you figured out where to look. Piecing all those things together."

Mira's eyes didn't leave the door. "It's what I do."

"Do you think he'll let you go?"

"Of course. The trick," Mira said, "is to mention Shade. I suspect that might be the only thing he's really afraid of."

"Aren't you?" Farideh asked. After all, if nothing else was clear about her, it was apparent Mira knew a great deal more about Netheril and the more ancient version that had birthed it than anyone Farideh had met.

Mira smiled softly. "Not really. The Empire of Shade is a danger, of course, but they're not fools. And as long as your enemies listen to reason, well, they're practically allies." Her dark eyes flicked over Farideh's bare mark. "You know that well, I suspect."

Farideh fought the urge to cover the brand, to rub it as if she could rub the scars back into her skin. "You make it sound as if you work for them."

Mira laughed. "Broken planes, no. Shade is for zealots. I merely think there's good mixed in with the bad—maybe not much, but there's something there. Nobody's perfect, and no kingdom is an unremitting horror."

And a pact is a tool, Farideh thought, not a damnation. "As long as you're careful," she added, as much to her own thoughts as to Mira's words.

"That goes without saying," Mira replied with an uneven grin.

"And this . . . cavern?" Farideh asked. "This Tarchamus—closer to perfect or unremitting horror?"

"Ah," Mira said, a zeal in her voice that Shade couldn't tap, "that's the question isn't it? What lasted to the current age suggests it could be either. One reference makes it sound as if he was often arguing with the other High Mages of Netheril, implying that their courses of study were bound to doom them all—which they did, eventually. The other . . . well, let's say Tarchamus could have used some other arcanist telling him to stop ripping holes in planes."

"What sort of planes?" Farideh said too quickly.

Mira gave her a curious look, and Farideh blushed a little. "I mean," she said, "dangerous planes? Or . . . more like planes one would visit?"

"Dangerous," Mira said. "Somewhere fiery for certain. He's supposed to have created a spell that made a flame powerful enough to burn one of their floating cities from the sky by opening a gateway to someplace."

Farideh wet her lips. "Whatever you find is going to be astounding, isn't it?" she said. "I'd like to see that."

Mira considered her a moment. "That fellow, Dahl—he's been showing you rituals."

"Only as many as he has to. He's not a terribly patient teacher," she explained, when Mira arched an eyebrow. "But some, yes."

"Did he show you any that decipher languages?"

"That was first," Farideh said. "I can read Draconic already. If it helps."

Mira shrugged. "Who knows? But I will need clever hands and strong backs. Uncovering a site like this—with the limits having that scoundrel on our heels creates—it's a lot of work."

"If I come," Farideh said, "then you'll have my sister as well. She can't cast the ritual, but she'll be useful at clearing the space—of rubble or of creatures."

Mira nodded to herself a moment. "Fair enough. And your Mehen? Will he worry?"

Yes, Farideh thought, terribly. And for a moment, she thought about telling Mira to forget the offer, she couldn't run off like that, especially when Mehen was taking so long to come back from Cormyr. *You can hardly carry a weapon through the wilds without the proper writ.* She took a deep breath—Mehen was fine. Lorcan was the one in trouble.

"He's supposed to contact Tam. So if Tam's along with you . . . we can simply return the message that it's all fine." And then deal with the consequences afterward, she thought.

"Then that all sounds perfect," said Mira.

"There's just Tam," Farideh said.

Mira leaned back over the map, taking up a pair of calipers and setting them along a planned path. "Don't worry. I'll convince him."

Farideh smiled. Perfect. "How is it you know Tam?"

Mira's calipers stopped.

"He didn't mention?" she asked. Then, "No, of course he didn't. It's exactly the sort of thing he'd forget to say. Three damned days, and he never says a word. Just assumes it's been handled." She slammed the calipers down on the table. "Gods."

"I'm sure it's just that things are so hectic," Farideh said quickly. "Whatever it is, I didn't mean—"

"He's my father," Mira said. She looked up at Farideh, the same lazy smile she always seemed to wear painted on her mouth, covering up all trace of her outburst. "Did you think we were colleagues?"

"Perhaps," Farideh said, suddenly very aware of Mira's resemblance to the Calishite priest. "I didn't know Tam had any children. It's not the sort of thing he talks about—with me, at any rate."

"And what do you talk about?" Mira asked, turning back to her maps.

She spoke as if she were doing Farideh a favor, as if she were leaving the conversation open for the younger girl to amuse herself. But under it, Farideh suspected, there was an old anger. She thought of Mehen, of the way he favored Havilar and the way he fought Farideh so hard when she wouldn't break the pact. She and Mira might have more in common than she'd expected.

"About how I've done the wrong thing, usually," Farideh said. "But mostly, we don't."

"I wouldn't worry," Mira said, straightening and eyeing the inked path she'd drawn through the green patches marking the forest. "Really, the only one who is ever truly right with him is Tam Zawad."

Which was true, Farideh thought, recalling how often Tam's conversations had been centered on how she ought not do something she ended up perfectly capable of doing, or how she ought to avoid something she'd never ever intended to do. Or how he'd streaked off to reclaim the page and stone without once consulting Dahl or herself.

And yet she wouldn't have agreed with it, not outright. Enough persuasion and Tam could be convinced. He would see reason. But then, she supposed, much like if someone were to ask Farideh what she thought of Mehen while they were mid-argument, Mira wasn't interested in that side of things.

The thought of Mehen sent a nervous pang through her stomach, and the patch above her tail tensed. She hoped indeed that Tam was right about that much.

"Has it been long since you've seen him?" she asked.

"A few years."

"That must be hard."

Mira looked up, her smile even more insistently unconcerned. "Not in particular. Are you ready to leave soon?"

Farideh frowned. "Now?"

"Well," Mira said. "My father's clearly gone to get permission or coin or what have you from his superiors—else he would have said *something* about where he was going. Once he has that, I suspect we'll be well underway. All of us, most likely, and I would think by morning. So you ought to get your things together. Your sister, as well." This time, Farideh thought, Mira's smile was genuine. Fond, even. "And this time next tenday we'll be in the cavern of Xammux," she said. "Amid the treasures of Tarchamus."

·:⁀:·

Brin watched as Havilar lunged at the mercenary, the butt of her glaive aimed at her leading knee. Pernika darted out of reach, letting the glaive strike the packed earth. The women slipped around each other, so fast Brin wasn't sure how they'd both managed to keep their balance, coming back into firm-footed stances before lunging at each other again, graceful and deadly.

"It's like watching a dance, isn't it?" Brin said. The man beside him made no reply. "I mean, I know people say that all the time, but . . . it really is with those two."

Beside Brin, Maspero only grunted.

Pernika swung the flat of her sword hard at Havilar's back, but the tiefling was quicker than she'd expected and rolled under, bringing the shaft of the glaive down on the mercenary's wrist. Pernika hissed and leaped back, shaking her hand.

"Sorry!" Havilar cried, dropping the batting-wrapped glaive and scrambling to her feet. "Ah, *karshoj*, sorry. I didn't break it, did I?"

Pernika chuckled under her breath. "I'm a little less fragile than that." She clutched the wrist all the same.

**LESSER EVILS**

Panting, Havilar grinned and wiped the sweat off her brow. "Good. Again?"

"Give me a minute, stripling," Pernika said. She came over to the bench, Havilar trailing. "You'll get another chance to make up the score." She pulled at the collar of her shirt to stir the air. "Balls, but it's hot. Where'd you learn that style of glaivework? You're quick."

Havilar's grin grew wider, and she shot a little glance at Brin. "Around," she said shyly. "You're really good. I haven't sparred with anyone so much better than me in ages."

Pernika gave Brin an amused look. "Well, you can't expect to spar with someone in your safekeeping. Might as well challenge a tree."

"I am *not* in her safekeeping," Brin snapped.

Pernika's black, tapered eyes glittered. "My mistake."

"I liked that move you did," Havilar blurted. "The one before the big lunge where you feinted. If I shortened the swing, it might work as a chop."

"Maybe," the mercenary said, and Havilar was off and chattering as if she could fill the tense silence with talk of guards and parries and glaives and swords, making complex gestures with her hands to show the angles of blades and strikes.

But Pernika kept staring at Brin, and he turned away—who cared what some mercenary said? He was of the blood of Azoun after all. Constancia was right—that couldn't change. For all that it meant . . . probably half the nation of Cormyr could trace their ancestors to the promiscuous king.

Yet Brin had been trained by the holy champions of Loyal Torm, the god of duty. He'd been blessed by the god . . . and not taken the oaths that would have made him a true priest, all too aware he wasn't always the god's best representative.

Brin wiped sweat from his forehead. You're fooling no one, he thought. He could be anyone's descendant, any god's devotee, and it didn't make him braver or cleverer. He was still himself, no matter what titles he might lay claim to.

No one had doubted his capability in Neverwinter. No one had called him a coward. No one had made him take up a sword and defend his friends against the horrors of the Spellplague Chasm. No one had protected him when he faced the corrupted priest, Brother Vartan.

Even if the half-elf priest had been mad and distracted, he'd been dangerous, seething with the otherworldly powers that infected his mistress, Rohini. And Brin hadn't had a hope of staying alive without aiming for the good brother's heart. He still dreamed of killing Vartan, still woke shaking some nights, remembering the hideous slime that poured out of the corrupted priest's wounds. Vartan had been a kind man, once.

"Are you ready?" Havilar asked Pernika.

Pernika didn't answer, but started rolling up her sleeves, baring the intricate inkwork of tattoos that swirled from wrist to elbow and perhaps beyond. "Where'd you two hook each other?"

"We're not . . ." Havilar's tail flicked across the dust. "We're not *hooked*, or anything." Brin's stomach tightened and he watched the edge of the wall along the training ground. He could still hear her embarrassment—*fssk, fssk*.

Pernika chuckled. "She means," Maspero said in a surprisingly light voice, "where'd you start traveling from?"

"Neverwinter," Brin said flatly.

"You're from Neverwinter?" Maspero asked.

"He's from Cormyr," Havilar supplied.

Brin cursed to himself. He turned back to find Pernika giving him an appraising look as she leaned on her practice sword. "Interesting."

"Is it?" he said blandly. "There're a great many people from Cormyr in the world. You go to the right places you might think half of Faerûn's Cormyrean."

"Easy there," Pernika said. "Just making chit-chat. You want to know, I came out of Erlkazar. Maspero here is Westgate's dear scion." She swung the wooden blade up onto her shoulder like a yoke, and Brin stared at her arms. "There—now we're all interesting."

Brin's mind scrambled for something to say. Something to put the mercenary off his birthplace, his identity, or whatever else she might have been digging at.

But the words escaped him, his thoughts far too occupied with the tattoo nestled in the lines of inkwork of a black clawed fist, clutching at the air. Of Pernika's mad dancing eyes, and the implications of a mercenary who marked herself with the ancient symbols of the god of tyranny.

"I'm from Tymanther," Havilar said.

Pernika's eyes lingered on Brin a moment more. "Now that," she said, "is terribly interesting. Point for you, stripling."

Havilar smiled nervously. "Shall we go again?"

Pernika traded glances with Maspero, whose expression hardly flickered—a slight tightness around the eyes, a momentary purse of the lips. Still, a fleeting annoyance crossed Pernika's foxlike face before she turned back to Havilar. "Not today. Sun's too high. And you're too skilled for me to go half measures."

"All right. Tomorrow?"

"If we're still here," Pernika said, collecting her things. She and Maspero headed back through the tower, toward the city beyond, never saying a word to one another.

"That," Havilar said, once Pernika was out of earshot, "was *fantastic*. Did you see me get past her? That wasn't easy."

"Was it?" Brin murmured, turned away and watching Pernika's back.

"No it *wasn't*." He turned back to find Havilar frowning at him. "What's the matter with you? It's not . . . It's not because of what she said before, is it?"

"No." Brin beckoned her nearer. "I think Pernika's a Banite. We need to tell Tam."

Havilar didn't react. "Sometimes," she said after a heartbeat, "I think you say things like that to make me ask what you mean."

Brin nearly cursed again—how could someone possibly know so little of the gods?—but he bit it back. Havilar might look like a tiefling, but the ways of the unbelieving dragonborn lined her marrow. "She worships an evil god," he hissed. "The kind of god whose followers enjoy killing people to prove they can. And," he added before she could speak, "not in a fair fight, or because someone needed protecting, or any of that."

"Oh," Havilar said. She stood on her tiptoes and peered over his head at Pernika's retreating form. "Are you sure? She didn't try to kill me before."

"She has a tattoo," Brin started.

"She has a *lot* of tattoos," Havilar said. She rocked back down on the flats of her feet. "Maybe I need a tattoo."

"Havi!" he barked. "Stop being daft and *listen*."

Her brows went up, and her mouth tightened. "I *am* listening," she said. "And I think you're imagining things. Pernika's not trouble—she didn't hurt me before, she didn't hurt you either, and I don't think a tattoo makes the difference."

"A tattoo of a dark god's symbol?"

"Sort of like a devil's brand?" she said sharply and set to unwrapping her glaive. "Tam knows what he's doing. If *you* can spot some stupid symbol, then so can he."

Brin flushed. "Whoever she is, she doesn't need to know where I'm from," he said a little stiffly. "I'd appreciate you keeping that to yourself."

"Pernika doesn't *care*," Havilar said. "As you said, half the world's Cormyrean." She wrapped the batting into itself. "Although I don't think that's so."

"I was *exaggerating*," Brin said. "And I still don't want you telling."

Farideh appeared in the tower's doorway and made straight for her sister. "Are you through?" she called.

"Got too hot. But she only took me five times of seven. I'll catch up tomorrow."

Farideh glanced at Brin. "They're leaving tomorrow," she said. "Mira said she has clues enough to find the place finally."

Havilar's face fell. "Oh. Drat." She considered her glaive. "Do you think any of Tam's people might spar with me? Or maybe you two—"

"I want to go with them," Farideh said. "And I think you should come too."

"What?" Brin cried.

"Really?" Havilar clambered to her feet. "Isn't it supposed to be dangerous? Caves and evil wizards and maybe that creepy codloose Netherese?"

"It's just a ruin. We've handled worse."

"Well, right, but you were worried the whole time." Havilar peered at her. "And what about Mehen?"

Farideh bit her lip. "He said to stay with Tam. We have to go along to stay with Tam."

"That's true!" Havilar grinned. "And he knows we're *here*. He'll know we're there too."

"You're not at all worried about Mehen?" Brin asked. "I thought he was meant to be back almost a tenday ago." The twins looked at him.

"Tam says Cormyr's terribly complicated," Farideh said. "That everything is bound up in officials and papers and things."

"Well, yes," Brin admitted. "But wouldn't he have *said*—"

"What could happen to him anyway?" Havilar said. "It's *Mehen*."

From the open windows of the tower, came the sound of Tam's raised voice. Farideh flinched. "Mira," she said, "was going to talk to him about our coming."

Good, Brin thought. If Tam hadn't agreed yet, there was a very good chance he'd stop them from going. Even if Pernika weren't a Banite, she was trouble. He *was* sure about that.

"*Karshoj*," Havilar sighed.

"I think she'll win," Farideh said. "I just hope he's not too mad once they're done." She looked down at Brin. "Did you know Mira was his daughter?"

"Yes," Havilar said mildly. "Who else would she be?"

Farideh looked at her and shook her head. "Anyone else in the world. Did he tell you?"

"No. But their faces. She'd have to be his daughter. Or . . . his much younger sister. Or maybe a niece."

Brin looked up at the window, imagining the man and woman beyond its shadows. "I didn't know he had children. He'd be strange to have as a father." The words had no sooner left his mouth but he regretted them: an itinerant spy was far less strange than a dragonborn bounty hunter. The twins let the conversation fall.

"I'm going to pack," Farideh said. "Come up soon?"

"Yeah," Havilar said. "A moment." Farideh went back into the tower, leaving Brin and Havilar standing on the training field. Not looking at one another.

"Will you come?" she asked abruptly. "Or are you going to stay here?"

"Dunno," he said. Just say you're sorry, he thought. "I certainly won't go where I'm not welcome."

Her mouth was still tight and furious. "Well I guess that's for you to decide. Don't want you to have to muck it with us *daft* folks." She turned and stomped back into the tower.

# CHAPTER NINE

## *The Silver Marches*
*14 Flamerule, the Year of the Dark Circle (1478 DR)*

**T**HE EXPEDITION WAS NOT WHAT MIRA HAD PLANNED ON—HALF AS many helpers, only two of them Harpers with any sort of training for artifacts, her father ready to run back to Everlund at the merest sign of Shade—but she had not gotten to where she was without a knack for adaptation. Convincing her father it would be too dangerous to leave his hangers-on behind at Everlund—without him to watch over them—had been the first step, and one tenuously made. All it would take, she thought, looking over the group as they set a camp by the roadside, was a word from Tam, and her expedition would crumble. Fortunately, she had the long ride to the caverns to accustom herself to the ragtag bunch that hung on her father like they were his children. If Tam decided to undercut her, she would be ready.

Havilar was the simplest—so enamored of Pernika and her blade that Mira suspected she would follow the mercenary into the Abyss. At least for the next tenday. Mira had made a point of nudging Pernika into sparring sessions, taking on her share of the campwork to make certain there was time enough for it.

And if the tiefling wavered, there was Farideh who was—Mira suspected—almost as interested in Tarchamus's magic as she was. Mira could count on the warlock to slip up beside her at least once a day with some nonchalant question about the arcanist's powers. Whether she was greatly underestimating the gulf between his skills and hers didn't so much matter, because one thing became abundantly clear watching Farideh beside Dahl: the girl was stubborn.

And if she wants magic, Mira thought, there are ways I can give that to her.

Dahl was still a puzzle, but Mira had seen enough to gamble that if Tam ordered a retreat, he would refuse, at least at first. He wasn't stubborn so much as ornery, ready to take everything as a slight. Dangerous to cultivate, Mira thought. That sort could turn on you quick.

And Brin . . .

Brin was watching her, even now. As if he were trying to determine the face that lay behind a mask. Keep on looking, she thought with a little smile. I was born to this.

Mira pulled her haversack from the cart and from it took the book she'd pressed the page into, a relatively crisp and thin atlas of the Sword Coast. The creases had been largely flattened out, and the ink no longer pooled along them as it shifted lazily. She could hear the whispery madness of its speech—*ashenath enjareen nether pendarthis.* Through rock and flood I've come to *this.*

"*We will bring you back,*" she said in Loross. "*Tell us where.*"

The ink jumped, as if she'd startled it, but the page didn't reveal anything new before continuing its regular pattern of scrawlings. The schema had come up briefly the first time she'd offered, but never again. It was time for new efforts. She closed the book and sought out Dahl, sitting alone beside the fire.

The trouble was she spoke Loross, but the modern sort. She did not speak the Loross of Tarchamus, five thousand years old. For all she knew she was offering a pronunciation the page didn't understand. Or one that threatened or insulted it. For all she knew she might, Mira thought, sound like nothing so much as a madwoman screaming from the street corner.

A blessing she had access to the sorts of rituals that solved such problems.

"Well met," she said, dropping down beside Dahl. He eyed her warily, but nodded and returned the greeting. "Am I right to understand you can cast a translation ritual? I hear you're rather talented at it."

That flustered him. "Yes, well. I can cast it. Yes."

She opened the book to show the magical page. "I need this particular dialect of Loross." He studied the page—a necessary sacrifice, she thought. As much as she'd like to keep a tight rein on what the Harpers knew about this mission, she couldn't restrict everything. If he saw any of the page's secrets, she'd deal with that later.

"It would be terribly helpful," she said, after several long moments of his study of the page. "I can read it but I can't be sure I'm speaking to it. And I'm no ritual caster."

"I could show you," he offered offhandedly, "so you don't need others to cast it."

Mira smiled and tucked that reaction away as well. "As lovely as that would be, I understand your services are already engaged." She nodded at Farideh, who stood off at the edge of the grove, stretching a kink from her neck. Dahl's expression closed.

"She's not a very good pupil."

"Really?" Mira asked. "She seems eager enough. Capable. What's the matter?"

Dahl hesitated. "What she wants to learn . . . I can't teach it."

Planar magic, Mira thought. "Can't or won't?"

His whole demeanor had shifted, tensed. "Both."

"I see," Mira said before he pulled too far from her. "Shall we get to it?"

"You'll have to wait until he sets the circle," Brin interrupted. He was still standing on the other side of the campfire, arms folded. "Won't she?"

Dahl glowered at him. "I know what I'm meant to do."

"Well, Farideh can handle that," Mira said. "You already taught her to lay a protective circle."

"No," Dahl said, still glaring at Brin. "Not yet."

Not yet, but Farideh had said he would teach her back before they left Everlund. Very interesting. Usable.

"Mira!" her father called. "No one's seen to the horses."

Mira stood and dusted off her breeches, irritated but well aware she couldn't do any more at the moment. "Sounds like we both ought to attend our tasks," she said wanly. "But find me later. I could use your help." She left without looking back, sure that they were both still glaring at each other. At least Brin had stopped watching her.

She was rubbing down the cart horse, contemplating the two younger men, when Maspero cornered her. "This isn't what you sold me on." Maspero's voice was a sheet of lace, so fine and light, it was a shock to hear it coming from such a big man. But if Maspero was talking to you, you'd soon realize the lace was tatted of razor wire, and you would be lucky to live to repeat such comparisons.

"Well met, Maspero," she said mildly.

"Half as many. Only two of them Harpers, and your father—"

"This is better," she assured him. "You'll get your weapon."

Maspero grabbed hold of her wrist and jerked her around to face him. "You said Harpers would be best," he reminded her. "You said they'd know how to look and what to look for, that you could get ones who wouldn't ask questions."

"We'll manage," she said, ignoring the pain in her arm. "May I have my hand back? I'm sure you don't want anyone asking questions about why my mercenary is manhandling me." Maspero narrowed his eyes. "It's not as if we've drafted a gaggle of idiots. It was they who recovered the page, remember."

Maspero snorted and released her, and it took all of Mira's focus not to rub her wrist. "I heard about that," he said. "Tell me why it is that shitting Graesson knew about the revel and the treasures. I believe I told you to be discreet."

Mira returned to brushing the horse's coat. "He already knew. Sent two assassins to kill me and steal it. I just . . . made sure he had the means to continue his search. And keep Adolican Rhand and his guards distracted in Graesson's normal, dramatic fashion." She bent to attend the horse's legs. "The chaos was extraordinary."

"Godsbedamned Cyricists," Maspero muttered. "And if he'd managed to gain my treasure?"

"He didn't."

She straightened. Maspero was glaring over the cart horse at the rest of their party. "Pernika thinks the Cormyrean boy's worth something," he said.

"Tell her to keep it to herself until we're done," Mira replied. "The last thing you need is Pernika's mad plans destroying your allies."

"So now they're allies?" Maspero said. "You told me 'tools' before. I don't want Harpers as allies . . . A danger and a weakness. We deal with them as soon as they're not necessary."

Mira didn't blink. "Best of luck with that."

"Are you implying you aren't with me, Mira?"

"I'm implying I don't trust you not to kill me too," she said simply. "Especially if you're insisting I 'deal with' my own father because he wears the pin. He trusts me, so he trusts you too. Our goals are all in line, Maspero. What we want and what they want aren't so far off. We get extra hands, extra eyes, and so do they, so why stir the pot? Especially when we all have a common enemy in Shade and Adolican Rhand."

Maspero narrowed his eyes and muttered a curse for the Netherese gentleman. "If he beats us there, I'll throttle your father myself for delaying us."

"Oh, you'll have to get in line in that case," Mira said. She handed him the hoof pick. "It would do to look busy."

·:⌒:·

Farideh hissed and pressed a hand to the sharp pain on the side of her head, drawing her ritual book closer like a shield. "Damn it, Havi, I said you could braid my hair, not yank it out by the roots."

Havilar, who was busy scrutinizing the trio of slender braids that lay against a sleeping Pernika's cheek, let the strands go looser. "Sorry," she said, not looking away. "The back . . . she's lying on it, but it does a funny curl, I think." She squinted at her sister's hair. "If I tuck this bit . . . D'you have a stick or a pin or something?"

Farideh held up her stylus. "Wipe the ink off, please. Why don't you ask Pernika how she does it?"

"This is more fun," Havilar said. "Did I tell you she said I was very skilled? She was impressed I got past her with Devilslayer, especially all battened up and off balance."

*Run darling, Lorcan says. Run fast and run far.* "I wish you wouldn't call it that."

"What? Devilslayer?" Havilar said. "I like it." She gathered up the thicker braids at the back of Farideh's head and twisted them against the base of her skull. "Besides, it's not like I called it

'Half-Devilslayer.'" She stabbed the stylus through the layers of Farideh's hair in one sharp stroke, slicing across her scalp.

"Ouch!"

"Sorry," Havilar said. "It's a bit precarious. Needs real pins. Here, look at me."

Farideh reached back and gingerly touched the knot of braids that pulled all her hair taut and made her scalp ache. Havilar straightened the three smaller plaits that she'd threaded under Farideh's right horn to run from her temple to her collarbone.

"Well?" Farideh said.

"I think it will look nice on me," she said. "And Mehen can't complain—there's hardly anything to grab hold of." She considered her sister a moment. "You should probably do the little braids on both sides if you like it—doing it only on one makes it seem like you're trying to draw attention to one eye over the other. Makes your face a bit uneven."

Farideh shoved the smaller braids behind her ear. "I'll just . . . leave things the way they are."

"Suit yourself." Havilar looked ahead of the cart they rode in. "I think . . . It looks like the miners' camp is ahead."

"Good," Farideh said and yanked the stylus free. "I'm tired of the cart. Though I suppose walking won't be easier. Or riding." Havilar sighed.

*"You were right, by the way,"* Havilar said, switching to Draconic. *"Brin isn't fond of me."*

Farideh bit her tongue. She wasn't glad—how could she be glad at Havilar's expense?—but she wasn't disappointed either. In all the world, she had only Havilar and Brin, and if they went off together—or worse, fell out—everything would change. *"I'm sorry,"* she said. *"Did he just . . . tell you? Like that?"*

*"No,"* Havilar said, as if Farideh were an utter fool. *"Why would I ask him? Gods, that would be embarrassing. No. I can just tell."*

"Oh."

*"Don't say* 'oh' *like that,"* Havilar said. *"I'm perfectly capable of telling."*

"Could you two stop pretending I'm not here?" Dahl scowled back at them from the driver's box. "I know *enough* Draconic to tell you're gossiping."

Havilar rolled her eyes at Farideh. "Fari, do you wonder why Dahl's such a grouch?"

Farideh smiled. "Perpetually."

"*I* think," Havilar said, her eyes on Dahl, "he wishes we'd gossip about Mira." Dahl's scowl tightened and he turned back to guiding the wagon toward the stream ford.

"I like Mira," Farideh said, closing the book and slipping it into her haversack. "She's . . . very good at getting what she wants."

Havilar sniffed. "Sometimes you shouldn't get what you want." She stood and heaved herself over the side of the wagon, her glaive in hand. Farideh sighed—gods, whatever she meant by that, it surely meant a fight later on. Perhaps she was mad about what Farideh had said about Brin. Perhaps she hadn't wanted to come along. Perhaps she, like Farideh, wasn't expecting Brin to come as well.

"She's wrong, you know," Dahl said abruptly.

Farideh leaned over the edge of the wagon so she could see him better. "About what?"

"About him. Brin." Dahl looked back at her. "Every time he catches her talking to me he turns icy as a Nar foot bath."

"I thought you were tired of gossip."

He looked down at her. "I'm tired of half-understood gossip. This . . . I'm glad. I'd been thinking he was just another lordling ass looking down on the common folk."

Farideh laughed. "Brin? No. Not in the least." She considered Havilar, splashing up the other side of the stream toward where the others had stopped to arrange stables for the horses. Toward where Brin and Mira stood outside the lodge, talking. "I hope you're wrong. I think she doesn't like him so well as she pretends."

"Certainly," Dahl said dryly, as the cart sloshed down into the streambed. "That's why she's gone ahead to keep Mira from 'getting what she wants.'"

Farideh cursed to herself. He was right—Havilar headed straight over and slipped into their conversation, drawing all their attention, her body language tense and angry. She was definitely going to pick a fight with Farideh later.

"Do you think we'll stop long enough for another ritual?" she asked.

Dahl's expression closed back up, like a book being shut. "I doubt it." He was quiet as they eased through the water. "Master Zawad says you're supposed to be resting in the wagon anyway."

Farideh rolled her eyes. "I'm rested. Rested and rested and rested."

"And you know better, do you?"

"Do you really think it takes a tenday to work a single dose of poison from a body?" she demanded. "Tell me honestly that you think that's true, and I'll rest until we're back to Everlund."

"It could," he said defensively.

"But it doesn't. Not in this case." She scowled. "And still I'm supposed to rest and not cast and not take anything to help me sleep." Tam had made the wagon a condition of her coming—along with insisting that if one of them came, *all* of them came.

"One separated is a weak point," he'd said when Brin had informed Tam he would rather stay behind. "If Rhand comes through here looking for clues, I don't want him to have options." Mira had been as good as her word, and though Brin was clearly irritated to be painted as a weak point, the expedition was underway.

"Do you think he'll catch up to us?" she asked Dahl. "Rhand, I mean."

Dahl stared at her as if he were waiting for her to break down and confess all manner of crimes. She stared back, fighting the urge to turn away, to hide from his scrutiny.

"Look," he said finally, "I didn't *know* he was going to be that dangerous. You can't blame me for that."

"I wasn't."

"But you do," he said. "It's patently obvious you do."

Farideh bit back a curse. "How very clever of you to know my mind." Forget him, she thought, get out and walk. She came unsteadily to her feet. "Perhaps your Oghma favored you with the knowledge?"

The look on his face, so shocked and frankly hurt, showed the barb had gone deeper than she'd meant, but Farideh was too angry and too embarrassed to smooth things over. She moved unsteadily to the rear of the cart and slipped off as the wagon came up the muddy banks. If he wasn't going to help her, she didn't have to work at being pleasant to him—especially if he was going to treat her as if she were slow and wicked and plotting something fiendish by learning how to put glasses back together.

The miners' camp marked the last bit of habitation before they reached the canyon Mira had marked, and it was the only place to leave the wagon and horses Mira had procured. There was no path to Mira's cavern—they'd have to spend the final day of travel picking their way through the foothill forests.

"You planning to *carry* back what you find?" Pernika asked.

"I plan," Mira said, "on finding out what we need to carry out before staking valuable horses out to make a highsunfeast for dire wolves. Unless you'd like to coax them into the caverns?"

"Are you suggesting we *all* need to traipse into the caverns?" Tam asked.

"Who knows how big they are? If we leave people behind, they'll have no idea whether the rest of ous are lost or just following a particularly deep cave path. More inside means more who can carry a message out, if need be—and in pairs. Always in pairs. But that's well ahead of us." She shouldered her pack. "All we have to do is find the cave mouth; the rest should be easy enough."

The forests of the Nether Mountain foothills were packed with larches and laspars with their shags of needles, and gnarled felsuls clinging to hollows of rock matted by their own shattered bark. In between, all manner of wildflowers and weeds, snags and bogs of old needles, and thick slicks of moss slowed them down. As Farideh picked her way through a matted patch of fireweed, a great flock of moths the size of doves swirled up around her. They battered blindly into her, and where they landed, they clung to her clothes and hair. She yelped and swatted wildly, trying to cover her head and knock the creatures off her armor at the same time.

She heard Brin crash back through the underbrush to her and the weight of the moths came off her hair one by one.

"Laspar moths," Brin said. "They're harmless."

She shivered and rolled her shoulders, trying to rid herself of the sensation of them. "They're too big to be harmless," she said. The rest of the group was looking down the rise at them. Particularly Havilar.

"Thank you," Farideh said to Brin. She started forward again, but he fell into step beside her.

"She's angry, isn't she?" he said. "Did she tell you why?"

Farideh hesitated. "I think it's complicated."

"Not that complicated," he said irritably. But by then they'd caught up to Havilar, and he wouldn't say any more. There was a moment between them so awkward and prickly that Farideh didn't dare guess at its source, and then Brin was picking his way across the bare rocks.

"What did he say?" Havilar demanded.

"He wanted to know if you'd told me why you were angry. And I told him you hadn't."

*"Hmph."* Havilar kicked a larch cone over the hump of granite. "If he doesn't know, he could ask me. I almost wish he hadn't come. Or we hadn't." She watched the group ahead of them for a bit. "Do you think we shouldn't have come?"

"Why are you mad at him?"

"He called me daft," Havilar said. "And some other things. But, I mean, I wonder if we shouldn't have come because of Mehen. I keep expecting any moment Tam's going to hear one of those senders and it'll be Mehen roaring curses about how much trouble we're in. We're going to be in so much trouble anyway, you know? And then I wonder if maybe Mehen's in trouble."

"Maybe he's just accepted we're grown. We can go where we like, when we like. He can't really stop us—"

Havilar grabbed her arm. "You're *not* leaving."

"No," Farideh said, shaking her sister off. "But I could. You can. Or we can go off for a bit without Mehen and be trusted to come back. Maybe he's seen reason."

"Mehen?" Havilar said skeptically.

"Well what makes more sense?" Farideh asked, as the cliffs came into view ahead of them. "Mehen's all right with us having a little adventure? Or he's gotten into trouble standing in line for forms and approvals?"

"Well, yes." Havilar's tail slashed the fireweed. "I don't know. What if . . . it's Constancia? She might—"

"Want to keep us and Brin away?" Farideh interrupted. "Isn't she more likely to . . . I don't know, ransom Mehen? Or something more knightly to try to get Brin to come back?"

"That letchy fellow with the beard—"

"Would want us to go back to Waterdeep and bring the page with us." Havilar went quiet and there was only the sound of their breaths and the crunch of dry moss underfoot.

"Devils," Havilar said firmly. "What if it's *devils*? Who . . . are trying to get us trapped somewhere . . ."

Farideh pursed her mouth. It was close—awfully close—to all she feared. Could Sairché have found out about the expedition? Could Sairché be manipulating Mira's plans? Ahead, the dark-haired historian had stopped and was consulting her compass with a furrowed brow. Farideh would have called her independent, maybe carefree. Never the tool of another. But she would have called the cultist who'd nearly killed both her and Havilar kind and well-mannered. Her opinions of others weren't all that trustworthy.

Mira had handed Dahl her map, and the Harper was holding it open for her to scrutinize. That opinion, Farideh thought, she trusted wholly.

"Lorcan would do it," Havilar said.

Farideh watched Mira dart off over the rise, down toward a stream valley. "No, he wouldn't."

"He *hates* Mehen. And he tried to kill me."

"No, he didn't. He *expressly* didn't, all right?" And he wouldn't— he'd promised she was safe. They were both safe. Only so long as he's alive, Farideh thought. And then who knew what would come? "It's not Lorcan."

"You don't know that."

Farideh yanked her sleeve up to her shoulder, displaying the angry red scars of her brand. She took Havilar's hand and pressed it to the marks. "Cool. See? I'll tell you when it's Lorcan."

Havilar scowled. "All right, fine. Maybe Mehen just trusts us."

"And we were perfectly right to come."

"You're acting strange," Havilar said, as they started after the others, "you know that? You're supposed to be the worried one. I'm supposed to be the one demanding adventures."

Farideh shook her head. "Maybe that's why you're worried. Because someone has to be."

"That's stupid," Havilar said, but Mira's cry of discovery from up ahead forestalled any argument. They had found the cavern of Xammux.

․⁚⌒⁚․

For all of Mira's assurances, nothing was simple about entering the cavern, in Farideh's opinion. First, there was a climb up a nearly sheer rock face, the stream that seemed to trickle out the broken door pouring down on her head. She hauled herself up onto the narrow ledge behind Mira, not wanting to consider how they would get back down.

The stone here was the same strange pattern as the fragment, layers of sharp circles over the dark grain of the granite. One door still hung in place, held to its ancient frame by the remains of one stone hinge. The other was half gone, its base nowhere to be seen. All over, mad writing scratched the pale stone's surface—runes in Dethek, Draconic, and languages Farideh had never seen before. *Xammux*, they said. *The Many.*

And beneath those, in firmer, more formal lettering, was the Draconic that wasn't Draconic.

"Not our door," Mira said. She kneeled down and ran a finger over the broken edge. She shook her head. "No, it wouldn't be."

Farideh looked back down the cliff face, at Tam who'd nearly made the top. "So we're through?" she panted.

Mira looked up at her and blinked. "Through with what?"

"It's the wrong door."

"No," Mira said. "Just not the door that fragment came from. This is an old break. Ours had sharper edges. And none of this." She waved at the scrawls crisscrossing the façade. "We have to go deeper," she informed Tam as he climbed up beside her.

Tam peered at the door himself, easing across the slippery rock to touch the carvings. "The marks of our cultists."

"Possibly," Mira said. "But I don't think they're around, if they *have* been around any time of late." She pointed across at the canyon wall, where one of the spongy funguses was crawling slowly toward them, the patterns of its skin shifting as it eased over the rocks. "The caverns must have flooded recently—and violently. Those things certainly look as if they'd rather be inside. And that's likely where our fragment came from." She pulled a slim book from her haversack, and the page from the center of that. "Perhaps you would too," she said to it.

Second came the long and stumbling trek along the uneven streambed as it wound deeper into the ground. The wet, marshy smell of the funguses still hung in the air over the cold, clammy smell of wet stone. Rocks polished smooth by their passage out of the mountains turned under Farideh's feet, and the water that covered her boots at the beginning swiftly rose to her knees. Mira led the way, the page in hand. *Ashenath enjareen . . . Tarchamusi enpuluis . . .*

At least Farideh could see well enough. Something greenish and shimmering coated the broken edges of the walls, the points of stalactites, and it threw off enough light for her sensitive eyes to pierce the dark, leaving both of her hands free to catch her balance on the walls.

Dahl came up beside her, holding one of the sunrods Mira had passed around and staring up at the strange glow. "Cavern botfly nymphs," he said. "We'd best burn our hose as soon as we're out of the water."

Farideh looked back over her shoulder. "Why?"

"They lay their eggs in the water to find purchase with some passing host. They lodge in the knit of hose," he said blandly, and he passed her by without further explanation, leaving Farideh eyeing the dark, chilly water uneasily.

Soon enough, the tunnel widened into a cavern as broad as Everlund's training yard and longer than Waterdeep's market. The path was a broken, sloping thing, inching upward to another cavern beyond. The river pooled into a lake that covered half the floor. More of the botflies glowed along the sunken walls and stalactites, matched here by a strange, bluish luminescence in the water itself. The ceiling shimmered with their reflected light.

"Wait," Tam ordered. No one needed to be told—even Farideh and Havilar knew that color of light often meant a pocket of the wild magic left behind by the Spellplague. Almost a hundred years had passed, but here and there the remains of unbound power left by the death of the goddess Mystra could still be deadly.

But this . . . Farideh felt no pull to it, no sense of power. Tam seemed to be considering it with the same uncertainty. Blue might mean spellplague, but it could mean plenty of other things as well. He edged toward the water.

The light brightened as he neared the pool's edge. But the waters stayed relatively calm, stirring gently toward the beginnings of the stream. If it had been plaguechanged, there would have been a greater strangeness—a twisting of reality, an unfolding of the stone and water, a wrongness that would have been clear in the growing light. Tam's shoulders relaxed.

"Why is it getting brighter?" Havilar asked.

Tam looked back over his shoulder at Dahl, who shook his head. "It's likely something living in the water. Some little plant or something. Like a sea sparkle. Might be a signal of some kind."

The lights flared and shifted, as if the glowing creatures parted, leaving the center dark. Farideh crept a little nearer. "What in the world would a plant be signaling?"

A mass of serpentine heads lashed out of the dark water, all bellows and teeth and glowing eyes. Farideh shouted and leaped backward, away from the water, away from the burst of acid that spewed from the nearest mouth and hissed against the wet rocks.

The hydra's near head snapped after her, more acid dripping from its jaws. The rod was in her hand with hardly a thought, the surge of the Hells in her blood, and a blast of crackling purple energy shot out and caught the hydra head along its cheek.

She called on her pact once more and slipped through the gap in the planes that opened. It spat her out farther left as the hydra dived toward the spot she'd been in before. Havilar shouted at her from across the way. "Get its head up!"

Farideh stabbed upward with the rod, a plume of flames searing the beast's softer throat. It bellowed and thrashed itself away from the fire, but the Hellish magic clung to it.

"There!" she shouted as the head's arc peaked, and it started to crash down.

Havilar sprinted up from behind her to plant the sharp end of her glaive below the falling head like a spike. With a great bloody *crunch*, it speared through the jaw and split the fragile base of its skull, spearing its brain.

A second head swung low, its jaws wide to snatch Havilar, the glaive, and the dead head in one gulp. Farideh cast another stream of fire into its mouth instead. It veered off. Havilar wrestled the weapon free.

Farideh grinned like a madwoman, exulting in the pulse of power, the strength of the spells she cast. Let Tam think her too weak to manage. Let Dahl treat her like some grasping apprentice. She knew what she was doing.

"Fari! Duck!" Havilar cried.

The second head slammed into her side and threw her into the lake.

The icy water shocked her every nerve and she nearly gasped in surprise. The blue light of the water was all around her, and for a moment she couldn't tell where the surface was and where the lake bottom lay. A current stirred the water around her and pulled her gently toward some other shore. She turned, trying to find some purchase, some touchstone that would point the way.

And found herself facing a dark, jagged hole in the rock.

She hung there, her lungs screaming as her eyes adjusted to the dim light. A flat surface surrounded the hole, a square that broke the natural shape of the lake's wall. And if that was the wall . . .

Farideh made for the surface, took another breath of air, and dived again, swimming closer. She ran her fingers over the freezing stone, the chiseled edges of runes still clear.

No wonder it had been lost to the ages.

The hydra plunged a head into the water beside her. She swam frantically backward, away from the bloom of acid, the snap of its teeth. The rod was still in her hand, but she couldn't breathe let alone speak the trigger word. Back and back and back—chased by the lunging jaws, until its neck was stretched to the limit. Her muscles ached with the cold. She pulled out her sword and stabbed at the creature, only making it madder. It caught the edge of her cloak in its teeth and yanked. Pulling her near enough to take a bite. Pulling her near enough for Farideh to shove her sword into the soft back of its mouth.

The hydra pulled back, spitting acid. She swam for the surface again, and made for shore. The wounded head reared up over her, the hilt of her sword still protruding from its mouth.

"Dive!" Tam bellowed across the water, and she did, but not before she glimpsed Dahl and Pernika both taking their swords to the creature's heart. From under the icy water, the *crack* of the hydra's neck slamming into the lake's surface sounded all around her. It drew up again, and its death scream reached even Farideh's ears.

She broke the surface again. The last head lay sprawled across the stony shore, and Havilar was clambering over it. As Farideh paddled nearer, Havilar kneeled at the edge and held out her glaive end. "Gods, here! Are you all right?"

"I th-think I f-found it," Farideh gasped. She grabbed hold of the proffered end of Havilar's glaive and hauled herself up out of the freezing water. Her teeth chattered and her bones ached, but still she grinned. "There's a hole, a passage in between two rocks. It's hard to see, but there's writing on part of it and the broken part's the right size."

Mira had been standing over Tam and Dahl, but now all her attention was on Farideh. "Where?"

"Along the cave wall, on the left." She pushed the wet hair out of her eyes. "It's fairly far in, though. Someone not so winded should check it."

Mira was already stripping off her armor and gear. She waded into the water and started toward the cave wall.

Havilar pulled her cloak from her haversack and draped it around Farideh's shoulders. "Here. Bad as swimming in the tarn too early?"

Farideh pulled the cloak around her. "Easily."

"*Brrr*," Havilar said sympathetically. "Can I borrow your sword a breath?"

"Get it out and you can."

Tam yelped in pain. "Shar and hrast!" Dahl held Tam's right hand by the raw and ragged fingers. The hand below it hardly bore any skin and had swollen twice its normal size.

"Broken," Dahl said. "Can you heal it?"

"Not without my right hand," Tam snapped. He winced as Dahl smeared an oily substance over the ruined skin. "Hrast. Brin, get over here. Dahl, go start a fire."

"The salve will help," Dahl said.

"Not fast enough to make my hand good for the next thing that needs healing." Brin dropped down beside the silverstar and started praying. Dahl looked away—but seeing Farideh watching, he scowled.

"Start a fire," Tam ordered again. "One of us is half frozen and it's about to be two." He looked over at Farideh. "What happened to 'no powers until you're well'?"

"Better than being eaten," she replied. "And I'm fine."

Out on the lake, she heard Mira break the surface, draw another breath and dive again. Farideh drew the cloak nearer, shivering in sympathy. Dahl finished off the spell that made a cheery little campfire burst smokelessly into being. She settled beside it, wishing it were bigger, just as a hydra head rolled past her and into the growing flames.

"Don't you dare!" Dahl cried, jumping forward and kicking the head out of the fire. It rolled a short distance and sat steaming on one scaly cheek. "The air's bad enough down here without adding burning hydra to the mix."

"Do you have a better plan?" Havilar had planted a foot on another one of the hydra's necks and started hacking at it with the sword. The hydra's head came loose, and she kicked it away from the body, toward a hollow in the floor, before doing the same to the next one.

"What are you doing?" Maspero demanded. Farideh startled. The mercenary had said hardly a dozen words since they'd left Everlund, and his soft, light voice still surprised her.

Havilar kicked the second head so that it settled against the first. "Taking heads."

"Why?"

"Every head grows another hydra," Havilar said as if he were slow, "unless you burn them. So we'll *have* to burn them. Fari, will you?"

Even with Dahl's little fire, Farideh still shivered, and in a moment Mira would too. A quick gesture, a whispered word, and a bolt of flames sizzled from her open palm to engulf the hydra heads, hot enough to send up a cloud of steam and set the skulls to popping wetly. She caught her breath—Dahl was right, it smelled fouler than foul. But the chill in her bones started to recede.

Mira pulled herself from the water, her grin answer enough and her skin taking on a bluish cast. "Thank your gods, da," she said through a chattering jaw. "We've found it—ah, piss and hrast, what is that stench?"

"Prevention," Havilar said solemnly.

"You're cold, even if you're excited," Farideh said, pulling Mira toward the fire.

Brin cursed and clutched his head. "I'm sorry," he said. "That's as best I can do." Tam's hand was still swollen and raw looking. "I can try again in a bit," he offered, "but if I push it—"

"Neither of us will be well," Tam finished.

"Bad luck," Pernika put in. "Are you sure this is the right way?"

Havilar kicked a fourth head into the fire. "That's all of them. No more hydras."

Tam's attention went to her. "Hydras have seven heads."

"This one only had four. The other three necks are just stumps." Havilar looked down at the carcass and wrinkled her nose. "Nasty-looking stumps."

Tam sat up straighter. "Old wounds?"

"Old enough to putrefy," she said. "I said nasty. I meant nasty."

Tam cursed. "Then someone else has been this way recently. We don't have time to dally."

# CHAPTER TEN

## THE CAVERNS OF XAMMUX
*15 FLAMERULE, THE YEAR OF THE DARK CIRCLE (1478 DR)*

DAHL LAID THE LAST OF HIS COMPONENTS OUT, TRYING HARD TO ignore his audience and the stink of burnt hydra. Two rituals atop each other—a spell to keep the cold out and a spell to make travel through water possible. If he slipped, either one could be weakened and someone could well die.

You wanted responsibility, he reminded himself as he poured sea salt in a circle large enough to hold all eight of them, around several neat piles of powdered metals. "Step inside," he said, pulling the leaves from a dried stalk of herbs.

"You're too far from the water," Tam said. "We'll suffocate."

Dahl shook his head. "Not necessary. This is a refined version." He set a vial of fresh water beside the pouches laid out at his feet, and then a very small vial that held a drop of white dragon's blood. "The older rituals mimicked the original spells—the ones with the gills and such—but this one's one of Procampur's experiments. Shouldn't affect anyone's ability to breathe normally. Well, I mean," he added, "apart from being able to breathe water."

When the leaves had been sprinkled in a cross through the circle and he had everyone facing outward, Dahl took his place in the center. He shut his eyes and held the vial with the dragon's blood out.

Oghma let this work, he thought. He dropped the vial.

An icy gale blew up from their feet with a terrible roar that reverberated off the cavern walls. As the wind threw the leaves into the air, the magic that streamed upward found its way into Dahl's nose and mouth—into each of their noses and mouths, he hoped—and flooded his lungs with a cool, green taste. The wind turned warm, then hot, then faded away and left all eight standing there, looking tumbled and confused.

All of them were staring at Dahl.

He dusted the salt off his jerkin, hefted his haversack onto one shoulder, and trying not to look nervous, stepped into the water.

It was warm as a midsummer mill pond, and he sighed in relief. "Come along," he said. "It will wear off eventually."

Dahl had breathed water before, but that didn't make the experience any less unnerving. It might have felt like breathing strangely cool, strangely humid air, but the pressure of the lake around him was still there, the currents of the water still pulling at him like the wind never could.

It did not surprise him to see Farideh holding her breath—the instinct was hard to fight—but it annoyed him. He'd mentioned that, hadn't he? He pulled her aside and took several exaggerated breaths. She gave him such a plaintive look as she continued to hold her mouth shut. Dahl rolled his eyes—no, it didn't feel pleasant, but it wasn't going to hurt anyone.

*Breathe*, he mouthed.

She fought it until her air ran out, and she tried to swim for the surface. Dahl caught her arm and held her until she had to take several great, frantic gulps. He mimed again—*keep breathing*—and headed after the others, his thoughts unkind but wholly deserved.

The ancient door had been pried open, the remainders of the seal knocked away. Mira swept the lake bed, picking out the broken pieces and adding them to a sack. The current flowed into the doorway, pulling Dahl's feet toward it. Mira considered her collection and pulled the drawstring shut. She pulled a length of thin rope from her sack and tied one end to her belt, then passed the coil to Tam before heading into the tunnel. It left little time for each of them to tie in before following Mira into the dark, and no room at all for discussion.

She was, Dahl thought, as he took the coil from Maspero and knotted the rope to his sword belt, a much more palatable leader than Tam. He passed the end of the rope to Farideh and headed in after her.

And Mira's enthusiasm made the trek seem less like some ridiculous make-work quest handed down by the Fisher. This *mattered*, to

Mira at least, and if they did not find this wizard's secret hoard of magic items and scrolls, it would not be for lack of effort from Dahl.

The current picked up. Suddenly it felt like trying not to tumble down a steep hill. The water sucked at his legs and arms and swirled around his head, tossing his hair into his eyes. He tried to move with the current, only to find himself caught. He glanced back to see Farideh edging along with one hand on either side of the tunnel, her brow furrowed in concentration. The current sped up as they passed over a rise, and Dahl stumbled, catching himself on the bare rock, and he jerked against the rope at his back. From the corner of his eye, he could see her speaking, asking if he was all right, but he turned back to the path instead. He was fine, of course.

There was no hint of how much time had passed as far from the sun as they were, and Dahl began to worry. The spell would protect them from the water for only an hour—and there was no sign of any break in the ancient passageway. Only the same, close, endless walls. The same unbroken ceiling.

Another age passed—for all Dahl could be sure of they were traveling on accidental time. Did they know? Had he mentioned the time limit? He must have. But he couldn't recall.

He pulled on the rope that bound him to Maspero, but the sellsword didn't turn. Dahl tried to haul himself through the water, but Farideh weighed him back like a stubborn anchor.

Gods damn it. He should have been early into the watercourse, close enough to be able to make them turn back if need be. If only he hadn't delayed to make sure everyone took to the water properly. He dug his heels in to halt the procession—

The rope jerked at his waist once, and suddenly there was no tension from the front. In the darkness ahead he could not see Maspero, but the end of the rope danced in the current like a lure outlined in the glow of the sunrod.

He hardly had time to curse before the water suddenly surged over another rise pulling his feet out from under him and tossing him down a sluice so steep it broke his grip on the rocky walls and pulled him through the tunnel. Behind him the rope went taut and pulled Farideh along with him. The current snatched the sunrod from his hand.

All instinct, his limbs went wide, clutching at the faces of the watercourse, digging into the stone—but it was all smooth. Then there was a break in the surface of the ceiling, a gap of air where the stone had not worn as smooth and where light pierced the darkness. And a rope dangled down into the water.

There was no room to fail. He caught the rope and as the current tried to pull him away he planted both feet against the wall's edge, pulling himself up and into the air pocket. The rope still tied to his waist went taut as Farideh's weight pulled his feet from the wall, and threatened to break his grip on the rope.

Wrapping the rope once around his left arm, he dared let go and plunged his right hand back into the water. Farideh caught hold of his arm and Dahl shoved her up and out of the rushing water, to waiting hands, before hauling himself up and out of the hole beside the tiefling.

"Gods!" her sister cried, at Farideh but also at Dahl. "Are you all right? What happened? Maspero climbed out and you were just *gone*."

"Fine," Dahl said, avoiding the string of questions.

Farideh was still crouched on the ground, her arms shaking. "Thank you," she panted. "Gods, gods. Thank you."

Dahl looked back at the shaft and the swirling water below. "Yes. Well."

As odd as the water-breathing felt, coming back into the air was stranger—at once he was heavier and the air in his lungs so much thinner. And while the water had still rushed over his skin with definite wetness, the spell had kept everything—clothes, gear, leathers—bone-dry.

Almost everything. Beside him, Farideh squeezed a river from her hair, and Dahl bit back a curse—at least if the ritual had weaknesses, they were minor, but she'd surely point them out, wouldn't she?

"We have to do that again to leave," she said, "don't we?"

"If you'd stop fighting every step and breath, it's really not that bad," Dahl said. He straightened. "Some climbing gear for the last bit . . . Who in all the shattered planes bought that godsforsaken . . . rope." He trailed off, his attention fully taken by the cave around them.

The pale stone of the walls glittered wetly in the light of the sunrods, but the floor had been ground flat and smooth. A line of white marked the tool-chipped floor where the river beneath had once flooded nearly up to the threshold of the enormous doors that dominated the space.

Time had ravaged the first set of doors, the ones which marked the caverns' entrance. Water had hidden the second set, and damaged its seal. The third set of doors looked as if they would have brooked no such interference from the rest of the world. Taller than Dahl by twice over his own height, the massive entry depicted a figure of a man in chased metalwork, an elderly human with a staff and a long beard. His eyes were formed by deep green chunks of jade, and a fat garnet had been set in the pendant he wore around his neck. Draconic runes covered the field of the door, like the delicate claw marks of some erudite and frantic beast.

"This is it," Mira said. "This is it!" She pointed to the runes. "This says 'Tarchamus.' And this one 'Netheril.' " She glanced back at them. "We should take a moment. Get the rituals working, study the structure and check for any lingering spells. It's best to be sure—"

Maspero strode past her and slammed his shoulder into the door. The stone edifice shuddered and creaked open wide enough for Maspero to shove both hands into the gap and pry the door wide.

"Looks fine," he said, and he passed through the entry.

Mira went very still, watching Maspero vanish into the darkness beyond. She did not look back at the lot of them. Tam started toward her, frowning, but without so much as a glance, she squared her shoulders and passed into the cave after Maspero. Pernika followed.

Leaving Tam to pointedly not look at Dahl, Brin, or the twins.

"They are stranger," Havilar whispered, as they eased around the door after Tam, "than you and Mehen."

"Hush," Farideh said. "Everyone has arguments."

The doors covered an unfinished cave that angled down into the earth with no trace of the stream that ran so near to it. Tam and Mira and the mercenaries were nowhere to be seen, but their footfalls echoed up the path.

"What do you think it will look like?" Havilar whispered. "A pile of coins and swords?"

"He was a wizard," Farideh said. "I suspect it's more magical things."

"Arcanist," Dahl corrected.

"What's the good of that?" Havilar asked. "I thought the Spellplague broke all the magic from the olden days."

"It's . . . mendable," Dahl said, even though he was certain she wasn't speaking to him. "Some of it. A spell becomes a ritual, a magic item can be tapped for residuum. Sometimes they can be adjusted to fit the Weave as it stands. It just takes the right mind."

"And that's you?" Brin said. Dahl glowered at him.

"I didn't say that."

Havilar snorted. "If we've come all this way for a bunch of junk . . ." She trailed away as they came out of the tunnel, to the overlook where Maspero, Mira, and Tam stood, gazing out at the cavern that held the treasures of Tarchamus.

It could have held a dragon. It could have held ten dragons or even twenty. The dome of the cave sparkled with hundreds of magical lights that lit even the farthest corners. The floor—where it could be seen—had been laid with slabs of limestone, polished smooth, and carved columns held the space between.

And rolling away in wave after wave was a sea of bookshelves.

•:⌒:•

Tam followed his daughter down the stairway, unable to keep his gaze still. A library. Not a treasure hoard. Not a stash of weapons capable of unmaking the world. Not an open portal to another plane. Scrolls and books.

Scrolls and books that held gods knew what, he reminded himself. A weapon of ancient Netheril could mean the destruction of an entire kingdom. But any one of these books or scrolls could contain the information to craft a thousand weapons, a thousand spells—enough so that no one would have to decide which one kingdom to aim at.

"It has to date from before the fall," Dahl said, amazed. "It's . . . I've never seen so many books. This has to be all the knowledge of ancient Netheril."

Tam regarded him solemnly. "Even what Shade has lost track of."

"How long do you think we have before we're tracked here?"

Ahead Mira moved down the path with a breathless wonder, touching the stonework of the shelves, the spines of the codices, her eyes on everything they could spy. The same decoration as the door was repeated in miniature on the ends of the shelves. "Not long enough," Tam answered. "Hours. Days. We won't be able to search it all before we're found."

"Pity it wasn't a weapon," Dahl said.

Tam agreed. A lost weapon could be assessed, dismantled, or dragged away. There was no hope of assessing every piece of writing here, let alone taking it away. What secrets and wonders of that lost world might be waiting in those shadowy shelves?

"I found something!" Havilar called from off to his right, off the path and into the stacks.

Farideh shouted a curse. Tam turned to grab her arm with his unwounded hand as she sprinted toward her sister's voice, heedless of the possible danger. He missed.

"Damn it. Everyone stay here," he ordered and ran after the twins, reaching for the holy symbol he wore pinned to his shoulder, his wounded arm cradled to his chest. He hadn't said to stay to the path—he shouldn't have had to say it.

At the end of the aisle in a small room carved into the wall of the cave stood a lectern shaped like a stooped gnome, holding up an open book. Havilar picked up the tome. "The runes are all shifty just like—" She broke off, her eyes squeezed shut as if she were flinching from the text.

"Havilar!" Farideh cried. "*Karshoj*! Put it down!"

Havilar started coughing, and she dropped the book to the ground, just as her sister reached her and grabbed hold of her shoulders. "Havi? Havi?"

Havilar swatted her away. "It's just dusty."

*Tuor aripotvych*, a voice spoke in Tam's thoughts. *Darastrix wux thric?* Both twins froze and stared down at the book. *Vivex axun?*

"*Ak—Akison,*" Farideh said.

Tam took hold of his holy symbol, edging toward the lectern. "Fari," he said quietly, "what's it saying?"

She looked up at him puzzled. "It wants to be sure we're not dragons."

"What does?" Mira said from behind him. She stepped out of the shadows, watching the tome. "Blessed Watching Gods. Has anyone touched it?"

"You need to stay back," Tam told her. "Everyone needs to stay back until we know—"

*That isn't necessary,* a disembodied voice, aged and sharp, rang in Tam's thoughts. *I don't bite. You must pardon my confusion. I heard the girl's shouts and assumed . . . but of course Draconic isn't the proper tongue.*

Mira kneeled and gingerly touched the very edge of a page with gloved fingers. "I think I have something for you." She pulled the atlas from her haversack, and the page from the atlas. The hum intensified.

*Oh my,* the voice said. *Yes. It's been . . . My goodness, it's been longer than I'm sure of.* It chuckled, sounding almost uncomfortable. *It makes me sound a bit mad, doesn't it? Would you mind? It belongs in the end.*

Mira flipped to the last few pages, handling the rest with evident care. Where the ragged edge of the missing parchment showed itself, she laid the wildly shifting page in place. A sizzling green light etched its way up the tear, and when it faded the parchment was whole and the inks settled into neat lines of Draconic letters.

The voice sighed. *I'd forgotten how I'd missed that. You have my thanks. They call me the Book—unimaginative, I know. They always lacked in that area. But you'll find, I hope, that I've earned the moniker. I contain the knowledge of the ages, and what I do not contain, I can direct you to in the shelves.*

"What is this place?" Tam asked.

*You don't know? I thought surely . . . This is the fabled library of Tarchamus the Unyielding. Here lie the secrets of the greatest arcanist of Netheril, for those worthy of them.*

"Think your man's got some competition for that title," Maspero said.

The voice chuckled, and Tam had the impression of an older man, indulging the foolish insistence of youth. *Many would claim to be such.*

"Not so many now," Tam said. "Old Netheril has fallen—"

*Yes, yes. Many ages ago now, with only Shade returned from where it fled. And risen again, in the wake of the goddess's death?* The Book chuckled again. *"Knowledge of the ages" is a trite saying, but not entirely untrue. Events so great as*—the voice hesitated for the barest moment—*the Spellplague, reach even down to this depth. And you are not the first to come to Tarchamus's hoard.*

"How many?" Mira asked. "What did they take?"

*Nothing but knowledge. And in one case,* the Book added, dryly, *my page.*

"What about the spellbooks?" Mira asked. "Where are they?"

*Oh,* it said, *here and there. The library is arranged chronologically and by topic. If you know the specific spell, I might be able to find it.*

"The one which creates the volcano."

The Book was silent a moment. *I'm sure I don't know what you mean.*

This was too much—Tam brushed past Mira and scooped the book up in one hand to set it back on the pedestal. It was heavier than it looked, and in his weaker hand it felt as if it might snap his wrist off . . .

And then suddenly it felt lighter, and his throat itched fiercely with the dust. He cleared it and set the book back on the pedestal, flexing the remains of the cramp from his hand.

"Extraordinary," Mira murmured.

Maspero snorted. "Plenty of dumb objects out there with a voice."

She shook her head. "Not so many with a whole library memorized. Not so many that can claim to be aware of the world beyond." She cast another glance at the Book, as if all she wanted was to sit and study it, then dropped her heavy pack and yanked the mouth open. "Everyone who can, cast your ritual, get your eyes used to Loross, and start taking notes. Our goal is Tarchamus's spellbooks, or those of his contemporaries." She took out a stack of slates and started handing them out. "But I want to know what you find and where you find it in the searching."

"That will take ages," Tam said. "Lifetimes. We can't possibly make that much of a dent in it before the Netherese catch up. We ought to seal it properly and—"

"There is no sealing it properly," she said, pressing a slate into his hands. "Not with Adolican Rhand and whatever might Shade has put behind him at our backs." She wet her lips. "If he knows enough to have counted those pieces precious, he knows well enough who Tarchamus was."

"We can't be sure—"

"He knows," Farideh said, and Tam was surprised to remember there were six others standing around, listening to him and Mira. The tiefling shifted. "He mentioned. Before. When he was . . . bragging. He said Tarchamus had blended planar magic with the Weave to destroy a rival."

Tam's heart sank. "Then you think he wants the same spells."

"What else?" Mira asked. "Do you think Shade would put agents into play for old ledgers and collections of folktales? I would give *lifetimes*," she said more quietly, "to study this place properly. To find the sorts of secrets an arcanist would hide away—secrets of the gods, the planes, his contemporaries, even the mundane records of Ancient Netheril. The location of the ruins of Tenish, I would give my left hand for. But you are absolutely right: we don't have time for that now. So we scour the place for the spellbooks, and we don't come back without reinforcements. Agreed?"

No, Tam thought. We should leave now. This moment. But everything she said made sense. If he refused—

*Beg pardon,* the Book interrupted, *but did you say that there are Netherese after you?*

Tam and Mira exchanged a glance. "I think you misheard," Tam said.

*Oh, don't worry,* the Book said. *Tarchamus had no love left for Netheril—you'll not find her secret allies here. There are wards protecting the library from magical intrusion to keep Netheril's arcanists at bay. And, as you've seen, this place is difficult to discover, and more difficult to reach. Consider it a test. One you passed; one few others will.* The Book chuckled to itself. *And you have me, to give you the lay of the land—so to speak—and to point out the traps.*

"Why should a library have traps?" Tam said. Mira frowned.

*Tarchamus was very protective of his knowledge, as you can well imagine. Worry not—I know all of them, and most are merely illusions meant to frighten and harry the weak-willed from this place. I'm sure none of you are such cowards.*

"Surely," Tam murmured. He took Mira by the sleeve and pulled her aside. "This doesn't sit right. None of it."

"It's the lost library of a mad arcanist," she said lightly. She looked out into the library beyond, a faint smile on her lips. "It shouldn't sit right."

"Mira." He turned her away from the rows of bookshelves. "We are far, far from support and there are Netherese agents following us. We don't have time to search. We need to seal this place and get out."

She stepped back, out of easy reach. "I'm not one of your Harpers."

"Perhaps not. But four of these people answer to me—"

"Do they?" she said. "It seemed before you weren't all that keen on having subordinates. Don't like people weighing you down?"

Tam bit his tongue—better not to start an argument with her when she was in a mood like this. "Let me get word to Everlund and Waterdeep then," he said. "And we are out in three days—no more. There's nothing here worth dying for."

"Are you certain?" Mira said. "Perhaps Tarchamus preserved some half-remembered relic of Selûne. Some secret weakness of Shar. We have no idea what is hidden in those books." She handed him a stylus. "Not until we start looking."

*You are subjecting them all to danger,* he thought. Indulging Mira too far could mean the deaths of all of them—surely she knew. Surely he wasn't the one who had to stop things. He watched as Mira gathered the half of them with no eye for Loross, directing them to set up camp at the library's center. She had every one of their attentions.

Beside him, Farideh stared out at the library, chewing her lower lip in a distracted fashion. As tempted as he was to tell her to ignore Mira and go rest, he bit his tongue. There was no amount of resting that would undo the fact that something terrible had very nearly happened on his watch. He wondered whether it would compound the matter to tell Mehen what had happened, or to leave it secret and let Farideh have her privacy.

"Rhand won't find us," Tam said.

"I hope not." Farideh looked over at him. "Do you wonder," she asked, "who was here before us? And what knowledge they took?" Her voice became softer, "Why none of you have heard of this place before now?"

The library stretched off into the distance, a labyrinth of shadows and lost knowledge, of secrets, good and evil.

# CHAPTER ELEVEN

*The Lost Library of Tarchamus*

FARIDEH JERKED OUT OF SLEEP TO THE COOL AIR OF THE CAVERN-library, her skin chill and damp with sweat. Panting, she surveyed the little courtyard in which they'd established their camp—the circle of shelves, the stillness of the library, not a hellwasp or a devil or a ruined wall to be seen.

Only Dahl, perched on a camp stool, holding a mug of something hot and watching her with one raised brow. His gray eyes were softly bloodshot, as if he'd been up most of the night as well.

"Sleep well?" he asked dryly.

Farideh didn't answer, but straightened her clothes and rebuckled her jacks. Her head ached and her hands were shaking, and she did not have the reserves to deal with Dahl's surly mood. Not when her brain still trembled with the images of Lorcan being torn apart and Havilar laughing over it.

She pressed her hands to her eyes. Perhaps Tam was right. Perhaps Rhand's drugs were still undoing her.

"What kept you up?" she asked, standing and straightening her bedroll.

"Nothing," he said. "It seemed better to start work than to sleep." He sipped from his mug. "Mira and I stayed up, searching the shelves. Don't," he said, when Farideh smiled at the admission. "I am not being pulled into you and your sister's silly gossip."

"You are full of so much more silly gossip than either of us," Farideh said. Havilar might have teased him, but Dahl was the one sorting out her sister's imaginary love life for his own amusement.

He scowled at her. "We're marking the shelves we've searched with chalk to keep a better record. Pull a book every few levels to get an idea of what's shelved along that row. Write that down on the slate and put a cross on the end so no one else comes back to search it."

"I kept a slate fine yesterday," she reminded him. She hesitated. "Are you ever going to show me the rest of those rituals?" she asked. "You owe me seven more. And you said you'd show me the protective circle."

Dahl sipped from his mug. "We haven't got time."

She waited, but he said nothing else. "Convenient." She scooped up a slate and stub of chalk before she said anything she would later regret.

Only a few of the nearest shelves had been marked with quick slashes of white. Farideh found an unmarked line and pulled several texts—all very old scrolls to do with military orders that were at least interesting, but not terribly applicable to the world they lived in now—and added her own mark before moving down a row. The scrolls and tomes stretched off into the darkness.

It would take ages to find Mira's spellbooks, no doubt. And ages more to stumble on the planar magic that she did not know the name or the shape of that might make a path for Lorcan.

*You have to figure this out,* she thought. *He's going to* die *if you don't figure this out.*

Perhaps she should tell someone else what she was looking for . . .

"Well met." Farideh started at the sudden voice. Havilar came around the corner to stand beside her.

*"Karshoj,"* Farideh swore. "Don't sneak up on me like that."

"Was I sneaking?" Havilar said sweetly.

Farideh scowled at her. *"Yes."*

"Have you looked at that book I found yet?" she asked. "It's *amazing.*"

"I was *there,*" Farideh said. "I saw it just like everyone—"

"You should be reading it. Everyone should be."

"Why?" Farideh said sharply. "Is it going to tell me dragons' toenails are made of gold or hydras sprout from heads or some other nonsense?"

Havilar's brow furrowed and Farideh let her tirade die. She rubbed her face. "I'm sorry. I'm just . . . I haven't been sleeping well, you know? I didn't mean it. Honestly. I'm sure the book's plenty interesting, I just haven't done any sections."

To her surprise, Havilar only shook her head, as if Farideh were being silly. "I think it does know everything," she said. "I'll bet it knows how to make you sleep. You should ask it."

Farideh waited for Havilar to lash out at her, but she just stood there, giving her sister the same, almost puzzled, look. As if Farideh were the one acting strange.

"Maybe you need some rest too," Farideh said. She frowned. "Havi, where's your glaive?"

Havilar shook her head again. "In the camp. Where else? You should see what the Book says about your problem, anyway." She turned and slipped back in between the shelves, no doubt to seek out more traps.

*Karshoj*, Farideh swore to herself. She hoped Havilar wasn't acting strange over her fight with Brin. Because gods knew how that was bound to shake out. If she'd just been a little more careful and not . . .

Farideh rolled her shoulders against the knot in the middle of her back. Calm, she told herself. Calm. Havi's keeping busy. She's rooting out traps. She's reading that book. Farideh reached for a scroll . . .

The Book. It had said it knew the library. That it could find spells if you asked for specifics. She closed her hand into a fist. She'd only be able to read Loross a few more hours—if that; there was no hope of telling time down beneath the earth. She'd have to stop and recast the ritual anyway.

No one else was standing in the alcove where they'd left the Book, and Farideh stood just at the edge of the shelves considering it. There was a good reason, she was sure, that everyone was avoiding it but Havilar. She thought of the way the Book hadn't known where the spell was that Mira mentioned, the thing that Rhand wanted. *Perhaps it's just not that clever*, she thought.

*Can I help you, dear girl?* the Book spoke. Farideh moved closer, watching the pages. Someone—Havilar, no doubt—had left it open on the lectern again, and the pages crawled with spell-enhanced lines of Draconic written so neatly they might have been printed.

"I think . . . perhaps," she said. "I don't want to be a bother."

*Nonsense,* the voice said, sounding more like a pleasant old man than anything else. *Do you see anyone else bothering me? That callous woman earlier made it sound as if you were in a hurry. As if you had agents of a floating city on your heels. And yet no one's here asking for my help.*

Because you didn't know the spell we need, Farideh thought. "I need to find a ritual. Where would I find such books?"

*Ritual . . . ritual . . .* the Book mused. *Ah—do you mean the spells of the new era? The magic cast to rebind the Weave?*

"Yes?" That certainly sounded right. Like something Dahl would utter.

*Fascinating study. Alas, that variety of magic is the work of more modern minds. We did not need such measures before the Blue Fire.* Its voice grew wistful. *Before, the Weave of magic was like a tamed beast, if you had the right sort of mind, the right sort of sight. No need to tie together errant wildlings of power—just let your spells work with the natural flow of Mystryl.*

"Of course," Farideh said, not sure about half of its assertions and not wanting to ask. Her stomach twisted, remembering Lorcan's bloody, empty sockets. No rituals in the library. None but Dahl's and Tam's.

*Is there something in* particular *you need?* the Book asked. *Magic has certainly changed, but it's always possible to adapt, to reinvent. Perhaps the spell you require already exists in another form?*

"Perhaps," Farideh said. The runes were shivering, as if they might swirl into something else, the way the page alone had. "I need to summon someone from another plane," she said, leaving the book on the plinth.

*Someone willing?* the Book asked. *Or someone . . . coerced?*

Farideh hesitated. "Yes, willing. I mean, I believe so."

*Well there's nothing simpler!* the Book said. *There are half a dozen spells to do just that, and Netheril mastered the art of interplanar travel very long ago. It would help,* the Book went on, *if I knew where your someone needed to be gathered from.*

Farideh hesitated again and looked around to make certain no one was near. "The sixth layer of the Hells."

*Your friend is in Baator?* The Book sounded genuinely surprised. *In the domain of Moloch?*

She frowned. That didn't sound right—Lorcan answered to a mistress, an archdevil called Glasya—but whether the Book was wrong or the Book was remembering something long ago, she couldn't have said. Did archdevils have successors? "Things," she said, "may have changed somewhat."

The Book harrumphed. *Even evil is inconstant. Nevertheless—you should start with the details of the planes and the fabric between. The scrolls you need are in an antechamber on the western side of the library.*

"There are other chambers?"

*Something your leader should like to know, eh? Let her come and ask then.* It chuckled once more. *Follow the outer ring of the shelves until you find a large column with a rune on it. Now that rune locks the antechamber, so before you so much as touch the door, you need to disarm it. Eradicate the mark and that should break the spell. The door is a score of paces beyond, between the maps of the Eastern kingdoms and the star charts.*

"Thank you," Farideh said.

*Not at all,* the Book said. *Come back when you've found your information and we'll see about finding you the right sort of spell.*

Farideh followed the Book's directions along the curved path that traced the library's outer wall. The shelves along it stretched to twice her height and were laden with thick, leather-bound tomes. The sounds of the others echoed back across the dim cave, but no one was working here. She was completely alone.

She stopped and drew a deep breath, trying to still her thoughts to match the quiet. How long had it been since she'd been truly alone? No Havilar asking her what she was thinking. No Lorcan telling her what to think. Not even the anonymous bustle of Waterdeep.

It was strangely unnerving. She wondered if the arcanist had enjoyed the solitude.

The columns along the outer edge were wide enough to wrap her arms around and polished to a sheen. Farideh kept her eyes high, studying the veins and grains of the stone, searching for anything that might have been a rune. She needn't, it turned out, have looked so hard.

Six columns from the Book, a rune scarred the stone high above her head, a deep black mark shivering with a greenish light that echoed the pulse of the swirling lights and swarmed in the space between the shelves and the ceiling. Eradicate the mark, she thought. She took the rod from its pocket.

*"Adaestuo."* The ball of jagged violet light crashed into the column almost as soon as it came into being, just beyond her outstretched arm. The spell and the rune combined in a blinding burst of light, a pop, and a shower of stone dust.

When the flare of the blast had faded and her eyes had adjusted, she could see the polished exterior of the column had been destroyed, blasted into powder. The powers of the Hells that had surged up through her when casting slipped back into their places, trailing down her nerves like a lover's fingers.

She rolled her shoulders, trying to shake the sensation. The bones of her neck popped past each other.

Then . . . more popping. Like a campfire.

She turned and saw the camp, the full moon casting shadows with the broken remnants of ancient walls. The campfire tossing them back. Akanûl, she thought. Scarcely a tenday out of Arush Vayem—the village she'd grown up in, the village that had cast her aside when she took the pact. They had come down far enough from the mountains that winter had all but lost its teeth, and only the night air had a bite to it. The grass and scorched stonework beyond glittered with frost.

She blinked and Lorcan's portal opened, in the heart of the campfire. Whether because of the noise, the smell of burning brimstone, or the fluctuation in the air as one plane intruded on the next, she heard Mehen stir as the devil stepped toward her.

"You shouldn't be here," she blurted, dimly noting that she said it because she *had* said it that winter night. "He'll wake."

Lorcan didn't stop, but passed her by and so she followed between buildings to a roughly flat field that had once been a road. "First it's that I can't come around while he can see me," he said. "Now it's not while he might wake. Honestly, darling, I'm going to have to insist you give me more options. Or give yourself a little more space."

"You should stay away," she said.

He moved around her, and she held her breath waiting for the hand that slipped around her waist, over her hip. It didn't come. He smiled with that wicked way he had. "You should give yourself a little more space."

She frowned. That didn't sound like him. "Do you want me to show you what I've done?"

"I want you to . . ." It was as if her mind turned over, as if other thoughts spilled into this one, and suddenly the air was Neverwinter's all over again, all humid and threatening storms. "Run, darling," Lorcan said, urgent and fearful. "Run fast and run far."

She blinked hard. "What?"

Lorcan crouched a distance away and scratched a rune into the layer of frost and dead moss: a sinuous thing of smoothly angling lines that seemed to suggest a much more complex symbol, as if there were lines to it that Farideh couldn't perceive.

"You still think like a soldier," he said, coming to stand beside her. "Remember, darling." And his voice shifted, turning into Tam's. "There's nothing here worth dying for."

Farideh jumped away from him, and once more she was in the lost library, alone and standing in a dusting of powdered stone. Her footsteps alone marred the dust—she'd walked twenty feet, back the way she'd come.

She pressed the heels of her hands to her eyes and cursed. She'd been so sure the poison had passed, but to see things this mad . . . If she told Tam, he'd be after her to lie down and give up the pact for the rest of her days. And then what would become of Lorcan?

Lorcan . . . She would have been embarrassed to admit just how real the hallucination had seemed. How much she had been waiting for his hand on her wrist, his arm around her waist, his breath on her neck . . .

She blinked up at the ceiling, as if she were waking from a second dream, and cursed under her breath. It was the spell she was remembering, she told herself firmly. The echo of the dream. Everything else was just her being silly. She was through with that. They were . . . comrades. And she owed Lorcan her life. Get the scrolls, she thought, then go and lie down.

She found the door to the antechamber easily enough, noting the maps and charts for Mira's sake, as she pressed the smooth stone inward. The hinges moved silently, admitting her to a room packed with scrolls.

"*Karshoj,*" she swore. She could be hours searching all of it. She pulled a scroll from near the door and unrolled it—something about a city made of brass. She pulled one a few feet farther in—details about the fauna in a plane of ice. She kept on, pulling scrolls from different shelves, looking for anything that might hint at a way to link to the Nine Hells. There were notes on planes that housed gods and planes full of nothing at all; worlds of flame and stone and metal; a dimension where nothing stayed on the ground and another that could be sailed to by launching a ship across the stars. Planes above and below and just to one side of Toril.

The next scroll she pulled was rolled as thin and tight as a reed. Open it stretched only the length of her arm. But there, in vibrant shades of red and violet and stark black was a map of the Hells, each layer spiraling down into a smaller, more concentrated realm. *Avernus, the Last Outpost. Dis, the Iron City. Minauros, the Endless Bog. Phlegethos, the Heart of Flames. Stygia, the Frozen Wastes.*

*Malbolge,* the spidery writing read, two-thirds of the way down. *The Tyranny of Turmoil. Be cautious and do not . . .*

The runes dissolved into gibberish before her eyes, and Farideh cursed and nearly crushed the parchment in her frustration. The ritual had run out. She'd have to go back to the camp to recast it.

"Think like a soldier," she murmured, recalling Lorcan's words. "Take what you might need and sort it out later."

There were at least a score of scrolls in the same niche as the map had come from. She pulled every one out and scanned the foreign marks for familiar signs—eleven bore the cluster of runes that seemed to mean Malbolge. She gathered these in her arms and left the rest in a tidy pile where she could find them later.

It was a start, she thought, making her way back to the camp at the center of the library. She knew better than to hope the arcanist's notes were less confusing than a ritual scroll like the one Havilar had found. But it was a start—a better start than she'd had in the last month—and she dared to hope she'd found the solution.

A month . . . and her spells still worked. She wouldn't pretend she understood the ways of the Hells, but having seen Lorcan's monstrous sisters at battle, it seemed strange she might still have a chance to save him. If someone had asked her before Lorcan had vanished, she would have said the erinyes would surely have slaughtered anyone they took prisoner.

She remembered watching one slice a man in half, so quick he had time to grasp for his legs, as if he might pull them back on like trousers—before Lorcan turned her face away.

Maybe he *is* dead, she thought. Or maybe someone else has already rescued him. She held the scrolls closer. Maybe he'd decided to be done with her.

Farideh took a deep breath and pressed on. She wouldn't know until she tried, and if she was wrong, at least she would know. She owed him that much. And if he was free, well, he would have found her, and said so. Wouldn't he?

She walked more quickly, as if she could outpace the worries that wouldn't stay down.

As she passed an open aisle, she glimpsed her sister. Havilar sat on the floor beside a hole left by the slab of polished limestone she'd somehow levered out of place. In its absence, the workings of the pressure trap were laid out like a strange skeleton. She disconnected one of the pieces, a copper spring made verdigrisy with age.

"Hey," she called as she drew nearer. Havilar looked up at her. "I . . . talked, I suppose, to the Book."

"Which book?"

Farideh frowned. "The . . . talking one?"

Havilar tilted her head. "Did you? Was it more interesting than before?"

"I suppose," Farideh said. "It's odd talking to a thing, you know?"

"I guess. Aren't you supposed to be reading the scrolls and stuff though? I thought Mira said to forget the weird book for now." She held up the spring. "Isn't this odd? It's as if there's air flowing under the floor."

Farideh shook her head and let it go. "How many have you dismantled?"

"Three," she said. "This one nearly got me." She pointed with her chin at the nearby shelf, now plastered with a sticky ooze. "Mira's going to have a fit, isn't she?"

"She'll understand," Farideh said. "How many other traps are there?"

Havilar shrugged. "I found two others that are magical. I'm not fussing with those. I think there's something over on the east side. There's a big rune on the wall there."

"Didn't the Book tell you where they were?"

"No," Havilar said, prying one of the levers from the mechanism. "Why should it?"

Farideh did not press and made her excuses. Given the world of questions Havilar might have asked the Book, she supposed as she wound through the maze of shelves, one that would give her less to do to distract her from worrying about Mehen or Brin, or maybe even Farideh probably wouldn't rank high . . .

Farideh stopped in the middle of the shelves, the hairs on her neck on end and sure as she'd ever been that someone was watching her. "Well met?" she called, looking back the way she'd come. "Is someone there?" Only quiet.

Havi, sneaking around again, she told herself, her eyes locked on the darkness. Mira, being quiet. Maspero, creeping around like Mehen does.

There was a thickness to the air. A strange quality she almost recognized—as if something were about to be there. As if something had just left.

"Is someone—"

A hand fell on her shoulder, and she spun, scattering scrolls across the aisle.

.:⌒:.

Tam flexed his hand and winced. It had taken Brin several more tries, and though the skin was healed over, and the bones were all set, it was stiff and aching. Not worth wasting a healing on, he thought, but it annoyed him nonetheless. He eased himself to the ground and pulled down another batch of books.

In the sepulchral silence of the library, the sounds of the others echoed and refused to settle into any clear location. The repeated *shush* of Mira pulling book after book, one at a time past its fellows, might have been several rows ahead or on the other end of the cavern. The occasional shuffle and *thud* of Maspero carting the texts she set aside to the camp in the center of the library might have come from beside him or farther on. The wooden clatter of Havilar and her glaive setting off one of the traps might be anywhere. The sound of Dahl and Farideh sniping at each other should have been nowhere.

He sighed. Gods, he did not want to play caretaker. Not for the first time he cursed Mehen, cursed the Fisher, and then cursed himself for not refusing the two of them.

They don't *need* a caretaker, he reminded himself, opening one of the books. You don't *need* to stop Farideh and Dahl from arguing or stop Havi running around.

Except he did—they were all his responsibility in the end, and if he couldn't keep them alive and unharmed and watching out for one another, they might all be doomed. He rubbed the beginnings of a headache from his forehead. They shouldn't have come—*he* shouldn't have come. Only the moon above knew what the Fisher was letting happen out in the world. He set the book, a collection of folktales from Eaerlann, back on the shelf.

He wished he'd been able to detect the spellbooks from among the more mundane texts, but the magic of the library seemed to blur and bounce his senses every which way. He wished he'd insisted on leaving the cavern, on being out in the open one time more before they settled into this all-but-futile task. He'd have liked to perform the rites to have a moment to himself and Selûne before being buried under the ground.

Mira had a point, he reminded himself. More important, perhaps, he hadn't wanted to take that point, that authority away from her. Something was wrong—she had always been unflappable, reserved even. And all he knew to do was let her have the room she insisted on—to step back so she didn't need to push.

But this time, he thought, returning the next two tomes to their spots, it didn't seem to be doing the trick. More than anything he wished he could sit her down and get her to tell him what was going on. Good or ill. He was still her father after all.

The sendings to Everlund and Waterdeep hadn't worked. The components had lain there, unspent as the ritual failed. The wards, Mira reminded him. The Book had mentioned them. They keep outside eyes from seeing in, so wouldn't they stop messages from getting out? Perhaps—there was no telling, as old as this place was, as many changes to the nature of magic as it had seen. He tried again, just past the doors, and while the ritual cast, he got no answers. There was no way to be sure where the Shadovar, the Zhentarim, or even Mehen were.

"Shepherd," a voice, an old voice from the recesses of his memory, said, "what do you think you're doing?"

Tam blinked. The book was gone. His hands rested on the marble altar of Selûne he'd used for so many years, in the chapel at the center of Viridi's complex. Above, the leagues of stone had vanished, replaced by a clear and cloudless night sky.

He reached for his chain as he looked back over his shoulder—the shelves, the library, and the sounds of his team were gone. It was the chapel, as surely as it was Viridi, stern-faced and richly robed, standing there beside the stone table they used for resurrections, leaning on a cane.

Tam remembered this. It was two months before she'd died, her lungs failing her at last. Only Tam had known her time was short, and she'd caught him praying for the power to heal her.

He swallowed. "Let me do this. Let me *try*, at least."

Viridi didn't budge. "It's effort wasted. You know that. My time is what it is." She seemed to vanish, to skip across the room when he blinked. She was sitting behind the resurrection table, as if it were a desk. "Your people say you're difficult to work with, you know?"

"It's not that, I—" he started, then he stopped, puzzled. "I don't have people. I work alone. I always have."

"You are never alone," Viridi said. "You're a link in a chain, a knot in a silk rug. If you leave now . . . your people will owe you quite a few favors. Even if they don't know it."

"Stop talking about my 'people,' " Tam said. Stop talking at all, he thought. She didn't sound right. She didn't sound like Viridi. "I don't have people. I work alone."

"We're on the same side," she chided, standing again and moving. Moving toward him.

Tam shook his head. They'd had this conversation before . . . but it had been different, as if the words were out of order, landing in a pattern that wasn't from the spymaster's tongue. He looked down at his hands, at the thick veins and thicker knuckles. He'd been younger too, when they'd spoken last. She took a step toward him, and he remembered.

"You're dead," he said to Viridi. She gave him that patient look she'd worn so often, the one that said he was missing something, and she wasn't about to tell him what. He started to stand, but his knee seized, forcing him back down.

Viridi leaned down the shadows settling into the hollows of her eyes and the sudden collapse of her cheeks. The dead spymaster spoke and he could have sworn it was his own voice speaking back to him: "There's nothing here worth dying for."

Tam fell backward onto the stone floor of the library, and the chapel, Viridi, and moon above were gone. He blinked at the shelves surrounding him, his pulse still pounding. There was no sign of Viridi. There was no sign of what had just happened to him.

"Well met," Brin said, coming around the corner. "Do you think you could recast—" He stopped and his eyes traced the path of Tam's gaze. "Is everything all right?"

"Fine," Tam snapped.

"You look like you've seen a ghost," Brin said.

You haven't, Tam told himself. Viridi is buried in Erlkazar, hundreds and hundreds of miles away. You've had her in your thoughts is all. That and not enough sleep. You're overtired and overworked. It's why you were supposed to rest, remember?

"I just . . . ," Tam said, standing. "I'm going to go lie down a spell. Excuse me." He pushed past Brin, heading off toward the camp, the conversation with the illusory spymaster rattling in his thoughts. *You're a link in a chain. If you leave now . . . your people will owe you quite a few favors. There's nothing here worth dying for.*

Havilar slipped back into the presence of the Book. She glanced around, to be sure she was alone, before edging up to the Book once more. Picking it up initially had been completely boring—but after Farideh admitted to talking with it as if it were *something important*...

She scooped up the tome in both hands, perhaps a bit too eagerly, as the puff of dust hit her again and made her cough. It wasn't as heavy as it looked, and she turned so that she could look at it and watch the aisle to the camp in case someone sneaked up on her.

"You're supposed to know everything?" she asked.

*Not everything*, the Book said. *But plenty.*

Havilar eyed the open pages and the shifting inks. "What's the best way to counter an attack that comes from both the left and the right side?"

*Depends on the weaponry.*

"Axes," she said, after a moment. "And you have a glaive."

*I'm afraid I would have nothing at all*, the Book said with a chuckle. *But it seems that the Liquid Blades form would do best in those circumstances. Get both attackers to one side, and likely trip one into the other if you move correctly.*

Havilar frowned. "Tell me what a nentyarch is."

*A ruler of frozen Narfell*, the Book said. *Demon-binders. Are you interested in demon-binding? Nar history?*

"No." She stayed silent for a long time, considering the Book in her hands, her tail slashing over the floor behind her.

"What does it mean," Havilar finally asked, "when you're fond of a boy and you think he's fond of you—he *acts* fond of you, anyway—and then he doesn't tell you that he's secretly a prince and then he starts acting like he's fond of you half the time and not so fond the rest?"

The quiet stretched taut, hanging after Havilar's question like a rope with too much spring.

*I beg your pardon?* the Book said.

"What," Havilar said a bit louder, "does it *mean* when you're fond of a boy and he acts fond of you, but he doesn't tell you he's a secret prince of Cormyr, and when you find out, he starts acting confusing?"

*You can ask me anything,* the Book said, *and that's what you choose?*

"Then do you know?"

*Let us say it is not in my purview.*

Havilar all but tossed the book back on the pedestal. "Rubbish," she muttered and stalked away, into the shadows of the library's shelves, leaving the Book to ponder what exactly had just happened.

The Book—and Pernika, who stood watching from the shadows with a sharp smile and a sharper knife.

# CHAPTER TWELVE

*Malbolge, the Hells*

LORCAN SAT CROSS-LEGGED ON THE BONE-TILED FLOOR, WATCHING HIS Phrenike heir attempt to summon a book imp and trying to quell the tic he'd developed under one eye. He twirled the leather scourge pendant between his fingers, back and forth, and tried once more to get that idiot tiefling's attention. The Phrenike heir shook his head at the summons, as if trying to dislodge an unpleasant thought.

Bastard, Lorcan thought. Not for the first time, he wished he'd worked the same spells on all his warlocks that he had on Farideh. At least Farideh *noticed* when he called. He reached for the mirror. And stopped.

If you call her, he thought, Sairché wins and Glasya will have no problems with her killing you. Gods be damned, there had to be a way out of this.

He waved a hand over the mirror's surface and called up another warlock's image. The heir of Titus Graybeard was probably among the least valuable of his warlocks, not merely because of her ancestor's potency, but also because she was not particularly adept at the pact. He called her as well, watched as she lifted her head and looked around, and watched as she retreated into ever more private environs, waiting for Lorcan to appear. He gritted his teeth. Stupid cow—*clearly* he needed help.

He was painfully aware that he had no plan but this. If he couldn't get a warlock to call him back to Toril, he would have to face Sairché again. And likely soon. He'd started ranking the secrets he held, the only currency he had with which to stall his sister. She wanted Farideh, so what could he tell her that would make her think she could get the tiefling's pact? What would keep her busy and keep Farideh safe, but more importantly, keep him safe?

Shit and ashes, he thought, I hate the whole Lords-blasted hierarchy.

Lorcan had turned the mirror's focus to a third warlock when he heard the door open. His pulsed jumped—too soon.

"Have you come to gloat some more?" he asked without looking up. "Or are you finally going to kill me?"

"Oh gloat. For now," Sairché said. He let the mirror go dark, so that it reflected his sister in her shining, false armor, standing in the doorway, flanked again by Bibracte and Noreia.

And holding a terrified-looking Farideh. She shoved the tiefling into the room, tumbling her to the ground.

He had not been locked away from the viciousness of the hierarchy so long that he couldn't stop himself from reacting—the curse that he would have liked to shout bitten back, the urge to leap forward and catch her tossed aside. He checked himself and came to his feet with a cool expression—it did none of them any good to let Sairché think the warlock mattered too much. "I see you didn't need the mirror."

"Nor do I need you," Sairché said, her chin high.

He smirked, even though his blood was suddenly full of rage worthy of his mother's kind. Kill her, it said. Dash her head against the floor.

"Is that so? Nothing you've forgotten?" Farideh scrambled to her feet and came to stand near him, watching Sairché and the erinyes in horror.

Sairché chuckled. "Lords, you do act foolish when your options are spent," she said. "Say your good-byes, Lorcan. Make them count—I don't expect she'll be seeing much of you at all." She turned on her heel and let the door seal shut behind her.

"Shit and *ashes*!" he burst out, once the door was gone. He should have taken the chance and attacked Sairché. He should have at least *tried*. Now he was doomed.

And so was Farideh.

"How did she find you?" he demanded. He turned and startled to find her standing just behind him, all wide-eyed and fearful. He stepped around her.

"I don't know," Farideh said. "All of a sudden . . . there were just so many of them!" She covered her face with her hands.

"That is *why* you have a pact, you little fool," he said. "Tell me I at least leave the world a sister shorter."

"I did what I could."

"And Mehen? Havilar? That snot-nosed Brin? Did they just stand there and watch?" Sairché must have frightened her badly, he thought, when she merely shrugged and hugged her arms to herself, looking cold and lonesome, instead of lashing out at him for blaming her family. "You do understand I'm going to *die*," he tried again, "and you're not coming out of this much better."

"I'm sorry." She moved nearer to him, watching him intently. Tears sprang to her eyes. "Tell me what to do."

Lorcan stepped back from her reflexively, and caught himself. "Did Sairché do something to you?"

She bit her lip, as if she might break down, but her gaze didn't waver. "Bruises," she said. "Those . . . devils with her were rough." She swallowed. "What does she intend to do?"

"I don't know," Lorcan said. There was absolutely no reason to have dragged her to the Hells—a foolish move if he'd ever seen one. Sairché *must* be getting desperate to make such a wild gesture. "She's likely going to shift your pact."

"To another devil?" Farideh said. "Oh, gods, you can't let her!"

"Well you were happy to do it yourself before," he snapped.

"No," she said, tearful. "I'm sorry. Please. You must have a way to send me back?"

"You know I don't," he said. "The portal is gone."

"Please," she said, coming nearer. "I'll do *anything*."

He took another step backward. Something was very wrong here. Farideh was still staring into his eyes, still leaning awfully close. Still acting, he realized, as if she weren't in the Hells with her life in peril, but in some sort of ridiculous narrative . . .

*Those . . . devils with her were rough*, she'd said.

She knows, he remembered, what an erinyes is.

Oh, he thought as everything came together. To the pit of the Abyss with you, Sairché. She really did think he was an idiot.

Lorcan grabbed hold of Farideh's shoulder and shoved her backward, rocking her off balance. He snatched her arm as she threw it out for balance and turned her so it was wrenched behind her. He grabbed the other too and held her tight—he had to keep her hands off him.

"What are you doing?" Farideh cried, struggling to break free. Hells, but this one was strong. "Let *go*!"

Instead he slammed the succubus against the floor and held her there with all his weight, one hand on the back of her skull.

"The trouble," he panted, "with going off of Sairché's memories is that she's seen this girl twice. Too many details to get wrong."

"What do you—"

"She *knows* what a shitting erinyes is," he went on. "And you're about an inch too short and a shade too pale, and *entirely* too forward, so quit pretending I haven't figured you out!"

"Close enough to confuse *you*," the succubus said, calmer now. She wriggled under him. "Maybe you just like this version better."

At that moment, Lorcan figured he'd had enough succubi for an eternity, regardless of who they did or didn't look like. The shape-changing devils were renowned for their skills of seduction—a well-deserved reputation, he knew—but he'd also seen close up how dangerous they could be. Even one low-ranking enough to be compelled by Sairché.

"Are you watching this, Sairché?" he called.

"Please," the succubus said. "You underestimate how much she loathes you. She doesn't want to see you enjoy yourself."

"So that's her clever plan? Seduce the way around the warlock's binding spell out of me? Did you really think that would work?"

"No. She thought you'd show me the way back. But no one said I couldn't amuse myself." The succubus arched her back, and he fought to hold her down. "I can always do it the hard way."

He didn't doubt it—if he let her get too close, she'd have him charmed and his thoughts spread out like wares on a market blanket.

"You can't hold me forever," she said.

"I can do it until Sairché comes back and sees how you failed," he said, even though he wasn't sure that was true. If she changed form and sprouted wings again she'd knock him right off. "I'll make you a deal," he said, piecing together secrets and scenarios. This might work. "But you stay on the other side of the room, understand?"

"You're going to take *my* word?" she said. "How sweet."

**ERIN M. EVANS**

207

He moved off her, swiftly as he could, and was back, in front of the window, before she gained her feet. "You'll find I'm a lot more . . . accepting than my sisters. If you wanted to stay a demon, you had the whole Abyss to hide in."

The succubus didn't change her form and so Farideh stood there leering at him in a disconcerting way he didn't want to think about. "What's the deal?"

"What's Sairché want from you?"

"She wants the warlock. Nothing less."

"And I can't give her that." Not a lie—Farideh had to take Sairché's offer as much as he had to undo the pact. "But I can tell you why she can't find her."

The succubus shook her head, sending Farideh's dark locks shifting unnaturally in the dim light. "Not enough. She wants the key to undoing it."

Lorcan eyed her a long moment, weighing his options. "I can tell you how I managed it."

"And I can take that from you, easy as you please."

"Or," Lorcan said, "you can trade with me. Make no mistake, if you try to take it, I'll go down fighting, and even if you win, I'll make sure it's not easy."

The succubus smirked. She'd made the upper lip too thin, he thought, and the lower too full. "That's what they all say. What do you want to trade?"

"I want to know why she's stopped torturing me," he said, "and who her buyer is. And I want a message carried for me."

"Back to the warlock?"

"No," he said. He took a deep breath, hardly willing to ask it. But he needed a portal, and quickly. If he gave Sairché the information about the protective spells, she'd be one step closer to Farideh—and one step closer to killing him—unless he could move quickly.

"To the succubus aeries," he said. "To Invadiah."

The succubus didn't laugh like Farideh either. "That I'll do, just to see her face when I tell her that her traitor son wants a boon."

"A boon that will thwart her twice-traitorous daughter," he said. "Invadiah is vicious but she isn't a fool. By now it should be clear that Sairché doomed us both. You have portals to the other planes in the aerie—tell her I beg use of hers. Tell her it will bring about Sairché's downfall. And tell her it will exile me; I won't come out of this well either. Find out what she wants for that."

The succubus nodded. "That I can do. I don't know the buyer—I've heard things, here and there. A collector in Phlegethos. A collector in Minauros. Another archdevil. People talk, even about the dull fancies of collectors, but this one . . . it's clear there's something else going on. It's a *select* group that wants this one."

"Why?"

She shrugged. "That wasn't part of the deal. But we can always renegotiate." She paced along the wall, daring closer. "Tell me the key."

Lorcan wished she'd change form already, but the succubus seemed to sense his discomfort, and relish it. She'd edged closer, still technically on the opposite side of the room. "There's a protection laid on her," he said. "Laid thick. If it's not the result of some god's old interest, then I'm meant for Ao's army. No amount of scrying will get around it, no matter the method. And whoever Sairché's found to take up the pact will find that connection isn't enough either."

"But *you* found a way?" the succubus said skeptically.

"There's more to me than first blush," he said. He waited, holding tight to the last secret, turning it over as if there were some way to substitute it with a lesser detail. "She'll regret what she's doing," he said. "Or perhaps, someone could make sure she regrets it."

"And how is that?"

"When I was taken, before I was brought here, the archduchess spoke to me. Told me to be careful as she would have need of me and the Kakistos heir in the future."

Farideh's odd eyes narrowed. "What for?"

Lorcan hadn't the faintest idea. Glasya's counsel had come without warning, and her presence had vanished the moment she'd delivered it. "Now that wasn't part of the deal," he said with a smile. "Especially when I gave you Glasya's interest in Farideh for free."

The succubus tilted her head. "Farideh. Is that her name? How ugly." She sucked her lower lip, deep in thought. "They say it's because of Glasya that Sairché stopped torturing you."

That surprised Lorcan. The archduchess was well known for her elaborate methods of torment. "That hardly seems likely."

"Well, we all know she had you close to death," the succubus said. "I hear she had plenty more surprises for you too. Then the archduchess called her to court out of nowhere and said if she'd like you to be tortured, then she should hand you over to her lordship's tender mercies." Farideh's gold and silver eyes flashed with the succubus's amusement. "Sairché declined, they say. How could she do anything else, if what you're saying is true? You might tell Glasya what Sairché needs to know. What *I* need to know," she said, coming nearer, close enough now to reach out and trail her knuckles down his arm. Shitting demoness, he thought. "You want to renegotiate? I'll tell you what I've heard about your Brimstone Angel. You give me a peek inside."

Lorcan kept himself from flinching. What a perfect example of Malbolge, here in front of him—something to make him want to recoil in horror and throw himself headlong into corruption at the same time. Maybe he'd been locked away too long. Maybe he was tired of waiting to die. Maybe he did like this version better.

"It's very boring, I assure you," he said. "Go ahead and see for yourself, if you really want to be pulled into the archduchess's mess." The succubus's piercing gaze wavered, and she eased back, hardly at all, but enough to notice. Enough to be confident she wouldn't touch him.

"You owe me still," the succubus said. "The key to getting past the protection."

Lorcan shrugged, insouciant. "She has to find something that isn't affected by the spell."

The succubus reached out and wrapped a curl of his hair around one finger. "Is that all?"

"Simple as they come," he said, fighting to keep his voice steady. "Just make sure the warlock holds onto it."

"Hmm." The fingers that had been toying with his hair lengthened into talons, tangled in the locks, and she wrenched his head back. Her face was feral and terrible and so far from his warlock as she loomed over him before lunging in with a kiss she had no need to disguise from what it was: she meant to devour him from the inside out.

His mind went blank, black, and then thoughts began to race across it—out of his mind and into the succubus's. Neverwinter and the ruins and the racing anger in him as she fled . . . the rod at his throat, the rod pointed at his attackers, the rod he'd stolen from Invadiah to protect her with . . . *You should have run. You aren't worth this* . . . Her face in the firelight, the beat of her pulse . . . *Does it hurt? You'll be fine. No, I mean you. Does it hurt you?* The ring of the Kakistos heir. Havilar and her knife on the other side of the summoning. The book, the fire, the brand, the knife in his hand and the slit he made at the center of the brand, the extra wound she never noticed. The vial he squeezes the blood into . . .

He broke through the succubus's spell and threw her off of him with a forearm across her throat. He scrambled back as, panting and wild-eyed, she came to her feet and spread her wings, the illusion of her shape shed as the ill-fitting robes fell away into a succubus's leather armor. She kept a face that hinted at Farideh's, but the eyes had become red as rubies.

You *are* such a shitting idiot, Lorcan thought. He let his hands fill with flames—not enough to kill her, but certainly enough to do a little damage if she tried that again.

She smirked at him. "Oh, none of that. I have enough to make your sister happy."

"Sairché? I doubt that."

"We'll have to see. Blood magic? Clever, clever." She licked her teeth. "I was expecting a trinket you connected to. I think she was too."

Lords, had she seen the focus? No—surely not. He'd stopped her at the vial. "What are you going to tell Sairché?"

The succubus shrugged. "We'll see. I don't like having a cambion lording secrets over me. Especially not when I'm doing them favors." She backed away from him, out onto the balcony. "Maybe Sairché will send me down to Toril," she said. "Maybe she'll have me wear *your* skin for the Brimstone Angel to bring her into hand. Won't that be fun?"

Lorcan bit back a laugh. "She'll see right through you," he warned.

"That's what they all say," she replied. "I'll let you know what Fallen Invadiah says." She launched herself off the balcony and into the sickly skies of Malbolge.

Lorcan stood a while, watching her fly toward the aeries built into a cliff of hip bone, rolling the copper-tipped scourge he wore around his neck between two fingers, the blood-stiffened thongs splaying as it spun.

.:⌒:.

"*Karshoj*!" Farideh shouted at Brin. She swatted at him with the last of the scrolls. "Don't creep up on me like that!"

Brin kept his hands up in a gesture of calm, glad she hadn't been *really* surprised and unleashed a spray of fire at him as he came up behind her. "I wasn't being all that quiet," he said. "It's this place, I think. It makes people jumpy." He bent down alongside her to help gather up the fallen scrolls. "Tam nearly took my head off earlier."

"You're very lucky I wasn't Pernika," she said. "Or Havilar."

At the moment, Brin thought that anyway. "I need you to do the ritual for me. Mine's run out and Tam's not feeling well." He handed her the pile of scrolls.

"Ask Dahl," she said. "He has all the components."

Brin would rather have asked Pernika for a shave than ask Dahl for a favor. "I can't find him," he lied. "You don't have enough for even one?"

"I have enough for one, but mine's run out too. Don't you have a ritual book?" she asked, as they started back toward the camp. "I thought . . . I mean the priests . . ."

"I didn't take it with me," Brin said. He'd had the same conversation with Mira when they'd first arrived. "They're heavy, and I don't need it."

"You need it now," Farideh pointed out. "Maybe you can help Havi with the traps."

He could, he thought. Maybe she'd need help. Maybe she'd be glad he offered and apologize for that stupid fight, for ignoring his concerns about Pernika.

"You should tell her you're sorry for calling her daft," Farideh said. "She won't forget, but she'll forgive you."

"Stop doing that," Brin said irritably. "I'll say my apologies when she does."

"Oh, gods, Brin, just . . ." She shook her head. "Be the bigger one. We'll all be happier for it." She left him standing just beyond the camp's edge.

Brin cursed to himself, looking down the wide corridor that led to the gates. He *was* tired of being angry, tired of avoiding Havilar, and of her avoiding him. And maybe . . . she seemed as if she was tired too. Maybe, he thought, heading out into the library, listening for the sounds of Havilar springing traps, she would admit he was right.

Because the more he thought about it, the more he watched Pernika and Maspero, the more he was certain something was awry. These weren't the sort of people with whom you wanted to be caught in a dark alley.

Which meant, the more he thought about it, Mira wasn't either.

She'd known the two mercenaries. She'd said she had worked with them before. He couldn't pretend that she was possibly foolish enough to *not* notice the emblem of Bane on Pernika's upper arm. She couldn't have missed Maspero's dark expression.

And Brin couldn't possibly ignore the fact that Mira was definitely not giving orders to Maspero. What that meant, Brin wasn't sure, but the memory of the black-clad assassins in Waterdeep was hard to shake. The Shadovar weren't the only ones who wanted what Tarchamus had left behind. And Cyric wasn't the only god the Zhentarim held dear.

He was mulling over what exactly he ought to say when Havilar stepped into his path. "Well met," she said.

"Well met," he said, surprised. "I was looking for you. Are you . . . in the middle of anything?"

"No," she said, not moving. "Would you like to be in the middle of something?"

He squinted at her. "What is that supposed to mean?"

"It means," she said, reaching behind his head and sinking her fingers into his hair, "I think you should come with me."

"I . . ." Brin shut his mouth, blushing furiously. He looked away, but from the corner of his eye he could still see her staring at him. "Isn't this a bit . . . abrupt?" he managed.

She smiled and took him by the arm, her hand like ice through his sleeve. "Come on. I want to show you something."

Yes, he thought. All right. "Havi, wait," he said. "You can't just pretend we're not arguing about—"

"You were right," she said, still pulling him along. "I see that now. I found the answers in the Book of Tarchamus." She turned to face him, still pulling. "You should see it. That's where we're going."

"Wait, we're going to look at a book?" he demanded. "What about . . . all that . . . ?"

"Later," she said.

Brin dug his heels in. "What in the Hells and Abyss would a five-thousand-year-old book know about Pernika any—Havi, let *go*."

She yanked him closer, and her eyes were like lanterns. "Promise you'll follow," she said.

"I will," he said, "if you promise to stop acting like this. Gods damn it, let go!"

She released him, and the blood rushed back into his arm. He rubbed his wrist. "What is the matter with you?"

"I'm sorry," she said. "But you'll see." She beckoned to him and, rather than risk her trying to lead him by the hand again, he followed. She didn't look back as they wound through the maze of shelves toward the Book's alcove.

Loyal Torm, it shouldn't be this hard, he thought. It shouldn't be confusing and I shouldn't have to fight her on so much.

It shouldn't take a goddamned book to get her to trust that he might have something to say. And, he thought, raising his eyes to the back of her head, well aware he was making himself blush, you should not have a crush on a girl with a tail no matter what her legs look like.

"Here," she said, when they reached the alcove. She waved him toward the pedestal, and Brin pointedly didn't look at the tormented-looking gnome that made the base. "Pick it up," she urged. "Ask it something."

Brin glowered at her and scooped up the Book, so roughly he must have sent a cloud of dust up into his eyes. He winced and coughed to clear his throat. Havilar stood by, watching eagerly and completely missing the fact that he was angry at her.

"How much time," he said acidly, "is this wasting while we're being tracked by Netherese and Zhentarim and the gods know what else?" Havilar smiled at him blithely—gods, she didn't listen at *all*.

*I believe you're in a better position to answer that*, the Book chided. The ink swirled, making pictures of scholars in a scriptorium. *But is the search for knowledge ever truly time wasted?*

It is if it's the difference between living and dying, Brin thought irritably. "Thank you," he said, and he dropped the Book back in its spot. "I don't need more."

*No, no*, the Book said. *It's my pleasure.*

"Happy?" Brin said to Havilar. But when he looked up she was gone. "Havi?" he called. He could almost feel her watching from a distance. Or someone watching. "Havi!" he called again. There was no answer. "Damn it." What in all the broken planes had that been about? Brin wended his way back to the camp at the center of the library.

She doesn't listen, he told himself. She doesn't care if you're angry. She doesn't bother to wait around when you've done as she asked. He could practically hear Constancia clucking her tongue. "It will run its course," he could imagine her saying. "Just bide your time and ignore her 'til it does."

The camp was empty by the time he made it back—a blessing and a pity, he thought. He didn't want to talk about Havilar to anyone else . . . but he'd even talk to Dahl if it meant he could be distracted for a bit.

She probably went off to find *him*, a little voice in his thoughts chimed in. He shook his head—so what if she did? Bide your time. It will pass.

Stlarn and hrast, he thought bitterly. He couldn't sit here waiting, all useless and full of nerves. There was a library full of paths, full of potential distractions. He set off into it, wending his way through the shelves and stacks, sunk in his own bad mood. He pulled a scroll or two, but none were in any language he knew—fitting, he thought. As if the whole place were keeping him from being diverted. Footsteps echoed through the caverns, his companions everywhere and nowhere. None of them crossed his path.

Brin walked until he found himself in an open space near the outer wall, a little courtyard with a statue of a wizard looking up at an enormous glowing rune. He followed the statue's gaze—not a trap, he thought, if he remembered his lessons right. It looked more like a seal or a ward or—

"Well, here we are," a woman's voice said. Brin turned to see Pernika standing a dozen feet behind him, and his stomach dropped.

"You and I have business to attend to, Lord Crownsilver."

⁘⌒⁘

Once again, Dahl thought, you're stuck following orders that make no sense. He marked the end of his shelf with a cross of chalk. And wasting components, he thought grimly. How long had they been down here? A day and a half? Two? There was no way to tell, and though the piles of codices and scrolls were growing in their little camp, no one had found the promised spellbooks.

"Keep looking," Mira had told him earlier, when he'd expressed his doubts. "The spellbooks are somewhere. But in the meantime . . . there's not a thing wrong with seeing what else is here. Surely there's *something* of interest to you. Some topic that strikes your fancy? Some question you want answered?"

Yes, Dahl nearly said. But he kept his thoughts to himself—what he wanted to know was surely not kept in an arcanist's library.

The sound of voices bounced past him, and it took Dahl a moment to recognize them: Tam and the Book they'd found before. The Book Mira had said to leave where it was. He followed the curving shelves back to the alcove, where Tam stood over the text. "Such wonders," he said to himself.

Dahl stopped short, eyeing Tam. "Thought you were supposed to be searching the inner shelves."

Tam did not look up. "You haven't consulted the Book yet, have you?" he said.

"I've been busy," Dahl said.

"A pity," Tam said. He looked up at Dahl with that patronizing expression. "You really ought to make time. There's much here to be enlightened by."

"You know," Dahl said, struggling to guard his words, "you might find I'm not so utterly unenlightened."

Tam shrugged, with that same bland smile.

"For example," Dahl continued, biting off the words, "do you have any idea how many books and scrolls are in here? I've counted one hundred and twenty shelves radiating out from the center—and that doesn't even address all the bits that seem to be tucked in here and there like afterthoughts. We are talking about hundreds of thousands of texts. Even if a tenth of them were Tarchamus's spellbooks, we couldn't find every one of them without a lot more time than you're giving us."

"I think you're underestimating, actually," Tam said.

"Then my point stands all the stronger. This is a futile effort—we have no time to search, and we have no plans for contingencies."

"Such as?"

"Such as what in the bloody planes do we do when the Shadovar find this place if it's so full of dangerous information? Even if we find the spellbooks, all you have are vague notions about sealing the doors and gaining reinforcements. Have you even contacted Everlund yet?"

Tam strode nearer and laid his hand on Dahl's shoulder so lightly he hardly felt it. "Perhaps you should look for answers in the sources we've been left." And with another patronizing smile, he turned and vanished into the stacks.

Watching *Gods*—Dahl fought the urge to kick something. He wasn't a fool and he wasn't an innocent. He didn't need someone chiding him to do his research and check his sums. It didn't take a seer to divine that the Harpers needed capable agents—so why was he being forced through paces so remedial he might as well have been a lame pony?

*Tarchamus's peers never truly appreciated him either,* said the voice of the Book, breaking the silence. *It's partly why he hid all of his knowledge here. Not everyone is worthy of knowledge.*

"All are worthy," Dahl murmured. He looked back at the Book. " 'Knowledge is not to be hidden, not from the world and not from the self.' "

*An Oghmanyte?* the Book said. The text shivered into the shape of Oghma's harp, the lines of hymns. *Well, well.*

"I . . . no," Dahl said. "Once."

*Nevertheless*, the Book said, *we can agree—can we not?—that . . . display was unworthy of you. You are a bit old, by my reckoning, to be his apprentice.*

"I'm not his apprentice," Dahl snapped.

*Precisely*, the Book said. *Why are you no longer an Oghmanyte?*

"The gods are fickle." He stared after Tam. "Have you texts on the worship of Oghma here?"

*But of course. What do you want to find in particular?*

Dahl hesitated. "Spells. Covenants. The laws of paladins."

*Paladins of Oghma? An interesting course of study*, the Book said. *One might surmise this is personal for you. If you ask the question you're looking for answers to, I may be able to cut your search short.*

Dahl considered the shifting inks. "Never mind."

*What if I guess?* the Book said. *Might it be that you . . . know someone, someone who had been sworn to the Binder's church? But who has been unceremoniously cast aside?*

When Dahl didn't answer, the voice chuckled. *There's few enough who realize that gods like Oghma have paladins in service to them. Fewer still who realize even a god as . . . fickle as Oghma has rules.*

"I said 'never mind.'" Dahl started to follow the aisle back to the camp at the center.

*I think I have your answer.*

He stopped.

*Eight rows on, follow the shelf to your left. You'll cross two paths and find a column with a rune carved onto it.*

Dahl turned. "Go on."

*The rune holds the power to a trap that guards the shelf you need*, the Book said. *You need to destroy it before you go any further. Once that's done, go around the column and down the path there. There's a narrow set of shelves, and the volume you want is a slim one, bound in blue cloth.* It chuckled again. *That whole shelf is probably something that woman who led you here would like to see. I'll let you be the one to tell her, though.*

You should know better than to hope, Dahl told himself as he crossed the cavern and came upon the column. It was one of the few, he noticed, that seemed to reinforce the ceiling.

The rune shimmered halfway up the limestone column. It was some language older than Loross, older than Draconic perhaps. Add it to the list, he thought, digging through his pockets, of things I do not know. Right below runic magic.

He found what he was looking for: a leather bag of a powdered, potent acid collected from basilisk droppings. He poured a measure of water from his canteen and tied it quickly shut. He counted to twenty, and just as the rehydrated powder had dissolved and started to eat through the leather of the pouch, Dahl hurled the pouch at the column so that it burst across the rune. The sizzle of the acid ate into the stone column and destroyed the rune.

"Right," Dahl said, trying not to be *too* pleased with himself. He passed the column and found the short path the Book had mentioned, the narrow shelf. He moved with caution, but the trap didn't spring. Well done, he thought.

The volume the Book had suggested turned out to be a handwritten text . . . a diary, it seemed. Dahl pulled another book down, and another—all the same. Personal journals.

Not spellbooks, he noted. Though they were marked up with notes on spells being created or broken down in between the long stretches of day-to-day tedium. Perhaps worth mentioning to Mira anyway . . .

The diary in his hands had belonged to an arcanist by the name of Emrys, and the dates—gods' books, five *thousand* years past—made him a contemporary of Tarchamus by Mira's estimates. Magic slicked the pages, somehow, even after all the years and all the powers of the Spellplague. The entries began in the summer, focusing on Emrys's successful execution of a spell that brought a storm of ice to earth.

*The potential for defense is extraordinary*, it read. *Let us see that fool Arion "accidentally" unleash his winds on us again; we shall see! Have warned Sadebreth repeatedly that he has a poor grip on his council, but to no avail. The ice shall be my own warning. Tarchamus is terribly amused, in his fashion, says preemptive measures are appropriate. I do not agree, but the thought of Arion waking up to find his city encased, that false look of perpetual surprise genuine for once, did keep me laughing.*

Dahl frowned. Not only a contemporary, but a friend, it seemed. And a powerful wizard. He skimmed ahead.

The pages that followed painted a world where the arcanists wielded astounding powers over the ordinary Netherese who lived under them—often literally, beneath their floating cities. A world where the wizards bickered like gods, tormented apprentices, and stole wildly from one another. Emrys, as it was his own narrative, came off a bit better than others. As did Tarchamus.

Until Dahl turned past the center of the diary. It was autumn then, a few years on.

*Sadebreth has finally granted me audience,* Dahl read. *After the disaster that brought Tenish to ground, how could he refuse? It did not take much to convince him that censure is not enough for Tarchamus. He will convince the council to come together and work spells to block Tarchamus's access to the Weave completely.*

Dahl's stomach tightened. Not a simple thing. Magic had changed in so many ways since then, but . . . to block access to the Weave, they might have needed the goddess of magic's intercession to keep Tarchamus from reaching her Weave. To teach him a lesson. To rein him in.

No god would have done that, he told himself.

*I must regretfully confess,* the entry went on, *I struggle with the probable fallout—not only the possibility that Tarchamus will manage to carry on with his planar magic, but also the precedent this sets.*

He closed the diary, the very notion of what the Book seemed to be suggesting intolerable. That couldn't be what happened to Dahl. It would be too simple. And who would have done such a thing? Not Jedik, surely. Jedik had never made an example of him like that . . .

But others . . . others had. If nothing else, it was a possibility he hadn't considered. He tucked the book under one arm to read later on.

•:⌒:•

The last of the texts the Book had sent Farideh to find was perched on a shelf high over her head, past the big rune Havilar had mentioned and on the other side of a little courtyard around a statue of a wizard. It was a thick tome bound in green brocade that looked like nothing so much as the sort of robes she'd seen for sale in Waterdeep—and she said a little thanks for that. It was easily spotted at least. She set the other scrolls on the ground and hauled herself up, climbing the shelf like a ladder. Just this last one, and the Book said it could help her construct a ritual. Her outstretched fingertips hooked the top of the book.

"Well met? Do you need a hand?"

Mira's sudden presence surprised Farideh, and she yanked the book down. Mira caught it before it hit the ground, and Farideh managed to catch hold of the shelf again, before she lost her balance.

"Many thanks," Farideh said, coming to the ground again. Mira handed back the book. "I suppose . . . I haven't really searched this section yet."

Mira waved her off. "Look when you can. We have time."

"Do we?" Farideh gathered her remaining scrolls from the floor. "I know I don't want to be here if . . ." She didn't even want to say Rhand's name. "If the Netherese are on the way."

Mira shrugged, unconcerned. "They haven't come yet. I have something for you." She pulled a rolled sheaf of parchment from her jerkin and handed it over. It was a copy of a ritual—the protective circle.

"Heavens knew Dahl wasn't going to show you," Mira said. "And it sounded to me as if you wanted it rather dearly."

"Thank you," Farideh said. "That's very kind."

Mira bobbed her head as if it was and it wasn't. "Consider it a gesture of friendship," she said.

Farideh looked down at the scroll. "Thank you," she said again. "I need to get back."

"Of course. I'll come with you."

Farideh would rather she didn't. She wanted to read what she could of the texts she'd gathered before she got back to the Book. But Mira fell into step beside her regardless.

"You know," Mira said, "I've been considering taking on an assistant. You have a good eye, a sharp mind, and"—she nodded at the pile of scrolls in Farideh's arms with a smile—"a *bit* of an interest. You also have a little ritual magic, which should come in handy. I could help you find whatever it is that you're looking for."

Farideh looked down at the other woman. "What makes you think I'm looking for something?"

Mira chuckled. "Please. It's your business, and I certainly don't begrudge you that. But I know all too well exactly what it looks like to be consumed by something you're not keen on sharing. We're not that different, you and I." She grinned. "And, I'll bet you've heard that before. I know I have. But let's just talk about *this* case in which we're similar. After all, are you planning to sign up with the Harpers when this is through? Or are you still looking for something else?"

"At the moment," Farideh said, "I've got enough to keep me busy. But I'll think about it."

"Do," Mira said.

Farideh watched her head off into the deeper stacks, turning over the strange offer in her mind. She'd never thought of being a historian, and couldn't imagine what made Mira think she ought to consider it.

*Are you planning to sign up with the Harpers when this is through?* There'd been a bite to that, a reminder she wasn't welcome in those ranks. A reminder Farideh ought not to be choosy—it rubbed her the wrong way.

Then again, Mira had gotten Farideh the protective circle spell, and she appreciated the gesture. She unrolled the parchment again—gods, that made everything a lot easier. And Mira *had* been right without Farideh telling her that she needed the spell. Maybe there was something to her assertions . . .

She frowned. She knew the handwriting, and it wasn't Mira's. The steeply slanted letters were the same ones that made the reports Tam had written on the way back from Neverwinter. The silverstar had copied the ritual. She pulled the sheaf flat—the left-hand edge made a gentle curve instead of a straight line. As if someone had sliced it from the book that bound it.

Farideh shut her eyes and cursed: Mira had stolen it straight out of Tam's ritual book.

Later, she told herself. Later she would have to confront Mira. Later she would have to give it back and hope that Mira did the right thing. Later she would have to decide if she would tell Tam.

Right now, she thought heading into the Book's alcove, she had a ritual to unravel.

Brin composed himself as Pernika stalked toward him, as if he weren't already rattled, as if he weren't already sure she was trouble. As if she hadn't just called him 'Lord Crownsilver.' "

"Well, well," Pernika said, stalking toward Brin. "I hear you've been holding out on us. Hear you've got some . . . royal roots."

Brin stiffened. "I don't know what you're talking about."

"Of course you don't. But let's pretend we're past the part where you lie to me, and we argue, and then I point out I heard it from your idiot girl's own mouth." She smiled and Brin's stomach clenched. "Let's get to the part where we all agree you've got some deep pockets behind you."

"I also have some friends with sharp blades," he said, all cool and courtly. Gods damn it, Havi, he thought. Even after he'd told her Pernika wasn't to be trusted, she'd just blabbed away. How much had she said? How much could he deny?

"Calm down," she said. "No one's got their knives drawn. I've just got a little offer for you. A . . . *partnership*."

"I'm not interested."

"Hear me out. Sounds to me like there are people who are awfully concerned about your well-being, seeing as you're . . . 'a secret prince.' Hmm? People who might be willing to pay a goodly amount to secure your safety?" She waited for him to say something, but Brin knew better than to give her the satisfaction. "I'll demand a ransom. We'll send them one of your fingers or something for effect. Then they'll gather up the coin, and we can split it. You don't even have to get hurt."

"Aside from the finger," Brin said dryly. Cool, he thought, calm. Like you're in audience with Helindra. Pernika won't do a thing while you're down here. His stomach was twisting all the same, and when he tried to move past her, she blocked his path.

"We can always send someone else's finger," she said, "if you're too faint of heart."

"I believe I'll pass."

She leered down at him. "Don't believe I gave you the option," Pernika said. "After all, I can always carry on without your permission once we're out of this miserable place."

"Hey!" a voice called. Pernika turned, and Brin could see past her shoulder, Havilar and her glaive looking perfectly deadly. "Try that again."

"Which part?" Pernika asked, unconcerned, as Havilar stormed across the space. "Did you want in on it too?"

"The part," Havilar said, "where you assume you're going to get away with that rot. Leave him alone, if you know what's good for you." She set herself, toe-to-toe with the mercenary. "He said he passes."

Pernika smirked at her. "You only got by me twice. Don't think you'll do it again."

Havilar didn't budge. "That was sparring. I was going easy on you."

"Were you, little girl? You know how many people have threatened me? Cemeteries worth. Sparring's one thing. Blood's another."

Havilar snorted. "I've brought down devils and orcs and a whole *room* full of cultists. In the last month. One mercenary past her prime will be *nothing*." She leaned a little closer. "You leave your guard open on the left when you do that silly lunge. Doesn't matter sword to sword, but a glaive . . . a glaive goes a lot farther. And next time you'll wish I broke your wrist."

Pernika's smirk seemed to flatten out, as if she were no longer convinced Havilar was just a stupid, overconfident girl. She stepped back and tossed a glance Brin's way.

"Consider it," she said, and she backed out of the camp, her dark eyes once again locked on Havilar, and her smirk still mocking, despite the changing odds.

"Stay away from him!" Havilar shouted after. *"Karshoj,"* she said to Brin. "The gall of her! I thought we might be friends, but now. . . *ooh*!" She stomped her foot. "*Tiamash*. Are you all right?"

Brin could not have wished harder for the floor to open up and swallow him. Gods damn it, she thought he was too weak to do anything. She thought he was a coward too. And worse—she'd spilled the only semblance of a secret they'd had.

"Perfectly," he said coldly. "Only I'm getting fed up with trying to convince you that I can take care of myself."

"I know that," Havilar said.

"Then stop rescuing me. I don't need it."

Havilar looked at him—surprised and hurt and confused. "You want to have that madwoman bothering you?"

"Well," Brin said, "she wouldn't have bothered me at all if you hadn't told her who I was." His cool failed him. "How could you? Didn't I say it was private?"

"I didn't. I've hardly said a word to her that wasn't about traps since we came down here."

"She was pretty clear she'd heard about my family from you," he said.

"Why would I say anything about you and your family . . ." Havilar waved her hand vaguely. "See, I don't even know what I'd say. You won't tell me a thing about them unless I find out by accident, and *you* haven't said a word to me since we got down here that wasn't about *pothac* books."

"Well someone told Pernika I'm 'a secret prince,' " he said. "Which doesn't sound like anyone else I know."

Havilar's cheeks colored. "Oh."

"So you admit it?" he demanded. "You told her?"

"No. I . . . I said that to someone else."

Gods, it just got worse and worse, he thought. "Who?"

Havilar looked as if she would have liked to vanish into the floor as well, and Brin feared the worst. "That book," she said. "The one that everyone's asking questions of. I know you said it was private, but I thought—"

"Why in the Hells and Abyss were you asking that thing about me?" he demanded. "It's not your business. Why do you care about my family?"

Because they're wealthy, he thought. Because they're powerful. Because you're a madman for rejecting all of that. She didn't have to say—it was the same reasons anyone cared.

"Because I wanted to know why you're acting like this!" Havilar shouted. "I didn't *ask* about your *pothac* family, I asked why you're avoiding me, and the Book didn't know either!"

Brin's anger fled. "Avoiding you?"

"You act like you're fond of me," she went on, "and then you act like I'm no one, and then you won't tell me things as if you don't trust me or you want me to keep my distance. And then you call me daft. But whatever it is that's bothering you, I just want to help. But when I help you get angry."

Flushed and flustered, she folded her arms around the glaive and tugged on the end of her braid. "I give up," she said. "I don't know what I'm supposed to do. It's not like chapbooks at all."

Ah, ye Watching Gods—someone could have knocked the floor out from under his feet and he would have felt surer. For a moment he was almost afraid to breathe. It shouldn't have hurt her feelings for him to keep such a secret, but it had—there it was. He didn't know what he was supposed to do either.

"Listen . . . ," he started. He glanced around to be sure Pernika had gone and no one else was near, before taking her by the hand. She stiffened, but followed him into a little nook of shelves around an ugly bust of some ancient arcanist.

"Oh, just *yell* if you're going to!" she said. "Everyone can hear anyway."

"No," he said, and he sat down on the floor, sure this was the right thing to do, even though every part of him rebelled at it. She eyed him a moment, but sat down beside him at last, laying the glaive on the floor.

"Listen," he started again. "The thing is . . ." He pursed his lips a moment—these were the last seconds before everything changed again. "I do trust you. So I'll tell you everything. But it's . . . more than a secret. You can't even tell Farideh."

Solemnity didn't suit Havilar, but she wore it for the moment. "All right."

"My mother," he said, "she was a Cormaeril—parts of this aren't going to mean anything to you, right, but let me finish. Her father's father's father was the king of Cormyr, back before the Spellplague. Azoun Obarskyr the fourth. Not an 'official' son, but . . . the king claimed him anyway. So she has a little royal blood—but not enough to inherit anything, right? And my father . . . everyone thought my father was just a Crownsilver for ages, just the old lord's eldest son. Nothing special.

"But then Granny—on her death bed, mind—announced that he wasn't the old lord's son at all. That she'd dallied with the prince, the current king's brother. And so my father was really an Obarskyr by blood. Everyone went *mad* and there were fights in the halls and arguments in the king's court, and tests and sworn statements, and for a few tendays my father was in line for the throne. Until he died . . . Until someone had him killed."

"Oh," she said. "Oh, Brin, I'm sorry."

"Which means," Brin said, feeling as if he might throw up the words if they didn't get spoken, "when you put them together, I'm . . . I'm in line to be king."

She stared at him a moment, then shook her head. "Aren't a lot of people?"

He had been ready for a lot of things—for her to pull away, for her to start in on some wild fantasy, for her to laugh hysterically at him—but nonchalance was not one of them. "What?"

"I mean, in stories there's always a line of succession that goes on for ages and then some catastrophe happens and everyone dies and some swineherd's the king. You're some kind of lord—I figured that out—so of course you're ahead of the swineherd." She looked thoughtful for a moment. "I might be in a line of succession for all you know."

"No," Brin said. "I mean, yeah, you might, I don't know. But I mean . . . Right now it's the Crown Prince, then his son and his daughter, then Baron Boldtree, the king's nephew, the old prince's other bastard." He took a deep breath.

"And if I go back to Cormyr, my Aunt Helindra is going to tell everyone the truth: that because Granny loved the old prince, the line goes: the Crown Prince, his son, his daughter . . . and then me."

Now her eyes were like saucers. "Holy gods!" Havilar said, pulling back as if to get a better look at him. "Are you serious? That . . . that doesn't even take a big catastrophe for everyone to die and then you're the king. One nasty carriage accident! A bad cauldron of soup!"

"I know," he said glumly. "And no one else has any idea. Aunt Helindra let people think I died in a featherlung epidemic when I was eight, before people figured out I land ahead of the Baron. It's going to shock a lot of people when I turn up not dead."

"Gods," she said. "Well, no wonder you ran away."

"It's not because I'm afraid."

"I know," she said, as if he were reminding her that he was human. "You're terribly brave."

He felt his face grow hot. "Don't tease," he admonished. "My father didn't die by accident, and he didn't die alone. There are a lot of people who take that line of succession very seriously. It's the best thing for me, for my family, and probably for Cormyr, too, if I just don't exist. It's them I'm afraid for."

"I'm not teasing!" She took his hand and squeezed it, and he was never so aware of his hand as in that moment. "Look, you said that they're mad, your family—and I'm sorry, if your cousin is the good one, then the rest of them are pretty *karshoji* lunatic and ready to do some stupid things. But even if they're lunatic, they're family, so why would you want them to get hurt for you? And," she added quickly, taking her hand back, as if she'd just remembered herself, "that *is* terribly brave. I couldn't bear to leave Farideh and Mehen. Even if it were for their own good."

Ye gods, he thought. You don't give her enough credit. "Yes," he said. "They don't . . . they don't really understand that. Not many people seem to." He looked down at his hands, wondering if she'd object if he took hers again. "I'm sorry I called you daft."

"I'm sorry I didn't listen about that *henish*."

He smiled. "And I'm sorry I yelled at you before. It's just . . . sometimes it doesn't seem like you're listening."

"It's all right. You're not the first person to say that," she said. "I do think you can defend yourself, you know. I'd just hate it . . . if something happened and I could have helped." She looked down at her own hands. "I hope you don't think I'm a nuisance because of that. Sometimes I think you're the only one who doesn't, and if I've wrecked that . . . I don't know what I'll do."

He sighed. "No. It's not you. It's . . . Where I come from, the stories aren't usually about princes getting rescued by pretty girls. It's hard not to feel sort of stupid and useless, even if it makes a lot more sense to put the sword in your hands, right?"

"Oh." Havilar went very stiff and flushed, her mouth clamped shut as if she were trying to keep herself from speaking.

Oh gods, Brin thought. "What?"

"Do you think that?" she said very quietly. "That I'm pretty?"

"Um." He wet his mouth.

For all the time spent on teaching Brin what to say and how to say it; how to tell what parts of information were better kept close to the chest like a trump card, and which were to be played early, to lure others into putting forth details they ought to have held close—for all of that, Brin hadn't any idea what to do next. For a moment, in the dark of the library, his thoughts scrambled, trying to form a play, trying to decide how badly he'd tipped his hand, and whether Havilar had tipped hers at all. Trying to form a strategy when he didn't even understand the game they were playing, but he was pretty certain he'd made the wrong move when he wasn't paying attention.

Havilar was still staring at him, unmoving. Looking like he could break her heart with two words together.

Gods. She wasn't trying to get something from him, he realized, and he didn't want to hide from her. He'd said it without thinking, because he meant it and frankly, he didn't care if she knew so. And if she wasn't fond of him, if this was all a stupid game to her . . . well it didn't change how he felt. He'd bided his time long enough.

"Yes," he said, more terrified than he'd been in a long time and ignoring it. "I mean, at first . . . It snuck up on me. But you're very pretty. And funny. And if someone's going to save me from assassins or Zhentarim or hydras, I'd be glad it was you." She was still watching him as if blinking might make him burst into flames, her face growing more and more flushed. "I am," he said, because if he didn't get it out, he'd hate himself for being a complete coward forever, "really fond of you, and if—"

She kissed him. She kissed him and every explanation went out of him. Every twistable word, every affectation, every notion of play and counter—this is what he wanted to say, he realized. Just this.

Havilar pulled back. "Is that right?" she asked. "It seemed right. But I'm mostly guessing."

"It's a . . . pretty good guess," he managed. "Does that mean you're fond of me?"

"Of course," she said. "Wasn't it obvious? It felt awfully obvious."

Brin laughed. "No. I thought you might be fond of Dahl."

Havilar wrinkled her nose. "Why? He's bossy. And rude."

"And 'good-looking,' " Brin reminded her. "And smart. And . . . tall."

"Well, you can kiss him then."

He took her hands. "I'd rather kiss you."

She blushed all over again, as if she hadn't already done both of those things herself. "You know," she said, suddenly quiet, suddenly timid, suddenly nothing at all like Havilar, "I think those things about you."

"That I'm bossy and rude?"

Havilar giggled. "No. That you're smart. So smart. And I do think you're nice looking, and you always laugh, but never at me." She smiled. "And you're terribly brave."

He was brave then and kissed her, several times, all the while marveling that it was actually quite simple, once you stopped thinking so hard.

"You know," he said, "I like this better than before. That was . . . I don't know, did you read that in a chapbook or something?"

She pulled back, puzzled. "What do you mean?"

"When you were going on about the Book. You were . . ." He waved his hand, not sure how to put it. "I mean, I don't mind a little, but I like you the way—"

"Wait," she said. "I was going on about that Book?" He nodded and her brow furrowed. "You're not the first person to say that either."

# CHAPTER THIRTEEN

*THIS WILL NOT BE SIMPLE,* **THE BOOK WARNED FARIDEH.** *TARCHAMUS WAS a very powerful arcanist.*

Farideh had spread the map of the Hells, her ritual book, and the three other texts the Book had sent her to search for—two scrolls on planar powers written in the same spidery hand as the notes on the map, and one thick tome about the theory behind ritual magic. The text was so complex and dense, Farideh despaired of ever understanding it before Lorcan suffered his sister's wrath. Dahl, she suspected, would have called it a nursery story, if only because it would make her feel stupider.

"At least I have your help," she said, searching for a passage outlining alternate power sources. In truth, the Book was the one doing most of the work of it. Farideh simply served as its eyes, a hand to do calculations, a pair of feet to crisscross the library in search of more texts.

"Do you think it was easier before?" she asked, copying a series of runes from the scroll—once the keys to Malbolge and, with some careful adjustments, perhaps a backdoor now. "The Weave sounds . . ." She paused and looked over the complex net in the ritual book's illustrations. "Like having a hundred pacts, a hundred tethers to the next plane."

The Book chuckled. *So you're not a wizard*, it said. *Your magic comes from somewhere else . . . a binder? A warlock?*

"A warlock," she admitted. "But I'm not . . . It's not a wicked thing. I swear." You are defending yourself to a talking book, she thought. She turned back to the parchment. "Only I draw magic from the Hells, I suppose."

*How very interesting*, the Book said. *A style of magic the Netherese never truly mastered. Much has changed . . .*

Not a word of it sounded like chastisement—Farideh smiled. "Do you know much about the world since Netheril?"

*Some*, the Book admitted. *Not nearly enough. Long gone are the days when like minds came to share their knowledge with me. It's quiet now. But . . . there are events that shake the plane to its foundations, that seep even into the ground at this depth. The death of Mystryl and the fall of Netheril. The death of Mystra and the fall of the world. The phaerimms' tricks and the return of Shade. The Ascension of Asmodeus . . . Not even Tarchamus's fears could seal away the library from events that shook the worlds so.*

How old and strange the world was, she thought. To imagine the way it must have looked when the library was buried: no Spellplague, no dragonborn, Netheril a sprawling empire. Did people fear it then the way they did now? She felt so lost, not recognizing any other of the events the book listed.

Except for one, she realized. Asmodeus. She heaved the book from its pedestal and held it a little closer. "Have you ever heard of the Toril Thirteen?" she asked quietly. "It would be . . . much more recent, but . . ."

*Now let me think*, the Book said. The script on its pages seemed to shiver and squirm. She shifted the tome onto her lap, trying to find a more comfortable position. When she'd settled it, she must have stirred up the dust from its pages. She flinched at the sudden itch in her eyes, her nose, her throat.

*Ah, yes*, the Book said, and the text flowed into red, spiky symbols she didn't know, *the followers of the Brimstone Angel.*

Farideh's heart sped up. "Was that . . . were they involved in one of those events? One of those things that shook the world?"

The voice was silent for a long moment. *They are all that stood between Asmodeus and powers the likes of which none have seen.*

"What do you mean? He's a god, isn't he? What could be worse?"

*Oh my dear girl*, the Book said. *You cannot imagine how it was in the days before . . .*

*Asmodeus was not a god, but still the king of the Hells and craved every scrap and snippet of power he could gain. The tieflings in the world, well, their lives hung on his balance. He sought to make them all his slaves, because he could.*

*But a devil loves a deal, and Bryseis Kakistos offered him the chance to become greater than an archdevil, a very god if he took the chance—but only if he agreed to spare the tiefling race, to let them master their own souls. Those first thirteen warlocks took the pact with Asmodeus to appease the Lord of the Ninth's vanity, and to spare their loved ones the yoke of the Raging Fiend. Doing so gave him the power of the gods, but gave them all the chance to escape his traps.*

*Ah! How he gloated to think he'd won! Without a doubt, every being on Toril and beyond, every being remotely sensitive to the music of the planes, heard the God of Evil's crowing. But to look at the facts ... those thirteen knew what they were doing. Sometimes the only choice we have is between two evils. Sometimes the only right choice is a sacrifice.*

Farideh hardly knew what to say. All her life she'd been warned that she stood on the edge of utter damnation, that the wrong decision would awaken the fiendish blood that flowed through her and doom her as it doomed every other tiefling. Since taking the pact, the worry that she'd leaped over the edge was as inescapable as a literal fall. But if Bryseis Kakistos had led the Toril Thirteen for the good of the world, if she took the pact for good reasons—perhaps, perhaps Farideh wasn't doomed. Perhaps none of them truly were.

"Thank you," she said. "I think it's a story people have forgotten."

*Easy to do. And it is my pleasure to enlighten you. When you are finished with this part of the spell, perhaps we can delve further into these lost tales. Perhaps there are other things that have been kept from you.*

She smoothed the map open and searched the spellbook for the incantation the Book had mentioned, her heart a little lighter . . . but she couldn't help but wonder why Lorcan had never told her. Even if he'd kept secret the nature of collector devils and the implications of a Toril Thirteen set, the story of Bryseis Kakistos would have made her far more comfortable with the pact far sooner.

Maybe he thought you'd give in and corrupt like any other warlock, a little voice said.

*Tell me*, the Book said, *who laid those spells on you?*

Farideh ran a hand over her upper arm, feeling the raised edges of the infernal shapes through the thin cotton. What else could it mean? "It's part of the pact. It ties me to the Hells. To a devil in the Hells."

*A most . . . protective master*, the Book mused.

She pursed her mouth. "He's not my master."

The Book chuckled again. *Your pardon.*

She finished the line of runes—neat enough, she hoped. "What now?"

*There should be a very long section near the center of the book about components.*

Farideh paged ahead, past field after field of neat, close-spaced handwriting describing the long development of ritual after ritual.. She could only imagine how many years it had taken someone to craft the tome.

She frowned. "Where did this book come from?"

*Where do any books come from? The imagination and effort of the wise and determined.*

"No," she said, "I mean, this is a book about ritual magic, and you said there was no such thing in Tarchamus's day. That there was no need for such things."

*There wasn't*, the Book said. *The rabble of wizards made all sorts of magic by abusing the powers of the Weave. And a few worked around it, like Tarchamus. If you should like to know more about the origins of magic like yours, I should be happy to point you in the proper direction.*

"Tarchamus was a warlock?"

*Oh my, no*, the Book said. *But he did come up with terribly clever ways around the limitations of the Weave by seeking the powers of the planes.*

"And the ritual book?" she said. "How did it get here?"

The Book was quiet a moment. *Left by some earlier visitors, obviously,* it said. *I don't know why you couldn't figure that out.*

Farideh didn't argue, and went back to searching for the pages on components, but in the back of her thoughts, she couldn't help but wonder what sort of person would abandon a book so clearly valued as this one.

Mira made herself close the book, but marked it for later. Just a misfiled ledger of caravans passing through Low Netherese cities—no hint at all of what she was supposed to be looking for there—but, Watching Gods, how many little jewels of information lay gleaming just under the surface of such ephemera! Why did this city need so much lumber when it lay near a forest? Conflict with the elves? A rot afflicting the trees? Border skirmishes with another city? Why did that city see half as many caravans? Fewer people? More resources? A more insular council?

A whole world came to life in such mundane details. Patrons like the Harpers might want magic scrolls and spellbooks, maps to lost ruins and treasure hoards. But a graveyard? A midden heap? A record of commerce? Mira would trade a hundred magical weapons for such rich artifacts.

A shadow fell across her as someone stepped into the space between the shelves.

Maspero. She pulled down another book. "Can I help you?"

"You can tell me you're not wasting my time," Maspero murmured. "You know well what happens when my time is wasted."

Mira gritted her teeth. "We've found the library," she said, "ahead of the Shadovar. You'll have your spells. I don't see how we're wasting your time."

"And yet your Harpers can't find my spells," he said. "I have to wonder, is it because they're not so clever as you said, or because they're stalling until those reinforcements they keep mentioning arrive? Those two need to be taken out. Now."

She mastered herself and turned. "Why would we do that?" she said, sweeter than she felt. If there was one danger to working with Maspero, it was managing his impatience. "Everyone is getting along fine, everyone's working so well. You kill any one of them and you'll lose the rest. Would you like to dig this place out with only *Pernika* to assist you? I promise this is the best way to get what you want."

Maspero sneered. "What *you* want doesn't seem to be what the Zhentarim want."

"To be honest, Maspero," Mira said coldly, "I don't think the Zhentarim *know* what they want. Graesson sends assassins after your people and prizes, Naliah cuts off your caravans, and that damned Vaasan nearly killed you two months back. 'The Zhentarim are a fractured organization, imagining they still have world-spanning powers,' isn't that what you said?"

"And the Harpers are a bunch of dandies playing hero in the twilight," Maspero said. "It makes neither of us less dangerous." He grabbed her arm and pulled her nearer. "And regardless of what the Cyricists are doing, *I'm* in charge of this expedition, understand? You play nice or your dear old da will get a chance to see how much the Zhentarim are *not* dandies."

Mira smiled, even though Maspero's grip was hard enough to leave bruises. "The Zhents may sneer at how far the Harpers have fallen. They may tell themselves again and again that the lot of them are only fops with secondhand harps and grand ideas.

"But you ought to know better," she went on, even as he twisted her arm. Her eyes watered. "You've seen my father. You've seen his chain. And let me tell you, in case you've missed it: nothing would suit him better than playing hero to save his only daughter from a mad Banite."

Maspero held her tight. "You're playing both sides," he accused.

"The only side I'm playing is the one that gets this site examined properly."

"When they figure out who they're working for, your site won't matter."

"You miss the plane for the portal," she said. "Listen: the Harpers loathe Netheril. Their hatred of Shade is the only thing that kept them from dispersing altogether. This library may be the only place in the world that holds the secrets Shade lost when it shifted planes. No Harper would stand aside and let the Shadovar take those secrets back. In particular, not Tarchamus's eruption spell."

"I'm well aware—"

"And," Mira went on, "it was Risen Netheril who destroyed Zhentil Keep. Who brought down the Black Network enough to let the Cyricists take control from your god and his exarch. The Harpers may not wish to bow to the Zhentarim—and my father least of all—but when the choice is to work alongside each other or bow to Shade and Shar over them . . . no one would choose the latter."

Maspero was quiet a moment. He let go of her arm.

"If they work out who *we* work for," she said, rubbing the bruise, "remind them of that. My father in particular prides himself on being reasonable. If there's a zealot among them who wants to act out some chapbook scene, he'll put a stop to it *for* you. So long as you stay reasonable."

A slow smile crept across Maspero's brutal features. "Hells," he said, "but you're devious."

"Prudent," Mira corrected. "This is the best way to get what we *all* want."

That, she thought, should keep him still. Harper, Zhentarim—Hells, even Shadovar—Mira didn't care who she worked with if it meant she could be the one to unearth the ancient ruins. The history, the discovery—these were what mattered. If it took the promise of a powerful weapon to get that aid, then that was how things sat. They could fight over it once it was found.

She smiled at Maspero, but secretly, she hoped he prevailed and took the plans—it would mean every other Zhentarim leader on the Sword Coast would come down on him and wipe that sneer from his face. A hundred years ago, the Black Network had been something to fear indeed—across the continent, every Zhent answered to the same calculating, determined master, and the organization hid itself in every city, in every layer of power.

When Shade destroyed Zhentil Keep, the heart of the Zhentarim's power, the cracks had already begun to form. Those who worshipped Cyric, the god of strife and madness, rose up and seized power from the more orderly Banites, leaving the widely scattered cells to their own devices. Every few years, it seemed, one of them—Cyricist or Banite—rose above the rest of the rabble and tried to seize power over his neighbor cells. And every few years there was another brutal internecine battle.

But as fractured and fractious as the Zhentarim were, Mira could not deny she was one of them.

What she'd told her father before had been the truth, only the details were lies—far more than guardwork, being employed by the

Zhentarim meant she had the funds to do what she wished. If they wanted a particularly valuable artifact, well, at least they left the rest of the site to her. If they wanted to exploit her contacts among the Anauroch's desert tribes, at least they never damaged their trust. If they wanted her to get them past zealous guards and into parts of the world that didn't often see human eyes, well, at least they let her lead them to actual ruins when their business concluded.

Still, Mira had not gotten to where she was by being a fool. Maspero grew more dangerous by the day, his rivals more bold, and the certainty that one would decide Maspero needed to be stopped became surer. For all her bravado, she wasn't certain he'd keep his temper steady. She wasn't even certain he'd let her return to Everlund unscathed. He knew—all the Zhents knew, she was sure—that Mira didn't care so much about their goals, about their machinations, about who had stood in whose way. She might be one of the Zhentarim in name, but patience for Mira's lax loyalty was finite, and running out.

But without her ties to the Zhentarim, she was merely another copperless historian, pleading for coin from patrons who had to be convinced to care more about the ancient world than their new wardrobes, or—worse—patrons who only wanted her to look for and confirm what they wished to be true. That their race had been in that valley first, or that the Spellplague had spared *their* temple or touched *their* ancestral home.

She hoped her father wouldn't press the issue. She'd rather not decide where she stood when the lost treasures of Tarchamus were here within her grasp.

As if her thoughts had called him, Tam appeared at the end of the aisle, smiling pleasantly. Maspero took a step backward.

"Well met, Mira," Tam said. "How are your studies going?"

"Fine," she said. "This section's all natural studies it seems. We ought to—"

"You might find it better to do more searching," Tam chided. "And less talking." Mira pursed her lips in annoyance.

"I've been doing plenty," she said. "Have you found anything?"

He gave her a small, tense smile, a vague expression that ignored her tone and her anger and the fact she had a very good point. "I've been thinking," he said. "Have you considered discussing your search with the Book?"

She had—and had dismissed it. It was a fine artifact, to be certain; it's quick denial of the existence of Tarchamus's eruption spell meant it was also far cannier than it seemed. The arcanist's most famous spell and the curator of his library had no knowledge of it? Unlikely. There was no being certain about the mind-set of a creature like that. Her father ought to know that—and hadn't he been the one shouting at everyone to stay clear of the thing at the start?

"In due time," she said. "Right now I think we're better off narrowing our search area."

Tam shrugged. "I think it's worth looking into. Ask it where your city is. Or why not start with something simple? See what it knows?"

"You do that," she said, turning back to her shelf.

"Why don't *you*?" Maspero said with a significant look. "Nail down the necessities." Prove you're on my side, he did not have to say.

Piss and hrast. Mira gave them both a false and flimsy smile. "Why not?"

Her father brightened. "Wonderful. Come along."

Following after Maspero, Mira took several deep breaths. She was not going to lose her temper. She was not going to let her anger show. And she was certainly not going to stoop to her father's level and act like the child he was treating her as. At least, she thought, as they headed toward the center of the library and the Book's alcove beyond it, it was warmer here, and brighter too.

She looked back the way she'd come. The lights had moved away from the shelves, casting them in dreary shadow. Unlike the sanctum at the center of the library, it seemed colder, more forbidding. Odd—she thought. She'd been standing there reading a moment ago, with no trouble. She looked up at the cavern ceiling—the magical lights were drifting back toward the center of the library in that section. As if the library were discouraging anyone from wandering into those shelves.

"Oh clever, Tarchamus," Mira murmured, and she headed back the way she'd come.

"Mira!" her father called. "The Book is this way."

The lights didn't follow as she pressed farther into the darkness. She pulled a second sunrod from the kit at her belt as she passed the books she'd been examining.

"Stlarning Hells!" Maspero shouted after her. "I don't shit those things!"

"Mira!" her father scolded. "Come back here!"

There was something here—there had to be. The darkness warred with the glow of the sunrod as she moved past the shelves to the face of the cave. More shelves lined the wall here, stretching up beyond the edges of the sunrod's light. She pulled a scroll from the shelf—a copy of the *Teachings of the Path of Enlightenment*—and farther down, another—Earlanni myths. Not the spellbooks. Nothing to hide. The sunrod's light moved along the shelves with her.

And then, abruptly, broke in a neat line. A corner.

Mira rounded it and thrust the sunrod into the darkened alcove. Where the rough and rippling cave wall should have been, the surface was smoothed stone, decorated with the figure of the same elderly man as the outer entrance. Mira felt the edges of the space—a seam in the rock all the way up both sides and across the top. Her grin spread so wide her cheeks ached.

A door.

"Maspero!" she shouted. "Da!"

Eyes locked with Tarchamus's jade ones, she held the sunrod high, listening as the two men's footsteps clattered ever nearer. Maspero reached her first and she beckoned him to come nearer, until he stood facing Tarchamus's likeness too.

"There!" she said. "I will lay down coin that what we're looking for is in there." Maspero started toward it, but she put up a hand to stop him. "It's sealed by some means. If you shove it open, you might well trigger one of those traps that blasted book mentioned." She spun on her father. "Did you know about this?"

But she found she was demanding answers from the darkness. Tam Zawad was nowhere to be seen.

·:⌒:·

"Something's odd," Brin said. Havilar had no memory of their argument in the stacks, of telling him to find the Book, of flirting shamelessly with him.

"That doesn't even *sound* like me," she said, wrinkling her nose. "You must be stupidly fond of me to fall for that."

He ignored her. "But what's the point of making a replica of you just to . . . what? Get me over to the opposite side of the library?" Brin shook his head. "And who would do it?"

"Pernika?" Havilar guessed. "She was trying to get you aside. Maybe she made an illusion to get you away from the others."

"I don't know," Brin said. "I think she'd have to be a fairly powerful wizard. That was . . . a very solid illusion." Havilar dissolved into completely inappropriate giggles.

"Be serious," he admonished, but gods, he couldn't stop smiling. "I'll go find Tam," he said. "I'll tell him about Pernika and whatever that was. You find Farideh and ask her about what she saw. Meet back at the camp?"

"Yes," she said, her grin creeping back. She darted forward and kissed his cheek. "If you see me again, be sure it's really me, first, all right?"

He laughed. "Come on, this might be dangerous."

"So?" she said, still grinning. "We can be happy and cautious at the same time. It's not like swimming and eating at once or something." She considered him. "You are happy, right?"

"Yes," he said, and he was—not just because the looming question of what she thought was gone. It felt as if things were fitting together where they wouldn't before.

He paused. "Are you going to tell Farideh?"

"Yes," Havilar said. "Of course . . . Would you rather I didn't?"

"No," he said. Yes, he thought—how much more complicated would everything be once other people knew? This was pleasant and a little exciting. But he knew full well he was going to hear a lot of nonsense from a lot of people. Even Farideh.

But—gods—Havilar looked so glad, so *excited* to tell her sister that Brin had kissed her. To *brag* about it—complicated or not, he wasn't about to complain about that sort of compliment.

While Havilar hurried off toward the center of the library, Brin made for the Book's alcove. He'd find Tam, but if whoever it was that was so interested in getting him over to that area, perhaps he'd missed something about it. He moved cautiously through the library, keeping a lookout for traps and watching eyes, and trying very hard to keep his thoughts on the present moment and the serious problem of Pernika and the strange double.

He reached the alcove with no trouble, and found it quiet and still. Farideh sat sleeping on the floor, one leg tucked in and leaning against the chest of the wretched little gnome that made the pillar of the book's lectern. A variety of books and scrolls and maps lay spread across the floor in front of her, and a stylus was bleeding ink on a fresh parchment.

Hrast, he thought. Maybe she'd just stay asleep while he searched. But his footfalls had disturbed her and she started awake, clutching at the air as if trying to grab hold of someone. She blinked, her breath uneven as she came around and caught sight of Brin.

"Sorry," she said blearily. "How long have you been standing there?"

"Not long," he said cautiously. "Have you seen Havi?"

Farideh stretched her neck with a wince. "No. Why? Was she looking for me?"

"Yes," Brin said after a beat. "I think she is probably looking for you."

"Are you two talking again, then?"

Brin nodded. She paused and gave him a peculiar look. "Brin, I don't know if . . ." She paused. "Havi may be under the wrong impression about some things."

"Such as hydras?" He stooped to gather her collection of books from the floor, all the better to avoid her eyes.

But he could still feel her gaze boring into him. "I just don't want her getting hurt," she said after an interminable silence.

"Does anyone?" he said. "Don't worry about Havilar. I'm sure she'll be fine."

She was still staring at him, as if their secret was written all over his face. Why couldn't Havi have found her sister first? *He* didn't want to have this conversation with Farideh—without quite being sure why, he suspected she wouldn't like it. And Havilar would probably be furious he ruined her chance to tell Farideh.

"Do you know what I'm talking about?" Farideh said hesitantly.

"Maybe," he said. "But does it matter? I agree with you. Let's keep Havi safe." He smiled at her. "When's the last time you slept properly?"

Farideh groaned and rubbed her face. "My ritual wore off. So . . . I suppose it's been awhile."

"Dedicated to the treasures of the ages, eh?"

She didn't laugh as she came to her feet. "Something like that."

"I think Havilar was heading back to the camp," he said. "If you want to find her, that's the most likely spot." She nodded, too tired perhaps, to remember that Brin was the one who wanted her to find Havilar.

"Have you seen Tam, by the way?" he asked as he handed her the collection of books and scrolls she'd had open.

"I haven't seen anyone," she said. "This place is a maze. And the echoes . . . you know people are out there, but it's as if the sounds all come around the corners. He could be anywhere."

Brin sighed. "Damn. All right." The scrolls were threatening to tumble out of her arms. "What *are* you doing with all of this? Did you find Mira's spells or something?"

"No," she said diffidently. "It's a ritual."

He cocked his head. "A ritual? Where'd you find a ritual in here? That's new magic, I thought."

She shook her head, as if the question were unanswerable. "There's a little of everything in here, I suppose," she said too lightly. "Except Mira's spellbooks. If I see Tam, I'll tell him you're looking for him." And without leaving him any room to ask what sort of ritual it was, where she'd found it, or why she was acting so cagey, she turned and vanished in between the shelves. He frowned—he'd tell Tam about *that* too.

There was nothing out of the ordinary around the alcove, and nothing odd—or odder, at least—about the Book itself.

*What sort of tampering?* it wanted to know when Brin asked.

"Any sort, really," he said. He shrugged, and wondered if the thing could appreciate the gesture. "Perhaps I'm imagining things."

*What exactly are you imagining?*

There was an edge to that question, as if there were an answer that the Book wouldn't like, and Brin hesitated. How much did it really know? "Shapes in the shadows," he said. "There was a concern, when we found the cavern, that the Netherese had beaten us here."

*Aside from those who founded it?* the Book said. It chuckled. *I assure you, there are no assassins left walking in the shadows.*

Brin left it then, uncertain of what he'd discovered, and wound his way back toward the center of the library, hoping to find Tam—or at least someone who had seen the silverstar—before he ran into Havilar and Farideh. Loyal Torm, he hoped that went well enough.

He came around a shelf of neatly packed scrolls and found himself facing, not the rows and rows of books that he expected, but a room. A little room, with a little bed meant for a penitent priest, and a window that overlooked a courtyard. He crept toward it, knowing that he'd see brick red tiles, and scores of milling nobles in dark clothes. A bell started tolling, and he listened to each of the thirty-four peals with bated breath, as if the bell falling short might mean it was another's years it honored.

"Aubrin," someone said behind him. He turned. Constancia stood in the doorway, framed in the light of the low afternoon sun. She wore a charcoal gray gown instead of her ubiquitous armor, and she was still young. Younger than Brin was now. Fifteen, he remembered. Fifteen when she'd last worn mourning.

Grief pressed down on him suddenly—ages of sadness, far too much for a boy his age. "Must we?" he asked, his throat aching with the effort of not crying. If they just stayed where they were, if they didn't go to the bier then perhaps, perhaps, his father would still be alive and everything wouldn't be falling to pieces.

Constancia sighed. "You'll regret it if you don't." She beckoned and turned down the hallway.

Brin followed, and found himself wishing that she'd taken his hand. That little gesture . . . it would have meant the world. He watched the drape of her skirt spread over the stone floor as she walked and walked and walked.

It had meant the world, he realized. Because she'd done it. She'd taken his hand in hers and walked as slowly as he wanted, and the dour squire they'd made his nursemaid had suddenly changed from a monster, a symbol of everything that had gone wrong, to a friend.

**LESSER EVILS**

And they'd gone to the gallery, behind the screens, to watch his father's funeral from where no one could see that Brin was still alive, still Helindra's tool, and he'd wept great spots into the soft wool of her dress. Then she'd given him the little flute she'd rescued from the midden heap—one of his father's carvings. Brin carried it all the years after.

A decade, he thought. *It's been a decade since this happened.*

"Where are we going?" he asked hoarsely. The hallway had become impossibly long, the muffled *tap, tap, tap* of Constancia's hard-soled shoes beneath her skirts interminable. She didn't turn. She didn't answer. "Constancia?" he tried again. "Where are we going?"

He reached out to grab her shoulder, but she seemed to skip out of reach, as if he'd blinked too long and missed her motion. She looked back over her shoulder, her mouth open, but hesitating, wordless.

"What is this?" he asked.

Again, in the space between blinks, she went from girl to woman, her dress traded for polished and well-worn armor. "I think you ought to see it," she said, her voice shifting as wantonly as snow on a cold road. "You're never really alone. You haven't been."

She beckoned again, and again she was the girl in mourning, and there, behind her was the balcony behind the screens. Brin crept forward and put his eye to the gap in the panels. There on the bier lay the cold, bloodless body of Halance Crownsilver, a tapestry drawn up under his beard to hide the dozens of burning arrow wounds that riddled his chest and arms.

Brin's throat tightened and his eyes welled with tears again.

*It's not real,* he reminded himself. *He's already gone.* He looked back at Constancia, who was regarding him with a grim expression.

"There's nothing here worth dying for," she said in Tam's voice.

And all at once, Constancia, the hall, the screen, and the sunshine disappeared, and Brin was left standing all alone in a corner of the library he hadn't explored. Where the screen had been, there was a shelf loosely stocked with books bound in very soft leather.

And beyond it, where his father's bier had lain, there was a body.

# CHAPTER FOURTEEN

For the second time since they'd arrived, Tam waited just beyond the doors to Tarchamus's library for an answer to his sending, but still there was no answer. He studied the ceiling of the smaller cave, and wondered if his messages had even reached Everlund and Waterdeep.

He gathered his supplies and returned to the camp. He would simply have to broach with Mira the subject of retreating. The hours went by, quicker than any of them could appreciate, and while searching the whole of the library for a few spellbooks had originally seemed like trying to empty a lake with a beer mug, having attempted it made it clear "a sea with a teaspoon" was a more apt comparison. They were running short of supplies and very likely short of time. At the very least, they needed a report on where the Shadovar might be.

The library was a fraction of what Netheril had known. The sprawling empire of wizards had gained more knowledge than mortals were meant to have, and so had collapsed under the weight of their own hubris. All that remained was the City of Shade, which escaped to another plane as Netheril fell. And now Shade wanted what Netheril had possessed. Shade felt entitled to an empire and all its trappings.

*It is a wonder*, Tam thought, as he reached the camp, *that they haven't found this place and torn it apart.*

The camp was empty except for Farideh, sitting on her bedroll with an assortment of scrolls and books open in front of her. Tam cleared his throat, and she looked up guiltily. She all but threw the book in her lap onto the pile of scrolls . . . but not before Tam marked the map that lay nearest to the top, the descending spiral used to illustrate the layers of the Hells.

"Enjoying the rarities of Tarchamus?"

"While I can," she said.

"Which, I hope, won't be much longer," he said. "We need to contact Everlund. You need to go back to Mehen." She nodded absently. Tam frowned. "What are you doing with all of those scrolls?"

"Brin's looking for you," she said and did not answer his question.

Tam cursed to himself—he'd forgotten Brin was asking for something earlier. *This is why you work alone*, he thought.

*You're a link in a chain, a knot in a silk rug.* You haven't worked alone, truly, since you took up with the Harpers, Viridi might as well have said.

"Tell me what you're doing," he said. Farideh looked up at him skeptically, as if he were trying to trick her. There were dark circles under her eyes. "Good gods. When's the last time you slept?"

"Just a bit ago," she said. She looked past him. "You're missing Brin."

The younger man walked past the camp. Tam cursed again. "Stay here," he said to Farideh. "We're not done." He sprinted to catch up with Brin, coming to a stop just before him.

"I'm sorry I didn't find you," Tam said. "It's been rather busy. But I'm . . ." Brin walked right past him, staring fixedly at something just ahead. "Farideh said you were looking for me," Tam tried again. The younger man kept walking, his pace quickening.

"Where are we going?" he asked.

The hairs on the back of Tam's neck stood on end. Something wasn't right. He unpinned his holy symbol and started after Brin.

They followed the aisle for another thirty or forty feet, when Brin drifted right between two shelves. Tam sprinted to catch up, glimpsing the blue sleeve of the younger man's shirt as he wove through the maze of shelves—left, then right, then right again. Tam stepped out into a narrow passage, towered over by shelves packed tightly with thick tomes. Brin was nowhere to be seen.

"Brin!" he shouted. He ran one direction for a dozen feet, then back the other way. The door that led between the shelves was all but invisible until he came right up on it. A narrow shelf of small leather-bound volumes, dripping a trim of ribbon placeholders, stuck out from its neighbors. Behind the books, Tam could see Brin, standing stock still, and peering through a gap in the shelf in front of him. He could also smell the corpses.

He pulled on the shelf, which swung open smoothly on hidden hinges, just as Brin cried out and leaped back from the shelf. Tam caught him, and he shouted again.

"It's all right! It's all right. What happened?"

Brin shook his head dumbly and swallowed hard as if he'd been overcome. "I don't . . . Where are we?" He glanced back at the gap in the books, at the dead body of a man in inky leathers and a deep emerald cloak who lay sprawled on the floor, looking up at them with staring, hollow eyes. His belly was a ruin, rotting around a deep cut that his hand was still buried in. The stench was powerful but peculiar—the sweet rot of death smothered and blunted by a staleness, an almost muskiness . . .

"Oh, Loyal Torm," Brin swore and clapped a hand over his mouth. Tam guided him back out the door and down to the ground.

"Put your head between your knees," he instructed. "And breathe." He pushed his sleeves up and went back behind the partition, fearing the worst with the scent of shadows in the air.

The man looked up at him with eyes as ebony as an eclipse, his skin a shade of gray that death couldn't explain. And as Tam watched, a wisp of shadowstuff rose off his waxy cheek.

"Hrast," Tam swore. A shade. The man had been dead at least a few days, and judging from the bloodstains on the floor, he hadn't been alone.

Tam followed the path of black, stinking footprints around a blind corner. There were two more bodies, weapons in hand, lying on the floor. Both shadar-kai. One had a chain wrapped around his throat. The other had a sword in her back. Both seemed somehow less substantial, as if their bodies were slowly returning to the Shadowfell.

Brin still looked pale, but he was well enough to lift his head when Tam came back out. "We have a problem," Brin said. "A few problems."

"I'll say." Tam pulled him to his feet. "We need to get out of here. How did you know there were dead Shadovar behind that wall?"

"I didn't," Brin said. "That's the first problem." He described what had happened in his mind as he raced past Tam—the memory that shifted and changed from the truth, the strange sound of Constancia speaking in broken words. Tam schooled his expression—but with every word of the strange vision the hope that his dream of Viridi had been brought on by fatigue and stress faded faster than the dead shade.

"Walk," Tam ordered. They had to get back to the others—if Brin had been pulled into an illusion real enough to lead him halfway across the cavern, who knew what the others had experienced. "Did you have the sense she—it was trying to trap you? Hurt you?"

"No," Brin said. "Only . . . it was hard to live that again." He swallowed once more. "She didn't do anything else though—only showed me the dead body."

"Which sounds an awful lot like a threat to me."

"She said there was nothing here worth dying for."

Cold horror poured over Tam. "I'm inclined to agree. Whatever's happening, we're not equipped to handle it, few as we are." They reached the wider aisle. "At least the other problems can't make things worse."

"Much worse." Brin stopped walking. "There's another kind of illusion," he said. "And we haven't got as many allies as we thought."

Tam swore, but before he could get more of an explanation out of Brin, a scream split the silence of the library.

·:⌒:·

"*There* you are!"

Farideh nearly leaped out of her skin as Havilar bounded out from the maze of shelves into the open space of their camp. Farideh tucked the scroll she'd been studying—and its guilty infernal runes—under her ritual book. Havilar dropped beside her sister, practically vibrating with energy.

"I," she announced, "have been looking *everywhere* for you."

Farideh had been sitting in the camp since leaving the Book's alcove, trying to sort out the ritual before Tam came back to scold her. "I don't think it's been everywhere."

"It might as well have been," Havilar said with a giggle. "You will not *believe*."

"You're in a good mood," Farideh said, returning to the text in her lap as her sister settled down beside her. "What happened? Did you find another trap?"

"I kissed him."

Farideh looked up, startled at her sister's smug, gleeful expression. "Brin?"

Havilar snorted. "No, Maspero. *Yes,* Brin. Right on the mouth." She grinned and hugged her knees to her chest. "And *then* he kissed me back. Can you believe it? I was so sure he wasn't fond of me."

"What . . . When did this happen?" Why did she feel as if someone had punched her in the chest? Brin hadn't said anything, she realized. He'd stood there and let her think everything was the same as always.

"Before. We were talking and he said I was pretty, and I wasn't sure at first if he meant it or if maybe he meant the both of us, right? But then . . . he said the nicest things. And he is fond of me. So I kissed him." Havilar squinted at her. "Are you *angry*?"

"No," Farideh said. "I . . . just surprised." She swallowed. "Was it . . . How was it?"

Havilar blushed. "Nice. Not like you'd expect, right? But nice. Sort of terrifying."

"If it's terrifying, maybe you shouldn't be doing it," Farideh said, before she could stop herself. You can't stop any of this anymore, she thought.

Havilar looked as if Farideh had slapped her across the mouth. "Many thanks, *Mehen*," she said. "I don't care what you think. I did it. I'll do it again." She stood. "Besides I'm sure it's a thousand times more terrifying to kiss Lorcan, and that's never stopped you."

Farideh blushed so hard her face ached. "I've never kissed Lorcan."

Havilar rolled her eyes. "Well he's kissed you then. It still counts."

"No!" Hells, but there had never been a conversation Farideh wanted to have less. "Really. We've never . . . on the cheek and that was only to bother me."

Devils don't love, he'd told her once, and even if he was half a devil, that still meant Lorcan. Every touch, every sweet word, even that burning kiss on her cheek—they were all to keep her guessing, to make her unsure of where she stood. Not a one was "nice."

It doesn't matter, she thought. You wouldn't kiss him. You have an agreement, that's it.

Havilar was staring at her. "Really?"

"He's not some boy. Why would I?"

"Because you're not blind," Havilar said. "No, even if you were blind I'd still be surprised, since your ears and hands would still work. How many times have you snuck off with him and you never even tried—"

"Are you not the one always telling me to get rid of him? To stop talking to him?"

"And you should," Havilar said. "But it's not like you haven't already ignored me for ages, and gods, *do* come on!"

"I am not talking about this with you," Farideh said. "Go talk to Brin about how faulty I am. You can share that too."

Havilar scowled at her. "I'm not blind either. So quit pretending you're so much more virtuous." She turned on her heel and stalked off into the labyrinth of the library.

Farideh watched her go, torn by the urge to chase Havilar down and make it all right and to leave her be, to let her cool down.

*This isn't going to last. He's going to break your heart. He doesn't belong in our world. He's going to leave us both.* She didn't have the words in her to explain to Havilar why this was a terrible, terrible thing, and she didn't think Havilar would have heard them if she had.

She will call me jealous, Farideh realized. And to a point she would be right.

Not of Brin—though Havilar would never believe that, she was sure—but that Havilar had things so easy. A nice boy, a decent boy, a boy brave enough to get close to Havilar, and he liked her horns and all. Even if Farideh had half a chance at such luck, the pact would probably frighten anyone decent off.

Unbidden, Adolican Rhand popped into her mind and she shuddered. That was what she was allotted. No thank you.

*I'm sure it's a thousand times more terrifying to kiss Lorcan.*

Farideh ran her hands through her hair, under her horns, and squeezed her eyes shut. How could Havilar even think that was an option? And, even if it were . . .

Even if it were, she thought, you wouldn't. You couldn't. And neither would he.

She opened her eyes and suddenly the floor was dark, and canted woozily, as if half the library had sunk. But there was no library, no books, and no maze of shelves, the floor was clear but for the trash of a life someone had fled ages ago and the splash of moonlight across the floor.

Neverwinter, she thought, and the powers of the Hells surged up through her, trailing pennants of shadow. Neverwinter and they were all in terrible danger.

"I'd never hurt you like they will." She turned, and there was Lorcan, standing by the window. She remembered this—she'd been furious with him, and all over again a cacophony of emotion slammed into her, so heady and tangled she fought to rise above it.

But here he wasn't wearing that petulant scowl. He wasn't trying to confuse her. He kept his distance, tense and watching, his wings' tips flicking with agitation. She shouldn't be angry, she thought. And she shouldn't want to run to him.

She slipped a hand under her collar and pulled the amulet out. She'd bound him with it, hadn't she? Yes—he'd threatened her and she'd bound him, but he didn't flinch to see it. "You hurt me enough," she said.

His wings flicked again and again, as if she were blinking and missing the motion. "I would have died anyway," he said, and the voice was his but angry, far angrier than his expression. "You could run. Run, darling. Fast and far."

"No," she said. "I'm not leaving you." Not again, she thought, remembering the hellwasps. But that had come after, well after. And he hadn't been so angry at her until they'd left the tilting building. She pressed the heel of her hand to one eye. Gods, what was this?

When she looked up—for the barest of moments—it wasn't Lorcan standing there, but a bearded man, thickset and sad-eyed. And then it was Lorcan, no one but Lorcan. She took a step back.

"What is this?" she said.

"You will be *dead*, and there is nothing I can do to fix that." He shivered again, like there was too much heat between them, and his wings flickered. "There's nothing here worth dying for," he said.

It wasn't Lorcan's voice. It was Tam's. "What?"

He was staring at her now, imploring, willing her to hear the words he wasn't saying. "Trust me here. Run, darling. Fast and far."

Farideh took another step back, flame and shadow pouring down her arms and into her hands. "Who are you?"

His red skin darkened, mottling with bruises. His wings collapsed, broken, and blood poured from his mouth when he spoke in a patchwork voice, "Run, darling. Run fast and far. There is nothing here worth dying for."

"Don't listen to him." She spun toward the voice. Tam was suddenly standing there, in the shadows of the broken room in Neverwinter. "They're all lies. Every word."

"It's not what you think," Farideh started.

"Run, darling," Lorcan, or something like him, said again.

The moonlight through the window cast the priest's sharp features in a ghoulish light as he moved toward Lorcan. The half-devil flickered, then the room. Farideh stepped between them, but Tam kept coming, his dark eyes hateful. She threw an arm behind her to push Lorcan back, out of the way, but she couldn't find him. Tam lunged forward, shoving her aside.

Farideh screamed.

And everything—Lorcan, the room, the moon shining down—vanished.

She blinked, trying to reorient herself—the shelves, the little cookfire, Maspero's bedroll under her feet. She stepped off of it quickly. Her pulse was racing, her arms aching with unspent magic. The vision of Lorcan, battered and bleeding, wouldn't leave her thoughts, and she felt as if she might break down and weep; it had seemed so real, so certain. She swallowed the urge and tried to shake the flames from her hands.

"What was that?" she demanded of Tam, who was still staring at the empty air with such a look of fury and disgust as she'd never seen on him.

"Nothing," he all but snarled. He turned to her and smiled, but the rage was still there behind his eyes. "An illusion. Never you mind."

She stepped back. "How did you know?"

"Paltry magic like that shows," he said. "How are your studies coming? You've been doing a lot of reading, I noticed."

She searched his face but it betrayed nothing. "Well enough," she said. He said nothing but moved nearer, still wearing that peculiar, distant expression. The miasma of shadows seeped up from the churning powers flowing into her. "Are you going to take me to task for learning something new?" she asked. "It's not as if the others aren't doing the same thing. Dahl and Mira—she's piled a whole cart's worth of books here."

"But you've gotten a lot of help from Tarchamus's book of knowledge, haven't you?" Tam said. "You've taken plenty." He grabbed her forearm, and his hand was colder than the waters of the cavern lake—so cold her skin ached. "Why don't you come give something back?"

*Something is wrong*, a little part of her thoughts shrieked. *Something is very wrong.*

But the greater part of her lit with an animal fury. "Don't touch me." She twisted her arm and brought her elbow down hard on his forearm, to break his grip. But he didn't so much as flinch at the strike, only twisted with her, his icy grip tightening. She pulled back to strike the center of his chest, to knock him back and off balance the way Mehen had taught her.

But as her palm connected, the powers of Malbolge showed dark in the veins that writhed over the bones of her hand. As she struck the priest in the sternum, she spoke the word that triggered a great lash of flames, and engulfed him in fire.

She leaped backward. The blaze raced over the priest as he stumbled and unleashed an unearthly howl. She snatched up the nearest bedroll to smother the flames—oh gods, oh gods.

"Shar pass us over," Tam said from behind her. Farideh froze and looked back to see the priest, his expression stunned. He unhooked the chain from his waist and the pin from his collar, as Farideh's spell extinguished itself. "Move," he said, his eyes locked on the double of himself, now riddled with empty patches of angrily shifting light.

Light, bright as a full moon on a clear night, seared Farideh's eyes, the echoes of Tam's voice reverberating in her ears alongside his screams. Both faded and, through the floating spatters of her vision, she saw Tam—the Tam who she'd cast her spells at—thrash against the light, throwing off the priest's skin. For a moment, it seemed as if another man stood there—a gaunt, clean-shaven man with a nose like a knife. The creature roared and shifted to become only a dancing distortion in the air.

But Tam—the Tam who had cast the Moonmaiden's magic—slung the length of his spiked chain at the ghost, another crackling blessing skipping along the links.

Farideh leaped out of the way as the blessing burst free, enveloping the ghostly creature. The air pulsed with a frantic sound, so low it made Farideh's ears throb. The promise of flames and poison throbbed in her hands, and the memory of her brand's ache.

She cast again—the burst of energy that came so easily, it might as well have been an exhalation. The Hellish magic caught the ghost just as Selûne's magic subsided, and the pulse became a sharp, high screech. Something popped like a drum skin breaking. Then there were only the sounds of Tam and Farideh, trying to catch their breath.

"What was that?" she demanded, her eyes on the empty space where the creature had been. Her arm kept aching, and she realized it was not the brand at all, but the place where the ghost had seized her. "*Karshoj*—what was that?"

"Nothing good," Tam said. But even with her nerves so shaken, she could tell he was just as unsettled. "Did you try to set fire to me—to it?"

"I didn't *try*." Still trembling with adrenaline, Farideh shoved her sleeve back up past her elbow. The dark marks of the ghost's fingers stood out luridly against the frost-pale skin. "And if you ever grab hold of me like that," she said sharply, "I'll do it again."

"Hrast." Tam took her by the wrist. She flinched, and he waited until it passed and she let him examine the bruises. "Not an illusion then." Tam set his fingertips against the wound and murmured something. A silvery light bloomed from his fingers and spread over her skin with a prickling sensation she had an urge to rub away. But when it faded her skin was smooth and only ached when she pressed against it. She hugged her arm to her chest all the same.

"Thank you," she said. "I'm sorry I thought . . . That wasn't like you."

"Loyal Fury," she heard Brin curse from the other end of the camp. He looked winded, as if he'd chased after Tam. "Are you all right?"

She turned away, too embarrassed to look at him. "Fine."

"The second one's not an illusion," Tam said to Brin. "It's a ghost. Or it was." He looked up at the ceiling, as if there might be more there among the stalactites. "We need to find the others."

.:⌒:.

In the alcove of the Book, there was a silence, like the space after a drum's beat. A silence shivering with sound just beyond hearing—a vibration just beyond sensation. If any person had been standing in the empty space, they would have been struck by the feeling that the space did not seem empty at all.

*I want more time*, the Book said to the emptiness.

The air thickened, taking on a whining drone, the sound of a trapped fly, amplified to fill the space.

*Of course he's hungry*, the Book said quietly. *He's always hungry. We're all hungry. But you had those last three in hand and what happened? It's not my fault he's woken up without a proper meal.*

The air thrummed and turned colder. The strange presence divided, separated into three smaller nodes of thick air. In each was the suggestion of something more solid, and human-shaped. The notion of a face. The one opposite the Book—a lithe and twisting form that recalled a young woman with her hair in a thousand tiny braids—popped and crackled like a wet fire.

*And whose fault is that?* the voice sneered. *You overplayed your hands. It's as if you've all been corrupted by his impatience. So I will not weep for Bois—there is tragedy and there is the inevitable end of one who cannot think beyond his next task.*

The strange ghost's noises grew louder and more insistent. Threatening, one might have thought, and then dismissed. The space was empty after all.

*I want more time*, the Book repeated. *I haven't gotten enough from even* one *of them.*

Another of the ghosts, the one that may have been an older man with a short beard, picked up the thrumming whine. The air grew colder still.

*Perhaps they are cleverer than you think,* the Book said sharply. *Or perhaps it is Emrys's doing. Either way, you may look into the runes, no one is stopping you. Or leave it—there is no need to slow down those who might find the library after all. Tarchamus never wanted the wards, you'll recall.*

A pop. A screech. A whine that crescendoed into a faint roar, like a rush of wind.

*Fine,* the Book said. *Take one or two. And leave me the warlock and the paladin at least. They show promise.*

The strange presences swirled and clamored, drawing together once more. The roar of a phantom wind bounced around the space, and the disturbed air shifted from wall to wall to ceiling, before shooting off to other parts of the library.

*Idiots,* the Book muttered. A silence. Then, *I know you are there, Emrys. Do not pretend I am such a fool as those children are.*

The space shifted, and if the Book had possessed eyes, it would have seen the alcove as a brightly lit room, all paneled in rare, blond woods, with an enormous window looking out into an endless blue sky, and the rolling country far below. There was a bearded, thickset man standing by the window, looking down at the Book.

"You are asking for betrayal," he said, as the ghost plucked words from different memories the Book held of the man. "You are lying. They will wonder."

*They are zealots,* the Book replied, *beholden only to the rotting plans of a man without enough vision. They will not even think I might have surpassed Tarchamus as they knew him.*

The illusion's power wavered. "You ought to consider. You ought to forsake their plans. They do not matter."

*Let the visitors free?* the Book said. *Why? Better rescuers are underway. Or do you have some other method to keep him distracted?* The bearded man did not answer. *Forget these people, Emrys—they are as doomed as every soul that enters the library. Everything you might have done slipped out of your reach five thousand years ago,* it said bitterly. The illusion collapsed, returning to the cold, empty library. *Your chance to win me over has passed.*

# CHAPTER FIFTEEN

FROM THE MOMENT THEY'D SET FOOT IN THE LIBRARY, TAM HAD BEEN certain they needed to leave. There weren't enough of them to clear the site. There weren't even enough of them to seek out the spellbooks Mira wanted. They needed reinforcements to defend the entrance, and to keep information flowing from Everlund and Waterdeep about any movement on Netheril's part.

Now, he thought, with a dead shade and unnumbered ghosts, more than ever.

"Pack everything up," he told the rest of the expedition once they'd found them all and brought them back to the camp. "Our safety's been compromised."

None of them moved.

"Were you planning to *ask* if we wanted to leave?" Dahl said.

Tam turned on him. "Were *you* planning to hear me out before deciding you'd rather stay?"

What was it about Dahl that made Tam wish he could abandon him here? The question seemed too obvious for words. He was surly and disobedient—but then so were the twins by turns, and they didn't rankle Tam. He had a smart mouth and he was too ready to call Tam's bluff, even when there was no such agenda—but then much the same could be said of Brin, and the boy mostly amused the silverstar. But Dahl ought to be more, ought to do better. If he was the next generation of Harpers, he ought to be following orders, learning from his elders.

Did you? a voice in Tam's thoughts asked, and it sounded so much like Viridi, he momentarily feared another illusion. When you were so young, did you follow? Or did you fumble your way into a Shadovar agent's quarters and murder him without a plan for escape?

No, he thought, noting the look of fierce stubbornness the younger man wore. Dahl probably would have had some semblance of an escape plan. But at twenty, Tam had been no one to emulate. He'd settled down since. He'd learned the way of things, the rules of an agent moving through the world without disrupting more than necessary.

And you still work alone, the same voice all but laughed. You still won't settle for orders you don't like. You still, it added, as Tam considered Mira's stony expression, would rather avoid fragile, difficult things like *people*.

"By all means," Mira said quietly, "elaborate."

I shouldn't have to elaborate, he thought. And again, he could hear Viridi laughing at the stubborn old man he'd become.

"A few hundred feet from the entrance," he said sharply, "there's a dead shade and his lieutenants, rotting amid the arcanist's tomes."

Mira startled, shut her mouth, and he nearly regretted throwing the revelation at her. "How long?" she asked.

"Hard to say. Shades don't rot like the rest of us do. No more than a few days. We would have walked in on them if we'd come any quicker. Netheril knows about this place, you can be sure of that. And if they've sent a shade, they're going to be wondering where he's gone off to sooner rather than later."

Mira bit her upper lip, deep in thought. "What about the spellbooks?" she asked after a moment.

"What spellbooks?" Tam said. "Have any of you found a damned thing that looks like a spellbook?"

"They *are* here," Mira said.

"Oh, they're here all right," Maspero chimed in. The big man stepped up behind Mira and laid a hand on her shoulder. "Your girl knows best, after all. I didn't come down here for garbage like old maps and ledgers." He squeezed her shoulder, and Mira's mouth went small and tight.

Ah, Silver Lady—Tam's hands itched to take up the chain, to show that brooding bastard what his veiled threats were worth, whoever he was. Not here, he thought. Not now. Not with so many bystanders. Maspero gave him a smile full of violence.

Priorities, he reminded himself—Netheril came first.

"Are you planning on dragging us out of here?" Pernika folded her arms and regarded him lazily. "Maybe not all of us are afraid of shadows."

"Oh, ye gods!" Brin cried. "Just leave them here then, and let the ghosts turn them in circles until Shade can sort them out. It's *stupid* to stand here arguing."

We haven't got as many allies as we thought, Brin had said, and now Tam was cursing himself for not hearing the boy out then and there.

"What ghosts?" Dahl demanded.

"Two of them," Brin said. "At *least*. They look exactly like Tam and Havilar. You think you're having a conversation all normal and . . . mostly normal, anyway. And then they're suddenly trying to coerce you into going and using Tarchamus's Book."

"Oh," Farideh said. She blushed when all eyes turned to her. "I didn't know there was one that looked like Havi. I've seen her too." Her eyes slid to Havilar. "Unless you *were* adamant I read the Book?"

"Are you serious?" Havilar cried. "It's bad enough Brin couldn't tell, but you're my *karshoji* sister."

"Perhaps they're very convincing," Mira said quietly. She chewed her lip.

"You've seen one too," Tam surmised.

She hesitated. "Do you remember chasing Maspero and me from the door? Chiding me about my scholarly pursuits?"

Tam's eyes narrowed. "What door?"

"The door we discovered shortly before you hauled us back here," Mira said. "The door, which I intend to open before I leave here. It may lead to the location of Tarchamus's spellbooks."

There was so much of her mother in that face—the set of her jaw, the purse of her mouth. It was a stark reminder that she wasn't a child anymore. There was a balance to be struck if he wanted her to follow him out of this place, he knew.

He also knew there was no time left for cajolery.

"What do I have to say to make it clear to you that you are in danger like you've never been before?" he demanded, low and quick. "Do you want to hear what they will do when they find you in their way? Do you want to hear how they will hunt you down? Do you want to hear how the shadar-kai amuse themselves with captives? Because, Mira, I wish I didn't know. Don't make me tell your mother I left you to die at the Shadovar's hands."

Mira's expression betrayed no fear. "So you'd rather I left the spellbooks to them."

"Pack everything up," Tam said. "This isn't a discussion."

"I think you've made your point, Harper," Maspero said. "And you're free to go. We're not leaving until we have those spellbooks." He looked over at the twins, Brin, and Dahl. "And if any of your charges would rather stay and assist us, they're welcome to."

"Could we not just send word to Everlund?" Dahl asked.

"Do you think I haven't tried?" Tam asked. "The wards on this place block any such magic. If the sending's going through, the replies aren't."

Dahl folded his arms. "Well if there's a ward that can block sendings, I assume that held true for the Netherese who came before us too. Which means Netheril doesn't know—"

"We can't be certain of that. They might have found a way around them. They might have had compatriots in the woods. They might have agreed to report back at proper intervals and now that they aren't, Netheril will come looking."

"Shouldn't we at least see if we can find the spellbooks?" Farideh asked. "Isn't that why we stayed in the first place, to keep those things from Shade?"

Tam regarded her levelly. "Do you want to protect the spellbooks, or are you looking for something else in the arcanist's hoard?"

She flushed angrily, and folded her arms as well.

Havilar sighed. "If Farideh's going to stay, I have to too."

"What is wrong with all of you?" Brin demanded. "Have you not been listening?"

Havilar shrugged. "Fari's staying."

"Well, I'm not," he said. "There are dead shades in the stacks, imposter ghosts on the prowl, illusions sucking people in—"

"We're worrying about illusions now?" Dahl said.

Brin scowled at him. "They're powerful. They pull out old, dreadful memories and twist them around. Make you think you're in another time and place."

"Very frightening," Dahl said dryly.

"Watch your mouth," Maspero said.

"You too?" Tam asked.

Maspero eyed him a moment. "Thought it was just the spirit of the place or something, rattling my thoughts. Had me thinking of a girl I knew as a lad, Blind Jhaeri. Pretty thing, quick with a lock." He looked away and nodded to himself. "She died of some sickness that swept the docks one summer. Haven't thought of her in ages, and all of the sudden, I'm caught up in an old argument." He met Tam's eyes. "Glad to hear I'm not the only one."

"The Book mentioned traps," Mira said. "Illusions to drive off people who weren't worthy. Could it be that?"

"It doesn't matter," Tam insisted once more. "The ghosts are a danger, the illusions are a danger, the traps are a danger, and it may well be that whatever killed our shade and his comrades is some other horror we haven't discovered. And none of that matters if Netheril is looking for their lost agents."

"And if they aren't?" Mira asked.

Tam bit back a curse. "Humor me. Please. Come back out onto the surface and we'll contact Everlund and Waterdeep. We'll see what they say."

"And then?"

And then, he thought, I do not care how old you are, I will drag you out of this place myself if you won't come. What deal had she gotten tangled in to be under the thumb of someone like Maspero?

"And then," he said out loud, "you'll have better information."

She bit her lip again, staring down at the mess of their camp. "Leave the heavy supplies," she said finally. She looked up at him with those clear, dark eyes. "We'll be back soon enough."

It wasn't what Tam had hoped for, but at least she gathered up her personal items, and the rest of them did the same. They put out the coals of the cookfire, bound up their bedrolls, and gathered their haversacks.

Silver Lady, he prayed. Don't let us be too late.

Farideh came to stand beside him. "Do you think," she asked, "we ought to take the Book? It seems like the worst thing to leave in a wicked person's hands, after all."

Tam hesitated. If the ghosts were pushing them toward the Book, would they know once someone removed it? Would they try and stop them? Or would the Book?

It had insisted it didn't know the location of the spellbooks. Would it say the same to Shade?

"Come with me," he said. She followed him through the winding aisles, back toward the Book's alcove. "Shall I pretend your interest in staying is all altruistic?" he asked. "Or are you going to tell me what you've been up to?"

Silence. "Is there something wrong with being interested in rituals?"

"You had a map of the Hells," he noted. "There is something wrong with tampering with that sort of ritual." Silence again. "Did you never think," Tam said, "that you might be better off without that devil? That his death might be a blessing?"

"If he dies," Farideh said tightly, "then I lose everything."

"It might feel that way now—"

"No," she said, stopping as they reached the Book's resting place and facing him. "If he dies, I lose *everything*. I lose my pact. I lose my powers. I lose the protection I have against other devils. They'll seek me out. They'll seek out Havilar. I'll lose her too. Lorcan isn't perfect, I know that. But he's worlds better than being helpless and at the mercy of uncountable devils."

Tam shook his head. "There are ways to deter fiends. Don't you see? You could be so much more than a warlock."

Farideh regarded him, her temper barely leashed. "Whatever I can be," she said, "I can be that as well as a warlock. Otherwise, let's be honest, I could never have been so in the first place."

"Be reasonable."

"What do you think, Tam?" she demanded. "That I could renounce the pact and be a Harper? And then when you put me to work with someone like Dahl, then what? He leaves me for dead in a fight because I'm just some tiefling? *You* be reasonable. You sound worse than Mehen." She glanced back the way they'd come. "And frankly, if you're going to act like Mehen, you can start by worrying about your own daughter."

He frowned. "What is that supposed to mean?"

Farideh colored. "Nothing." She scooped the Book off its pedestal and started determinedly back the way they'd come. "Forget it."

*Where,* the Book asked, *are you taking me?*

"Back to our camp," Farideh answered.

Their things packed and ready, the expedition returned down the stunning main aisle, back to the enormous double doors. Tam stayed to the rear of the procession, his eyes sweeping the shadows on either side, ready for the ghosts to strike again, for the illusions to overwhelm someone. He couldn't shake the sense that someone was watching them pass, and his imagination was full of shadowalking warriors.

We are nearly done, he reminded himself. We are nearly safe.

He spoke too soon.

The doors were shut tight at the end of the passageway. For a moment, Tam wondered why Dahl and Maspero at the front of the group had shut them—they had been open when Tam returned from trying to contact the Fisher. But both men were straining at the portal, trying to pull the doors wide again.

"Now we have a problem that trumps Shadovar," Mira said as he caught up to them.

Green-tinted magic glowed all around the egress, the mark of the spell that sealed tight their only exit from the arcanist's library.

·:⌒:·

*I did warn you*, the Book said, when they'd returned to camp. *Tarchamus littered this place with traps to dissuade those who weren't dedicated to knowledge.*

Farideh stood, holding the tome open, so everyone could see the shift of ink. "And sealing the door?"

*I haven't the faintest idea*, the Book said. *I suppose no one's tried to leave before they were meant to.*

"Are you implying," Tam asked, "that the arcanist is deciding what's best for us?"

*Nothing of the sort. I'm merely suggesting possibilities. Perhaps one of you did something to trigger a lock. Perhaps these ghosts you mentioned are to blame. Perhaps it's the work of someone on the outside.*

"Perhaps we weren't meant to take you out of here," Tam said.

*I would have known about that,* the Book scoffed.

If they all had been hesitant to listen to Tam's concerns before, now everyone was watching the silverstar for answers.

He must love that, Farideh thought bitterly—even if Tam had been right. His lecture still smarted, as did the embarrassment that she hadn't been as subtle as she'd thought she was being. You wouldn't have to be, she thought, if anyone gave you the slightest benefit of the doubt. If anyone *asked* what was so dire.

"All right," Tam said after a moment. "Pair off. No one goes anywhere from now on without a partner." He set a hand on Maspero's shoulder with a very tense smile not even Tam could pretend wasn't threatening.

Farideh set the Book down and started toward Havilar. But she'd hardly taken a step before Havilar's hand intertwined with Brin's. Farideh looked away. Pernika moved to stand beside Mira. Farideh shut her eyes and cursed.

"Anyone approaches alone," Tam said, "assume it's one of the ghosts. Your partner stops reacting to you, assume they're caught by one of the traps. Mark its place. Maspero and I will go search the Shadovars' bodies for clues on what sort of timeline we're talking about. Mira, you and Pernika go search the lower floor. Find us a rear exit." *And put the Book back,* he mouthed. Mira nodded once.

He frowned at Brin and Havilar, hesitating a moment. "Can I trust you two to guard the camp?" he asked finally.

"That's it?" Havilar said.

"Twice the ghosts turned up near the camp. If they want us to stay, it makes sense they'll be back," Tam said. "Besides, I thought you'd like the chance to deal with your double."

Farideh gave a very small sigh. Was Havilar that predictable, or was Tam that smooth? Suddenly her sister was not only determined to defend every inch of the camp, but also *not* to slack off at it and spend her time kissing Brin.

Hells, Farideh hoped so. It was too easy to imagine a ghost like the one who'd looked like Tam catching Havilar around the throat with his icy hands, because she'd been too busy staring into Brin's eyes . . .

She cursed again, angry she was annoyed. Annoyed she was angry.

"You two," Tam said, considering Farideh and Dahl. He sighed. "Try and fix the door. Farideh, don't set the place on fire. Everyone meet back at the camp as soon as you've found anything. There's no keeping track of the time, but be sensible. If we have to come find you, there had better be a good reason." They dispersed.

"What rear exit?" Dahl muttered as he gathered up his sword and haversack. "It's not a stlarning inn."

"There's fresh air coming in from somewhere," Farideh said, recalling Havilar's trap. "There are vents under the floor."

"Excellent," Dahl said. "We can shinny a thousand feet up a crack the size of a hay straw." He started off without waiting for her.

Farideh gave her sister one last look. "Be careful." Havilar folded her arms and turned away. A sick feeling tightened Farideh's lower back, and her tail started thrashing. She hurried after Dahl.

The magic glowing around the edges of the door had not faded. Dahl dropped his haversack on the floor and prodded the gaps with the tip of a dagger. The green light seemed to have completely filled the space between the doors.

"I might be able to jump through it," Farideh said. Dahl looked back at her as if she were insane. "Humor me," she said, "and rule it out. We're going to both feel like fools if it turns out the door could have just been opened from the other side." He stepped out of the way.

Farideh drew the powers into herself, enough to make the little tear in the world that would let her leap through space and even the thin stone of the door. The pulse of Malbolge surged, the shadows around her deepened . . . and nothing happened. The magic broke around her with a crack and fell back, through the planes to its faraway source.

"There we are," Dahl said. "Tarchamus had a little more power than you."

Or her link to the Hells was damaged, she thought, and the spell weakened. Could it work that way? The urge to pull all the scrolls and notes from her haversack and attempt the cobbled-together ritual of the Book was strong. She quashed it, burying it down under more pressing worries. She couldn't attempt anything with Dahl watching, anyway.

"I never said he didn't," she replied. "It was just supposed to go around his spells."

Dahl broke off. "Never mind. You were right. It needed to be ruled out." He stared at the door, silent for a long moment. "I don't suppose you were eager for this assignment either."

She folded her arms, doubting anyone was eager to be matched up with Dahl. "I expected to be left back at the camp with Havilar."

"I take it," he said, pulling out his ritual book, "that means your sister and the lordling have some kind of understanding? Not pleasant being abandoned, is it?"

She laughed. "Oh, what in the Hells would you know about that?" His expression closed, and he looked down at the tome in his lap. Sulky *henish,* she thought, but her ire softened slightly. She didn't have to coddle Dahl or coax a reason out of him not to find him impossible. But she didn't want to be a *henish* herself.

"There are runes on the walls and the columns," she offered. "They lock some of the doors. Maybe there's one for this." She thought back to her earlier conversation with Havilar. "I think there's one on the wall near here."

Dahl gave her a puzzled expression. "Who told you there were rune-based locks?"

"The Book," she said. "Look, we'll just go, break the rune, and see if it does any good. It's worth trying."

He turned back to the door. "How far is it?"

"I don't know. Not far, I imagine."

"Why don't you take care of it?" he said. "I'll stay here."

She nearly laughed again—who could have guessed her example for Tam was so prophetic. "And if the ghosts find us? The illusion triggers?"

"The ghosts don't look like you or me," Dahl said dismissively. "And we've tramped through here enough that I'm certain there's no trap to trigger. Go test your theory. I'll be here."

Farideh started to protest again, but she caught herself. The scrolls in her haversack were still calling. She could go, destroy the rune, and try the ritual—if it didn't work, she needed every possible moment to find a way to fix it before Tam made them leave and she was back to not knowing where to start. She had the components—borrowed, begged, and gathered from the library and her comrades. She just needed space, time, and to be as far from anyone else as possible for a few moments.

"All right," she said. "But be careful."

She followed the wall to the west, where Havilar had said she'd seen the large rune. The library was darker here along the edges, but her eyes were sensitive enough to make the path clear. Not so sensitive to make the space less eerie. She listened for a moment, but not even the echoes of her comrades reached her.

The rune had been etched into a space between shelves, a letter nearly as tall as she was drawn in strokes as thick as her leg. It glowed faintly, as if reflecting the light of the orbs overhead. The floor around it was open, as if the shelves had been arranged to better display the rune, and a statue of a man in wizard's robes stood opposite it.

First the ritual, she thought. Better to break the rune right before she went back to Dahl, in case he decided to come find her once the doors opened.

If she listened hard enough, could she hear the motions of the ghosts of the library? At least now if anyone came toward her alone she'd know better. Anyone but Dahl, she amended. She looked back the way she came—a gloomy path through the shadows and the sickly cast of the arcanist's greenish magic tracing the walls. Which would be worse—Dahl or a ghost playing at being Dahl coming across her now?

Farideh kneeled near the statue and opened the ritual book—Dahl could take care of himself, and if he came upon her, it didn't matter, she'd already be well underway. She started drawing the runes one by one in a careful circle, slowly so the shaking of her hand wouldn't muss things. Her thoughts raced. What if Lorcan wouldn't come? What if he couldn't? What if someone else had already rescued him and he was somewhere else entirely?

Worse, she thought, chalking the rune carefully over a seam in the tiles, what if he never needed rescuing at all? What if he's only grown tired of me?

You should be so lucky, a little part of her thought. A very little part.

She didn't want Lorcan back the way he was, the way Havilar seemed to remember him—chasing her down and trying to drag her through portals, sending assassins to kill her friends because he didn't like them—but when the forces of the Hells had appeared to take him back . . . He'd changed, she thought. By then he was different. By then he'd been kinder, maybe gentler. His nobler side, she thought, coming through. He wasn't all wicked. Neverwinter proved that. Surely.

Farideh finished the circle and thought of the night in the winter woods, after she'd taken the pact, after she'd fled the village. The heat of him and his burning hands grasping her wrists . . . Perhaps a little wicked wasn't so bad.

Gods, now she was making *herself* blush. She rubbed her hands over her face, as if to scrub away the memory. She wasn't fond of Lorcan. She was rescuing a . . . comrade. Returning a favor.

You *are* a terrible liar, the same little part of her seemed to say.

She trailed a line of the silver dust over the runes. As the line closed into a circle, the runes took on a soft, white glow.

Farideh's heart was in her throat as she kneeled again, a little ways off, the ritual book open in front of her. What if he didn't come? What if he couldn't? He might be dead, after all, she thought. He might have died at his mistress's hands so I wouldn't.

Or Glasya might have killed him anyway, with or without Farideh . . .

Or his terrible, monstrous sisters might come instead. . .

Or the ritual might fail . . .

She started speaking the words of the spell, her mouth moving as if on its own, as if it had decided to go ahead and try even though her thoughts still raced, screaming that the magic wouldn't work, that she was wasting time and components, that she was going to break her own heart. The cadence of the ritual was powerful and rhythmic—it pulled itself out of her, drawing strands of the frayed Weave together, and she couldn't stop any of it even if she'd wanted to. The air in the antechamber thickened and her hands began to ache as the powers of the Hells rose in concert with the powers of the Weave, straining to be set free.

Just when Farideh's words began to run out, just when she was sure she could not handle another strand, another syllable, the magic split the air, neatly as a razor.

---

"Son of a barghest," Dahl muttered, considering the spent remains of yet another ritual arrayed around the base of the door. The green light of the magic sealing the portal and the yellowish light of his sunrod made it all look like a sickly mess. He could not pass through it, unlock it, break it down, melt it with heat, crack it with cold, or ask it nicely to open up.

That marked the last of his ideas. He blew out a breath.

"Would you let me try and shrink you down?" he asked, looking back over his shoulder. "It probably won't work, but . . ."

Farideh was still not there.

He walked a little ways down the tunnel, to where he could see the library beyond. Nothing. Damn it.

Dahl walked to the opening of the tunnel and scanned the shelves. If he went looking, she might come back to the door while he was out. If she came back and couldn't find him, gods knew what she'd decide to do next. He made his way back down the tunnel to the sealed door and pulled out the diary he'd taken. She'd be back. Surely.

He'd read several years' worth of memories—and with each successive entry, he found himself wondering more and more what he was meant to gain from it. For though that late entry remarked on the intercession done to prevent the arcanist's access to the Weave, as he paged through earlier comments, there was little to remark on but Tarchamus's biting wit and disdainful nature.

He turned to a later page, one dated to the spring of 1374, by Netheril's calendar.

*Tarchamus has made fools of us all. We should have known better. Censuring him has only driven him to find more dangerous sources of power. Last night I called on him to make some amends—more the fool am I. I thought I owed him that—and over wine he asked after my eruption spell. I told him, quite honestly, that it progressed well, but I have reconsidered its need. Such a feat of magic would wreak more destruction than anything we've attempted thus far. He scoffed—what is the world for, if not so that we can remake it to our imaginations? Better to devise such feats as might destroy what came before than to sit in our halls making lights and plumbing for the unfortunate worms unwilling to seek the knowledge of the spheres.*

*"That is the sort of talk which led to your censure," I said to him.*

*He replied, "It is the sort of talk all you fools are thinking. Thinking, but not brave enough to speak. Burn the lower cities if it gives you greater insight. Melt the mountains down and boil away the rivers if it shows the gods what greatness we can achieve without them. There will always be more—mountains, rivers, men."*

*I said, "I think you forget yourself. You are talking of humans. Of our subjects. You can't treat them like simple gnomes or elves."*

*I shall never forget his answer: "They are as far from us, Emrys, as they are from the gods." And then he showed me the scroll on which he had written his own spell—one which would take a relatively small amount of magical effort, applied just so, and tap into the planes in such a way as to create, if not a volcano, then its near simulacrum. I have copied it to the best of my memory on the following pages, because of what came next.*

*We fought. He accused me of envy. I accused him of callousness. I warned him I would turn him over to the council. I left, but I did not go to Sadebreth. I told myself it was merely Tarchamus's temper and if he were allowed to cool, things would return to the way they had been.*

> *The next morning the ground beneath the city of Tenish had erupted, burning Arion's fortress from the sky, and laying waste to his vassals below.*

"Gods' books," Dahl muttered. If the arcanist was truly the misunderstood scholar that the Book had painted for Dahl, there was a lot of explanation missing from Emrys's diary. His thoughts turned circles trying to find a way to understand Tarchamus's actions as anything but horrific. Perhaps this Arion had been a greater threat? Perhaps someone had stolen Tarchamus's spell and used it? Perhaps it had gone off by some accident?

But still: he had crafted a spell to destroy vast tracts of land and had not cared if it killed those who stood in its way.

He could not help but wonder what Jedik would have thought of it—a thought experiment for a novice loremaster if Dahl had ever seen one. If knowledge was not meant to be hidden or hindered, how did one act when the freedom of some knowledge led to death and destruction?

"The knowledge is not to blame," he murmured, as if at lessons, "only the use of such. The actor controls the action, not the potential for action." A pretty answer, but Dahl—perhaps, he thought bitterly, since his fall—found it hard to accept. A spell to birth a volcano from the fields might well sit quietly on a shelf, an example of one wizard's careful, brilliant study . . . but that counted on the goodwill and self-discipline of a great many people who weren't known for such things.

He turned the page to see Emrys's scribbled diagrams, full of questions and strange symbols he'd marked as provisional. Dahl rubbed his eyes—even with the ritual's help, the pages were barely comprehensible.

The voices that carried through the door on the other hand—

"*It's right!*" he heard a man shout in Netherese. "*It's right! There's the old bastard. Pull the wizard out, you idiots.*"

Dahl slammed the book shut and pressed his ear to the door. Movement—plenty of bodies. More muffled Netherese. And then a voice he had been sure that he'd never have to hear again.

"Well done," Adolican Rhand said, so close, Dahl could picture him admiring the garnet in the arcanist's pendant. "Get them open."

Dahl scrambled back from the door, one hand on his sword and his ears ringing with nerves. The doors started to shudder with the impact of a ram. The green magic held them shut and whole, but they'd soon realize that and try other means—he had as long as it took Rhand to come to drastic measures. And he couldn't sit here and wait.

Dahl snatched up the heavy haversack and tossed it back down the tunnel, before pacing out a distance between the doors and the point where he'd have to cast the ritual. He yanked the bag open, digging through the bottles and vials and pouches for the right pieces, stringing together in his head the two rituals he needed, and the way to cast them both as one.

The sentry was simple—a spell for a student, a spell he could have taught Farideh and been done by highsunfeast. He set the two components—crushed quartz and basilisk spines—to one side. The other, the amplifying ritual was much trickier and would take all his concentration.

Or, he thought, all he could give while the rhythmic crashing of the ram demanded his attention.

Salts of copper, powdered silver, the splintered roots of a Feywild tree, and a chip of diamond the size of a flea. He worked feverishly, fighting to keep his focus on the spell and not the door, not the *boom, boom, boom* and the inevitable point when the ram stopped its futile efforts and the wizard went to work.

The sentry came together quickly, an invisible watcher left in sight of the doors but as far down the tunnel as possible. It wouldn't see Dahl or the others but it would be very quick to spot the Shadovar.

The second half took longer, the broken strands of the Weave fighting against Dahl as the spell pulled them together, winding them down into the secret substance of the sentry, down around the core of its spell. The booming slowed.

Dahl's grip on the magic started to slip. He spoke the last words of the ritual in a rush, all gasped together in one breath of air. The magic snapped tight around the sentry, and a flash of colorless light filled the tunnel. Dahl dropped to his knees, panting.

What he'd told Farideh before was true: ritual magic wasn't for fighting. But the amplification spell he'd been part of creating back in Procampur would make a simple workaday ritual feed into itself, casting at a hundredfold its prior power without changing the intent of the original spell.

In this case, the sentry would scream when its range was breached. Hopefully loud enough to shatter Rhand's ear drums and echo off the farthest walls of the library. It would buy them time to prepare.

The ram stopped. He scooped his components and books back into the haversack. He had to get back to the others. But first, he had to find Farideh.

Dahl sprinted out into the stacks, and had no more than hit the last stair before he heard Farideh's cry of alarm echo through the library.

"Shit," he cursed.

With only a vague idea of where she'd gone, he followed the nearest to the wall, calling her name. He shouldn't have to pay attention to her comings and goings. He shouldn't have been asked to play nursemaid. Damn it, he thought easing around one of the enormous columns—if anything happened . . .

Gods, he hoped this was just her being foolhardy and easily excited. Could one of the ghosts have lured her away? Could they have killed her the way they had the scouts? Or gods, worse—what if the shadar-kai found a way in? What if they didn't need to breach the doors?

You ignorant fool, he thought at himself. Tam would skin him alive.

The pathways through the library twisted onto themselves, throwing shelves up into his path and dwindling into dead ends with dead-eyed statues. The farther he went, the more worried he became. He'd sneered at the notion of the ghosts. He'd not believed they were in danger, and now he'd lost Farideh *and* himself in the maze of the library—

There. Voices. Farideh and . . . someone else.

Calm voices, he noted, and he slowed down, easing his way toward the sounds. What did the illusions look like from the outside? Would he know?

Who else would she be talking to? he wondered. He came around the corner, his sword at the ready, and froze.

# CHAPTER SIXTEEN

LORCAN DROPPED FROM NOWHERE, AS IF STUMBLING INTO THE WORLD.
Farideh sprang to her feet. "You're alive." Such a stupid thing to say, but gods, she hadn't been sure—even when the spells had worked, she hadn't believed. For once, Lorcan had no witty barb, no charm and cajolery for her. He stared at the cavern, at the circle, at Farideh as if he didn't believe a one of them was real.

"How?" he finally gasped. He started laughing. "*How*, you perfect little . . . ashes, but I could kiss you!" He pulled himself to his feet, staring at the cavern beyond.

Gladly, since she was blushing furiously—he'd spoken and what had gone through her thoughts but, *Yes, you could.* An old thought, she told herself. She twisted her hands into each other. "It took some work," she said. "But—"

"But Sairché can eat that shitting room," he said. He laughed again, triumphant, and found her eyes. "Darling, you are worth twenty of any other warlock. I can't believe I doubted you." He started toward her.

And hit the barrier of the circle.

The magic rebuffed him solidly as a brick wall, and he stepped back, startled. He pressed a hand against the empty air. A crackle of gold energy spidered off his palm where it pressed the plane of the line of runes, and he pulled it back with a hiss.

"What is this?" he said, low and deadly. "Let me out."

Farideh swallowed. "It's for your own good."

Lorcan closed his hand into a fist. "Is it? Or is it just a way to get what you want?" He paced the edge. "I see you've improved on your sister's design. What's the requirement? Hmm? Do you want me to release you from the pact? Or stand against another unbeatable force out of the Hells before you send me back into Sairché's tender mercies?"

"No, I—"

"Did you just learn the spell to punish me?" he raged. "First that godsbedamned amulet, now a binding circle? What comes next? Will you leash me like a disobedient dog?"

"No!" she cried. *Karshoj*, she thought, you idiot. He is the same. He is exactly the same. "Here! Here."

Farideh crossed carefully over the line of runes, into the binding circle. The magical barrier created a narrow wall of chilly air that sent goosebumps over her skin. She shivered. Wary, Lorcan stepped back. She spread her hands in a gesture of appeasement.

"You can't escape them here," Farideh said. "I haven't figured that part out yet. But whoever has you can't find you—I don't think they can find you—if you're trapped in the circle. Isn't that right?"

Lorcan scowled. "Yes," he spat.

"So it's just temporary. Just for safety. The only binding is that you ask me to send you back." She swallowed—gods, but she was out of practice talking to him. "Do you have a way? Something to keep . . . whoever from finding you?"

"No," he said glumly. He dropped to sit on the floor. "It's a clever notion," he allowed. "Although, *such* a waste—what's the point of giving me a few moments respite if you're just going to send me back?"

*It's a thousand times more terrifying to kiss Lorcan, and that's never stopped you.* Farideh looked away.

"I thought you might know a way to block them," she admitted.

"Sairché," Lorcan supplied.

"Oh," Farideh said. "That's . . . well she's not the worst, is she?"

"She's kept me captive since you left Neverwinter," he snapped.

"But you're alive," Farideh said, smiling despite herself. "And . . . I mean, Sairché hasn't bothered us again. If nothing else, she's been distracted."

"Something like that," Lorcan muttered. "Is that dragonborn going to come storming over to pin me with his falchion?"

"Mehen's not here," Farideh said. She looked down at him again. "He's in Cormyr."

Lorcan's eyebrows rose. "Really?" he said, and she knew that tone. That tone was dangerous, far more dangerous than his ire. "And where is here?"

"The Silver Marches," she said. "It's a buried library, a Netherese wizard's collection."

"What have you gotten up to, darling?"

"It's too long a story," she said.

"What do I have but borrowed time?"

Farideh started to protest that *she* was the one short of time. She hadn't expected the spell to work, to be honest, and now she was all too aware of how long she'd been away from Dahl. Her eyes drifted up, away from Lorcan, and she saw he held his wings at an awkward angle, pinned together. She moved to better see the iron pin that had been stabbed through the thin membrane and bound around the bone. Black blood oozed from the wound.

"Oh gods," she gasped and reached for the powers of the Hells, the powers to shatter the awful thing to dust.

Lorcan grabbed her hand out of the air. "No," he said. "Don't touch it."

He didn't let go of her hand. "Doesn't it hurt?"

"Of course it hurts," he said. "But it will hurt ten thousand times as much if I go back and Sairché sees it missing. She's not so self-absorbed as to miss *that*." He glared at her hand, as if he were holding something he couldn't decide what to do with. She drew it back.

"What do you plan to do now?" he asked.

She sat down beside him, as aware of the barrier of the circle as if it had been a solid wall. It might have been no impediment to her passage, but it was the last layer of protection she'd had from him. From what stupid things she might do.

"Do you know of some spell I should be looking for?" she asked. "Something that would keep you safe? There's . . . so many books here, it's possible I've just missed it."

Lorcan looked at her, as if he weren't sure whether to laugh or not. "You're serious, aren't you? Lords of the Nine, you mean that."

Farideh held herself a little straighter. "Of course I do. You saved us. I owe you this much. I can't just leave you there." She looked down at her lap. "Tell me what I need to do?"

"Buy me passage to another layer?" he said bitterly. "Kill Sairché?"

"Something I *can* do."

"If I knew, darling, I would tell you," he said. "But you'd better think of something. She's only interested in me to get ahold of you, and I am fast running out of options. If you don't figure something out, I can't promise I'll be able to hold onto that little secret Sairché doesn't know about."

Havilar. Farideh's heart stopped. "You wouldn't."

"Darling, you're clearly not aware of the myriad tortures my sister has at her fingertips." He looked away, scowling up at the statue of the dead wizard. "I wouldn't, but I might not have the choice."

"No," she said. She pressed the heels of her hands to her eyes. "Why is she doing this?"

"It's complicated."

No doubt, she thought. Everything in the Hells seemed complicated, but when it came out across the planes and threatened her, Havilar, and everything she held dear, it was not too complicated to explain.

"It has to do with Bryseis Kakistos, doesn't it?"

Lorcan stiffened, but he kept watching the wizard. "Sairché told you that, didn't she? Not someone you'd normally listen to, darling."

"I don't see another answer." He didn't react. "Tell me what it is."

Silence.

"I know," she said. "About Bryseis Kakistos. About the pact with Asmodeus."

Lorcan froze, turned, and for a moment, eyed her with such breathless horror that he might as well have been expecting her to smash his teeth in and tear out his tongue.

"Why didn't you tell me?" she said.

"If you know," he said, still watching her cautiously, "I think you can appreciate that wasn't the obvious course of action. I had thought . . . Well, I expected you to be upset, darling, and why would I want that?"

"Upset?" She frowned at him. The story the Book had told her was so much better than what she'd feared. Better than anything she dared imagine. She couldn't guess what Lorcan thought she'd be upset about.

"Because," she ventured, "I owe her better? Because she took the pact with Asmodeus to protect tieflings from being bound like this?" She rubbed her arm where the brand that marked her as Lorcan's warlock lay. "I don't think of our pact that way. Not anymore." She looked up at him. "It's a tool, not a punishment." Lorcan was staring at her as if she had suddenly started speaking in abyssal tongues.

"What *exactly* do you know about Bryseis Kakistos?" he asked.

Farideh's pulse was in her throat. "That she, that all of the Thirteen, took the pact with Asmodeus to protect tieflings from . . . from having to answer to fiendish lords. That she sacrificed her own freedom to . . ." Farideh let her words trail away. The dark expression on Lorcan's face said too much.

"Someone's been lying to you, darling," he said.

"It wasn't . . . Why would someone lie about that? They didn't know what it meant." Farideh shook her head. "How do I know you're not the one lying?"

"Darling, did you know that in the north, near Vaasa where your ancestress made her home, very naughty little tieflings are warned to be good, lest Bryseis Kakistos come and steal their skins off their bones? I didn't teach them to do that." He paused, then added, "Much as I wish I could tell you I had."

I am such a fool, she thought. "She was evil?"

"Vile," Lorcan said. "She was a madwoman, a killer of her own kind. In fact, plenty of people lay the credit for Asmodeus's ascension squarely at her feet. Without Bryseis Kakistos, there would have been no Toril Thirteen—there are those among them who did not enter the pact willingly. Without the Toril Thirteen, there is a fair chance Asmodeus wouldn't have had the power to claim the mantle of a dead god and fling the Abyss into the Elemental Chaos. Without the efforts of Bryseis Kakistos, the history of tieflings is a good bit different."

This shouldn't shock you, she told herself. This is what you should have known. But it did shock her, because some part of her had always hoped—no, had been *certain*—that she might be different. That she wasn't doomed like the rest. Farideh felt the blood pooling away from her. I will not faint, she thought. "That's not true."

"Likely not entirely," he said, as if they were arguing over a tavern tale. "These stories increase every time they're told. But, darling, no one in the Hells would give a mortal credit for anything they could claim the glory for, unless she'd definitely done *something*."

A swift stroke, she thought, is better than a thousand cuts. "What did she do?" Lorcan hesitated a moment, as if he recalled he should have been managing her differently, and Farideh's temper rose. "What did she do?"

"It's as I said," he replied. "What do you want?"

"The whole story," Farideh said. "Don't tell me not to worry about it."

"But you shouldn't," he said more sharply. "Darling, you can't change the past, and you can't change where you came from."

"I have you caught in a binding circle," she said. "Don't treat me like a child."

Lorcan's expression hardened. Gods, she thought, where did they stand anymore? She wouldn't bend to him, and he wouldn't treat her as something more than a plaything again—where was the middle ground? Was there any place left, she wondered, where they fit?

"If you go back in time, it was never a secret that the king of the Hells wanted godhood," Lorcan said. He spoke without softness, without care. As if he meant for her to feel every blow. "Whether they offered the sacrifices or he demanded them isn't clear. But thirteen tieflings made a pact with Asmodeus—a mass sacrifice of fiend-born, plus their own souls and blood, for the chance to wield the powers of the Hells.

"The stories are muddled. I don't doubt some devil has it written down—someone has everything written down—but the way it's told, the tieflings thought their blood would be spilled in offering, or maybe that they would die in a future sacrifice, but instead . . . their rites let Asmodeus take the very blood in their veins—in *every* tiefling's veins for his own."

Farideh frowned. "He killed them?"

"Then how would you be here, darling?" Lorcan said. "No. Before the Spellplague, tieflings . . . Well, it was harder to tell who was and who wasn't a tiefling, and what sort of being sullied the well. They might have horns or hooves or peculiar eyes or any number of things. Tieflings were descendants of all manner of creatures—demons, devils . . . fiendish things—and it showed. And after . . ."

"After we look the same," Farideh said, horror dawning on her. "Is that . . . she did that?"

"Perhaps," Lorcan said. "As I said, there's no way of knowing what happened precisely, short of convincing Asmodeus himself to tell you the tale. But there is no demon blood left in tieflings descended from those days. No scattered fiend's. The children born to tieflings after that rite were devilborn, the true-breeding scions of Asmodeus. A hundred years ago a body might have a little devil blood, and mixing with the right mortals could thin it all out. Mortals don't breed straight down after all, not even with fiendish blood in them. Now a dozen generations could go by, but the result will be the same. You are the descendents of Asmodeus, every one." His eyes darted once around the space, as if he were afraid the god of evil might be listening. "Whatever happened, those thirteen were in the middle of it and the magic was unlike anything Asmodeus had managed in ages."

Farideh covered her face, blocking out Lorcan and the library and all of it. A madwoman. A killer of her own kind. On Bryseis Kakistos lay the blame for Asmodeus becoming the god of evil, the fall of those first thirteen infernal warlocks, the undilutable blood that cursed the tiefling race.

She closed her eyes. Mortals don't breed straight down—but tieflings, ah, tieflings were the exception. Tieflings didn't mix, didn't dilute. A human and an elf might beget a half-elf, but no matter who lay down with a tiefling—human, elf, orc—the result was another tiefling. Her chest felt as if it were collapsing around her lungs. What else might carry down with that blood curse?

"Is that why you chose me?" she said, barely above a whisper. "Because you think I'll be like her?"

Lorcan clucked his tongue. "Lords, no, you're enough of a headache. I suspect your existence would make Bryseis Kakistos—and several of her descendents—spin in their graves." He paused. "I told you that you wouldn't like it."

"She had children," Farideh said. She stood, without any sense of where she meant to go. "How? Who would . . . ?" She trailed off. No one, was the answer. No one sane, no one with an ounce of decency, would take that risk and have a child with someone like Bryseis Kakistos. No one would seek to continue that line. Mortals don't breed straight down, she thought. And genocidal warlocks don't breed at all. Or they shouldn't.

No one sane, she thought, or willing.

"Darling, don't," Lorcan said, standing as well. "That's not a path you want to go down."

She swallowed to wet her mouth, but it did no good. "That's why they're rare. Sairché said there are only four Kakistos heirs. Five, if you count Havilar." She looked up at him. "You know who our parents are."

"Why ask? I can promise it doesn't matter. You don't need to know."

"Who, Lorcan?" she asked. "Please."

His wings shuddered as he tried to flex them against the iron bar. "I haven't looked into it. But . . . you're right. There aren't many likely options."

"And they're all wicked."

"It isn't common to have such a principled warlock," he agreed.

Of course it wasn't. Of course they were wicked. What other kinds of tieflings were there but those who were wicked to the bone? "Hasn't anyone tried to fix it?" she said softly, but she knew the answer. Who would try to undo it? If you knew, you were surely pacted . . . and telling yourself all sorts of fairy stories to make that all right. She wrapped her arms around herself.

"Ah, lords." Lorcan drew her closer. "Darling, *listen* to me: this is not yours to repair. You are not Bryseis Kakistos. You were not there, and if by some bizarre weft of the Weave you could be, do not think that you could have changed a thing. Don't think you *can* change a thing. Gods do not rise by a single act. Even if it is true, and the Toril Thirteen tipped the scales in Asmodeus's favor, there were dozens of other acts and powers that came first—the succubi's defection, the collapse of the Weave, the death of Azuth. Once Asmodeus discovered blood magic, there were a hundred ways he could have gained the power of a god."

She looked up at him. Close, so close she hardly dared to breathe. The first time she met him, she'd thought it was like being swallowed whole. There had been nothing, in that moment, but the man, the devil looking down at her, and she'd had no sense of when it would end. Or how. *I could drown watching him*, she thought. *I could do something foolish.*

*More foolish*, the little voice added.

"And Bryseis Kakistos," he said, taking her face in his hands, "would gladly let her devil rot in the Hells."

*It's a thousand times more terrifying to kiss Lorcan.* It would be, she thought. Like that first dip into the fount of the Hells' power. Like falling into darkness.

"I'll try," she whispered.

"If anyone can manage, it's you." Something in his expression softened, seemed almost human. "I suspect," he said, "that's more than true. There is not another soul on any plane who cares even a little if I die. No one but you, darling."

Tears sprang to her eyes. She turned her cheek into his hand, so she couldn't see him. So the breadth of his burning palm pressed against her face. "I'm sorry," she said. "I'm so tired. And I know, Sairché's bound to find me, to find us—"

Lorcan let go of her face, and she pressed her lips shut. "You need to take this." He took off the pendant he wore and pressed it into her hand. "It will keep Sairché from finding you. Don't ask what it is, just keep it safe. You can hand it back once you've solved the problem of how to keep her from finding me too."

She took the strange charm, a nine-tailed scourge with copper beads at its tips, and wiped her eyes with her other hand. "I don't want to send you back."

"Much as I'd love to tell you not to," Lorcan said, "it's for the best." He hesitated. "I may have an idea. Will you cast this again? In a day, no later?"

Farideh nodded. "I have the components for once more. But after I need to find a source of silver. And down here . . ." She swallowed—such a stupid thing to say when he might never come back to her.

"Well, you'll just have to make sure you only need the once. Good luck, darling."

"Yes," she managed. "Thank you."

Farideh hardly considered what she was doing before she'd already done it. Only the barest of seconds unfurled with the recognition that she was being an utter, utter fool—then she kissed his cheek, close enough to brush the corner of his lips, one hand on the opposite side of his beautiful face. He froze. Her brow resting against his temple, she shut her eyes tight, so that she wouldn't have to see his expression.

One arm slid around her waist.

"Please," she whispered, "be careful. I can't . . . I can't lose—"

"Oh gods' books." Farideh broke off and turned to see Dahl, standing at the edge of the shelves with a bare sword in his hand and a horrified look on his face.

⁂

Twenty feet from where Dahl stood, there was a devil in the library. Worse, the creature clearly had Farideh entranced. Dahl started forward, pacing around the devil, looking for a weak point. It hadn't noticed him—with luck it wouldn't until he was close enough to pull Farideh out of reach. He kept his eyes on her, ready to drop the sword and dive forward if—

He heard her breath hitch, and she darted forward, pressing her lips to the creature's cheek. Dahl stopped in his tracks.

Over her shoulder, the devil's nightmare black eyes met Dahl's, and narrowed. One arm snaked around her waist—possessive or protective or—

"Be careful," she whispered. "I can't . . . I can't lose—"

"Oh gods' books," Dahl said. Farideh turned, and her eyes went wide—with surprise, with horror, with what he couldn't have said.

"*Karshoj*," she said. "Gods. Damn it." She let go of the devil. The devil did not let go of her. "Wait, Dahl. Put the sword down."

"You *called* a stlarning devil," he said, still shocked, still dumbfounded. She all but told you this was what she meant to do, he thought. You should have seen that. Warlock. Tiefling. Gods. "I was so sure I'd find you in some monster's clutches," he said. "And instead you're off kissing the monster." And that—that was the polish on the whole mess. He'd had to stumble in on some bizarrely intimate moment.

She turned red as hot irons and shoved the devil's arm off her. "It's not what it looks like." The devil's wings twitched, bound by an iron pin. His dark eyes pinned Dahl to the ground.

"Where do you find all these broken holy men?" he drawled. "A cleric who can't be counted on. A fallen paladin pouting because he can't save you. Terrible taste, darling, or terrible luck?"

Farideh turned on the devil. "Stop it."

"Or what?" he said. "You've already got me in the circle." He glanced over at Dahl. "Are you going to do something with that sword, or do you just like holding it?"

Dahl's grip tightened. The devil might have powers he couldn't see, but Dahl was quick, the sword sharp. The devil was trapped in that circle. It would be better all around—

Farideh leaped over the ring of runes and put herself between Dahl and the devil. "Stop it," she said again, this time to Dahl. "He's *baiting* you. Can't you see that?" She swallowed. "Just let me . . . I'll send him off. Don't do anything rash."

Dahl found he couldn't look at her. He sheathed the sword. "Fine," he said. "But the next time you want to dally with fiends, *don't* do it when I'm supposed to be watching out for you."

The devil laughed. "I'm sure *you're* watching her ever so well."

"Lorcan, enough!" Farideh snapped. "It's not funny." Her voice was shaking. "Ask me to send you back."

"You'll call again?" he said.

"Trust me," she answered. "Now, ask."

The devil watched her for moments so long and taut that Dahl had to look away. "Will you send me back?"

He'd no more than spoken the words but the circle of runes burst into wild, leaping flames. The devil took on a searing, silvery light that grew and grew until, with a rush of air and magic, it overwhelmed Dahl's eyes. Farideh flinched away.

The light faded, the runes stopped burning, and the devil was gone. Farideh held still, facing the empty circle. After a moment, she looked back at Dahl.

"I suppose you're going to bring this up to Tam," she said.

Dahl shook his head, at a loss. He'd have to. What would happen if the silverstar found out and Dahl hadn't told him? She was putting herself in peril—putting all of them in peril by calling down devils.

"He's not . . . ," she started. "It's complicated. He's not that bad."

That was *it*. "You'll pardon me if I don't take your word on it. There are Shadovar at the doors, by the by. You might want to follow me." Dahl turned on his heel and stormed back toward the camp, not caring much if she followed. It was one thing to run off (you told her to run off, he thought), another to dabble with the Hells (you knew she was a warlock, he thought), but he was not going to stand there while she tried to tell him he ought to get to know her devil better.

The sound of footsteps came out of nothing, as if several people had suddenly materialized in the long aisle behind him, striding purposefully his way and making an absurd amount of noise. Dahl held his sword ready and turned cautiously toward the sound.

And saw, not the library of Tarchamus but the temple of Oghma, the Domes of Reason, in Procampur. And it was Jedik and the leaders of Oghma's paladins who were walking toward Dahl.

Cold rushed over him. He heard his sword fall to the ground, but when Dahl looked down at his hands, he saw as he feared: the blood-soaked bandage wrapped around the left, the ugly swelling of the broken bone. The floor beyond was no longer pale limestone, but rust-colored tiles, and there was no blade beyond. The shelves around him had become pews and reading stands.

No—he shut his eyes. Not again. Once was enough.

But before Jedik reached him, those old emotions surged up like an unstoppable tide. His world was in freefall, and no matter how hard he tried to catch hold, there was nothing to slow him down. His heart was pounding, and by the time his mentor stood before him, his stomach was sick and his head spun as if he might collapse.

"Nothing happened," he said, as he had seven years before.

"I know," Jedik said.

"I tried. I tried, and tried." Panic again clawed its way up Dahl's throat. "It's still broken and I can't fix it, I can't *fix it*!" The paladins behind the old loremaster looked on, stern and cold. Looking for all the world as if they had never thought anything of Dahl but that he was trouble and a nuisance. A poor use of the order's charity. A millstone.

"Please," Dahl said, tears rising to his eyes. "What do I do?"

Jedik set a hand on his shoulder and gestured for Dahl to sit. "It seems," Jedik said, settling himself beside the younger man, "that Oghma has seen fit to revoke your powers."

He had said it already, already the pain of it was seven years on, but all over again Dahl's heart shattered. "No," he pled. "No."

"Dahl—"

"Why?" he howled. "What have I *done*? How have I failed?" He was sobbing now, and he didn't care that the paladins were shifting uncomfortably to see him. Somehow he had slipped, he had transgressed without knowing how, and *fallen*. "I cannot. I cannot lose everything. Please. What do I *do*?"

Jedik laid a hand on his shoulder. "You are sworn to serve knowledge. 'Knowledge is not to be hidden, not from the world and not from the *self*. Tell me, Dahl . . . how does it serve you to lock yourself away here?"

Jedik waited as if he expected an answer. Dahl shook his head. "I don't understand. Where? In the temple?"

With a pitying look, Jedik set his gnarled hands on either side of Dahl's wounded one. But this time, he did not clasp his student's hand in his. He did not cast the spell to heal the wound . . . instead, Dahl watched as the old man's cheeks sank like a corpse's, his eyes becoming small and eerily bright as diamonds.

"There's nothing here worth dying for," he said, but it was Tam's voice that said it.

Someone grabbed ahold of him and pulled him bodily to the floor. He hit the ground, and once more the tile was limestone, the shelves hemmed him in, and his sword was lying on the ground all-too-near his cheek. And the tiefling was there, scrambling to her feet behind him, leaping over his prone form to stand as if ready to do battle with some unseen monster.

"You leave him be!" Farideh shouted. "Leave all of us be!" There were flames licking the edges of the air around the rod in her hand, the veins in her wrist black as streaks of rot. No answer came from the cold quiet of the library. "You can't chase us off!" she shouted. "We're not as weak as you think!"

Silence, but for the pant of her breath and of Dahl's.

She made a little shriek of annoyance and shook the flames from her hands. She looked down at Dahl for an interminable moment, her queer eyes flickering—and it took him a moment to realize she was assessing his state.

"Are you all right?" she said softly.

He looked down at his hands, but they were whole again. Not so his heart, once again ravaged by the knowledge of what he'd lost. He swallowed against the lump in his throat.

"Fine," he said, ignoring the hand she offered him. He dared to look at the spot where Jedik had stood. An illusion, he thought. A very cruel illusion.

"You were standing there," she said. "Talking to someone. Begging . . ." She looked away. "It was an illusion, wasn't it? You were reliving something bad."

He turned away from her and wiped the tears from his face—gods, that *hadn't* been part of the illusion either. "It's fine."

How had he come so under Beshaba's notice that not only did the illusion force him to relive his very worst memory, but then Farideh—of all people—had to find him at it, weeping like a child and shaking. He did not need her watching him all smug and piteous, while Jedik's words rattled his thoughts.

*It seems that Oghma has seen fit to revoke your powers. Tell me, Dahl, how does it serve you to lock yourself away here?*

No. That wasn't right . . .

Farideh was still there, watching him with that inscrutable expression. "What happened?" she asked more gently.

"It's *fine*," he repeated. "We need to find the others."

"You ought to tell Tam what you saw. He'd want to know—"

Dahl cut her off. "If you breathe a word of this to him," he snarled, "I will tell him *exactly* what I found you doing, and then I will leave you here in this bloody cavern with all that water to get through. Now leave. Me. Be."

For a moment, he thought she was going to pull the same ridiculous stunt she had back at the inn—flash her infernal powers as if rubbing them in his face. The tatters of smoke blurred her edges and she stepped back.

"You think," she said, "that you know *everything*, you think no one can possibly be as godsbedamned smart as you, but every other word out of your *karshoji* mouth is you jumping to another conclusion that *isn't* fair. At least now you know better than to sneer at the rest of us for getting caught by those illusions. I'll see you in the camp." The sound of her tail brushing the floor in an agitated slash chased her footsteps.

Good riddance, Dahl told himself. But it didn't work—that had been humiliating in every possible way, including telling her off. He didn't want to care. He dragged his hands through his hair. Once they were free of this place, he would find some other way to occupy himself—away from tieflings and silverstars.

*Tell me, Dahl, how does it serve you to lock yourself away here?*

It had been very nearly the same conversation they'd had on that terrible day, until the end. What Jedik had told him, Dahl had etched on his heart, repeating it over and over and over again: "Tell me, Dahl, how does it serve Oghma to simply give you the answers you've been sent to seek? When you are sworn to the God of Knowledge, you are sworn to serve knowledge, to seek it, to free it." He'd shaken his head. "It is in your power to know. So find the answers."

That had been three years ago. And Dahl had found nothing.

Not a soul would have called the Lord of Knowledge a cruel god. But after so long searching, Dahl had begun to wonder how dear Oghma's regard really was. He missed, still, the divine presence of his god, the surge of magic lighting his mind on fire and nearly stealing his breath away entirely, the shimmering notes of the harp that came sometimes with powerful prayers. He wondered how long it would be before he couldn't remember it any longer, and he both craved and dreaded that day.

He would have liked to keep on sobbing. He would have liked to have locked himself away with a bottle of zzar or three and get as maudlin as he liked. Three years and the wound was as raw as the day it had cut his life in half.

He wiped his face again, burying down all the sorrow and anger and loss and rage, all the while turning the difference between his memory and the illusion over in his thoughts, as if by some twisting he would find a secret to unlocking this misery. He pulled himself to his feet.

As he bent to pick up his sword, he saw one of the leather-bound books on the floor—fallen, likely, while he stumbled around begging shadows for mercy. It had landed open to the middle.

Dahl picked up the book, glancing at the text: . . . *Cormyrean line of succession as of 1478 DR.* He stopped, scanning the artful inking of a tree, laden with names. *King Foril Obarskyr . . . Crown Prince Irvel Obarskyr . . . Prince Baerovus Obarskyr . . . Princess Raedra Obarskyr . . . Lord Aubrin Crownsilver (Obarskyr) . . .*

"Gods' books," he said. He read it again, but the names and dates were all the same. Where in the Hells had such a thing come from? Where had it picked up the notion that Brin . . .

He raced after Farideh, toward the camp, still worried first and foremost about the Shadovar at the gates, but suddenly far more concerned about ghosts and illusions, and a certain over-helpful tome.

# CHAPTER SEVENTEEN

Tam never stopped watching Maspero, as the Zhent picked through the shadovar's belongings, and Maspero never stopped watching Tam, as the Harper examined the bodies of the Shadovar. The two shadar-kai still clutched angry-looking weapons, and wore the streaks of dead flesh that signaled death by powerful magic. The shade had bled out, both shadow and fluid, from the belly wound. Tam gently prodded it with the tip of a dagger.

"It looks like these two attacked the shade." Tam said.

"Shouldn't have killed him though," Maspero said.

Tam straightened. "Must have been poisoned. Doesn't look like he was healing himself like they do."

"You been around many shadow folk?" Maspero asked.

"Not many live ones," Tam replied. "Sounds like not as many as you."

Maspero smiled cruelly at him. "Are you implying something?"

"Why would I do that?" Tam wiped the dagger down. "At least we know it's not something *new* that killed them. Did you find anything in there?"

"Rations," Maspero said, pointing to each item he'd laid out on the floor. "Some candles. Bottle of poison—well, there we go. Map. A recreation of that stone fragment. Bloody thing." He picked up a slim leather-bound book. "Here. Can't read this."

Tam took it from him. The shade's handwriting was sharp and condensed—the runes of Loross, linked and shortened into script. The ritual he'd cast gave only the slightest hesitation at the variation.

"It's a log of their mission." He frowned. "It's mostly coded. 'Message to W. Six units past.' They started out right after the revel. Looks like Rhand was more prepared than we'd thought." He flipped to the end, the last entries before the party's death.

"There were five of them," he said in surprise.

"Five of what?"

"Five in their party. The shade, the two shadar-kai, and two humans." He skimmed the coy notes. "Definitely five. He was keeping track of supplies."

"You think they're still here somewhere?"

"If they are they're in trouble. Those rations look like the last of their supplies." Tam looked down at the pale eyes of the shade. "Attacking a shade . . . that's a fool's move."

"You think those ghosts engineered it?"

"Makes sense." Tam turned back to the journal, skimming ahead. "Looks like the doors sealed on them too. And . . . Hells."

"What?"

"There's a third floor. A third floor, and he had them retreat here to keep clear of it."

"Doesn't say why?"

*The walking dead themselves would flee*, the journal read. *Not flame, not blades, not the power of Shar Herself seems to halt it.* Tam shut the book between both hands and pursed his lips. "Not clearly." He cursed. "We need to get back. We need to pull Mira and Pernika out of there before they find that third floor."

Maspero grunted. "Could be he was keeping his people away from the good stuff."

Tam slipped the journal into his bag. "What's your business with my daughter?"

"Better to ask what's her business with me."

"I couldn't place you before," Tam said. "I'll admit, I was thrown by the mercenary act. Maspero of Everlund—you don't even bother hiding your identity." He faced him. "You work for the Zhentarim."

Maspero didn't flinch. "I work for myself."

"Oh, don't be modest," Tam said. "You head a cell of Zhentarim. You're gaining enough of a foothold in the North to be in Harper sights, anyway. I'm going to assume you're in a lot of rivals' sights as well."

"Not for long if your girl succeeds." He set his hands on his hips, on the hilt of his dagger. "People tend to leave you to your own devices when you make it known you have magic capable of destroying whole cities."

I could end him here, Tam thought. Leave him in the library and no one would know it hadn't been a ghost or a trap or one of the lost Shadovar.

But he'd done nothing. Yet. It would be murder, nothing less. And Tam wasn't the hot-blooded fool Viridi had found elbows-deep in blood and shadow.

"What's Mira owe you?" he said. "What are you holding over her?"

Maspero chuckled, eyeing Tam as if he weren't sure if Tam were serious. Then he chuckled again. "She's right about you, isn't she?" he said. "Always have to play the hero. Always saving people, even when they don't want to be saved."

"What's that supposed to mean?"

"You assume she owes me something," Maspero said, "that we forced her into this, and you can undo her debt? But it never crosses your mind, does it, that she might have come to us? That she might appreciate what the Zhentarim can offer her."

"You want me to believe Mira's interested in your power struggles?"

"Cold-blooded Mira?" Maspero chuckled again. "I wouldn't ask your glaive-girl to buy that nonsense. Mira's got her own agenda. Always has. But we all line up nice and neat, don't we? At least," he added, "so long as I get my spellbooks." He stepped around the corpse and back out through the swinging shelf.

Zhentarim. Tam had hoped he'd been wrong, guessing after Brin's intimations. That Maspero was only a mercenary with an overinflated sense of his own worth. He cursed under his breath. Once they left the library, he'd have to be careful—he'd have to get the twins and Brin and Dahl away from Maspero, away from Pernika.

Away from Mira, he thought. His heart squeezed. Silver Lady, let him be wrong. Please, he thought, please let them have found a way out. Please let them have found something to disarm the seal. Please, let Shar pass us by.

If the Lady of Loss could be persuaded, he thought, you'd have a much easier job.

Havilar leaped in front of him as he approached the camp, her glaive ready. "Are you Tam?" she demanded. Then, "Wait, how are we supposed to tell?"

"He's got Maspero with him," Brin supplied from behind her.

"Have the others come back?" Tam asked.

"No," Brin said. "You're the first."

"Right." Tam considered the camp, the supplies strewn across the space, the tall shelves of books surrounding them, and tried to imagine the mind of an arcanist who built such a fortress for his knowledge. The ghosts, the Book, the illusions—something wasn't right.

Footsteps pattered through the maze of shelves, and Farideh crossed the border into the camp, her fists balled and and her expression fierce.

Brin pointed his sword and holy symbol at her. "Stop. She's by herself." Farideh halted, glanced back over her shoulder, and cursed softly.

"No," Havilar said mildly. "That's definitely Farideh."

Farideh gave her a puzzled look. "How can you be sure?"

"How can you *not* be sure?" Havilar asked. "If the ghost could sound like you, move like you, look like you, and make that face you make when you're annoyed"—she scrunched up her nose and pursed her mouth in an exaggeration of Farideh's earlier expression—"well, then I don't think you'd have ever figured out they were ghosts, right?" She stopped, as if she'd remembered something, and turned back to her glaive with a scowl of her own.

"Where's Dahl?" Tam demanded.

Farideh's mouth tightened again. "Behind me."

Mother of the moon, Tam thought, give me patience. "What part of 'No one goes anywhere from now on without a partner,' did you misunderstand?"

She folded her arms. "My partner didn't seem to think that was important."

"Enough," Tam said, as Dahl returned a moment later. "Did you get the door open?"

"No," Dahl said sharply. "And worse, Rhand and his people are on the other side of it."

"Hrast," Tam spat.

"I set an alarm to go off if they make it through," Dahl said quickly. "It should slow them down and warn us too."

Maspero sneered. "Does it sound like a rockfall? How in the broken planes does an alarm slow a body down?"

Dahl spared him a glare. "It will be *very* loud."

"Good work," Tam said, assessing the situation. Six of them back, no way out the doors. Still no Mira. The shade's cryptic worries repeating in his mind. And Zhentarim—gods, the Zhentarim.

There was no more time to wait. "Everyone get your weapons ready and come along," he said. "We may have more trouble than we thought."

⸫⌒⸫

The ritual deposited Lorcan back in the room of the fingerbone tower as unceremoniously as it had dropped him in the cavern. He stood and brushed the traces of marrow grease from the knees of his breeches. His luck the spell would work so neatly—it couldn't have dropped him outside the tower, closer to some other portal, no. She'd had to do it right.

Gods be damned, he thought. Who had helped her? She'd distracted him with that nonsense about Bryseis Kakistos, and then . . .

It was probably that gawking paladin. Probably thought he was impressing her. Probably thought he could save her. Lorcan thought of the frayed feeling the divine powers around Dahl had possessed. A fallen paladin ought to be useful for keeping her virtuous streak in check. Just not that one.

Not *any* one, he thought, that waves swords at you and calls you a monster. Puts the wrong ideas in her head.

Self-consciously, he wiped his cheek. Was that the wrong idea or the right one? It meant she wasn't going to leave him. *I don't think of our pact that way,* she'd said. *Not anymore.* If she wasn't going to corrupt all at once in a spectacular collapse of morals for love of power, bit by bit through good intentions and fond feelings was nearly as good.

Except . . .

It was true, what he'd said. There was no one else on any plane who cared whether he lived or died or hurt. It got under his skin, right from the start, and he was glad she was worried about him.

And Lorcan wasn't completely sure that, had Glasya never said a word to him, he wouldn't keep defying Sairché all the same. Which was dangerous, he thought, scanning the room. Alliances were for players, tools of the hierarchy. Alliances tangled you in other devils' schemes and tied you to other devils' fortunes. Alliances mired you in the hierarchy, whether you were a miserable lemure or a Lord of the Nine, no mistake.

Glasya's voice echoed in his head—*Do be careful, little Lorcan. I may have need of you and her in the future*—and he shivered. He was already in it, up to his neck. Even if he abandoned Farideh, he was still caught in the Lord of Malbolge's plans.

All the more reason, he thought, to get out.

He turned toward the window and froze.

Leaning against the lacy bone balustrade was another succubus, one he'd recognize anywhere in any skin. She'd kept her deepnight hair and her eyes, sharp and shining gold. But her skin was as pale as dunes beneath the moon and the batlike wings that she held high, as if ready to launch into the air and attack her traitorous son, were mottled brown and bronze.

"Mother," he said, wondering if he could summon up a burst of flames fast enough. "I wasn't expecting you."

"I can see that," she said. As an erinyes, her voice had been as terrible as the roar of waves dashed against the rocks. Now when Fallen Invadiah spoke it was a melody that threatened to calm Lorcan, to make him drop his guard. "Nor does it seem you need me all that dearly. Does your sister know you have a portal?"

"She doesn't," he said. "And to be fair, I don't. I have an enterprising warlock with more ambition than sense. I gather you got my message?"

"I'd hoped it was that slattern's idea of a jest." Invadiah swept into the room, her wings filling the space. "That no son of mine was so foolish as to ask for favors from someone he wronged so deeply."

Lorcan bit back a laugh. "You'll recall, I was wronged right alongside you. Sairché's the one who pitted us each against the other. She's the one you want. She's the one we both want."

Invadiah gave him a pitying look, unsuited even on that unfamiliar face. "If you're going to try and sway me, kindly put a little effort into it. I'm not one of your mortals."

"What is there to convince you of?" he said. "Sairché's the one lording over *your* armies, decking herself in *your* treasures, wielding *your* authority. She's the one who drew Glasya's eye to your mission when Rohini turned on you. You cannot tell me you still favor her."

Invadiah's mouth quirked into a smirk, and now that she'd lost her fangs, Lorcan realized he'd inherited his mother's mouth. "An improvement," she allowed. "But I never favored Sairché."

"She had the *pradixikai* beat me within an inch of my life," he said. "You'll have to forgive me for painting her with too broad a brush."

"That temper doesn't suit you. You'll never have the power and the strength of an erinyes to follow through on it." Invadiah considered him, as a snake considers a vole. "I hear you'd like access to Toril again. I can provide that."

The change Glasya's punishment had wrought in Invadiah carried from her skin down to her very core—clever as she'd been as an erinyes, she'd been prouder and crueler too. If she'd come at all, she would have surely denied him and perhaps cuffed him for asking. He almost preferred the certainty of his mother as he'd known her.

"What's the price?" he asked.

Invadiah's smile shifted, flashing some measure of that missing cruelty. It was comforting in a way he was sure didn't exist outside of the Hells. "You know, it's a pity you and Sairché never got along."

"What's that supposed to mean?"

"She's a clever girl. Secrets unfold for her like a man's heart under a sword. But for all her cleverness she is not nearly so silver-tongued as you are. You might rather hide from what you know, Lorcan, but you know how to bring unlikely allies to your side." She tilted her head, considering him in the singularly predacious way succubi had. "How to make them forgive and forget you as a nuisance and nothing more. Together, you might have been something to make even devils quake. Together you might have proved me wrong."

"A pity Sairché sees a better use for me dead. What do you want for the portal?"

"Your sister's reign won't last forever," Invadiah said. "Nor will my demotion. Eventually the tide will shift and I will rise and shed this hateful form. When that happens . . . you'll serve me however you can until Sairché is overthrown."

Lorcan smiled. "Gladly."

"Don't be too certain." She held out a hand and in the center of her palm was a small pouch. He took it and found a pearl the size of his thumbnail inside. "Crush it," she said, "and have a good idea where you want to go. It will pull you through my aerie's portal."

The surface of the pearl seemed to swirl gently in the nauseating light. "And if I want to come back?"

"Then you wait until I come for you," Invadiah said, and she turned to leave. She paused at the edge of the balcony. "Sairché doesn't know, does she?" She looked back over her shoulder, over the curve of her wing. "She has no idea you've kept a spare all this time. Twins—it's clever really."

Lorcan held perfectly still. "I've only pacted one Kakistos heir."

"Of course," Invadiah said. "But it was her double that killed Rohini. You may leave the *pradixikai* to believe they saw one girl, but don't think I can't tell the difference." Without waiting for an answer, Invadiah vaulted over the balustrade, and flapped off to the edges of Malbolge where the succubus aeries lay.

Nothing to be done, Lorcan reminded himself. Even if he'd thought of a way to deny Havilar, there was no being certain Invadiah would believe him. And even if she didn't, there remained the protection that sealed the twins from searching eyes. Invadiah became no more than a dark spot on the plane's blood-stained sky. Lorcan rolled the pearl between his fingers, and wondered what she would ask of him eventually.

The stretch of land between the tower and the palace writhed with the movements of scores of fiendish creatures. None of them his sister. No matter—he could wait. She'd come back eventually.

He had not been bold enough to tell Farideh the extent of his plans: that if there were anyone who would know how to hide someone away, it was Sairché. If only he could tease it from her.

·:⌒:·

The door was as Mira had left it earlier, the image of the arcanist still glowering down at them. She bit her tongue as Pernika took a pry bar to the entry. Part of the silver chasing popped free of its channel, along with the garnet in his pendant.

The mercenary pocketed it. "Windfall."

Mira struck a fresh sunrod and said nothing, forging ahead down the stairs she'd been sure were there.

The lower floor was smaller than the one above, still roughly circular, and still ringed with shelves of scrolls and books. But these, Mira noted as they crept into the dimly lit space, were arranged in an even more tangled fashion, with hardly enough space to pass between two of the wooden shelves, that stretched two or three times her height to the ceiling. The floor was piled with stacks of books all along the widest aisle, and Mira had to sidestep more than a few teetering collections.

She picked one up and flipped through it—detailed notes, diagrams, and the crackle of ancient magic. She breathed a sigh of relief. Here, at last were the spellbooks. Maspero would be glad.

She traced the lines of runes with one finger, parsing out the Loross as best she could—the language of magic was complex and nuanced. But if she didn't miss her guess . . . this was just an apprentice's book, the spells simple cantrips and minor incantations. Nothing more deadly than a fireball. She plucked another from a different shelf—another spellbook, full of still more minor spells. Another shelf—another student's spellbook. Her heart sped, as she counted shelves into the dozens.

"Piss and hrast," she muttered. So close, so very close. But not close enough to stall her father. Not close enough to stall Shade, either.

"Think I found another exit!" Pernika called from farther in. Mira wedged the spellbook back on the overstuffed shelf and hurried along the walkway to the center of the floor, where Pernika stood, at the very edge of a pit fifteen feet across.

"Long fall," Pernika commented as Mira came to stand beside her. The light from the sconces and her sunrod wasn't bright enough to illuminate the bottom of the pit, but something down there cast a greenish light that illumined an uneven floor, scattered with detritus.

"We should explore the rest of this floor," Mira said.

Pernika made a disinterested grunt. "Send the Harper's people down. You know Maspero's going to want them killed when we're done." She grinned at Mira. "Even your dear old da."

Mira squinted at the bottom of the pit—lots of smooth-edged pieces of white stone. The remains of columns and intricate carvings, maybe. "It should be interesting to see you try it. Him, the one with the glaive, the warlock." She looked over at Pernika. "Haven't seen Dahl pull his blade, beyond the hydra, you could get lucky there. The lordling priest . . . But then you have plans for that one, don't you, Pernika?"

The mercenary narrowed her eyes. "Don't get clever. You're not better than the rest of us."

"Never said I was," Mira replied. She clenched her jaw—please, gods, don't let Maspero be so foolish. Please, gods, let us get out of here and not make unnecessary messes. Please don't let my father try to stop Pernika himself. "Help me search the rest of this place. We'll go up after and you can push whoever you can into the pit."

"Preening bitch," Pernika muttered. Mira took a slow breath and concentrated on not pushing the mercenary into the pit herself.

Mira pulled more books from the shelves on the opposite side, and found more of the same thing. Spellbooks, certainly, and these more learned than the first batch, but none of them full of the legendary magic of Tarchamus the Unyielding. She thought of Maspero's threats, and pushed deeper into the teetering shelves.

And found herself . . . not wedged between books. Standing in the middle of a room, a cottage, her mother's cottage. Too large though, she thought, looking around. It was as if she were . . .

A child. She looked down at her hands, and they seemed the same . . . No, they were the hands she'd always had, of course. Small and short-fingered. She was eleven. It was raining outside, and her father was leaving today. Again.

"Mira," he said on cue, "will you sit with me?"

She turned and saw him at the table, patting the chair beside him. She stayed where she was.

"I have to go," he said.

"You always have to go," she said. There was a knot in her stomach this time, too, and a lump in her throat. She'd cried the last time, and that had surprised him. As if he thought she was too old for that. But this time she wouldn't. No matter what he said.

"Mira, please," he said. "I will be back."

"As you say." Her father wasn't a big man, but he'd always seemed enormous. Larger than life. She knew better now, and it was strange to see him that way again—

The thought went through her head and startled her. *Again. Now.* When was it? Where was she? Her father watched her, his dark eyes sad.

"Mira," he said. "I have to go. And . . . so do you."

That startled her too. Go? Where? With him? He'd said it was too dangerous. Her mother had said it was too dangerous—even if Mira could hear the envy in her voice, the yearning for the life she'd left behind.

"You . . . could stay," she said, unsure. This wasn't how it went, she thought, and again the thought confused her. This has happened already, she thought. This isn't real. But the weight in her chest that threatened to drive her to tears wouldn't dissipate.

"Mira, listen," her father said, his voice uneven. Insistent. "It's not safe. It's less safe every time. You have to go. You have to go back."

"Go where?" she asked.

"Leave," he said. And then he was suddenly standing, suddenly older. Reaching out toward her. "There's nothing worth—"

He vanished. The cottage vanished. Mira stood, hemmed in on all sides by towers of books. And in the place of the fire's crackle, something else was crackling. Pernika suddenly shouted in surprise.

"Balls," Mira heard her say. "Where'd you two come from?"

Mira extricated herself from the books, trembling. Stlarning illusions, she thought.

"You want to make good on your little threats?" Pernika said. Mira heard her draw her sword. "I'm warning you."

Mira came around the corner—Havilar stood opposite Pernika, weaponless and watching. Brin came around Pernika's side, the same placid expression on his face.

Mira started to shout at Pernika, to tell her to drop the blades—even threatening her father's little tagalongs was a poor plan. But neither of them seemed bothered, only drifted around Pernika, to stand . . .

So that Pernika was between them and the pit.

"Move!" Mira shouted. "They're ghosts!"

The mercenary dived at Havilar, slashing out with her sword, but the ghosts were prepared. The blade seemed to pass right through Havilar. The one that looked like Brin shot forward, catching Pernika off balance and knocking her to the ground.

Mira pulled her own knives and sprinted toward her partner. Could a blade even harm a ghost? Hrast. Havilar looked up, saw her coming, and seized the shelf beside her, yanking it down with inhuman strength. Books scattered, tumbling into the pit as the heavy structure hit the floor, blocking Mira's path. She turned and raced around the other side.

Pernika's sword slashed across Brin's midsection—but as it connected, the ghost became incorporeal, dissolving into a cloud of shifting lights. Havilar took the opportunity to kick the side of Pernika's head, and when the mercenary rolled away, the ghost in the tiefling's form bent down, seized the knot of Pernika's hair, and leaped into the pit, hurling a screaming Pernika over the side with her.

Mira cried out and stopped in her tracks.

"This is what comes of hubris," a voice said behind her. She turned and saw something like and wholly unlike Farideh standing there. "You thought he could be stopped. You thought he could be silenced. You forget why they call him 'the Unyielding.'"

"The arcanist?" Mira said, her blades high. "He's dead." She wet her mouth, easing around the pit. Keeping the ghost from coming around her flank. This wasn't some spectre intent on luring her away. Threatening to bruise her and frighten her. "Do *you* know he's dead?"

Someone else's smirk showed through on the tiefling girl's mouth. "Death is no impediment to a true archwizard."

There was a *whoosh* like the sound of a fireball catching, and someone shoved Mira forward with a force like a charging bull. She fell to her knees, the knives skittering from her hands. She rolled to her back as the one that looked like Brin, solid once more, came at her with hands lengthening into claws. She kicked out and caught it in the stomach—her foot glancing off as if it were made of something both soft and resilient like old jelly. The ghost leaped aside, looking startled. As if it hadn't expected her to fight back. As if it expected her to be weak.

Mira snatched up her knives and rolled back to her feet. The ghosts slid around her, trying to pin her between them. A shimmer of light rose up from the pit, taking shape as it drifted over the edge, until Havilar's double stepped out of the air.

"You've given up your knowledge," she said. "Time to give up your life."

The only advantage Mira had on poor Pernika was knowing it was coming. She hadn't the mercenary's skill with a sword. There were three ghosts and not two. She was dead.

Mira stared down the ghost who had taken Pernika over the edge. She wasn't going quietly. "Come and take it then," she said, her knives ready.

The other two came up along her sides. The one that looked like Farideh sprang at her, latching on to Mira's right arm with a grip like a street dog's bite. Mira slashed at it with her knife, dragging the blade across the same viscous, not-quite-solid flesh. The ghost hissed and held her tighter, twisting the knife out of her hand. Another *whoosh*, and the Brin-shaped one was on top of her, pushing her toward the pit again. She struggled as the edge neared . . .

A corona of light seared Mira's eyes. The ghosts dissolved with a shrill whine. Mira blinked, eyes watering, and, as the light faded, saw Tam closing the distance, his chain shining with holy light. It lashed out and struck the ghost that had looked like Brin, sending sparks through the cloud of light.

"Move!" he shouted. Mira picked up her fallen blade and started toward the door. A cloud of crackling lights formed in her path, taking the shape once more of Havilar. Momentum carried Mira into it, and its arms wound around her, tight as steel bands.

She struggled and kicked and bit and thrashed—but the ghost reacted to her frantic strikes as though she were a child, having a tantrum. The edge came closer.

Light flashed again as Tam clapped a hand filled with the blessings of the moon goddess to the side of the ghost's head. The ghost howled and turned into light and shadow again. Mira stumbled free. Tam caught her arm and pulled her past him, toward the door. Toward where the rest of the party were descending the stairs. Realizing there was trouble.

And in the process, he turned his back on the third ghost.

Mira heard only the *thud* of him hitting the ground, the sound of the air going out of her father. She turned. The third ghost, leaking wafts of vapor and light where the blessings had hurt it, gave her a wicked smile, took hold of one of his legs, and dragged him into the pit.

His fingers scrabbled at the edge. Mira cried out and dived forward to catch his hands. She missed. She glimpsed only his terrified expression before he slipped over the edge and into the darkness of the pit, chased by the insubstantial forms of the remaining ghosts.

# CHAPTER EIGHTEEN

## *The Lost Library of Tarchamus*

**T**AM COULDN'T RECALL HITTING THE GROUND OR THE SNAP OF BONE. The fall, opening his eyes, struggling to draw a breath in lungs shocked from impact, and a pain so intense he could hardly think to calm himself; that much came to him in a rush. His ribs screaming where they'd hit the floor. The sharp edges of rocks and debris under him. His leg, the thighbone, the muscles contracting over the shattered limb. He was shouting, he realized, screaming on borrowed air.

Calm, hrast you, calm. He managed short pants, bringing his breath back into himself, mouthful by mouthful. Cooler air, stirring air. A bad taste. He looked around him and saw bones and bones and bones. An arm in leathers, an arm with a sleeve of tattoos attached to another body. Screaming that wasn't his.

Pernika lay bent and broken, farther away than his chain would have reached. Her arm was folded under and gravely dislocated. Her leg had broken at the shin, and a lump of bone protruded into her leathers. More than a body's worth of blood was thick and drying on the stones. Clumps of dark hair and sticky tissue spattered on the edge of a dais he could just make out, along with the jawless, half-skinned head of a man with matted hair.

And worse.

Sitting there, on the dais, a horror like everything the shade's notes had implied, was the mummified body of a man. He was folded into a pose of contemplation, his hands, like shriveled roots, set skeletal fingertip to skeletal fingertip and painted black with dried blood.

Around his neck was the garnet pendant every image had repeated. The arcanist, Tarchamus.

The arcanist lifted his head at Tam's curse, the empty sockets of his skull taking on an otherworldly green light.

Above him Dahl and Farideh were shouting, but to Tam's ears they sounded so far off, so garbled, they might as well have been shouting through the water that had brought them to this Hellish place.

"Don't come down," he tried to shout back. "It's not safe."

He might have bellowed or he might have only whimpered, but for certain one person heard Tam Zawad. The arcanist turned to look at him.

Tam struggled to sit up, to pull himself onto his good leg, but the pain was astounding. Magic crackled and shot over the arcanist's sinewy arms and legs, spidering like lightning over his protruding ribs, as he unfolded and came to his full horrible height.

In life, the arcanist might have been the elderly man the doors all depicted—but the magic that had given rise to the creature moving toward Tam had swelled and strengthened the arcanist's frame. He was as big as a dragonborn, and even if his muscles were dry and his skin leathery, it was clear the mummy could tear a person apart.

The bones littering the floor made it clear he had.

The mummy moved very deliberately toward them. Pernika's screams became frantic, piercing. The kind of screams that burrowed into a person's mind and never, ever came out. Tam tried to grab hold of the holy symbol he wore pinned to his collar, but his fingers couldn't find it and he could not look away from the mercenary lying in the mummy's path.

The arcanist reached down and picked up Pernika by her dislocated arm, as if she were a forgotten doll. The mercenary swiped at the creature with one blade, slashing at the mummy's desiccated skin. He regarded her a moment, as if puzzled by what she was doing.

Then he wrenched her waving arm from her body, as easily as plucking a flower from a wet field. A spray of blood red as poppies erupted from her body. The screams broke off as she collapsed in shock. The fountain of blood diminished pump by pump. The arcanist brought the end of the limp arm to his mouth and bit through leather, muscle, bone.

Silver Lady, Tam prayed, unable to look away, don't forsake us.

The air cracked and split with a gust of hot air and the acrid smell of burning stone, and Farideh leaped from the middle of nothing, pulling Dahl behind her to land lightly on his feet.

"Gods, devils and demons," Dahl swore. "What is that thing?"

Farideh didn't answer him, but pointed the infernal rod at the mummy. *"Adaestuo."* The powers of the Hells surged through her, racing black as soot along the veins of her arms before bursting out the end of the rod in a searing ball of sickly, violet energy. It broke over the mummy, clinging to his dry form in embers here and there. Tarchamus looked up from his grisly meal.

But now his full attention was on Farideh.

Dahl drew his sword, but Farideh laid a hand on his arm. "No. Don't get close. Get Tam fixed." She swept her arms together and with another infernal shout, sent a gust of burning air toward the arcanist as the strange green light gathered around him.

Dahl started to protest, but the arcanist's light burned brighter, gathering in his gaping mouth. The mummy's jaw opened like a yawn and Dahl leaped aside. Another crack and Farideh vanished and reappeared a dozen feet to the arcanist's left, just as the green light streamed out of the mummy, charring a streak through the litter of bones. Dahl's sword clattered on the bones and he dropped to Tam's side.

Time seemed to drag to an unbearable crawl as Dahl looked over Tam's injuries, the bursts of fire and green light flashing just out of sight and throwing shadows of their casters across the room.

"Hurry!" Tam tried to say.

"Right," Dahl said. "This is going to . . . be horrible." Tam hardly knew what was happening until another explosion of pain shattered his shock, and he realized Dahl had planted a foot to one side of his crotch, grabbed hold of the ankle of his broken leg, and pulled. The grind of bone sliding on bone made Tam clutch at the air as much as the pain did, and again he was dimly aware that he was screaming.

And still the arcanist roared and still the smell of brimstone was thick enough to make a man gag.

Now Dahl was binding his legs, one to the other with a solid piece of wood on either side of the broken bone . . . Tam looked down—not wood, some other poor soul's thighbone. He started to retch.

"You're losing blood," Dahl said, pressing gently on the broken leg. "The vessels . . . even though nothing's broken the skin, they're going to bleed. You need healing."

"I'll . . ." Tam started to reach for the symbol of Selûne he wore as a pin.

Dahl caught hold of his hand and pulled it away. "Wait for Brin. You need all your strength."

The *smack* of a rope hitting the floor beside him. The roar of the arcanist. The smell of bitter brimstone so sharp it burned the back of his throat. Mira landed beside him, her face suddenly hovering over him, pale and drawn.

I'm sorry, he wanted to say. I don't know what happened.

"Pernika?" she asked.

"Don't look," Dahl advised.

Mira said not another word, but tied the rope into a harness and—with Dahl's help—bound it around Tam. The flash of flames and ancient magic continued, just out of sight.

Then suddenly, there was a sickening *thud*. Dahl shouted and pulled his sword again. Mira went stiff.

"Haul!" she shouted. The rope jerked. He lifted his head and looked out across the tomb.

Farideh lay sprawled on the floor. The arcanist, still trailing bits of intestine and sinew, had stopped casting, was making his way over. Dahl ran across the bone field, blade out, but gods, no, Tam thought, he'll die. She'll die. No blade can stop that thing. No one can stop that thing.

Farideh pulled herself up, and stumbled.

No, he thought. You can stop it. You have to stop it. He clutched at the pin. And opened himself wide to Selûne.

The blessings of the moon swelled, so intense he could feel them in his teeth. Even here, so far from the night sky, so far from the Moonmaiden's fair face, the undeniable power of her poured into her servant, like water into a vessel. With all his strength, Tam pulled the pin from his collar and thrust it out toward the arcanist.

He cried out Selûne's name, and a silvery radiance exploded outward from the symbol. The light overwhelmed Tam's eyes, the spell sapped his strength. But he heard the arcanist scream and the sound of the mummy's body crashing against the farther wall.

"Gods damn it! Pull him up!" Mira shouted. The ropes around him tightened. He spun in the air as he was hauled upward, the roar of the arcanist suddenly splitting the air.

No, he thought, struggling to stay conscious. No, no, no. Arms pulled him out of the air. He landed on another hard floor.

*"Karshoj,"* he heard Havilar swear and swear and swear. Her voice echoed strangely in his ears as his vision closed. "*Do* something . . ."

There was a ringing sound, like a sword on a whetstone, and a woman's voice, singing softly. The pain in his leg multiplied, doubled, and tripled, and he was screaming again. The light, so bright he might have held the moon to his eye . . .

He sat up panting hard and nearly fell over. His leg was still in agony, his head still spun, but he no longer felt as if he were going to die. Brin, looking ashen, stood over him. Maspero held the rope, slung over a fallen shelf, hauling mightily against the weight of someone down below. Havilar pulled behind him, her feet sliding on the polished floor . . .

"Get this off me," Tam ordered, reaching for the splint of bones.

"Not until someone sees to you," Brin said. "I don't know if it's fixed."

Tam ignored him and tried to come to his feet, and stumbled, dizzy and sick. Brin caught him, like he was an invalid—damn it—and eased him down. "Don't move. I think it's still broken."

Down below the arcanist screamed again, and Tam pushed Brin away. Mira scrambled up the rope. The bookshelf the rope hung over splintered under their weight.

"Hurry, gods blast you," Maspero shouted down at her.

She wouldn't be quick enough. Tam took his pin in hand and filled his heart and mind with the distant powers of the Moonmaiden. A cool wave of intense magic rushed through him, along with the sound of faint singing. His thighbone knitted together with a cracking and snapping that he never got used to.

The bookshelf cracked and snapped along with him. The wood splintered. Mira reached the top of the rope and started swinging for the ledge. He pulled the chain from his belt.

"No!" Havilar screamed. The bookshelf broke—

Tam's chain lashed out and tangled around the rope. He hauled hard against it, keeping Mira from dropping any farther. Arms shaking, she scaled the rope to the edge of the chain and caught Brin's reaching hand. She half fell, half leaped the distance, and Brin grabbed hold of her as she did, helping her scramble over the side. She fell forward onto her hands and knees.

Down in the pit, where Farideh and Dahl still were, the arcanist howled.

⁂

Lorcan didn't have long to plan before Sairché returned, wearing more of Invadiah's treasured armor and accompanied by Bibracte again. Arisia and Cissa positioned themselves on either side of the door. Bibracte took off her sword belt and set it beside the door. Lorcan's pulse quickened.

"I suspect," Sairché said, "you thought you were being clever."

"It's possible," he said, pointedly not looking at Bibracte, standing there beside the door, all fang and muscle. He palmed the pearl Invadiah had given him. "I often am. What are we talking about?"

"The succubus."

"Ah," he said. "No. I wouldn't deign to call myself clever over that. I might suggest you were being a bit . . . let's say, overbold. As if I can't spot a succubus?" Bibracte was grinning at him. The memory of his mad half sister killing an Asmodean cultist for being near her sword, by slicing him completely in half, ran through his thoughts. Along with the sound of her cackling, like only Bibracte could, seeing him clutching at his innards. *Beshaba shit in my eyes*, he cursed to himself. *Bad, bad, very bad.* He could smash the pearl now . . . and hope picturing some cave on Toril would get him anywhere near where he needed to be.

"She told me," Sairché said, "what it was you talked about. The protective spells. Took some . . . convincing, but she was most forthcoming in the end."

"I didn't expect anything else," he said. She hadn't mentioned the blood magic. "It's more telling that she wasn't interested in sharing, don't you think?"

Sairché straightened the bracer on her left arm with a small, secretive smile. "Not so interesting as the fact that you thought you could keep her from compelling you. But that's all behind us now. I thought you should know I figured out how you got around the protections."

Lorcan met her golden gaze. "Did you now?"

"The rod."

He held perfectly still. Shit. *Shit* and ashes—he hadn't thought of that. The rod Farideh carried—a minor artifact from the first layer called the Rod of the Traitor's Reprisal—had been a fixture of his mother's treasury, gathering a greasy layer of wall spatter and bone dust for ages, before he gave it to Farideh. While Invadiah had been impatient and ill-tempered as a hornet's nest sinking in boiling water, she'd been remarkably thorough about her belongings. There would be records. Someone would have noted that Lorcan had taken it when he'd requested the weapon.

Which meant Sairché had a focus for her scrying that wasn't covered by the protection spell.

"It seems your girl is playing adventurer somewhere in Northern Faerûn," she said.

Lorcan smirked, though inside he was throttled by panic. If she'd found Farideh, she might know that he'd slipped out. That he might again. "That's an awful lot of world to consider. Doesn't sound like such a good solution after all."

Sairché smirked back. "Oh, not to worry. I haven't been able to find her precisely. She's somewhere with a forbiddance cast upon it. Some sort of temple, I'd wager. Fortunately, I have this lovely scrying mirror, already altered to pierce hallowed ground." She started toward the mirror.

Not a temple, he thought. A cavern. A cavern whose forbiddance had been broken down enough for him to pass through. It would be like greased tissue to the scrying mirror.

He rolled the pearl back between his fingers. Now. It would have to be now.

"What do you intend to do about the protection?" he blurted.

Sairché glanced back at him over her shoulder, puzzled. "Why should I do anything? By tracking the rod, I circumvent it."

Lorcan spread his arms wide. "Am I nothing if not an object lesson in the perils of relying on magic items? If you can track the rod, so can everyone else." He smirked, though he didn't feel terribly confident. "Not just the ones you're willing to deal with."

Sairché turned, eyeing him cautiously. "You didn't use the rod, did you?"

He shrugged, trying to look as impish and thoughtless as possible. "You may have noticed Invadiah only granted me that treasure fairly recently. Or you may not have."

She narrowed her eyes at him. "Dissolving the protection is a trifling matter, if you know anything about magic. I'll swap the rod."

"But you don't want it broken—that would merely send a signal to the entirety of the Hells that there's a Brimstone Angel to be had."

For a moment, Sairché looked as if she would sic Bibracte on him. She broke her gaze and stared deeply at the scrying mirror. "You might," she finally said, "have loosened the protection. Stretched it over yourself and her both. It would be enough to block her and you."

He snorted. "You're clever, but widening a spell is archwizard's magic. Not an option."

Sairché gave him a withering look. "Do you even *read* your pact agreements before you hide them away? You don't have to widen the spell, you just have to convince her to share her spell's effects . . . So that's not what you did." She shook her head. "Of course not. Then you'd have been stuck within the protection's boundary, and it wouldn't stretch between the planes."

She pursed her lips. "You'd need something she could carry without notice, something no one could take and something she wouldn't give . . ." Sairché's voice trailed away, and she looked up at Lorcan with the faintest suggestion of respect.

"Blood magic," she said. "That's how you got around the protection—called her blood with her blood. She can't lose it, she can't cast it aside, and you keep the protection." She cursed. "You shitting bastard. How could I have missed that?"

"I'm not the only thing you have to attend to," Lorcan said, as impudently as he could. But inside his thoughts were racing—now that she knew about the blood connection, she could find Farideh and take her own vial. There was a finite amount of time before there wasn't a damned thing he could do to stop Sairché.

But Sairché didn't know Farideh had pulled him out of this prison. Nor, he thought, did Sairché realize what she'd given away as she puzzled. Not the details he was hoping for, but a beginning, a possibility. And she wouldn't kill him until she had Farideh in hand.

Bibracte eyed him like a waiting vulture, as she pulled spiked gloves over her powerful hands.

Use the mirror, damn it, he thought. Anytime you like.

"Where's the connection?" she demanded. "It's one of your trinkets, isn't it? Which one has the sympathetic link?"

Lorcan shrugged. "You have all my belongings, don't you? Search them yourself."

"Oh, I will." Sairché glared down at the dark mirror, where it leaned against the fleshy wall. "Does it pain you to realize all you ever had to do was assist me?" she burst out. "It didn't have to be this way."

"When should I have done that? Before or after you went around bargaining with my warlocks?"

"I would have let you live."

"Then you should have come to me first," Lorcan snapped. "But we both know that was never going to happen. You don't want allies. It's not in your nature." It's in neither of our natures, he thought.

Sairché narrowed her eyes at his reflection and waved a hand to stir the powers of the scrying mirror.

It found the rod, the blast of Hellish magic that streamed from it, and Farideh's hand. Sairché forced the image to shift, to show the entire warlock—still down in the caverns where Lorcan had left her—and fighting alone against what looked to be a seven-foot-tall corpse spouting green fire.

Lorcan held his breath.

Sairché clenched her fists. "What is she *doing*? Gods be damned, I need her alive!"

"Welcome," Lorcan said, "to owning a Brimstone Angel." He folded his arms and kept his eyes off the mirror, off the sight of

Farideh putting herself in mortal danger. *There's nothing you can do,* he thought. *She'll dig her own grave.* "You don't even have a portal with which to gather her. Whatever shall you do?"

Sairche spun on him. "Oh, I've got plans to fix that. Irons in other fires. Once you're out of the way, it will take just moments. Don't worry," she added. "I won't take her right away. I want to make sure you suffer."

"If you really wanted my help," he said. "I would have considered it. Hells, it's not as if we couldn't convince some other heir to switch their pact, the two of us." He let the pearl drop to the floor behind him, where his heel could crush it quickly. "We still could."

Sairché regarded him, her expression puzzled and her grin slowly growing. "Really?" she said after a moment. "If I didn't know better, Lorcan, I would guess you didn't know."

That stopped him. "Didn't know what?"

"There are a fair number of devils interested in *a* Kakistos heir," she said, "and they'll pay well enough. But there are a much smaller number interested in *this* Kakistos heir. And what they'll pay . . . To be perfectly honest, even I wasn't expecting it."

Lorcan frowned. "Why?"

"Oh that's funny. You *don't* know."

"You intend to kill me anyway," he said. "Why not tell me?"

Sairché patted his cheek. "It's been awhile since you've had the upper hand, but trust me when I say it's far more satisfying to send you to your grave wondering. I do hope you've been a dearer brother to Bibracte than you have to me." The erinyes loomed over Lorcan, flexing her hands in the vicious wrappings, her fangs bared in a horrible grimace.

"Do be sure," she said to Bibracte as she headed out the door, "to leave something for the others to do." She glanced back at him. "We have to convince those watching that I'm a worthy successor to mother, after all."

Bibracte's spiked fist crashed into his face, hard enough to split his lip and bloody his nose. He reeled and felt his foot come down on the pearl. He caught himself before he crushed it and cut a glance to the mirror, to Farideh fallen prone across a field of bones. The paladin coming to her side, his sword drawn. The blast of silver, divine light, so cold he could almost feel it through the mirror. Now or never, he thought.

"Tell Sairché she'll have to try harder to succeed someone as cunning as Mother," he said, and he stepped back onto the pearl, smashing it to dust.

∴⌒∴

By the fifth time Farideh stepped through a rent in the world, she realized she'd gotten into more than she knew how to get out of. So many leaps through the strange passages were making her dizzy. As slow as the creature was, it didn't falter as it tracked her around the tomb. And as much as the fire seemed to pain it, none of her spells had brought it down—and it was getting angrier. The ghosts streaked back and forth across the crypt, diving near her, but always shying away as she drew on her powers.

Make for the exit, Farideh thought as the world parted for her, then cast the lava vent. If anything could stop it, it was that.

But as she stepped free of the cloud of smoke and brimstone, her foot came down on some unfortunate's skull. Her ankle turned, and she fell forward, smacking her face against a second skull.

That's what you get for being clever—the thought went through her head as quickly as the pain shooting from her cheekbone. Blood filled her mouth where her teeth had sliced her cheek. The creature's heavy footfalls, crunching through the field of bones toward her, shook her from her daze. She scrambled to her feet, collecting the fallen rod as she did, but her ankle threatened to buckle under her weight.

Her eyes on the creature and her rod in hand, the bones were equal parts obstacle and motivation as she limped toward the exit. The light between the creature's jaws started to build again. Farideh pointed the rod at it, drawing hard on the Hells.

Dahl all but tackled her, pulling her out of the blast's reach. At the same time a beam of silvery light streaked across the tomb, Selûne's magic slamming into the creature and throwing it across the chamber. The mummy screamed.

"Gods damn it!" she heard Mira shout. "Pull him up!"

"Come on!" Dahl hooked an arm under hers and started toward Mira and the exit and the rope dangling there.

The mummy screamed. The pain in her ankle surged to match it, but Farideh gritted her teeth and clung to Dahl and the rod. She glanced back over her shoulder. The mummy kept its pace toward the exit to the pit, its empty eye sockets seeming to focus past Farideh on the dancing end of the rope.

A sharp *crack*, a yelp of pain from Mira, and the remains of one of the heavy bookshelves rained down on the field of broken bones. Dahl cursed and jumped back, yanking her with him. She could hear Tam yelling and Havilar yelling and Maspero yelling. The crash of more shelves, another rain of spellbooks. The rope slapping the wall.

But the only sound that mattered was the howl of the approaching mummy. It was close, close enough to see where the pale jade bones of its wrists peeked through its flaking muscles, the fine, broken hairs that had been its beard, the garnet pendant hanging around its neck.

Tarchamus, Farideh realized.

The ghosts took shape at their master's side—no longer familiar faces, but apprentices in long mage's robes. A man with steel-gray hair and pale skin. A red-haired girl. A dark-skinned woman with her hair in braids. The cold light of the dead behind their eyes.

Dahl had left her and knotted loops into the hanging rope. He stepped into one, pulling it tight. He looked back and spotted the arcanist, now no farther than the reach of one of Farideh's blasts. "Let's go," he said, coming to her side again.

And then the portal opened.

Dahl gasped as he crushed her close, either to protect her or to claim some protection himself from the flash of hellfire and the fearsome figure that appeared in its heart: Lorcan.

For a moment, Farideh was sure he was nothing more than the aftereffects of Adolican Rhand's poisons, except Dahl could clearly see this devil too. She sat there, stunned: he'd found a way out. His wings were still bound, and his nose and lip streamed black blood. Lorcan's gaze fell on her and his wings flexed against the pin, but at the same moment the arcanist looked back and marked his presence.

He turned to consider this new threat—no, she thought, none of us are threats. We are nuisances. Prey. He knows he will have all of us eventually.

"Farideh, come on," Dahl said, finding his voice again.

He cannot fly, she thought, watching Lorcan. He cannot fight him. Even erinyes burn, but not Tarchamus. His eyes on the arcanist, Lorcan untangled the sword from Pernika's remains. The ghosts crept toward him. All Farideh's nightmares, all her hideous visions were about to come true.

"Run!" she shouted at Lorcan. He ignored her and cast a ball of energy at the mummy. The arcanist didn't so much as flinch. The boiling promises of Malbolge started whispering in her ears, burning in her veins.

"Go," she said to Dahl. She looked back at him. "Many thanks. For coming back for me."

"No—are you mad? That thing—"

"I can't leave him," Farideh said. She didn't wait for Dahl to argue. She stepped into another split—the last she could likely handle, she realized as vertigo snarled around her like a cast-off net—and landed off-balance near the northern wall, near one of the narrow alcoves that lined it.

Off-balance, because Dahl had grabbed hold of her arm and traveled with her.

"You are not," he said, drawing his sword once more, "making me explain to Master Zawad how I left you to die." He knew this was madness—she could see it in the grim set of his mouth, the verge of panic in his eyes.

"Stay back," she said. "Keep the ghosts off us."

The bursts of energy were enough to get the ghosts' attention, to turn them away from Lorcan. A rain of burning brimstone drew the arcanist's eye as Dahl's sword warded off the swooping ghosts. Lorcan cast again, and the arcanist's attention switched, still trying to decide which of them to take first.

"Shit and ashes," Lorcan shouted. "Will you run already?"

Green light collected in the arcanist's open mouth.

The erinyes poured out of the second portal, near where Lorcan's had opened. The center one she remembered all too well—the erinyes slicing one of the Asmodean cultists in half, laughing and toying with his innards, as Lorcan turned her face from the carnage. One of the *pradixikai*, the elite. The other two—one with red eyes, one with a broken fang—seemed smaller and less terrible but still fit for Farideh's nightmares. Their shining hooves crushed the field of bones as they strode from the portal, surveying the battlefield.

"Oh *karshoj*."

"What are those?" Dahl cried.

"Run, Dahl," she said. She pointed the rod at the mad erinyes. *"Adaestuo."* The bolt screamed past the arcanist and struck her wicked black armor. She focused her attention on Farideh, sneering . . . then turned away. Back to Lorcan. She pointed to either side and the erinyes fanned out to surround him.

As his sisters' gazes swept the tomb and each person in it, Lorcan had sprinted away—after the mummy. He scooped up a skull, a pelvis, poor Pernika's torn-off forearm, and hurled it all at the arcanist, between blasts of the bruised-looking energy.

The arcanist swung around to swat at Lorcan—but as he did, he released the building burst of magic. The green light screamed across the tomb and enveloped the erinyes with the broken tusk fully.

One moment the erinyes was stalking toward her brother. The next she had become nothing more than an ear-splitting scream and a wispy emerald vapor hanging in the air . . . before swirling together into a cloud that streamed back to the arcanist's open mouth, chased by the insubstantial forms of the ghosts.

Farideh clapped a hand to her mouth to stem the scream that threatened to work its way free. Even the erinyes seemed shocked. Then the mad one barked a command, and they broke wide to flank the mummy. The arcanist paid them no mind—the essence of the erinyes seemed to swell through him, and he threw back his head, making a hideous droning hum of pleasure. The ghosts chased each other around their master's form, sending a queer vibration through the air.

Lorcan ran to Farideh as if he meant to bowl her over, ignoring the death of his sister, ignoring the hideous sound coming from the mummy. "The bolt!" he shouted catching hold of the hand that held the rod. "Gods damn it, the bolt!"

Farideh tore her gaze from the arcanist. *"A-assulam."*

The bolt shattered into a rain of rust and sparks, and Lorcan's wings sprang open. He took another quick survey of the crypt and tried to grab her around the waist. "It had to shitting be Bibracte. Come on."

"Dahl," she said slipping out of Lorcan's reach. "We have to—"

The clash of Dahl's sword against the erinyes's interrupted her, and Lorcan leaped away from the sound. The mad-eyed erinyes—Bibracte—had circled around the arcanist, leaving him focused on her compatriot, whose own blackened sword swatted wildly at the ghosts as they swept near.

In the very core of her heart, Farideh was screaming. Compared to the erinyes of her nightmares, Bibracte was larger, fiercer, and more gleefully determined to tear through her brother and the tiefling before her as if they were made of parchment. Dahl blocked the erinyes's advance with sword strokes so clean and firm that Farideh could imagine Mehen directing her to pay attention, this was how it was done.

But Bibracte had a faint, amused smile—Dahl was a better match than she'd expected, but he wasn't built to cut down the enemies of archdevils.

*. . . the erinyes are a thunderstorm, unstoppable and rolling toward them out of nothing. Their hooves crack the cobbles, shatter the rune. Their crowns of horns threaten to spear the moon. Their swords are fire. Their swords are hungry . . .*

Farideh cast a stream of flames up under the erinyes's sword arm, forcing her back and burning the tender skin not shielded by her gleaming armor. If it hurt her, though, Farideh couldn't tell. Bibracte skittered back and snarled at her.

"Thank Sairché for your life," she spat. She swung a fist at Farideh, expecting, no doubt, to knock her flat.

But Lorcan's borrowed sword interrupted her—stabbing deeply into the gap of her spaulder and cuirass. Black blood oozed from the wound and Bibracte grunted as Lorcan pulled the weapon free again.

"Run, darling," Lorcan ordered, her nightmare starting all over again. But before Bibracte could punish her brother's impudence, the screams of the other erinyes demanded everyone's attention.

The ghosts had taken solid form again and pinned the erinyes to the ground. She was strong enough to lift them each from their feet, but they were three and she was one.

"Mother of nightmares, Cissa," Bibracte cursed.

The arcanist bent down, as leisurely as if he were retrieving a fallen coin, plucked the erinyes's armor away, and plunged a skeletal hand into her abdomen.

Farideh knew better than to watch after that, and focused only on the distance between them and the exit shaft, on being certain Dahl and Lorcan followed. The ghosts, no longer needed to hold down the red-eyed erinyes, streaked past, landing and taking solid form to strike at the trio before dissolving into smoke and light again. The old man slammed into Farideh with all the same strength the last ghost had had, knocking her into Dahl. But the Harper kept his feet and pulled her past so he could swipe at the ghost with his sword.

The other two hurtled into Lorcan, raking his flesh with their nails, tearing the wounds in his wings deeper. Farideh heard him cry out in shock and pain, but there was no time to stop.

The rope still hung down the wall's side, dancing as someone started down it. "No!" Dahl shouted. "We're coming up!" He pushed her forward. The arcanist looked up from his still-kicking meal, as if realizing he was about to lose them all. He roared and started toward them.

There wouldn't be time, Farideh realized. Not for each of them to ascend. Lorcan reached them. She shoved the rope into Dahl's hands.

"You go!" she shouted. "I can slow him down." She turned back to the monstrous creature and pointed the rod at the ground before it. *"Laesurach."*

The ground beneath the arcanist's feet turned molten, and a geyser of magma shot forth around him. He screamed, an unearthly howl, and the ghosts twined around and around and around. The mad erinyes retreated a distance, her sword drawn, waiting, it seemed, for the flames to die down.

Farideh looked over at Lorcan. "Can you fly?"

"Not well," he said. He took hold of her, and without explanation he plucked the rod from her hands. "Is your paladin out of the way?"

Dahl hauled himself awkwardly over the top. "Yes."

"Pity," Lorcan said.

The powers of Malbolge surged around and through them both, then burst out in a ring of flames that gusted up the exit shaft and under Lorcan's battered wings. She held tight as the burning air vaulted them both up, past the walls, past the lip, and out to the second layer.

"Back!" she heard Tam shout, as the flames burst outward, setting the scrolls and books left scattered by their efforts afire. She shut her eyes and curled toward Lorcan, shielding her face from the heat.

They landed in an awkward heap, the cuffs of Farideh's blouse singed and smoking. Havilar rushed her and pulled her up, and embraced her fiercely. "You stupid *henish*—don't *do* that!" she said. She tucked her head into her sister's hair. Farideh hugged her back, still trying to catch her breath. Below them the arcanist's screams of pain faded.

"Make a circle!" Lorcan shouted. "Someone make a godsbedamned circle!"

Farideh let go of Havilar, suddenly aware that *everyone* could see Lorcan and that only Havilar wasn't braced as if the devil was a new threat. Tam in particular, though he stood as if that were all he could handle, held the holy symbol of Selûne and his chain as if both would spring to life at any moment.

"Havilar," he said, "help your sister aside."

"No!" Farideh cried. She stepped back, closer to Lorcan. "Please, Tam! Lock him in a circle. Let me bind him, but don't kill him." She shook her head. "He hasn't done anything."

"Yet."

"Please," Lorcan repeated, without an ounce of scorn in him. "Please. I will go wherever you want, tell you whatever you need. Just make a circle. Now. Or they will find me and you will find yourself with still more to contend with, and I don't think you have the resources for that." He smiled and spread his hands in a gesture of peace. "We're on the same side for the moment, I promise."

The last erinyes started screaming, and though Farideh wouldn't have thought it possible, everyone grew tenser.

**LESSER EVILS**

"We'll need him," Dahl said, and Tam dropped the holy symbol to his side and stared at him. "We'll need as many as we can," Dahl added, "when we go back down."

"Next time," Havilar said, "you're taking *me*."

"No one is going down there again," Tam said. "Understood?"

Dahl shook his head. "We have to. The air shafts. Didn't you see? There are three of them along the far wall. That's our other exit."

# CHAPTER NINETEEN

"YOU ARE NOT *ALLOWED* TO DO THINGS LIKE THAT," HAVILAR WHISPERED to Farideh as they stood off to the side of the camp. "Especially not when we're fighting."

Tam cast a silvery circle around Lorcan, its powers pointing inward and hemming the cambion in close enough so that he had to hold his wings close. Whether that was Tam's goal or an effect of the priest's clear exhaustion, Farideh couldn't tell—the set of his mouth suggested one thing, and the way his eyes didn't seem to focus on the runes suggested the other.

"Tam and Brin wouldn't let me go down there until the rope was fixed," Havilar said. She'd only just let go of Farideh's arm, holding tight to her sister during the whole rushed trip back to the camp. Brin was watching them both, looking concerned. "And there were all those awful noises and then there were devils—where did Lorcan even come from? You said he was trapped and getting cut to pieces?"

Where *had* he come from? Farideh wondered. Lorcan watched her, looking annoyed as if it were her fault there were so many people there. He still held tight to her rod, as if it were a talisman. Had he been lying about being tortured and captive? Had he lied about being glad she'd pulled him here the first time?

"You have to ask him," Farideh said.

Havilar's tail made an agitated slash. "Are you still mad about Brin? Is that why you took Dahl and not me?"

Between all the Hellish powers she'd been channeling and the adrenaline that had coursed through every inch of her veins, Farideh's head was pounding and her muscles ached. She rotated her twisted ankle. "I wasn't thinking clearly," she said. "I thought, 'he used to be a paladin, he can heal Tam.' Which . . . was stupid, I know. But he knew how to splint his leg at least. Besides," she added, "you were at the back. With Brin."

"If you're mad, just say—" Havilar frowned at her. "What do you mean, 'used to be a paladin? As in he *fell*?" She scrutinized Dahl as he finished a a second circle of protection around the camp—his runes drew themselves in a flurry of chalk dust. He eyed her as she edged away from the border of the circle, as if he were trying to decide whether or not to yell at Farideh again. "Did he tell you that?"

Farideh hesitated. Havilar wasn't happy about Lorcan, and she'd be less happy to hear about his previous appearance. "More or less," she said.

"Huh. I wonder if that's why he's so touchy."

"I think it's probably just him."

Havilar looked at her, perplexed. "Do you *ever* read chapbooks? Paladins falling, that's a big deal. They decide to do something—for love if they're good, for power if they're evil, and for both if they're just tragic—and their god doesn't like it, so they lose all their powers. Forever. It'd be like getting an arm chopped off or something. I think."

Farideh shook her head. "That's chapbooks though."

"Well, they have to get it from *somewhere*," Havilar said. "Too bad *you* couldn't do something and lose Lorcan. Mehen is going to drop *eggs* when he finds out you called him back."

Farideh thought of all her fears that Lorcan might have died or been locked away forever, or forgotten her or tired of her or given her pact away to someone else. It might be as far as could be from losing the blessings of a god, but the result was the same. She would be lost and lonesome and always wondering what had happened.

*What have I done?* he'd wailed at the darkness. *How have I failed?* If Havilar was right—if all it took was a single misguided action—it sounded as if Dahl didn't even know what it had been. Considering how Dahl seemed to pride himself on knowing almost everything, it must be a wound that never closed.

Tam stood in the middle of the camp, looking so pallid and determined that he might have been a statue—had he not been swaying on his feet. "I hardly know where to begin."

"I think you start with what in the Hells killed Pernika," Maspero said, "then work your way around to why you've taken a devil hostage instead of killing him, too."

"Because I'm a good deal more useful than your dead swordswoman?" Lorcan said.

"Not another word," Tam snapped. He glared at Farideh. "Don't think this is permanent."

"But he's right," Farideh said. "We could use his help getting past the arcanist."

"What do you need help getting past a crumbly old wizard for?" Havilar asked. "Is that all that's down there?"

"It's not—" Farideh started. The air suddenly sizzled and Tam clapped his hands to his ears. Two voices broke the silence, both bellowing as if demanding to be heard first, both too loud and broken as if bits of them were falling away.

*Shepherd, drop the stlarning wards—*

*—no word since the twelfth and—*

*—and respond, damn it. Your fellow Rhand—*

*—Band of mounted shades with carriers spotted flying your way from—*

*—He'll be right on top of you and Everlund says he's got reinforcements—*

*—Get out of there immediately, agent . . .*

No one spoke as Tam straightened, as if dizzied by the effort of the sendings. "Received," he said. "Location . . . is secure. Looking for alternate exits. The wards . . ." He looked at Mira, as if he wasn't sure who she was. Farideh's chest tightened—a mix of fear and sympathy for Mira. She'd gotten that look before. " . . . are down. Send word if situation changes." The spell crackled again, as if it clung unevenly to the strands of the Weave, colliding with its own power.

Tam stared up at the ceiling, catching his breath. "When did the wards come down?" Tam demanded.

"A good question," Maspero murmured, turning on Mira. "You said this place was secure. That we shouldn't worry about Shade, because with the wards were in place, they couldn't find the spells faster than you. But that makes you wrong twice over, by my count."

Mira shook her head. "They can't have come down. They've lasted for years. Even the Spellplague didn't destroy them."

"Well, something did," Maspero said. "Else we wouldn't have dead shadovar in the stacks and sendings and devils coming through."

Mira backed away from him. "Then something changed. Runes don't unravel themselves."

All the blood pounding in Farideh's head suddenly dropped to her feet, dragging her breath behind. The runes were for doors, she thought. There must be different runes.

"You mean the marks on the walls?" Dahl asked quietly. "Those power the wards?"

"Yes. You see traces of similar spells in old Netherese ruins, but never intact like this. They're clearly meant to prevent outside eyes from looking in. Or they were." She shook her head. "The ones I found were still scintillating and when you said your sendings didn't pass . . ."

Farideh's thoughts were racing. She hadn't *checked* the door before she broke the rune. The Book had said not to. She swallowed. She had to say something.

"Well, we can't count on . . . their . . ." Tam swooned. Mira and Dahl sprang forward and caught him, eased him down to the floor. "I'm fine," he said, his voice faint. "Let me up."

"You're exhausted," Mira said.

Tam didn't seem able to look at her. "I'm *fine*."

"You are not," Dahl said. "And you're not in any shape to help us break out of here."

"I think I have a better idea of what shape I'm in," Tam said. "Help me up."

"Please," Dahl said. "You've run across this library end to end. Slung that chain around like a lariat. Broken your leg and then tried to heal it—and you're still hurting, we can all see it. Cast more powerful blessings than I can recall at the moment, and you haven't bothered to rest."

Tam bristled. "I know what I'm—"

"If it were me," Dahl said over him, "what would you say?"

Tam quieted. "It's not the same."

"You're right, it's worse. We need people who can heal and people who can cast to get past that thing and its ghosts. If you don't rest, we're down by one. The one we need most."

Tam rubbed a hand over his face. "We don't have time. We need a plan."

Dahl gestured at the larger group. "You have plenty of help. We'll come up with a plan while you sleep. You can tell us what we've done wrong when you can see straight."

Tam scowled at the floor, looking as if he were searching for an argument to hurl back at Dahl. But there was no denying how worn down he was, or how dearly his injured state might cost them.

"I have more of the tea in my bag," Farideh offered. "A little? To help you sleep?"

Tam didn't answer, but Dahl nodded. "Yes. Make extra." You need it too, his expression said. But they did not need her as much as they needed Tam. She dug out the little pouch and set a careful portion of water from their remaining waterskin boiling in a pot.

"There's a hitch," Tam said. He looked up at Mira, sad and furious all at once. "They ought to know who they're working with."

Mira stood a little straighter. "Does it matter?"

"Oh, I think so. I think when there are clandestine members of the Zhentarim pulling my people into danger, they have a right to reconsider alliances."

Farideh looked up from the cookfire. Mira had gone perfectly still, not taking her eyes off her father's. Everyone else watched them, uncomfortable and unwilling, it seemed, to step between and catch the sharp edge of the next words thrown.

"How could you?" Tam said.

"How could I not?" she said. "They make a persuasive offer. And it's not as if every alliance you've made is so innocent. Even I've heard stories of the Culler of the Fold."

"Being a paid assassin is not the same as being Bane and Cyric's playthings."

Farideh stoked the fire, uncomfortably reminded of half a dozen arguments she'd had with Mehen. But at least most of those times only Havilar had been watching.

"We want the same things," Mira said. "To keep these powers from Netheril. To punish Shade for what they've done—"

"To turn these weapons to their own advantage?" Tam demanded. "Don't be naïve."

Mira's expression hardened. "If anyone is being naïve," she said, a low edge to her normally calm voice, "it's you. Do you think for a moment that the Harpers will provide any sort of impediment to the Princes' expansion? Do you think you can really stand against Shade and do anything but die? Take the allies you're offered."

"Does it matter?" Farideh piped up, unable to bear the tumble of their conversation down its rocky, awful path. "We're all in this against Shade. Against Tarchamus. Perhaps against the Hells. And we barely stand a chance if we all stand together. Even if she meant to turn on us, you can't pretend she's foolish enough to do so with Pernika dead, and Lorcan on our side."

"Yes," Mira said bitterly. "Your warlock and her devil will keep us wicked mercenaries in line."

Farideh flushed and dropped her gaze to the simmering water. "Many thanks," she said, adding a few pinches of the tea. "I *was* on your side."

"Enough," Dahl said. "We don't have time *or* allies to waste, so I think we can all be trusted not to kill each other, yes? That includes Zhents. And devils. So your conversation will keep until later," he said to Tam and Mira. "First things first, we need maps of the lower levels—as clear as we can recollect—yes? Mira, that is obviously yours."

"I can draw a map," Tam protested.

"Farideh, if you have to pour it down his throat, make him drink that tea," Dahl said. "No one talk to Tam."

"Are we forgetting the shitting Netherese at the gates?" Maspero said.

"No," Dahl replied. "Take Havi and Brin and make certain the doors are holding—and on your way back, make as many obstacles as you can. Make sure if they do get through, they're forced to navigate the library as much as possible. But stay together, and let Brin scare the ghosts off if they get close."

"What about you?" Brin asked. "And Farideh?"

"Fari can come with us," Havilar said.

"No," Dahl said. "We need better information about the arcanist. And the library. I think I know where to find it." He glanced at Farideh, and it dawned on her that he knew about the runes. She'd told him. Ah gods. "She can help me when she's finished dosing Tam," he said.

Farideh cursed to herself. At least he wasn't going to call her out in front of everyone. Maybe he knew how to repair them. Maybe he knew how to make new wards.

*Maybe he just wants to be sure you know how badly you erred,* she thought, pouring the tea into a clay mug for Tam.

Tam was staring at Lorcan when she brought him the tea. "I cannot believe I have to tell your father you called that devil down. What were you thinking?"

Farideh kneeled down beside his bedroll. "He called himself. And then I was thinking it was awful handy to have someone fly me out of that mess."

He sighed. "And I cannot believe you are so flippant about this, Farideh. It's your soul, but you're treading a line you never had to, and I worry one day you will fall across it."

She held out the mug to him. "Will it matter? If I look like this, is a soul really a surety?"

"Those sound like someone else's words."

"Plenty of other people's. If you think I have a soul worth saving, you are well in the minority." Her gaze flicked over to Dahl. "Even in this company."

He took the mug, watching the steaming contents instead of her face. "Whatever part of you is devil, the greater part is mortal. And that part must have a soul capable of good. It would be a shame to damn that part of yourself because the fiendish part—if in fact some part of you remains irrevocably fiendish, mind—happens to control your outward features." He blew on the tea and took a tentative sip. "And unless you are a splendid actress, I think you *do* care. Don't let *him* tell you your soul is doomed."

Farideh pursed her lips and watched him drink several more sips of the tea. "Is it me you want to save, or Mira?"

And Tam Zawad was wise enough at least to know not to answer that question.

"There may be a line," Farideh said, "but I would hope crossing it had more to do with hurting people and being selfish, with letting bad things happen instead of stopping them and not stepping up when you've done wrong—with a great many things more important than the company I keep. I hope that's true for her as well." She stood, still smarting from Mira's last jab. "Although, she did steal the protective circle ritual from your book. You should know."

"Don't change the—" He broke off with a jaw-splitting yawn.

"Go to sleep," Farideh said. She sighed. "Being this tired just makes you surly."

Tam looked as if he would have liked to argue, as if there were a lot more he intended to say on the subject. But the tea was already seeping into his thoughts—his eyelids drooped and it seemed to take all the effort in the world just to blink. Farideh remembered the feeling. She left, and within a few steps, he had dropped to sleep.

"I do hope," Lorcan said coldly, "that he appreciates my silence. For all the good it did."

The devil sat seething in his silvery prison, passing the rod back and forth between his hands. His wounds hadn't been dressed, she noticed, but he seemed to pay them no mind. Farideh drew nearer to the binding circle. "Are you all right?"

"Oh, *cozy*," Lorcan said. "I see the paladin got over his aversions." He smirked across the camp at Dahl, who was half-watching them, half-reading a slim blue book. "Some of them anyhow. Aren't you *lucky*?"

"Leave him alone," Farideh said wearily. "We're in enough of a mess as it is."

"So it seems." He looked down at her, his black eyes cruel. "Once again, out of the frying pan and into the fire? Between this and Neverwinter, it hardly seems fair that I'm the one in the binding circle."

Gods, Farideh thought, pursing her mouth. Back to this. Back to sulking, sneering Lorcan. Why had she ever thought he'd be different? "I'm sorry you have to be in there. I didn't have time to find a solution yet."

He stopped passing the rod back and forth and glared at it in his hands. "Unfortunately things got rather heated on my end. I couldn't wait."

"Well, I'll keep looking," she said, and she turned to go deal with Dahl.

"How is your leg?" Lorcan asked. He was still looking at the rod as he spoke to her. "You were limping before. Is it all right?"

"Just a turned ankle," she said, waiting for the twist, waiting for him to spring some other nonsense on her. "Some bruises. I tripped on a skull."

"Well, that's . . . good, I suppose." He started fidgeting with the rod again.

"Can I have that back?" she asked.

Lorcan blew out a breath. "No. Not yet."

She frowned at him. "Why?"

"I need it."

Farideh started to protest, to demand to know what exactly he needed with a warlock's implement anyway, to insist he give it back—because what was he going to do from inside a binding circle if she just took it?—when Dahl came up behind her, still holding the little blue book.

"I need to talk to you," he said. "Now."

Lorcan gave him a wicked smile. "Sounds *serious*. Best do as he says, darling."

"We are not done," Farideh whispered to the cambion. She followed Dahl back across the camp, to the very edges of the circle, as far from Lorcan and Mira and Tam as he could get. Glancing back at the others, Dahl whispered, "You destroyed one of the runes."

Farideh felt the shadow-smoke start to pulse off her, the powers of the Hells stirring it up, ready for a fight. "I didn't know. I thought they were door locks."

"Because the Book told you."

"It's not that absurd."

"I'm not blaming you!" He ran a hand through his hair, glanced back again, and pulled her out of the circle and around the corner of the shelves. "I . . . I broke one too. The Book said it powered a trap I had to get past."

The shadows dropped back. "You did?"

"As you said, it's not that absurd."

"We have to tell them," she said. "What if there's a way to repair them?"

**Lesser Evils**

"Can you cast runic magic?" he asked. "I don't think any of them can. What's done is done. But . . . Look, what were you trying to get from the Book? What's it been telling you?"

She felt the blood burning up her neck. "I was using it to figure out something. A ritual."

"The ritual to pull the devil from the Hells," he said flatly. "Don't be coy. I was there. It drew it out? Had you coming back a lot?"

She nodded. "And . . . it sounds strange, but it lied about things, as if it wanted me to trust it and keep coming back. I have ancestors it claimed to know about, and it told me their history. Exactly what I wanted to hear." How stupid had she been to believe a word of it? And how terrible, she thought, would it be to tell Havilar the truth?

Dahl's face clouded. "It did the same to me. It . . . It gathered I had a problem," he said delicately, "and sent me to find a book that suggested it was none of my doing. That it was others manipulating me." He shook his head. "That I was like the arcanist."

"Was Lorcan right?" she asked softly. "Were you a paladin?"

Dahl studied the runes on the limestone tiles. "Once," he said. "I was dedicated to the god of knowledge."

Farideh knew if she told him she was sorry, he would snap at her and say he didn't want her pity. If she asked what made him fall, he would take it as taunting him. If she offered the parallel, the way her fear of losing her pact made her think of his losing his powers . . . well, that would only end badly, destroying the modicum of camaraderie they'd built up.

And if she said nothing, she would regret it.

"It sounds like something you were very suited to," she told him.

Dahl sighed. "Listen to the rest of what I have to tell you before you decide that. We're not dealing with just some old wizard." He opened it to a spread of pages covered with a hurried diagram and littered with notes. "This is a diary of one of Tarchamus's friends. I'm fairly sure this is a copy of the spell Mira's looking for. Only it's not an exaggeration. He really did burn a city out of the sky and destroy all the people living below it." He flipped back through the book. "Here: *'Tarchamus will not see me. He has not taken the council's intercession well—who would?'* " Dahl looked up. "They blocked him, the other arcanists and priests of the goddess of magic, from using the Weave after he destroyed that city. '*But his apprentices still come and go, visiting his former friends and rivals. Today, Nyvasha, who Tarchamus lured away from Tenish, came to see several of my own apprentices, carrying a tome of absurd thickness that she must have dug out of Tarchamus's attics for all the dust it carried.*' "—Dahl gave Farideh a significant look—" '*When I asked after her master, Nyvasha was suddenly quite shy of me and danced around an answer. When I asked if I might see Tarchamus, she was quiet and said only it would be a few years more, she suspected, before anyone saw him. Sadebreth tells me Lorull, the old man who has been Tarchamus's apprentice for such long years he must have more loyalty than sense, has flown for the mountains . . .* ' Wait, there's . . ." Dahl paged ahead. "Ah, here, the arcanist disappears and he gets ahold of his notes—'*the structure this suggests is not so much a hoard as a trap, a pit into which Tarchamus's hungry rivals may fall. It would take the likes of Tarchamus's eruption to breach it, but I must do as I can because within rests the only copy of the eruption spell, the last scroll bait for every fool arcanist in Netheril.*' " Dahl looked up. "Everything after that is notes about finding the place and trying to convince others to stop looking for it. I think he died here."

Farideh turned the pages back to the diagram, studying the runes. "This one," she said, tapping the center mark. "It's part of a spell I know."

"One that makes a lot of fire?"

"Lava. Not enough to burn a city out of the sky, but enough to do some damage," she said. The scrawlings surrounding the rune reminded her of the scrolls the Book had sent her hunting. "Have you shown it to Mira?"

Dahl shook his head. "There wasn't time before. And now . . ." He paused and wet his lips. "I'm afraid we might need to destroy this place. I'm sure we need to be ready for it."

"All of it?"

"I don't want to, all right?" he snapped. "The knowledge is not good or evil, but Shade will put it to evil purpose and people will die by the hundreds. Since Tarchamus isn't famous for his eruption beyond historians and maybe Shade, we have to assume that scroll never got out. And if we can't find it, we have to make certain Shade doesn't either."

Farideh nodded, surprised by the outburst. "Lorcan will know what the rune means. He might know what the spell does. He might know if we can reproduce it somehow."

Dahl scowled at the text. "I don't want to treat with a devil."

"I'll treat with him," she said sharply. She handed the diary back. "You could always ask the Book. It might let something slip."

"No," Dahl said urgently. "*Don't* pick up that book." He pulled another book from his jerkin, another slim leather volume. "I found this. Look at the dates."

Farideh frowned. "Fourteen seventy-eight? They couldn't . . ." She read the names. "*Karshoj*. Who made this?"

"Is it true?"

Farideh stared at the name bound in curlicues of stylized branches and marked with the number three: *Lord Aubrin Crownsilver.* "I don't know," she admitted. "He's . . . someone. But he wouldn't have just left this . . . or written it."

Dahl studied her face, as if he were assessing how much he could trust her and how much she trusted him. "Let's say you're right," he said, "Brin wouldn't have left it. What if this is what those ghosts are doing? What if they're driving us back to the Book so it can . . . pull things from our heads? Make new books? Hoard new knowledge? What if that's what this place is? A trap, to punish Tarchamus's rivals."

"And then they feed us to the arcanist?" She closed the book. If this was what was locked in Brin's head, it wasn't her business. "Where did you find it?"

"Near where you were casting your circle," Dahl said. "If I'm right . . . there might be something there about the scroll. If someone hid it or destroyed it, they might have given that knowledge to the Book."

"Maybe the memories of whoever got that page out of here?" Farideh held out a hand. "Stay here. Give me the diary, and I'll see about that first." And see about my rod, too, she thought as she walked over to Lorcan.

"I need to show you something," Farideh said. She opened the diary to the spell diagrams, the lines of Infernal letters arrayed around the center rune. "Do you know what it says?" He reached out to touch the center rune—the circle rebuffed him, and he flinched.

**ERIN M. EVANS**

"Phlegethos," Lorcan said. "The fourth layer."

" 'The Heart of Flames,' " she said, recalling the scroll. "What would that do?"

"Everything would burn," he said. "Perhaps even the caster. Phlegethos is hotter than a volcano's heart." Lorcan peered at the diagram. "Lords of the Nine, that's complex. What under Beshaba's wicked gaze are you doing with it?"

"Nothing yet. Could you cast it?"

"I'd be impressed if an archlord could cast *that*."

Not the answer she wanted. She shut the book. "May I have my rod back?"

Lorcan straightened. "Trust me, darling, you don't want it."

"I certainly do," she said. She held out a hand. "And it's not as if you can return it to the Hells at the moment. So please?"

"You can't just trust that I have your best interests at heart," he said, his wings twitching as if they might spread wide and shatter the walls of the circle. "Maybe you should have called Sairché—I'll bet she'd make a fine mistress."

Farideh shook her head, biting back a bitter laugh. "You know I thought things were different. I thought you and I . . . I thought you were done treating me like some *thing* you shift and prod and toy with, but that was never so. I spent *every* night worrying over you. I searched high and low for a gate to get you from the Hells—I put myself in the hands of *monsters* for you—and you can't even come up with a decent lie for why you want to cripple me?"

"This isn't about crippling you."

"Because you suddenly need a rod?" she demanded. "Because you'd rather I fight ghosts with weakened spells?"

"Because Sairché found you!"

"What?" All Farideh's anger froze. "How? You said she couldn't."

"She managed to scry the rod. But if it's kept within—"

Farideh pointed her bare hand at the rod. *"Assulam."* A flash of light, a low pop, and the rod shattered into a rain of splinters. Lorcan yelped and curled away from the explosion. Her stomach clenched. The implement and its enchantments had saved her more than once, and casting with it had made her feel far more powerful and in control than reality had ever granted her.

*Sairché found you. She managed to scry the rod*—and then it didn't matter what the Rod of the Traitor's Reprisal had done or not done or could do in the future. It was a lodestone for Sairché, and that was all that had mattered.

"Are you *mad*?" Lorcan hissed. "Do you know what that was worth?"

The splinters scattered over the limestone tiles, spangled with chunks of the quartz tip and flakes of gold leaf. Whatever magic had been in the Rod of the Traitor's Reprisal was gone. "Less than Havilar," Farideh said.

"She doesn't know about Havilar!"

"And now she never will," Farideh said. "No matter how hard she looks. Unless you were lying about that too."

Lorcan dragged his hands over his face. "Have you wondered why I'm the first devil to seek you and your sister out?" he asked. "The only one to offer either of you the pact? Your parents were likely wicked, but one of them may have had a change of heart—there is a spell laid on you, on both of you. A protection. You can't be scryed, not by normal measures."

She blinked, startled. "How long has that been so?"

"All your life, I'd wager."

"But you could find me," she said. "So how well does it work, really?"

Lorcan shifted. "Don't be angry, darling. Do you still have the charm I gave you?" She took it from her pocket and handed it over. Lorcan twirled the little scourge between his fingers. "Do you know anything about sympathetic magic? Like calls to like, and there's nothing more powerful for a sympathetic link than blood. The Weave, the planes, the scraps of wild magic that pulse in all manner of things—they cling to blood in ways only the gods can explain. That is how I found you."

She recoiled as his meaning came clear. "You bastard. You had no right."

"Oh come now," he said. "A few drops off your brand? That's hardly worth getting upset about. And without it I wouldn't have been able to find you again. I wouldn't have been able to give you those powers you're so fond of."

Whatever reasons he put to it, *stealing* blood from her was a step beyond everything she'd agreed to. *He's practically Lorcan without the devil-magic and wings,* Havilar had said. *All teeth and hands.* All greed and self-regard.

Lorcan thrust the charm at her, skimming the edge of the circle. "Here. Take it then. You'll have all your blood back."

And he'd never be able to find her. Farideh rubbed her arm. "You could have asked."

Lorcan lowered the charm. "And if I ask now? There is a *part* of the pact. An allowance. I can take a portion of the spells that are left affecting you. It's meant to spread the effects of curses and such, but I think it will contort the protection. But it uses blood."

"What do you mean," Farideh said after a moment, "a *part* of the pact? How many *parts* are there to this pact?"

Lorcan cursed. "It's just a little . . . perquisite."

Farideh bit back her anger. "One you didn't think I needed to know about."

"It isn't you. Look, do you think I want to deal with every lazy warlock thinking they can stroll through the world provoking each other without a care because they pestered me into being their shitting shield?" Lorcan demanded. "I would have brought it up if it mattered before. I'm bringing it up now. It should carry over part of the protection and keep Sairché from finding me as well."

"The binding circle does a fine job of that."

He narrowed his eyes. "Well, if you won't, then eventually you will have to make a decision: would you rather leave me to rot in this cavern, or break the circle so Sairché can have me? How do you punish me, then? How do you make certain I regret all that *I* suffered for you, all the tears and blood the erinyes made me spill instead of handing you over? I nearly died a *dozen* times over so that you can swan around with that shitting paladin and act as if I've ravished you by claiming a few drops of blood."

Farideh blushed to her temples. "I didn't say that. I didn't say any of that. I'll find a way to get you free."

"You don't have time to find another solution."

She didn't. There were already too many pieces hanging over them—the Book and the strange texts and the arcanist and the

Shadovar. She needed the pact and she might even need Lorcan. Farideh bit her lip. "What do I have to do?"

"Give me your knife."

She pulled out the blade, but when he reached to take it, she shook her head. "Tell me where to cut," she said. "I'll do it myself."

"I suggest the elbow," he said. "The skin is thin and no one will remark on the scars. Just a nick will do. And then you will have to hand me the knife. You're not the only one who bleeds this time."

Farideh pressed the tip of the blade to her skin, harder than she would have expected, until it broke the golden skin and freed a trickle of blood that smeared the knife. She grimaced at the pain that shot up her arm, but handed him the knife, hoping she wasn't making a terrible mistake.

*Another* terrible mistake, a little voice corrected.

Lorcan slashed his own arm, black blood smearing the knife blade. "Break the circle," he said, considering the mix of fluids. "This has to go quickly."

With one pointed foot she smeared the neat silver runes into nothing. The magic sputtered and collapsed, as the Hells' powers swelled around Lorcan. A steady stream of Infernal seemed to wind around them both like a serpent. Her brand started to throb. The blood burst off the knife's blade in a cloud of droplets, so fine she hardly felt its spray across her face and arms.

Lorcan drew her against him. She forgot to breathe.

The spell pulled and for the first time, Farideh felt the lines of magic that wrapped around her, as they stretched, tighter, farther, thin and sharp as wires in a net so fine it would have caught sand off a lake bottom.

Her sight shrank down to only Lorcan's black, black eyes. The pulse of the Weave grew stronger, harder to ignore, and it was harder to imagine she hadn't always felt it. Her breath quickened. Her own heart raced. Adrenaline stirred her thoughts into a blur and she was certain the spell would break and she would break under it, pushed over an edge she hadn't known was there.

Then suddenly, all of it vanished, and a great, gasping breath rushed into her. A wicked smile played across Lorcan's mouth. Dahl stood behind her, his sword drawn. Even Mira had broken away from her books.

"It's fine!" Farideh gasped. The sensation of the net faded from her skin. "It's fine." She brushed her shaking arms to be certain. "Did it work?"

Lorcan spread his hands. "No Sairché."

"Good. All right." Farideh swallowed against the knot in her throat. "I need to . . . I'm going to go with Dahl. So promise me you won't do anything while I'm gone."

Lorcan shook his head. "I'm bound to you and you're bound to me. You aren't going anywhere alone."

"We don't have time to argue this," Farideh said, turning to go, needing to be away from him. "Just wait until I get back, and—" She had gone no more than half-a-dozen steps before the sensation of the net cutting into her skin flared again and made her catch her breath. Behind her, Lorcan yelped and hit the floor.

"What was that?" Farideh demanded.

Lorcan scowled up at her. "I told you. You're bound to me and I'm bound to you. We're sharing the protection. If you try to go without me, the spell will pull." He stood, still looking furious. "Though apparently it remains *your* protection. Wherever you're going, I'm coming too." He glared at Dahl. "Like it or not."

# CHAPTER TWENTY

**T**HE SHELF WHERE DAHL HAD FOUND THE STRANGE LIST OF SUCCESSION held book after book after book of things and places and people who lived long after the arcanist had built the library, ending with a collection of bindings that could only have come from the current expedition. More, Farideh thought, than could be accounted for by someone forgetting a book they'd brought in or playing an ill-conceived prank.

Specifics of the Zhentarim cells and leadership along the Sword Coast and beyond. A dictionary of Tymantheran Draconic with notable gaps. A detailed and scattered text of strange secrets and underground knowledge set over the last twenty years that had the cadence of Tam's voice. A red-bound volume, in several hands, describing the current state of the city of Neverwinter lay open on Farideh's lap.

"Lords and gods damn it," Lorcan swore. Fire bloomed in his hands, illuminating the face of the ghost who'd taken on Havilar's form, skulking up the aisle. She bared her teeth and turned insubstantial again. The creatures had tailed them here, taking Brin and Havilar and Farideh's shapes, mocking them and trying to block their path, trying to herd them back to the arcanist. Then Lorcan had casually thrown a ball of fire at the one that had Farideh's shape, setting a rack of scrolls aflame and wounding it badly. The ghosts were more circumspect after that.

Farideh hoped they weren't giving Havi and Brin more trouble.

Dahl set the book back on the shelf and wiped his hands on his breeches. "Shadar-kai's," he said, grimacing.

"It doesn't seem as if it takes every stray thought," Farideh said. "At least there's that." She pulled down a book as thin as her ring finger, bound in deep crimson. *Mechanics of the Infernal Pact.* The frontispiece read, above an illustration that resembled a shirtless cambion reaching for the title. She slammed it shut and shoved it back where she'd found it. She didn't want to know which of her thoughts the magic had deemed important. "But it's enough. We're going to be looking forever at this rate."

"Oh, shit and ashes, kill me now," Lorcan said. Farideh bit her tongue, still furious Lorcan hadn't told her how the spell would end. If Lorcan had to stay six steps from her always, she wasn't sure if she would die first of anger, embarrassment, or want.

He was much easier to deal with, she thought, just as furious with herself, when he was just a rosy memory, wasn't he?

"You could have stayed in the circle," Dahl told the cambion. He took a step back, staring up at the enormous, half-filled shelves. "So the Book and the ghosts are working together to fill the library. And then they kill anyone who finds it." He shook his head. "I wish I knew what that thing was. Like a mummy, but too powerful. Like a lich, but dumb. Like an eidolon, but made of flesh. I don't doubt it was the arcanist, but what did he make himself into?"

"The Book would know," she said. "It would know about the scroll too."

"And then it would know we were making a run for the vents. And then the ghosts would know." He sighed and glared at the spines in front of him. "I should have asked the Book about Emrys from the start. We should have asked about the page."

Farideh turned around. "We didn't have a reason to."

"All the same . . ." Dahl frowned at Lorcan. "What *are* you looking at?"

Not the shelves and not the shadows—Lorcan's eyes focused much nearer. His breath had shifted, and his wings widened. Alarmed, Farideh thought, coming to her feet. Like his worst memories were happening all over again.

"Illusion!" Farideh reached for the rod and cursed as she found it missing. She grabbed hold of the strap that ran across the back of Lorcan's armor and pulled him away from the spot at which he was staring. He lost his footing and stumbled back, throwing both hands up and filling them with angry light.

"It's just an illusion," Farideh said, taking hold of his arm. "It's only—"

Dahl shouted, his eyes focused on something missing four feet in front of him. Farideh cursed and threw a small book at him, clipping his thigh.

"Ow!" Dahl clapped a hand to his leg. "Gods *damn* it."

Farideh started to warn him, but he was suddenly gone. The books, the library, the menacing ghosts, the cambion, and the paladin—all of it was gone. She stood on an icy mountainside, sword in hand, while Clanless Mehen ran her through another set of exercises at which she couldn't match his standards.

"Listen!" Mehen shouted. "Listen, please. You haven't got time. You need the words. The parchment." Something stung Farideh's arm. The image shivered and skipped across Farideh's vision. Vanished.

The library was back. Dahl was pinching her arm.

"What the shitting Hells is this?" Lorcan demanded.

"Stop it!" Farideh said, swatting at Dahl. "I think it knows what we're looking for."

"About the scroll?" Dahl said. "How can a trap know about anything?"

Farideh started to answer, but again the library vanished and she was standing in the middle of Adolican Rhand's ballroom, behind the settee where she'd been sick and where the page had fallen from the wizard's grasp. Dahl was still there, his arm splattered with vomit.

"Oh gods," she said, pulled into the illusion. "I'm sorry about that."

"The scroll," he said. "I know where the scroll is. I'm Emrys. You have to listen."

Farideh blinked. "Who's Emrys?"

Dahl's face shifted, fiercely annoyed at her. "The arcanist. The library. You know this. You don't have the words. I can't . . . I can't . . ."

The library. The arcanist. The diary Dahl had found. His gray eyes were boring into her, as if imploring her to hear the things he wasn't saying, the way Lorcan's had . . . when? Never. That had been an illusion . . . Like this was.

"You're the ghost of the other arcanist," she said.

"I have to *show* you," Dahl said. "This works poorly. You don't have the words. What *possessed* you? What *possessed* you to . . . ?"

The world upended and she was lying on the floor of the library, looking up at Dahl and Lorcan crouched over her, their swords and spells ready.

"Emrys," she said. "Let me up. Let me up!" She struggled past them. "The illusions aren't a trap, they're another ghost. The diarist. The arcanist who knew Tarchamus." She dropped her voice, in case the apprentices could hear her. "He knows where the scroll is. He wants to show us. But he can't build an illusion for it, not out of our memories."

Dahl shook his head. "What's he going to do?"

"I think he has to possess one of us."

"No," Lorcan said, still searching for signs of this new threat. "Darling, you know how that ends. This is a very bad idea."

I know how *this* ends too, she thought. With all of us dead under a mountain and Mehen always wondering what became of us. She pushed past them both to stand in the open space of the wider aisle. "Show me," she said. "Show me where it is."

The face of a sad-eyed, bearded man flashed before her eyes. Then the rush and roar of the ghost's magic drowned out the shouted protests of Dahl and Lorcan and her vision went dark, her senses overtaken by the burnt tallow and spilled ink scents of another library, another wizard, another time.

⁙⌒⁙

Brin considered the sealed doors at the end of the tunnel. Was it his imagination, or had the light filling the doors' seams grown paler? Dimmer? He couldn't recall.

Havilar twisted her neck, trying to find an angle around her horn that would let her lay her ear flat against the wall. "It sounds like wizards," she whispered. Maspero gave Brin a quizzical look.

"What do you mean?" Brin asked.

She straightened and blinked at him. "Dunno. There's maybe four of them all chatting and disagreeing about things. And someone chanting something. That seems like wizards."

Casters anyway. They'd given up on bashing down the doors.

"At least it's holding," he said.

"The light looks different," Maspero noted. "Bunch of fallen bookshelves won't stop Netherese wizards."

"It will give them something to use up their spells on, though."

"There are some traps I didn't undo," Havilar added. "We could funnel them toward the nearer ones." She thought a moment. "There's a sticky one and a pit trap near here. I put books around them to keep people off. If we have time to make them wind around a bit, there's a panel that shoots arrows. I couldn't figure out where it was reloading them from," she added apologetically. "I left a note in chalk on the floor. 'Don't walk here.'"

Brin shook his head. "It can't hurt, I suppose. It seems like they'll have someone skilled at spotting traps though."

Maspero considered the doors, his dark brows furrowed. "Not," he said, "if they're too busy destroying barricades of fallen books. Come on."

Havilar fell into step beside Brin. "It's lucky he's so devious," she said, pointing her chin at Maspero. "This will be interesting."

"Are you even a little afraid?" he asked. "I mean, we still might die down here."

"Terrified," she admitted, and she slipped an arm through his. "But we're not dead yet. And it's Farideh and you and Tam and devious Maspero, and maybe Mira and Dahl will be useful too. And Lorcan. I guess he made some difference in Neverwinter."

"I suppose," he said, glad she thought he was useful. He felt as if all he'd been doing since he got down into the caverns was getting in the way and being a prize for Zhents to fight over. "If you're going to be trapped between Shade and a monster and a mile of stone, it's not a bad roster."

She sighed. "But I do wish Mehen were here. Just in case."

Brin pulled her in a little nearer. "I know. Me too."

"*That* is how I *know* you're brave," she said with a little smile. "Even I'm not looking forward to Mehen finding out we kissed."

Farideh opened her eyes and found herself standing outside the doors of the library, looking up at the silver-edged depiction of Tarchamus. The rest of the entry cave was empty—no Shadovar and no flood of water.

She turned back to the doors and suddenly there was a man standing there beside her—the same bearded man she'd glimpsed in the illusion before. He looked younger than Tam, but the same grit and shrewdness showed in his face and in the stiff lines of his shoulders. "Are you Emrys?" she tried to say. But there was no sound. It was as if she weren't even there.

Emrys held a wand in one hand, a sword in the other, and stood as if steeling himself to do battle against the jeweled arcanist. He'd counted Tarchamus among his friends, she realized, the dead arcanist's memories filtering into her own. He'd known Tarchamus wouldn't be pleased by the intercession, the reminder that none of them are truly all powerful. But Emrys hadn't realized the chain of events it would set off.

He pushed through the doors, and Farideh followed him, down through the tunnel and across the much sparser library. The number of dead arcanists, both masters and apprentices, approached hundreds—talented wizards fooled by the promise of Tarchamus's eruption scroll and the lure of strange and wonderful magic.

The ghosts paced him, slipping through the spaces in the shelves. They took the forms of fallen colleagues and called out to him, to stay, to talk, to tarry. He pressed on. They took the shape of living rivals and taunted his efforts. He wouldn't leave here alive.

Emrys knew that was a possibility—and the memory, tainted by the ghost's long years, echoed with the sad knowledge that it was inevitable, that it had always been inevitable. Farideh hurried along beside the arcanist, watching as he crafted the six runes around the edge of the library, the warding structure that made a net over the hidden tomb. With each one she felt the magic take hold, sealing off the space from the world beyond. Keeping outsiders from scrying it. Hopefully blocking any other explorers until he could rescue the books and stop Tarchamus.

Or what remained of him. Emrys had seen the schemas, the remains of his friend's notes and spells. He knew what he'd been too late to stop: the four apprentices arrayed around Tarchamus's tomb, the Fugue Plane brushing near enough to steal some of its power. The flood of magic that would have overtaken the corpse of his former friend.

And the corpse . . . That was the part Emrys was most afraid to face. The scroll, he knew, would be down in the crypt, where those foolhardy enough to fall into Tarchamus's trap met their ends. The notes spoke of a ritual three years in the making—long and grisly and intricate. Changing the body as it slowly died. Emrys imagined, not for the first time, Tarchamus's last days, sealed in the stone box and channeling the scraps and spurts of wild magic that slowly overtook his body, saturated by his rage. The day he did not wake enough to respond to Lorull's knocking. The day his most trusted apprentices opened the case, and the body—no longer alive, but not quite dead—was buried for another year in sand and the torn pages of powerful spellbooks. Biding its time. Changing slowly. Changing without the magic they had barred him from.

The day the four apprentices performed the ritual around the mummified creature, waking it to life and becoming its undead guardians. Emrys had not been there to see it, but his memories of the apprentices—lovely, quiet Nyvasha; gaunt Bois; clever Kelid with her long fingers; Lorull, who was old enough to be an arcanist in his own right, old enough to have gray at his temples—and his memories of the notes were powerful. As the arcanist strode back through the library, toward the Book's alcove, the ghosts' taunts whipped the imagined scenes to the forefront of his thoughts.

As one, the apprentices would have spoken the words of the spell. The runes around their feet would have lit with an otherworldly glow and thickening illusions would have surged up out of the stone to encircle them. When the last grains of the hourglass fell and the planes drew near, as one, the apprentices would have finished—as one, plunging the knives to the hilt, up under the ribs to nick the heart, just as Tarchamus would have taught them three years earlier.

Fountains of blood would have sprayed out, drenching the mummified corpse of Tarchamus, the scroll, and the pages of the open Book.

Farideh may have been no more than a ghost in this illusion, but her stomach twisted all the same. The apprentices would have fallen to their knees, the illusions leaping over and into their bodies like waves over a rock. They would have screamed, even though they weren't supposed to, even though the sacrifice was necessary, even though the process was a trifle—Emrys knew Tarchamus well enough to be sure of his blind assurances. They would have thrashed against the magic that clutched at them, and the geysers of blood would have wet everything. Four lives ended so that they in turn could claim countless others. He knew this now—the ghosts still remembered.

And all because, Emrys thought, approaching the Book on its pedestal, of Tarchamus the Unyielding.

"What have you done?" Emrys asked the empty air. The ghosts all settled in the corners, making the air hum with a noise that was no noise. For long moments there was no answer to his sad question.

Then the Book spoke. *You blame me? I am as much a victim in this as Arion and his tragic vassals. It's him you want. Downstairs.*

The corpse—and Emrys's memories shivered with the simultaneous fear of what he might find, and knowledge of what he had found. "You were the architect more than that creature. I'm not the same sort of fool."

*That man is gone,* the Book said. *And I am left with memories and the knowledge of a wide world he never dreamed might hold value or the slightest interest. So which of us is the victim? Which of us suffers?*

"You will suffer more," Emrys said. "You'll trap no one else here. You'll take no one else's knowledge."

*My but you've grown honorable all of the sudden,* the Book said. *What happened to "the might of those willing to seize the power"? What happened to "the heirs of the gods"?*

"Your words," Emrys said.

*You agreed at the time. Perhaps you grow envious.*

"I do not envy a dead man. Nor the echoes of him." He wanted the Book to tell him—what? That it hadn't been because of the censure or the intercession? That it hadn't been because Emrys betrayed him? That, perhaps, this evil had always been lurking in Tarchamus, under that clever and biting façade? But even if any of those had been true, it would still mean Emrys had failed—he knew that now. He had caused it or hadn't seen it, and his fellows had died in scores.

And Farideh found herself thinking of Lorcan, of all the times he'd been wicked and dangerous, and all the times he'd been sweet. Where was the line, the point he couldn't come back from, and would she see it before something as horrid as Tarchamus's lost library came to pass? Would they ever come near such a point?

She found herself thinking of Bryseis Kakistos, and the laughing witch in her dreams who looked like Havilar.

*I suspect*, the Book said, sounding bitter, *you soon will. You can't imagine you will stand against him.*

"You can't imagine I won't try," Emrys said.

*You could take me. We could flee this place and its magic. There's such a lot of world I never saw.*

Emrys shook his head. "Farewell, my friend."

Down, down into the floor with the spellbooks—the shelves all still in place, the books fewer and more neatly stacked. The arcanist cast a spell and he floated down the sheer drop as gently as a falling leaf. The ghosts streaked past, all light and fury. The bones on the floor were fewer, scattered and largely whole.

The mummy was worse than he'd imagined—no part of the mummy resembled Tarchamus, and when he raised his head from his position of repose, if he recognized Emrys as anything more than a walking meal, there was no sign.

The scroll sat on a pedestal between the pit and the mummy, bait for the trap. The mummy unfolded himself, ponderously slow—slow enough to miscalculate, but Emrys was ready. Farideh had no names for the spells he cast, no understanding of the magic he wielded, but one thing was absolutely clear: he meant to destroy Tarchamus.

The mummy screamed the same beams of green magic and hurled balls of lightning. The ghosts swooped and dived, landing long enough to take solid form and hurtle around the battling arcanists, aiming to knock Emrys from his feet. The air sizzled and popped with magic as Emrys's spells shaped walls of flames, brought angels to earth, and made the bones rise from the ground and fight for him. Farideh found herself flinching at each remembered missle, each phantom blast that came near. Especially those which struck her guide.

Now bleeding, dizzy, and favoring a burnt and broken hand, Emrys might have meant to kill what was left of his friend, but it was quickly apparent that he could do no such thing. Tarchamus had been powerful when he died, and what he made of himself was meant for nothing so much as permanence. There was no spell in Emrys's book that could destroy the strange mummy. There might be no spell on the plane that could.

And so he cast a spell that split his form into three, and three again, and three again, overwhelming the space with Emryses and weaving between them as Tarchamus's horrible beams of green light vaporized the doubles in great swaths. It was enough to get the scroll in hand—the spell that had begun all of this. Emrys took it and ran for the exit.

Another spell lifted him up the shaft, chased by the howls of Tarchamus and the fearsome threat of his apprentices. They streaked ahead, took shape, and lunged at Emrys, digging great gouges into his flesh, and knocking him off his feet and into traps. Arrows pierced him. Flames leaped after him. Still Emrys ran.

The door was locked, much as it had been for them, and Emrys was failing fast. He tore down the aisles, the scroll clutched to his chest. The screams of the arcanist rattled through the library.

Farideh's blood ran cold—Tarchamus was no longer in the pit.

Emrys came to the little clearing with the wizard's statue. He needed time, he thought, he needed to rest. There was one spell left, one desperate spell. He wove the words and gestures and strands of the Weave together and the stone of the wall grew pliable and peeled back, making a little pocket the size of a man.

The ghosts were coming, and quickly. The screams of the mummy grew nearer and nearer. But Emrys kept his focus as the secret room widened to admit him—and the traces of Farideh that rode with him—and sealed the wall where he passed. He traced the rune—the one Havilar had found—and the wall lit with its power.

He'd meant to rest, to regain his strength and study his spells again. To be ready to find his way free of the library. To stop the ghosts and the mummy and somehow free the knowledge Tarchamus had stolen and hidden away. But the arrows were poisoned, and Emrys was already wounded and weak. As Farideh watched, the arcanist died, shivering and fevered and clutching the scroll tight in the failing light of a conjured orb.

*This is the legacy of Fallen Netheril*, the voice whispered in her thoughts. *The privilege of power, the claim to all knowledge, the right to the Empire. If they can set hands on it, then it is theirs. Tarchamus was not the rarity I thought. I did not see it in time . . .*

There was no saving the library, Farideh realized. She reached out to close the dead man's eyes, but her hand only passed through the memory his face and the darkness swallowed them both.

.:⌒:.

Farideh's eyes were a sliver of silver and a sliver of gold beneath heavy lids. She was there and she was not, her body limp on its feet. Lorcan did not watch for ghosts the way Dahl did. He watched for the ghost in Farideh. He wondered what would happen to the protection if the ghost didn't let her go.

Buried under a mountain, he thought, watching the unchanging curve of her eyes, menaced by an undead monstrosity capable of slaughtering Bibracte and both her underlings. And some godsbedamned Book putting ideas in her head—and pulling others out.

"This is a very bad idea," he said again.

"It's already done," Dahl snapped. "You should have talked her out of it."

As if it would have made a difference, Lorcan thought. Clearly the paladin didn't know Farideh as well as he thought he did. She'd made Lorcan keep his distance from the books they were searching, claiming the need for a sentry, but she was a terrible liar. He wondered if the paladin had managed to see any of the texts that blasted Book had made out of Farideh's thoughts.

Then her lashes fluttered. Her mouth twitched, as if she were struggling to speak.

"Darling?" Lorcan said. "Are you in there?"

Her breath hitched. She swayed on her feet, mumbling. Arguing with someone.

"Farideh?" he tried again.

With a great gasp, her eyes shot open, unseeing, and she lurched forward. Lorcan caught her as she stumbled, as if she were learning to walk all over again. Slumped in his arms, she looked up at him, wide-eyed and horrified for a moment, as if she did not know him, as if she'd never known anything like him. Then she seemed to focus and her eyes narrowed. A smile eased itself across her mouth. Lorcan tensed.

A smile that was not Farideh's.

She blinked at him languorously. "Caisys?" she said and chuckled.

Lorcan's blood froze. Not the ghost you were expecting, he thought. Oh Lords of the Nine—

"Farideh!" he shouted.

A jolt went through her, her lax muscles all tensing together, taking the weight of her body off his arms. She blinked, then blushed and scowled in equal measure. "What are you doing?"

Let her go, Lorcan told himself. You're imagining things, anyway. You have to be. "Would you rather I let you fall over?"

"Did it work?" Dahl asked, coming nearer.

"I saw the scroll." Farideh rubbed her head, pulling out of Lorcan's embrace. "I saw him fighting the arcanist's mummy—we're not going to beat it. But worse, it's not trapped down there. It can get out."

"Son of a barghest," Dahl cursed. "How?"

"I couldn't see." She pursed her mouth. "But if we're going to get past, I think we need to find out. Dahl, truly—it wasn't even trying before. What it did before was *nothing*. We won't be able to kill it. We need to get around it. We need to find the trapdoor."

"What in the Hells do you think you're going to do?" he said. "Ask it to come out?"

"No," Lorcan said, because he did know Farideh entirely too well. "She wants to try and trick that Book."

# CHAPTER TWENTY-ONE

When Tam woke again, Mira was sitting amid the piles of books and scrolls she'd gathered, sorting through them as somberly as if she were deciding which wounded could be saved and which would have to be left to die. The other five were all elsewhere. The devil was missing from his circle.

"Ah stlarning gods," Tam said.

"I wouldn't worry," Mira said, looking down at him. "She has him well in hand."

Tam started to protest that there was no such thing with regards to a devil—but Mira wasn't the one who needed to hear that. Farideh's admonishments still hung over his thoughts. "Your maps are finished, I gather?"

"Ages ago. Are you feeling better?"

"Much," he said. "You ought to lie down for a bit as well."

"I'm fine." She smiled to herself. "Not the life you wanted for me, is it?" she said, closing the tome on her lap and adding it to one of the stacks. "Better to be married to a farmer somewhere quiet, somewhere close to Mother. Keeping cattle, raising children."

"No," Tam sighed. "I could wish it a hundred times for you, but it would never make you happy." He sat up. "I just don't see how this makes you happy."

"You mean the Zhentarim," she said. "Just say it."

Tam ran a hand over his beard and tried his hardest to stop thinking of her as being eight and small. "I can't help but think," he said, knowing even as he did that it was the wrong thing to say, "that if I'd just done something differently things would have turned out better."

"It's possible," Mira said, still focused on her scrolls. "If you could go back, though, what would you change? Would you have stopped? Would you have stayed there, in that little house in Baldur's Gate? Would you have stayed away?" The tide of anger in her voice rose. "Never come around? Or would you go back, and never have noticed Mother—"

"Don't," he said. He sighed again. "Let's be honest, I wouldn't have done any of those things. And they probably wouldn't have made a difference. You make your own decisions." She looked up from her books, as if daring him to press her. It wouldn't get him any closer to understanding. "Silver Lady, Mira, *why* the Zhentarim?"

"They sought me out. They offered me a job." She smiled fondly. "You wouldn't believe the things I've seen. The ruins of the Serpent Kings. The traces of Athalantar. The stories of the Crown Wars, writ to the tiniest detail in the remains of an elven stronghold."

"The deaths of the Zhentarim's enemies?"

"Because the Harpers *never* kill anyone," she said acidly.

"Don't pretend they're the same," he said, sharper than he meant to. "You could see those things without the Black Network."

"Then maybe you should have offered me a pin."

That surprised him. "If I offered it now?" he managed.

Mira unrolled another scroll, her eyes flicking over the text so quickly, he was sure she wasn't really reading it. "If you offered it to me now, it would just be to keep me under your wing. Don't pretend it wouldn't be. I won't be kept—not by my father and not by some farmer."

"Mira, I could be hanged for letting you go. Do you understand that?"

"And for letting Harpers live with Zhentarim secrets, I could take a dagger in the back." And she chuckled to herself. "We do like to live dangerously, don't we?"

And despite himself, Tam smiled too. It should have broken his heart, he thought, that the fact that she trusted he wouldn't turn on her made him so glad. "Much as I suspect we both wish the other didn't."

"Yes," Mira said. Then, "Do you really think they'll hang you?"

"They can't spare an old warhorse like me," he added lightly. "They wouldn't hang me for anything short of pure treachery. And accidentally allying with an old enemy—and not the worst of our enemies—I'll make them see reason. I hope."

"If they try it . . ." Mira grew quiet. "There are rats in the Harpers' house," she said after a moment. "This isn't the only time the Zhentarim has gotten their hands into one of your missions."

"There's a traitor?"

"There are many," she said. "The Fisher, to begin with, is not to be trusted."

For all Tam wished, that surprised him; it fit more neatly than any other bit of knowledge he'd gained in the last few tendays. A Harper spymaster, traitor to his oath—gods. He didn't like to think how far and wide such a betrayal would reach. "How long?"

She shook her head. "You'll have to ask him."

Oh, and he would. He might not be a proper Harper by the Fisher's measure, but he knew the Code and moreover he knew what a spymaster owed his spies. Putting them into danger was part of the job. Putting them into enemy hands was not.

The thought of Mira in those same enemy hands didn't sit any better. Tam pulled his pack nearer and withdrew from the small pocket sewn into the bottom a medallion the size of a gold coin. Embossed with a harp and stars and shivering with enchantment. He held it out to Mira. "Take it."

Her brows raised. "A Harper token?"

"Just in case," he said. In case she changed her mind, in case she ran afoul of other agents, in case the Zhentarim turned on her and she needed to run. A Harper would know the signal. A Harper would keep her safe.

She looked at it, flat in the palm of her hand. "You aren't afraid I'll take advantage of it? Sully your good name?"

"It didn't even cross my mind," he said. "If you use it, I'm sure it will be because you need it." He reached out and squeezed her shoulder. "You *would* make a good Harper, you know."

"That isn't where the dice fell this time," she said firmly. But she tucked the token into a pocket all the same, and Tam took it for what it was: a start.

The rune still glowed where Farideh had left it. What would have happened if she'd shattered it, expecting the doors to the library to swing wide? Would the space have opened, revealing the remains of Emrys and the last scroll of Tarchamus? Would she have thought to take the scroll or left it there for the ghosts to reclaim, seeing the corpse as a warning?

"Why do you think the ghosts haven't smashed it?" she asked.

"They're afraid of magic," Dahl answered. "They know it hurts them." He considered the rune. "Which means it might discharge when it's triggered. We should keep back."

"He would have warned us."

Dahl shook his head. "He knows there's more than one of us. And he was Netherese. He probably wouldn't think to care if his spell killed someone not human." Farideh started to argue, but he cut her off, "Look, just move back and when you don't die, *both* of us can be happy."

From off in the distance came the din of the others pulling down shelves and books. Every crash made Farideh want to jump, to cast after the Netherese who might any moment break through the door. She imagined Adolican Rhand striding down the aisle toward her, and wished she hadn't. Farideh repositioned herself, and Lorcan with her—off to the left and as far back as she could go and still have her spells reach the wall. The cambion came up behind her.

"Here," he said, putting his hands over hers.

"I can handle it."

"It's not a lump of firewood. Plus your rod is in splinters. Take the assistance, darling. Stop being difficult."

She glowered at him over one shoulder. "Which of us is being difficult?" She positioned her hands again. "You don't have to like him, but stop trying to prod him into a fight. You're acting like an owlbear marking territory nobody wants."

"Oh, don't sell yourself short, darling," he said low and in her ear, and she shivered. She was almost positive he was looking at Dahl when he said it, too. Gods.

She cast the spell and left Lorcan where he was, channeling an extra burst of power through her, like a sudden flood of water forced through a narrow stream. The rune shattered with a sound like thunder and a burst of blazing light. The air smelled of sulfur and burnt cedar and stone dust, and there was no doubt if she'd been standing in front of the sigil she would have been obliterated by the blast. She stepped out of Lorcan's arms, toward the revealed room.

"See?" Dahl said smugly. "Now we're both glad."

Beyond the wall lay the scroll, untouched and shining pale as the day it was made, along the crumbling hand bones of Emrys's sad remains. The empty skull seemed to look up at her, its jaw hanging askew, with an expression of disbelief. "Poor fellow," she said.

Dahl crouched down, picked up the scroll, and carefully unrolled it. "I wasn't making it up before. The Netherese were terrible bigots. No one's worth as much as a human in their eyes. He really wouldn't have thought well of you."

"Well, he wouldn't be alone, would he?" *If they can set hands on it, then it is theirs. Tarchamus was not the rarity I thought. I did not see it in time . . .* Whatever Emrys had thought in life, she suspected the ghost had changed its mind, at least a little.

"Is it the right scroll?" she asked.

Dahl nodded, rolling the parchment back up. "It looks like the sketches." He considered the skeleton. "Maybe we could just destroy the scroll. Maybe we don't need to destroy the entire library."

"There are all the spellbooks," she said. "And the notes about breaching the planes. And the Book." She looked at him solemnly. "And the arcanist."

Dahl considered Emrys a moment longer. "You're right," he said. "It's such a shame. But you're right." He sighed. "At least I don't have to worry about what Oghma will do if I blow up a library." He frowned and looked up at her. "What did you mean, 'he wouldn't be alone'?"

She sighed and rolled her eyes, knowing he wouldn't be able to tell, and left the little hidden room. "If Mira's finished the maps, we should be able to find the best point to cast from. Maybe where the arcanist escapes." She was still turning that over in her memories—where had the roar come from? Where might the hidden door be?

"Do you actually think I would have let that explosion kill you?" Dahl demanded, following after her.

"No," she said tartly. "And I will be forever grateful you don't hate me as much as the wicked Netherese. Good work." She collected Lorcan. "We need to hurry. Before that alarm goes off and we don't have the time to plan."

"We may have a problem," Dahl said after they'd walked a ways. "If I'm reading this right, the caster ends up at the center of the eruption. With as much fire as this makes . . . it could kill a body. Quickly."

"How did Tarchamus manage it?"

He shook his head. "The diary didn't say. It could be he had a complementary spell. It could be he made one of his more dispensable apprentices cast it. It looks like there's a little delay—there's a plume of flames and then the ground opens. That should give everyone else enough time to get away."

Farideh pursed her lips. "I won't burn as easily," she said. "Give it to me."

"You *will* burn up if a volcano opens under your feet," Dahl said, as they came to the alcove. "We need another solution."

The Book sat open on its pedestal, the shift of its inks a frenetic swirl of runes. The air as they crossed into the alcove buzzed as if a swarm of bees were hidden in the shelves around it. As peaceful as the scene seemed to the eye, there was no pretending that they weren't walking into a special kind of danger. Dahl drew his sword.

"Do you have a plan here?"

"Well, *you're* the Harper," she whispered. "And he's a devil. I would think between the two of you I wouldn't need to tell you how to trick information out of someone." She considered the Book, and the conversations she'd had with it. "It's proud. It doesn't like getting caught in mistakes." She thought of the vision, of the Book's claim to be a victim of Tarchamus, same as the dead wizards. "It doesn't want to be here—or it didn't a few millennia ago. I think it hates Tarchamus." More than just hates him, she thought. And more than hated Emrys.

"It's never seen the Hells," Dahl said. "Maybe your devil's thoughts are prize enough."

"It's not going to make a trade," she said, cutting Lorcan's protests off. "I'm pretty sure it thinks it's smarter than you by a lot."

"Oh," Dahl said, surprised. "All right. I might know how to do this. Follow my lead." He strode toward the Book.

"This is the Book that told you tales of the Brimstone Angel?" Lorcan murmured to her as they followed. She nodded. "Perhaps if your paladin's plans fall apart, we can see how well tearing out the pages one by one works."

"Stop calling him that," Farideh said.

"You missed something," Dahl was saying to the Book.

*Did I?* The inks traced line after line after line of tiny runes. *I doubt that very much.*

"You sent me after the diary," Dahl said, all smugness. "You thought I'd side with Tarchamus. You thought I'd come back to you after finding out about the interession? But there was more there. Emrys mentions the scroll. The one you claimed didn't exist."

*Do you think I didn't know that?* the Book sneered. *I wanted you to find the scroll, wherever Emrys had it hidden. The promise of solving your puzzle was bait so obvious I worried you'd see through it.*

Dahl cast his eyes at Farideh. "Liar," he said, sounding petulant. "What good is the scroll to you?"

*Oh, I'm far past needing scrolls. But let's see what good it does you.*

Farideh frowned at the swirling text. Such an odd thing to say. When would a Book have needed scrolls?

Dahl hesitated. *Be nice,* he mouthed to Farideh. He jerked his head toward the Book.

"To . . . to be honest," she said, "it's Mira who wants the scroll, the woman who led us here. I can hardly see why. You seem more valuable."

*Leagues more valuable. Not that most people know it.*

Dahl mouthed more instructions. *Why not you?*

"Why is it no one's taken you from this place?" Farideh asked. "I mean, the scroll was hidden. But I would think they'd find you first, and then . . . well why bother looking further?"

*You aren't the first ones to be trapped in this place,* it said bitterly. *If anyone meant to rescue me, they'd soon need rescuing of their own.*

"Tarchamus controls the doors?" Dahl asked, genuinely surprised. "Not you?"

*Those brats of apprentices control the doors. And they answer to that rotting husk, not to me.*

"It sounds an awful lot like you hate Tarchamus," Dahl said.

*Our relationship is complicated*, the Book said. *All his relationships are complicated.*

The vision of the ritual, the mummy, and poor Emrys—*You could take me*, the Book had said. *We could flee this place and its magic. There's such a lot of world I never saw.*

*Farewell, my friend*, Emrys had said.

"Oh gods—you *are* him," Farideh said. "You're Tarchamus."

Dahl looked at her as if she had lost her mind entirely.

The Book paused. *Clever girl.*

"But the arcanist is in the crypt," Dahl said.

*I'm more him than what he made of himself*, the Book sneered. *Tarchamus duplicated his mind—his knowledge, his wisdom, his consciousness—and placed it in these pages. Quite a feat*, it said cynically. *One he never bothered sharing. The apprentices never acknowledged me—just hauled me around Netheril like a dumb object, taunting me with everything Tarchamus had kept from himself.*

Dahl shook his head in disbelief. "We mean to leave," he said finally. "We could take you with us. Destroy the creature Tarchamus became."

*You think to bargain with me, little boy? I have much better rescuers at hand. I have seen Risen Netheril—in your thoughts and in those of the ones who came before you. They will appreciate me. Once you lot feed that thing, he'll be sated enough for the army at the gates to swoop in.* It chuckled. *It's been two thousand years since I had a chance like this. I won't miss it. I'll tell them where to get the scroll and they'll take me out of this wretched hole in the ground.*

"Tarchamus won't open the doors until we're dead," Dahl pointed out. "And we're well-fortified and ready for a siege. We know to avoid the pit and we know the ghosts' tricks. If you wait too long, your rescuers are bound to give up. If you convince him to open the doors, they'll make much simpler prey."

*For one, I'm well aware that you are low on water in particular. My apprentices make careful note of such things. For another, Netheril is nearly through the doors on their own. My rescue is at hand.*

"So that your ghosts can chase them into the arcanist's pit," Farideh said.

*He'll be far too busy devouring you*, the Book said sweetly. *Your camp's not even far enough to make a decent chase.*

Farideh nearly sighed in relief. The trapdoor must be near the camp—with Mira's maps that might be enough to find it. Dahl pursed his lips, considering the Book for a long moment. He looked up at Farideh.

They couldn't take the chance that the Book might fall into Netheril's hands. If the doors opened and they didn't have time to do anything but flee, the Book was at least as important as the scroll. But both of them knew too much about their plans to escape, and had very little new knowledge with which to distract the Book.

"Lorcan," she said, "would you take it?"

The cambion picked up the tome in both hands, flinching as if about to sneeze as the Book's magic scoured his thoughts. *Well, well*, it said, sounding slightly rattled. *When did you come in?*

"Heavens to Hells," she heard Lorcan say, as they walked back to the camp. "What did you think you were helping my warlock to do? Those runes you had them destroy made space for a portal, and the spell you assisted her in creating pulled me through."

*I* assisted *nothing*, the Book said. *That girl was but my hands and eyes.*

"Of course," Lorcan said. "The heir of Bryseis Kakistos needed a Book to do her spellwork." He held the book close. "Did you enjoy spinning that tale for her?" he said, low and deadly. "Trying to undermine me? They say you can read people's thoughts—are you enjoying mine right now?"

The Book did not answer.

.:⌒:.

By the time the others finally returned, Tam was back on his feet and pacing a hole in the floor. He'd thought through a dozen potential plans—but every one of them needed more information, more hands, more magic. A riot of questions jangled his nerves.

"There you are," he said, as Dahl and Farideh returned, trailing the freed devil. "Where's my plan?"

"We're working on it," Dahl answered. He nodded to the cambion who was carrying the Book. He and Farideh wrapped the Book in cloaks and stuffed it into a haversack, then Dahl told Tam about Emrys and the scroll, about Farideh's vision and the escape of the arcanist. "That's the largest piece remaining," he said quietly. "If we can get the mummy out of that crypt and trap him up here, we're free to escape."

"Indeed," Tam said. "I don't suppose you took out any more of the ghosts."

Farideh shook her head. "Lorcan burned one fairly bad. They kept back after that."

Tam made a little *hmph* and she stiffened, as if braced for his reprimand, but Tam held his tongue. Not worth it. Not when the devil had been a help. Brin and Havilar came back then with Maspero.

"How are the doors?" Dahl asked.

"Solid for the moment," Brin said. "But they've gotten through fooling around with battering rams and such. There are wizards working on it."

"They'll have a time if they get through," Maspero said.

"Oh we made a *fantastic* mess," Havilar said. "Maspero, Brin, and me together are *excellent* at figuring out how to trick shady Netherese armies." She grinned at Farideh. "They might not even know they're being tricked."

"Should you get your arcanist free," Lorcan said, "I'll wager he'll make an excellent distraction for the Shadovar as well."

Tam ignored him. "Mira, you've got the maps?"

She spread out a pair of scrolls, neat lines and notes etched over what looked like a ballad and a hymn to the goddess of the sea. "They're not exact," she said. "I didn't dare go measure. But I think I can pinpoint the trapdoor." She laid a finger on the corner of the arcanist's crypt. "The floors actually rotate around a central point as they go down. This is the spot that overlaps with the floor we're on. If there's a trapdoor near to here, that is where it comes out."

"Where do you think the weak point of this place is?" Dahl asked quietly. "Structurally."

Mira frowned. "What do you mean?"

"If we were going to set off the eruption scroll," he said, "where would we need to do it to bring down the roof?"

Mira blinked at him, appalled. "You *can't*."

"I don't want to," Dahl said. He looked to Tam. "There's no getting around it though—this place is a trap, a tomb for people who were only seeking knowledge. We can't disarm the trap without destroying it. And destroying it is . . ." He sighed. "Compared to leaving Tarchamus's trap wide open, it's a minor sin."

"You can't ask me to do that," Mira said.

"Then we are leaving it all for Netheril," he said. "All the spellbooks. All the scrolls. All the information that a maniac wizard deemed precious. We are condemning whole nations to death."

"Mira," Tam said sadly. "Do what you will. But you know he's right."

Mira pursed her lips, as if willing herself calm. "The column at the centerline of the dome. The one to the left of the entrance, when you face the rear wall. It's not decorative. If you catch that in the blast, the ceiling will be damaged. It will bury the place." She tapped the door they'd found to the second level. "And if you keep it close to here, the lava should flow down and block the lower levels, if not destroying them. So about here." She drew a tight circle around the area beyond the Book's alcove.

"So you'd have to run for the trapdoor?" Tam said.

Dahl hesitated. "The scroll doesn't bode well for the caster. We need to find a way to protect them from the flames before worrying about how fast they can run."

"What do you mean?"

"The spell might consume the caster," Dahl said to Tam. "We can't be sure how likely it is without casting it, but by that point, they'll be dead or they won't be."

Is this your destiny then? Tam thought, staring at the scroll. If these were his people, as Viridi's memory had put it, then he couldn't ask any one of them to take the chance. He met Dahl's worried gaze—at least Tam felt sure the younger Harper would lead them out all right. He reached for the scroll.

But Lorcan's bright-red hand reached over him. "Give it to me."

Dahl pulled the scroll closer. "I don't think so."

"Unless you haven't mentioned the fact that you are the burning Chosen of Kossuth, *both* of you would certainly die if you were there when that thing goes off," Lorcan said. "Whereas I would find it unpleasantly similar to home." He made a face at the scroll. "Probably. And anything you were planning to do to assist would go a lot further."

"The ritual against the elements," Farideh said. "Could that do?"

Tam shook his head. "Even if it helped, it wouldn't be enough. That spell is meant for bad weather, not fire."

"But it's based off the object," Dahl said, staring at the devil with new eyes. "It couldn't boost a human's tolerance, but . . . the ritual I used on the alarm. It would make it stronger." He considered Lorcan. "Depending on how much heat you can take and how much the scroll creates, it could make the difference. If Farideh casts the ritual to fortify the both of you against the heat, Tam and I can . . ." He shook his head. "It needs silver—gobs of silver—and I'm down to a few grains. Without it, we won't—"

A haversack hit the ground between Dahl and Tam. Pernika's. "Search it," Mira said. "She chipped half the inlay out of most of these portraits. See if it's enough."

The twisted pieces of the edging made a tidy pile, and Farideh's destructive spells made short work of it. Dahl scraped the very last tracings of dust into vials. "Not enough," he said.

"Here." Tam took the holy symbol from his chest and the Harper pin from the inside of his shirt. They would be little use if he was dead, though he'd miss the mark of Selûne. He couldn't recall how long he'd had that one.

Longer than you've had Mira, he thought.

Maspero removed his silver rings. Brin and the twins turned all the silver coins from their pockets. Farideh pulled the amulet Tam had given her out from under her shirt. He was surprised she still had it.

"Hold on," he said. "See if we've got enough as is."

She pointed a finger at the pile. *"Assulam."*

The burst of silver dust glittered briefly on the air, before settling like an early snow across the field of limestone slate. Dahl scraped and swept it together, measuring the results.

"Close," he said. "But it should do."

"Good," Tam said. "Then, about the arcanist—"

Out of the library's silence, the sound they were all waiting for exploded as the Shadovar breached the doors and Dahl's alarm triggered, its wail bouncing off the walls of the cavern.

# CHAPTER TWENTY-TWO

As much as they'd all been waiting for each heartbeat to be interrupted by the alarm, Brin wasn't the only one who leaped at the sound. Even Lorcan's wings suddenly swung up and over them, as if he meant to fly out of the Shadovar's reach. Farideh grabbed him by the arm.

"Shar and hrast," Tam spat. He turned to Farideh. "Get to the weak point and wait for our signal. Mira, find the door and get it open. Havi and Maspero, keep the Shadovar off us and the arcanist on the Shadovar. Brin . . ."

Havilar's hand slipped into his, her tail twining nervously around his ankle. He could hear the words she hadn't said yet—*Brin can come with me*. And split her focus, he thought. You could get her killed that way.

"I'll go with Mira," Brin said, squeezing Havilar's hand. "If we can get the arcanist out, I'm the best person to try the air vents first. In case they're too narrow."

Tam nodded. "Excellent. Go."

Havilar held tight to him, and unlike before, she looked nothing short of terrified. "You *have* to be careful," she said, a little tremor in her voice. "You have to promise."

"*You* be careful," he told her. "I'm just doing a little climbing."

Havilar seized him in a fierce embrace, tucking her face against the crook of his neck. "Just promise, all right?"

"I promise," he said, and he kissed her quickly, before hurrying after Mira. Havilar looked around the camp, as if searching for someone—Farideh, he realized, but her twin had rushed off to help cast the rituals. Oh, Loyal Torm, he thought, seeing the sudden anguish on Havilar's face, don't let me have kept her from saying good-bye.

He broke into a run to keep up with Mira, darting around the twisting paths of the library's shelves. She stopped abruptly along a mostly straight aisle, lined with fat, leather-bound books on either side, and wide enough for Lorcan to have spread his wings. She scanned the floor.

"Here," she murmured. "It's the only place that's wide enough for that thing to get out."

"How . . . big is it again?" Brin asked.

Mira didn't answer, but dropped to her knees and started pulling at the corners of the tiles with a slim, sturdy wire. Brin bent low, studying the sand between the tiles for signs of disturbance. Off in the distance he heard the muffled *booms* of the wizards blasting their way through the obstacles. Ye gods, he thought. Where in the Hells was it?

Suddenly his ears felt thick, as if a storm were coming fast over the horizon, and the air seemed to vibrate. He looked up and saw the ghosts, still wearing the forms of Havilar, Farideh and himself take shape in the shadows. The booming grew louder, and Brin realized, as the ghosts edged closer, that not all of it was coming from the Shadovar's progress.

"Mira," he called.

"Have you found it?" she said, then she let out a little cry as she spotted the ghosts.

"It's found us," he said. He drew his sword and his holy symbol, and heard her take out her knives. The ghosts all eyed him as he backed toward Mira, as if waiting to see if he could do anything at all with the occasional goodwill of Torm.

One of the tiles started to lurch upward, out of place.

"Head for the others," he said. "I'll lead—"

"No," Mira said, firmly. "I'll lead it out. You get down there and make sure the air vents are a decent route."

Brin might have argued, but then the tile flipped out of place, and a hideous, skeletal arm as long as he was reached up out of the floor. Mira darted past him, scoring a slash along the thing's forearm, and the arcanist howled in rage. The mummy hauled himself up out of the trapdoor and for a brief, terrible moment, his glowing green eyes fell on Brin. He snarled and tossed his head, so bestial Brin could hardly imagine he had once been the architect of the library. Whatever the arcanist's howl had meant, the ghosts understood, and as the mummy turned to follow Mira, the three of them focused their cold eyes on Brin.

Loyal Fury, he thought, and he leaped down the trapdoor into the darkness. The drop was long enough that it shocked his ankles, but Brin ran past the pain, down the steep and winding passage. One of the ghosts streaked past him with a sound halfway between a swarm of bees and a stiff breeze, and his own self seemed to take shape fifteen feet before him. He held the pendant of his holy symbol up menacingly.

"The gods cannot hear you down here," the ghost said.

Brin gripped the emblem all the harder—if ever there was a time his fickle powers should come through, this was it. "Loyal Fury," he said. "Aid me."

The emblem took on a bright sheen, and the air rang with the sound of a blade against a whetstone. The ghost took a step back. Brin edged forward.

"Let me pass," he said. "Or I release it." He swung the holy symbol around to see the ghost in Havilar's skin creeping up on him. "This is the sort of magic that killed your friend," he warned.

She smiled, an evil, slippery thing. "He was already dead."

Which ghost lunged first, he couldn't have said. His eyes were first on Havilar's face catching fire in the sudden brightness that exploded from the pendant, then on his own, the ghost's gaping mouth filling with the holy light. His stomach churned up, but he had the good sense to run past the screaming creatures and swallow his sick back down.

They did not follow him into the crypt—whether they were dead or that fearful of him, he didn't know. He ran through the field of bones to the trio of niches along the far wall. Even though the air was dense with the rotten smell of the arcanist's victims, he could tell it was fresher than in the rest of the library, stirring the dank air into something breathable. He imagined the arcanist, his apprentices, or maybe their slaves—the wretched-looking little gnome of the Book's pedestal flashed through his thoughts—laboring in the dark and the murky air, and he shuddered.

Brin sheathed his sword and took the stub of chalk he'd been carrying since Mira gave out orders. He looked up the first shaft and saw no sunlight—he drew a rough *X* before the opening, and hoped it would deter the others if they came before he'd found the right way out. The second looked promising, but a quick scramble found the rock crumbling under his hands fifteen feet up. He slid back down and drew another mark before starting carefully up the third vent, his arms and legs screaming as he crept nearer and nearer to to the world beyond.

.:⌢:.

"You know," Lorcan said as Farideh poured the mix of metal salts into a circle around both of them, "there *is* a simpler way out." The sounds of Rhand's people making their way through the library made a strange complement to his calmness. He shifted out of the way as she came under his wing. "Not nicer, but simpler." She stepped around her open ritual book to finish the line. "If we break the protection, Sairché will be on us in a heartbeat. She'll pull us both out, quick as can be. Your sister too, I suspect."

"But not the others," Farideh said, calm because the alternative would undo her. "And then Sairché has us."

"And then we have at least a little longer to live," he corrected. "And a little longer to find a way out of the fire."

Farideh thought of Havilar, of the approaching voices of the Netherese scouts, and the inevitable presence of Adolican Rhand. "I think our chances are better this way," she said, even though she wasn't sure. "I *know* the others' chances are better this way."

"No doubt," Lorcan said. The echoing *booms* of the Shadovar's wizards blasting their way through Maspero's maze of shelves was getting closer. "What is your sister doing wrapped around the little wayward Tormite?"

"What it looks like," Farideh said mildly. She scrutinized the circle rather than meet Lorcan's eyes. He'd already seen whatever stunned expression must have crossed her face when Havilar went to Brin, all worried eyes and lashing tail—and not to Farideh. How many times had Havilar made her promise to stay safe when she wasn't going to be there to save Farideh? Enough that she couldn't shake the sense that missing that promise meant Farideh wouldn't come back at all.

"It sounds like that *bothers* you," Lorcan drawled.

"We are about to be overrun by a Shadovar army," she said. "I'm not gossiping with you." She looked back down the aisle where Dahl and Tam were bent over the ritual books, trying to transfer Dahl's spell to Tam's quicker than they ought to have.

A crash and a chorus of screams rang out as the Netherese hit the first of the traps. She looked back again for Dahl's signal. Tam still scribbled. Dahl still gestured wildly as he tried to explain how the spell went together.

"It does make a neat little pair, doesn't it," he said savagely. "She has her not-quite-paladin, and you have yours."

Farideh laughed once. "If Dahl is what I get then you can send me to the Hells right now. It would be much more pleasant."

"He cares an awful lot about what you think of him," Lorcan said.

Because he's a proud idiot, Farideh thought, but she smiled sweetly at Lorcan, "Does that bother you?"

He made a face. "Well done." She made the cross of leaves through the center, and looked back to Dahl and Tam. Now at least they had started, the lines of powdered silver gleaming in the light of the orbs overhead.

"What will you do if we escape?" Lorcan asked.

"Do we have to talk about this now?"

"What else should we do?" he said irritably. "The priest, no doubt, would tell you to be rid of me."

"I'm not sending you back," she said. She looked up at him, unsure of what to say. She wouldn't betray him, she couldn't. She wanted him near, even if at the same time she didn't. If nothing else—no threat of Sairché, no Brimstone Angel, no debt of gratitude—here was a chance to see where they landed, he and she. To sort out whether she loved him or feared him or resented him, or some unnameable combination she would never come by with a thousand unexpected visits.

"I owe you better than that," she finally said, and she thanked the gods that Dahl waved for her attention. The rituals were set. Once hers was finished, they'd make for the vents below.

She dropped the vial between them, and the magic surged through her, sucking the words of the spell from her mouth. The wind and the roar that rushed up between them was cool and then cold, blowing through Farideh's armor and raising gooseflesh along her skin. Light burned through the circle of salts, and Farideh felt the Weave's broken strands winding around them both, tying into tighter and tighter bands, before collapsing into them. The light and wind faded but a faint steam rose off of both of them, their flesh already scalding. She tucked the ritual book back into her haversack.

"Are you afraid?" she asked quietly.

"Not very, no," he said, unrolling the scroll. "Though I don't like to consider what comes after." He looked down at her with those black, black eyes. "I don't know which would be worse: oblivion or to rise into the ranks of devilkin already knowing I cannot win at the hierarchy."

She looked at him, surprised. A devil killed on Toril would reform in the Hells, but not a half-devil. He'd said so before. "If you're half-devil," she said slowly, "then you're half-mortal too?"

"Human, most likely," Lorcan said. "Just as fragile as a devil, when it comes to undead monstrosities."

Half-human means half a soul, she thought. You're not doomed, and maybe he isn't either.

"It's very brave," she said. "What you're doing. Even if you're not afraid."

"Let's see if it convinces the priest," he said. "Are you ready?"

There was not a syllable of the arcanist's spell that Farideh recognized, but every word sounded like magic. It made the pulse of Malbolge's energies strike a frenzied beat, fighting against her heartbeat. The flood of the Hells spilled into her, and she stepped back and back from the cambion, until the protection that linked them stopped her feet.

The flames of Phlegethos burst forth from the limestone floor, hotter than a hundred cookfires, even with the ritual's protection. The roaring stream of fire was nearly enough to drown out the ear-splitting screechs of the arcanist's mummy and the crashes of the Netherese approaching. The screams as the arcanist reached them.

Lorcan was thrown up into the air by the force of the spell, and for a moment he hung there, his wings buoyed by the shimmering air, his head thrown back in a cry of pain.

Then the fire caught. The edges of his wings started to burn.

Farideh rushed forward as he fell, the heat of the cracking ground forcing her back. She pressed on and caught him.

"Hurry," she said, hauling him up. "The lava's coming." He could hardly breathe for the pain of his burns it seemed, his eyes wild with the shock of it. She hauled him bodily toward the camp and the trapdoor beyond.

Mira raced across her path, knives out. Farideh called out to her, but she didn't stop. A moment later, the arcanist lumbered into view. He turned to face Farideh and Lorcan and opened his mouth. The green light began to swell between his jaws.

Lorcan held her tighter.

The arcanist looked up, past their heads to the fires crackling beyond and the lava that was flowing over the shelves and stone, making greater fires in its wake. The arcanist howled up at the ceiling, as the column behind them started to crack. He turned back the way he had come, back toward the door, and Farideh dragged Lorcan on, watching after the creature as they passed. He had thrown aside the fallen bookshelves and the Netherese mercenaries that swarmed at him. Magic crackled in his hands, a great storm of power that seemed to take all his focus—the Shadovar who attacked him drew no notice from the arcanist. The tattered remains of his three apprentices battered the score of blades at their master's feet, taking form and dissolving again and again.

As she got Lorcan past the aisle, she saw the arcanist cast some terrible power out the doors. As they came into sight of the camp, she heard the rush of the water pouring in. By the time Dahl and Tam reached her, it had covered the soles of her boots.

"He's hurt!" Farideh said. "Do something!"

Tam hesitated, and her heart threatened to crack under the strain like the stone of the column. Lorcan raised his head, his whole frame resting on Farideh now. It would be easy to say no, she could imagine Tam thinking. It would be easy to let the devil die.

The priest set his hands on either side of Lorcan's face. "Grant me, Selûne, our balm for this . . . unlikely ally."

If Lorcan's screams had been loud before, now they rivaled the roaring flames of Phlgethos. She held him tighter as the goddess's blessing racked a frame never meant to feel it.

For a moment, she was sure Tam had decided to kill him. But the charred flesh of his wings flaked away to reveal new, whole skin, and Lorcan straightened with a pained gasp. The hiss and crackle of the cooling lava carried across the caverns. The stone snapped and split as it cooled. Still the lava kept flowing over the river's efforts. The arcanist roared. She heard a sound like an explosion and more water poured in, the wall torn free to let in more of the watercourse beyond.

"Go," Tam said firmly, and he pushed her toward the hole where Dahl helped her down the steep drop. She ran down the slope, icy water rushing around her ankles, pressing her on. She nearly slipped in it and caught herself as she burst out into the crypt. Those were Mira's legs disappearing up the farthest shaft and she followed, not daring to hesitate long enough to look back and be sure of the other three.

Farideh braced herself against the sides of the shaft and inched her way up, panting and sore and pelted by the frequent rain of stone bits kicked loose by Mira, or whoever might be above her. For an eternity, she climbed, all too aware of the crumbling column, the swelling lava, the steam that was no doubt building up behind her as the river rushed into the gate to Phlegethos.

Suddenly, Mira was gone, and the light of the sun blinded her, and hands were helping her out of the air vent and onto the slope of a mountainside. Farideh helped her pull Dahl and then Lorcan from the shaft.

"Move," Mira said, pointing down the slope where an ancient path led down a nearly sheer face. "Around the cliff, quickly, before it blows." She reached down to catch her father's hands, and Farideh followed Dahl and Lorcan down the winding path, as fast as she dared to go, to find Havilar and Brin and Maspero waiting at the foot of a sheer granite wall.

Havilar threw her arms around her sister. "Oh," she said, overcome, and she buried her face in her sister's hair. "Oh." Farideh hugged her hard, glad she had been wrong, glad that nothing ill had come of not saying good-bye. She had no words either.

"Against the cliff!" Tam barked.

They broke apart and had just flattened themselves beside the others against the stone when the other side of the mountain erupted, blasting their ears and shaking the ground beneath their feet hard enough to send rocks bouncing over them and down the slope below.

They would hear later that it had ripped the peak of the mountain away, that it had rained down flaming stone and fat ashes on the High Forest for miles. The plume of smoke and steam would be seen as far away as Waterdeep, and Shade would quietly hide away any mention of the library, the mission, and the score and a half of Shadovar lost in the explosion. The books Mira had carried out would be passed from scholar to scholar, except for a precious few which would secure the strength of Maspero of Everlund for a few years more.

"Everyone's all right?" Tam asked as the rattle of falling stone slowed, and for the moment, it was the only thing that mattered.

# CHAPTER TWENTY-THREE

*WATERDEEP*

*1 ELEASIAS, THE YEAR OF THE DARK CIRCLE (1478 DR)*

TRAVELING BACK THROUGH THE WILDS OF THE SILVER MARCHES HAD been simpler than their first trek in some ways and far rougher in others, Farideh thought. They knew right away where to camp and where to ford the streams. They had little trouble finding food to supplement their trail rations, knowing where the likely sources were. Brin and Havilar weren't fighting with each other, nor were Dahl and Tam. The Zhentarim had separated from the Harpers' group as soon as possible, and so there were no more arguments about that.

But even though they skirted Rhand's Shadovar forces, they traveled with an eye on the road behind them, and another on the skies overhead. Plus it was plain that Mira's flight, expected or not, devastated Tam. Brin and Havilar were busy acting as if their time together was borrowed and about to be reclaimed. And the addition of Lorcan meant that no one was very happy with Farideh, even if his help had meant they had escaped the library after all.

Only Dahl had decided to make good on his promises finally, to teach her the last seven rituals from their bargain. He was still surly about it, and Lorcan still sniped at him given the chance, but for an hour or so each day, Farideh was grateful to have someone to talk to about something that wasn't how she was doing everything wrong or whether or not Brin's eyes were his best feature. Or worse.

"Are you planning to tell Havilar about what we talked about?" Lorcan asked, as they waited outside the coinlender's for Brin and Havilar to return. He'd hidden his true form, changing his skin for the appearance of a strikingly handsome young man, and passersby who weren't staring at Farideh's horns and tail were staring at him. "About the Brimstone Angel?"

Judging by his tone, Farideh thought the answer should have been "no." "She deserves to know."

"But does she deserve what comes of such a revelation? Knowing leads to more questions, leads to searching for answers." He gave her a wicked smile. "Leads to devils."

All worries Farideh had already had.

"Why didn't you take Havilar?" she asked. "She could have been your warlock."

"Easy, darling. Your sister wants things well within her reach." He turned that wicked smile to an older woman who was not-so-subtly assessing him. "She never needed help. Though," he added, as Brin and Havilar reappeared, "that can always change."

"Bad news," Brin said. "I don't have as much as I thought."

Farideh frowned. "I thought you said you had a kraken's load."

"He *did*," Havilar said. "Someone cleared it out."

"I think what I have might be exactly enough to buy back Squall and pay for an inn and stabling for a few days and then passage by portal for Squall and myself," Brin said with a scowl. "I might be off a little. I wish I'd never taken any of it."

At least he'd taken what was left. They were desparately low. When they'd parted ways from the Harpers earlier in the day, Brin had offered the funds in the safehold as a temporary solution while they sorted out what had happened to Mehen.

Farideh had managed to increase the limits of the protection spell, with painful, careful practice—she could be ten steps from Lorcan now without the spell snapping back. But as they walked through Waterdeep and Havilar and Brin fell into step, arms intertwined and heads together, she found it easier to keep pace beside Lorcan.

"Darling," he said, apropos of nothing, "you mentioned you were having nightmares. What did you see in them?"

"You," she said, not looking at him. "The way they might have been torturing you. Devils. Things that might be in the Hells. Why?"

He hesitated, studying Havilar and Brin's backs. "Curiosity," he said finally. "What sorts of things that might be in the Hells?"

**LESSER EVILS**

"Well, here you are," the innkeeper said when they returned to the Blind Falcon. "All that asking and once you leave, not an hour passes before your message from 'Mehen' arrives." He retrieved a thick envelope from under the bar. "And knowing how persistent you girls were, I held onto it."

A weight lifted off Farideh's shoulders. "Oh, thank the gods." She took the envelope. "Do you have any rooms left? We need . . ." She looked back at Lorcan and Brin, his hand still intertwined with Havilar's. "Three, I suppose."

"Two will do," Lorcan said.

"Two's all I have, so that's good to hear." He squinted at Lorcan. "Well, well. Where'd they pick you up?"

Farideh slid the coin across the counter, trying not to blush at what the innkeeper was thinking. "Cousin," she blurted. "On . . . our mother's side."

"Ah," the innkeeper said, clearly disbelieving. "Well, the two at the end of the hall."

Farideh thanked him and took the envelope. "I guess Tam wasn't exaggerating about the fuss."

Brin peered at the seal, a blazon of dragon with a crown muzzling its jaws. His eyes widened. "Oh no. Crownsilvers."

"Maybe they just lent him their paper," Havilar said nervously.

Farideh cracked the glossy yellow wax and withdrew the thick parchment letter from its envelope. The fluid script of a practiced hand flowed across the page, dense with the detailed language of courts and officials and the sorts of people who set bounties, not earned them. Farideh squinted at the text, trying to sort the meaning out from the nonsense. *Therefore the man identified as Mehen, being as he has entered Cormyrean soil . . .*

"They wouldn't," Brin said urgently.

*. . . the Crownsilvers' claim being paramount against the established bounty . . .*

"Well, maybe they're telling you he's on his way back," Havilar said. "Maybe they're saying thanks for returning Constancia."

*. . . and the complicating factors under consideration in the case of discreetness . . .*

"Maybe it's an invitation to join the dragonborn in their vacation home in the Feywild," Lorcan said, caustically.

*. . . until such time as reparations are made.* Farideh's stomach dropped. "Oh gods."

"What," Brin demanded, "does it say?"

"Mehen's in prison," Farideh said. "They think he kidnapped Brin."

·:⌒:·

As much as Tam Zawad had disliked the spy they called the Fisher, he entered the Harper stronghold with a heavy heart. Dahl and several more Harpers out of Everlund whose names he would have to learn followed him through the tavern on the ground floor, up through the narrow, sooty hallways to Aron Vishter's secret office.

In his arms, Tam carried a sullen bundle, wrapped in layers and layers of wool, and as they came to the door, he wondered if he'd made the right choice in bringing it. He would wonder over a lot of choices, he felt certain, in the years to come.

But not this one, he thought.

"Draw swords," he ordered and pushed in.

The Fisher sat at his desk, his golden rings in a pile and a measure of whiskey before him. He looked up at Tam with a somber expression. "Well met, Shepherd. Too afraid to do this, just the two of us?"

"You owe them as much as you do me," Tam said. "If not more." A little digging had turned up a dozen missions turned sour, all run out of Waterdeep. All crossed with the Zhentarim. More than a few ending with dead Harpers. "Watching Gods, Fisher. Was this all for coin?"

"Coin," the other spy said. "And the thrill of it." The Fisher drained his whiskey. "I think you might have let me run for it, for old times' sake. That's why you brought these bravos. I think you knew you couldn't trust yourself not to get soft for memory's sake."

Tam thought of Viridi, of the spymaster's willingness to bend her rules for him when it came to Mira. And of what Viridi would have done—to Tam, to any of them—if their actions had ended with agents dead. "Viridi would have made certain she had every one of your secrets before you died," he said, "whatever it took. So be glad I haven't dwelt too long in memories of the past.

"Aron Vishter, you have betrayed your oaths and disgraced the cause of the Harpers. You are sentenced to death by hanging." He signaled two of the Everlund Harpers—a half-elf man and a broad-shouldered Shou—to take hold of the spymaster. "But for the love of mercy, I hope you give us the names of your conspirators."

The Fisher gave Tam a wry smile as the Harpers seized his arms and hauled him up out of the chair. "You won't last long at this. Already told me you won't make me talk."

Tam shook his head. "I said be glad I'm not Viridi." He handed the bundle containing the Book to the third Harper, a brunette woman. "Don't touch it yourself," he cautioned. "And lock it up tight in the vaults when he's through."

*You will regret this*, the Book's voice said, as the armored Harper took hold of it.

"That I may." He looked at the gaudy silver pin perched on his shoulder, a harp and a moon on a round shield. Another thing to get on Everlund about. There had to be a less obvious way to mark themselves to each other. They led the Fisher away into the more secret parts of the stronghold. Tam watched him go, mourning the loss of a comrade, the loss of the last connection to a life he still missed.

"Where will you start?" Dahl asked. The younger man stood over the Fisher's desk, looking at the mess of documents.

"By purging the Fisher's traitors," Tam said. "Let us hope he is forthcoming. I don't want a changeling hunt." He looked over the cluttered office—he could clear it out while he waited for results. "And then . . . we need to start recruiting. Proper recruiting." He looked over at the younger man. "I hope you'll stay."

Dahl gave a bitter laugh. "I have nowhere else to go." He flipped through the papers on the Fisher's former desk. "And I think I'd prefer the Harpers anyway. Especially if I'm not going to be sent rifling through antiquaries."

"It would be a waste of your skills," Tam agreed.

Dahl nodded absently, in the way Tam had come to realize meant he was saying thanks, but embarrassed to do so. "Did you consider," Dahl asked, "recruiting . . . I mean, they're young but . . . Farideh seems like she'd be a decent ally. Absent the devil."

The girl was clever and quick, solving problems in the middle of everything falling apart as well as if she'd been put through the first years as the Red Knight's own. Havilar's glaive was, as they said, as good as her right hand and he would never need to ease Clanless Mehen's true heir into the bloodier aspects of protecting the balance of Faerûn. Even Brin, who was not cut out for the battlefield but was halfway to being able to lie to Cyric himself.

"I don't think they're ready," Tam said. "Nor do I think the Harpers are truly ready for them."

"I suppose you're right." Dahl looked down at the desk. "I suppose if she had been a Harper, we would both be facing a fair amount of trouble for what happened. Around the door. And such. It was awfully close to oath-breaking."

Tam sighed. There are rules you bend, he thought, and rules to which you hold firm. "You both survived and came out better for it, I'd say. No need for tribunal. But I wouldn't send you out together again, no." He regarded the younger man more seriously. "And I hope to the gods you are never that self-indulgent again."

"No." Dahl pursed his lips. "Do you mind? I have an errand or two . . ."

"Of course," Tam said. He followed him to the door. "When you get back I want a list from every available Harper of potential recruits. Anyone you know—from your past, from your present—who might make a proper agent. Think on it."

"I will." He stopped outside the door. "Have you any idea where Mira went?"

"No," Tam said, and it was the truth. They'd no more than skirted the Shadovar before she and Maspero vanished in the night—not a note, not a word, not a fond farewell. She'd taken the spellbooks she'd rescued and left Tam the Book of Tarchamus. That, he supposed sadly, *was* her fond farewell.

"She'll be all right," Dahl offered.

"Go," Tam said. "I need you back here soon."

Dahl left, and at last Tam was alone, in the secret offices of the spymaster of Waterdeep's Harpers. He'd been hiding from this for a long time, he thought. Running across Faerûn as if the best and surest way to protect things were to be the one who brought the threats down, tangled in his chain. As if he could avoid ever being the one who handed down the orders that didn't always turn out, that didn't always save the day. That didn't always bring Harpers home to their loved ones.

He looked up at the portraits the Fisher had hung along the ceiling's edge—Harpers of old, men and women, bards and assassins and casters and more. All exuding the shrewdness and determination it took to maintain the balance of Faerûn.

Less a balance these days, he thought, and turned to the window, looking out at the City of Splendors. More a dike against the tide of evil.

Someone must, he thought, and it reminded him so much of something Viridi might have said—the truth, said plain so that she could get to the business of doing something about it. *Someone must, and the best someone is you.* For all he wished his life had run a different course, it had not, and now the Harpers needed him and all the wisdom he'd gathered traveling the way he had. He hoped it would be enough. He hoped he would find himself suited to the spymaster's role.

Tam hoped it might help him keep Mira from harm's way.

He sighed and looked down at the sill, at the weather-damaged wood beneath his hands.

At the small, tightly rolled scrap of paper that had been wedged under the pane into the largest crack.

.:⁀:.

Dahl left Goodman Florren's shop, having gotten a better deal than he would have elsewhere, yet feeling very much like he'd been robbed by the roadside. He carried the paper-wrapped package under one arm and wended his way through Waterdeep's streets toward the Trade Ward. He hoped this was the right thing to do.

*He wouldn't be alone, would he?* Dahl had racked his thoughts trying to come up with what he might have said or done that made

Farideh put him in the same category as a Netherese wizard who didn't think elves or gnomes were worth as much as humans. Who wouldn't have thought a tiefling merited much concern at all.

And there *hadn't* been anything, he was fairly sure, that was worth such a declaration. Not any *one* thing . . .

But maybe, he had come to admit, *maybe*, he hadn't been the easiest body to deal with. Maybe he had said some things, here and there, that could have built up. Maybe he had managed to give her the impression that he thought less of her.

Be honest, he told himself, passing out of the Dock Ward, you did think less of her. Right from the very start. And even if he was right in one respect—she *was* allied with that devil—he was very wrong in a great many ways more.

*You think that you know everything*, she'd said, *you think no one can possibly be as godsbedamned smart as you, but every other word out of your* karshoji *mouth is you jumping to another conclusion that isn't fair.*

Knowledge is not to be hidden, the doctrine of Oghma said, not from the world and not from the self. And assuming you knew something, not even seeking out the answers . . . that was near enough to hiding from the truth.

Was this how he fell? he wondered. Was it something he took for granted that way? The realization hadn't brought his powers back—maybe nothing would. And he couldn't be the only one who let such assumptions lead him from time to time . . .

Maybe Oghma expects better of you, he thought, as he came to the Blind Falcon Inn. Maybe *you* expect better.

He climbed the stairs with absolutely no notion of what he was going to say to her. "I'm sorry"? "I thought you could use this"? "I feel like an ass and I just want you to know that"?

"You don't have to be friends with me," he muttered to himself, "but I promise I'll always be an ally."

The devil was sitting on a stool outside the door at the end of the hall, still wearing the skin of a human and flipping through a dog-eared chapbook. Dahl bit back a curse as he looked up.

"Well, well," the devil said. "The paladin come to call." He went back to the chapbook. "She's sleeping."

Dahl ignored him and went to knock on the door.

Lorcan turned swiftly and planted one booted foot on the opposite side of the door frame, barring the way. "I said, she's sleeping. So you can deal with me, or you can go lose yourself in the alleys." He nodded at the package. "What have you got there?"

Dahl considered for the briefest moment drawing his sword and running the devil through. The devil smiled as if daring him to do it.

But then he'd be the one having murdered what *looked* like a man in the middle of an inn for no apparent reason. And if Farideh seems to trust him, he thought, maybe you're missing something.

"Where are Brin and Havilar?" he asked.

"Buying a horse, apparently," the devil said. He held out a hand. "You can leave it with me. I'll make sure she gets it."

"You'll forgive me if I don't believe that."

"Normally? Yes." Lorcan chuckled. "But what would I do with it? This is as far as the spell lets me go. I could throw it halfway down the hallway, but what would be the point? Besides," he said, and Dahl could see why people made agreements with devils like him, "surely you expect to see her again. Next time she comes through Waterdeep? She'll seek out the priest, anyway. Maybe you. You can ask after your little trinket then."

"They're leaving that soon?"

"On the morrow," Lorcan said. "Pressing issues. So I'd recommend leaving it now." He held out a hand. "Unless you have the time to spare, sitting here and talking to me?"

Dahl thought back to Tam and the mountains of tasks waiting to be completed in the Fisher's absence. Agents to track and contact, missions to review, replacements to recruit. Traitors to uncover. And he owed his mother a letter still.

"Make sure she gets it," he said, handing over the package. "And tell her, please . . ." The devil smirked at him, and there was no way Dahl was going to say what he'd meant to. "Tell her I hope I see her again."

"Duly noted," Lorcan said. "And farewell, paladin."

.:⌒:.

**ERIN M. EVANS**

Lorcan watched Dahl leave, turning the package over in his hands. There couldn't be a next time, he thought. You will have to keep her far from Waterdeep from now on. Between the priest trying to convince her to undo her pact and the paladin who seemed a little too keen on gaining her good opinion, there was more trouble in the City of Splendors than Lorcan cared to manage. Especially given Sairché and her damnable secrets. Someplace quiet was certainly in order.

Lords look us over, he thought, picking at the knot of the twine wrapped around the package, and let her stay away from the Sword Coast from here on. Cormyr would make a good start.

The door beside him opened and Farideh looked down at him, bleary eyed. She glanced around the hallway. "Who were you talking to?"

"Delivery boy," Lorcan said, holding up the package. "I chased him off."

Her expression was stony. "What did you say?"

"I told him you were sleeping and not to wake you, of course. Here." He handed her the package. "A gift."

She regarded it warily a moment before peeling off the paper wrappings. Inside lay a rod, solid black and chased with inlaid gold leaf. The tips were cracked and cloudy amethysts. Lorcan held back a sneer—hardly better than kindling beside the Rod of the Traitor's Reprisal.

But Farideh smiled. "It's lovely. Thank you."

"It's not *that* lovely," he said reflexively. Then, "I mean, it's rather common. It shouldn't draw as much notice."

"That's . . ." She shook her head. "That's really thoughtful of you, Lorcan. How did you find it?"

He shrugged. "You ask the right people the right questions and all manner of things come to you." Lorcan studied her face, the easy delight in *this* smile. "Did you have any more nightmares, darling?"

# EPILOGUE

*Malbolge, the Hells*

**T**HE THRONE ROOM OF THE PALACE OF OSSEIA WAS EMPTY, BUT FOR Sairché kneeling on its patterned floor, her eyes downcast, and Glasya, Lord of the Sixth. The pit fiends and hellwasps who guarded the archduchess were gone. The devils who regularly filled the court, attending their mistress's orders had fled. Even Sairché's erinyes bodyguards had been repelled. What Glasya had to say was for Sairché's ears alone.

It wasn't lost on Sairché that she waited in precisely the same place her brother had, with precisely the same fate hanging over her.

The hierarchy was a dangerous place for a cambion, Sairché well knew. All the gains she'd made by turning traitor against her own mother threatened to collapse beneath her for want of a troublesome warlock. The mirror wouldn't call the rod. The mirror wouldn't show her anything close. It couldn't find Lorcan and when she sent it back to the place she'd glimpsed before, there was only a smoking crater and a score of shadow-worshipers crawling over the cooling rock. No rod, no cambion, no warlock.

To fall from her elevated status meant not just a return to skirting the edges of the *pradixikai*'s good graces, gathering secrets from greater devils like a child collecting scales in the wake of a dragon—the dragon had seen her. The devils wouldn't let her slip back under their notice.

*It is your own fault*, she thought, but she would never admit it aloud. She had made deals without having goods in hand, without knowing the archduchess's interest. She had overreached her station. And now, even Lorcan had slipped her grasp.

She stared at the floor and hoped beyond hope that this was not the end of her.

"You seem to be having trouble with your erinyes," Glasya said, her voice like a razor drawn over Sairché's eardrums. "Disobedience. Turmoil. Three dead."

"That was Bibracte's error," Sairché began.

"Bibracte is your problem," Glasya said. "And thereby your error. You are not a child, Sairché. It is not endearing to hear you blame your toys."

Sairché shivered. "Yes, Your Highness."

The silence that reigned in the court of Osseia seemed as if it were preparing to pounce on Sairché, to pin her down and smother her. She drew a noisy breath to keep it at bay.

"You are very lucky, little cambion," Glasya said. "I have uses for you still. We can forget this . . . novice's mistake. For now. Come here."

Sairché unfolded herself on shaking legs. She did not want to come any nearer to Glasya. She did not want to have a use to the archduchess. But more than either she did not want to die. The Lord of the Sixth looked down on her vassal, as beautiful and terrible as a crashing star. The smell of rotting flowers was thick enough to choke on. Glasya held out a scroll marked in shining red inks and ornamented with black and silver tassels.

"The king of the Hells begs a boon," Glasya said. "Something powerful is coming. Something the gods themselves may not be prepared for. He has passed down orders to every archduke—we are called to aid him."

The scroll seemed a leaden weight in Sairché's hands. "These are Asmodeus's orders?"

"A part of them. I would suggest," Glasya said very carefully, "that you read them and absorb them most thoroughly. My father's plans are ever delicate things, relying on a hundred thousand points to craft the whole. It would be . . . a shame, if one of those more critical points were to fail." Glasya's regard held Sairché in place as surely as nails through her feet would. "It might even cost him the godhood he prizes so highly, and then . . . well, then the whole of the Hells might rebel. We might find ourselves with a new king. Or queen," she added with a small smile.

Sairché swallowed hard. She would not die, but she'd been played into a terrible gambit. Glasya did not need to say she wanted Sairché to fail, but if she did, Asmodeus would surely punish her. But if she followed through on Asmodeus's plans, then Glasya would swiftly do away with Sairché.

Sairché nodded and clutched the scroll to her chest. *This is only the hierarchy*, she told herself. *This is nothing but the hierarchy made larger. You can defeat it. You can find a way around it.*

"How long do I have?" she asked.

"Some years. So I expect your very best work. You may go, Sairché. I suggest you choose a new commander for the *pradixikai*. Zela seems appropriate. You will be very busy in the years to come."

"Yes, Your Highness. Thank you." She turned to go.

"And do cheer up," Glasya called. "You'll be pleased to see our part involves your brother's warlock. And her twin," she added, as Sairché reached the doors.

Sairché froze and looked back at the archduchess. "Twin?"

"The one they say killed Rohini," Glasya said with a terrible smile. "Bear that in mind before you go bargaining with souls I have a right to: what the collectors think they know, what any of the devilkin think they know, is only ever part of the truth."

Sairché hurried back to her apartments within Osseia, sealed the door, and unrolled the scroll. The uncrossing of worlds. The uprooting of gods. A battle for powers that would come, and grow fevered as the final prophecies came to pass. If she didn't know better, she might think Asmodeus was completely mad.

But mad or not, Sairché had no choice but to play her part. She scowled—as much time as she had, there were a thousand ways to fulfill Glasya's responsibilities. She needed pieces, she decided. Better to start securing those now than scramble seven years down the line.

Farideh would be one. The elusive twin the other. She would have to figure out a way to find them. And then . . . as many fools with more ambition than sense, more ego than caution, and more power than reason as she could manage. She thought for a moment, then left, back to the little antechamber to which she'd had the scrying mirror returned.

The shadow-worshipers were still prowling through the mountain's remains when Sairché arrived through a borrowed portal, digging out the remains of books and stonework and grumbling to themselves. Not too busy to react to her appearance with drawn swords and thrown blades. The weapons glanced off the protective bubble Sairché cast around herself, and she gave the men a withering look.

"I want to talk to your leader," she said. "The wizard. Now."

The wizard who'd been all simmering temper and soulless eyes when she'd watched before, searching for the rod or the tiefling or her brother. The one who'd dashed off furious letters to Shade and to Waterdeep. The one who'd clearly failed someone, somehow. He did not come quickly, perhaps thinking he would bring Sairché down from her perch on the crater's edge. When he finally did come, it was with a sneer and a retinue of half a dozen other wizards. The eyes were colder in person, utterly without pity. He'll do nicely, she thought.

"I have a deal for you," Sairché began, and she made the opening play in the downfall of Asmodeus.

The epic *New York Times* best-selling series...

# R.A. SALVATORE

## THE NEVERWINTER SAGA

### BOOK III
# CHARON'S CLAW

Available in hardcover and ebook

*Also available in paperback and ebook*

### BOOK I
# GAUNTLGRYM

### BOOK II
# NEVERWINTER

Dungeons & Dragons, D&D, Wizards of the Coast, Neverwinter, and their respective logos are trademarks of Wizards of the Coast LLC in the U.S.A. and other countries. All other trademarks are the property of their respective owners. ©2012 Wizards.

## FORGOTTEN REALMS

# THE SAGA OF DRIZZT IS NOT COMPLETE WITHOUT

# THE STONE OF TYMORA

From *New York Times* best-selling author
**R.A. Salvatore & Geno Salvatore**

"The pace never falters, the cast is positively festooned with pirates and menacing magical creatures (such characters from parallel stories as Drizzt Do'Urden the Dark Elf also put in appearances)." —*Kirkus*

**Available from your favorite bookseller or ebook seller**

FORGOTTEN REALMS, D&D, WIZARDS OF THE COAST, AND THEIR RESPECTIVE LOGOS ARE TRADEMARKS OF WIZARDS OF THE COAST LLC IN THE U.S.A. AND OTHER COUNTRIES. All other trademarks are the property of their respective owners. ©2012 WIZARDS OF THE COAST LLC